EVIL DEEDS

INSPIRED BY ACTUAL EVENTS

JOSEPH BADAL

SUSPENSE PUBLISHING

Evil Deeds

by
Joseph Badal

PRINT EDITION

* * * * *

PUBLISHED BY:
Suspense Publishing on Smashwords

Joseph Badal
Copyright © 2011 Joseph Badal

PUBLISHING HISTORY:
Suspense Publishing, Paperback and Digital Copy, November 2011

ISBN: 0615556892
ISBN-13: 978-0615556895

This is a work of fiction. Names, characters, places, brands, media, and incidents are either the product of the author's imagination or are used fictitiously. The author acknowledges the trademarked status and trademark owners of various products referenced in this work of fiction, which have been used without permission. The publication/use of these trademarks

DEDICATION

To my dear son John, one of life's great sources of happiness and pride, and to Whitey, the dog that saved us from a lifetime of misery.

ACKNOWLEDGMENTS

As always, I want to thank my readers who have continued to encourage me in this great writing adventure through their kind words and willingness to step up to the counter and to the internet to buy my books.

My thanks go to Frank Zoretich and Brittani Lenz for their invaluable editing services. It's amazing how good you guys are.

I appreciate those friends who weighed in with suggestions about elements of this book, including Anne Beckett and Rosalie Sherman. I can always count on you both to tell it like it is.

I want to single out two authors for recognition: Tony Hillerman, who did everything he could to help me go from writer to author. The world lost a great man when it lost Tony. And Steve Brewer, who is always willing to listen to my complaints and frustrations, and is always a source of encouragement.

The contributions of John & Shannon Raab at Suspense Publishing were dramatic, and their passion for this project made the enterprise a great deal of fun.

And, finally, I thank Sara for her encouragement and "attaboys." Everyone needs a muse. I found mine.

PRAISE FOR JOSEPH BADAL

"Another tightly plotted, deftly executed page turner from a master of suspense and international intrigue. Joseph Badal writes timely stories with authority and compassion. Highly recommended."
—Sheldon Siegel, *New York Times* bestselling author of "Perfect Alibi"

With "Evil Deeds," Joseph Badal pulls together the 28-year saga of the Danforth family and their hair-raising adventures in the U.S., Greece and the Balkans. Action-packed and filled with memorable characters, "Evil Deeds" delivers on every level.
—Steve Brewer, author of "Lost Vegas"

"A rollicking adventure that will transport the reader to the Greek islands for a high-stakes treasure hunt that opens a Pandora's box if intrigue, deceit and murder. Joseph Badal serves up a rogue's gallery of sharply drawn characters present in lean, muscular prose that will always leave you wanting more."
—Philip Reed, author of "Bird Dog," "Low Rider," and "The Marquis De Fraud"

"Joe Badal takes us into a tangled puzzle of intrigue and terrorism; a page-turning mystery that gives readers a chance to combine learning of Greece and Greek politics with a tense, well told tale."
—Tony Hillerman, *New York Times* bestselling author

"Once again, Badal has crafted a superb thriller that grips you from page one and doesn't let go. "The Nostradamus Secret" has it all—compelling plot, intricate characters and a breakneck pace that will keep readers up well into the night. Another winner for Badal."
—Philip Donlay, author of "Category Five" and "Code Black"

AUTHOR'S NOTE

"Evil Deeds" is the first in a series, which includes "Terror Cell" and "The Nostradamus Secret." Although all three novels can be read as stand-alone thrillers, reading them in the order they were written will give the reader a feeling for the growth and development of the major characters, Bob and Liz Danforth, and their son Michael.

Part I of "Evil Deeds" is loosely based on the kidnapping of Greek children by the Communists during and after the revolution that occurred in Greece after the end of World War II. These children were taken across the northern Greek border into Communist Bulgaria and Yugoslavia. The Bulgarian orphanage mentioned in this novel is a creation of the Author's imagination.

For the sake of authenticity there are a number of foreign language words in this story. In order to facilitate the reader's experience, the Author underlines the syllable in these words where the pronunciation emphasis should occur.

There are several references in "Evil Deeds" to genocidal actions in the Balkans during the civil war there in the 1990s. Although the incidents noted here are purely fictional, they are similar in most instances to actual events that occurred during that conflict.

PART I

1971

CHAPTER ONE

Liz Danforth stood on the terrace of her rented home in the Athens suburb of Kifissia and watched the edge of the early morning Greek sun peek over the top of the six-foot-high stone wall at the back of the yard. The hills in the distance had already begun to turn bright yellow with the first of the May morning's sunlight. She closed her eyes and welcomed the sun's warmth on her face. All in all, not a bad way to start the day, she thought.

The sputtering sound of a motor scooter sounded from the street on the front side of the house, briefly overpowering her husband Bob's throaty laugh, two-year-old Michael's high-pitched giggles, and White Dog's frenzied barking. A hint of a breeze moved a few strands of her hair across her eyes, and she used the back of her hand to push back the blond wisps. She caught Bob looking at her and felt her heart swell. He seemed to revel in her slightest movement or simplest change of expression. How lucky could one woman be?

Liz had been afraid when the Army assigned Bob to Greece. She'd never been outside the United States before. The fact that Greece was ruled by a military junta only made things worse in her mind. But, despite her fear of living in a foreign country, she had acclimated well. And she'd take being with Bob in Greece any day over the year they'd been separated when he was in Vietnam.

"Okay, big guy," Bob shouted at Michael, "Superman time."

Liz watched Bob run over to Michael who chased White Dog, a long-haired mutt with a lot of Australian Shepherd blood and who knows what else running through her veins. Bob scooped up the boy and ran around the backyard, while White Dog trailed after them, barking ecstatically.

"Soup Man, Soup Man," Michael yelled in his husky voice, flying through the air, arms extended, a towel tucked into his collar floating behind like a cape.

Liz chuckled at her two-year-old son's pronunciation of *Superman*. Father and son, she thought. Except for the difference in age and size, two peas in a pod. Black-haired, hazel-eyed, high cheekboned peas. Her men.

Bob stopped running and extended his arm straight above his head, balancing Michael in one hand. Liz felt her breath catch.

"Bob, be careful!" she yelled. "You'll drop him."

"Not a chance," he shouted back. She saw a fleeting scornful look on his face and regretted having said anything. But the way he roughhoused with Michael scared her to death. She held her breath, anticipating what would come next, the way the game always ended.

Bob suddenly dropped his arm and Michael fell three feet to where his father caught him against his chest.

Michael giggled. "Again, Daddy," he yelled. "More! More!"

Bob nuzzled his son and kissed him on the cheek. "Gotta go to work, Mikey. But, I promise we'll play Superman when I get home."

Liz saw the disappointed look on her son's face—an expression midway between pouting and disappointment—when Bob carried him across the yard and up the four steps to the terrace. "No bye-bye, Daddy," he whined.

Bob again buried his face in his son's neck and gave him tickling kisses until Michael started laughing. Then he put Michael down and stepped to Liz, barely having to bend his six-foot-two-inch frame to kiss her lips. He put an arm around her back, then lowered his hand to the seat of her jeans. "Not bad for an old married lady," he said, squeezing a cheek. "You sure make it hard on a working guy. How do you expect me to keep my mind on my job, when the vision of you standing here in tight jeans and a tank top stays with me all day?"

"Don't give me that crap," Liz blurted. "It's Saturday. I bet there's not another officer working today. The General's probably playing golf, the Colonel's sailing, and everyone else is down at the beach. But not Captain Robert Danforth. Why don't you try coming home earlier than eight o'clock, for a change?" Liz said, giving him a shame-on-you look. "Then maybe we could discuss your visions . . . and other things, too."

Bob slapped her lightly on the butt. "I might do just that," he said, smiling lecherously.

"Yeah, yeah," Liz said. "Promises, promises."

White Dog suddenly barked and planted her two front paws on Bob's leg.

"See," Liz said. "She agrees."

Bob laughed. "White Dog always takes your side."

"I'm serious, Bob. Try getting home early tonight. We could all go out for dinner, then take Michael to the American Club Theater. They're going to show Cinderella. He'd love it."

Bob shrugged, and then leaned forward to kiss her; but she planted her hands in the middle of his chest and pushed him away.

"Dammit, Bob, I mean it."

She watched his face turn red and suddenly felt guilty for once again sending him off to work knowing she was upset. But she couldn't bring herself to apologize. She'd been looking forward to spending the day at the beach. This wasn't the first time Bob had broken his promise because of work.

"I'll get back here by noon," he said. "I promise."

She wanted to believe him, but she wasn't about to bet on it.

CHAPTER TWO

After Bob's Greek driver picked him up in the usual dented blue, decrepit Chevy pickup, Liz carried Michael through the back door of the house, into the kitchen.

"Dam-nit Bob, I means it," Michael suddenly exclaimed through a mischievous smile.

Oh boy, Liz thought. I'm going to have to watch what I say around little big ears here.

"You know what a workaholic is, Mikey?" Liz knew the best way to make her son forget something she wished he hadn't heard was to talk to him as though he was an adult. In five or ten seconds, he'd be bored to death. Michael stared at her with a wide-eyed look that seemed to say, Oh no, Mommy's at it again.

"It's a person who lives to work, not works to live. Daddy's one of those workaholics. He thinks he's the only man out there who's responsible for helping the Greeks defend themselves against the Communist hoards who are just waiting to attack Greece from the north. And, of course, there are the Turks to the east, who are going to swoop across Greece, raping and pillaging. But your daddy is the only thing that's holding the enemy back."

Michael wriggled out of her arms and slipped to a sitting position on the floor.

"Mission accomplished," she whispered.

But then Michael looked up and stared at her. "What's raping and pill–?"

"I'll tell you later," she said, then briskly walked back to the bedrooms.

Thirty minutes later, after making the beds and cleaning up the breakfast dishes, Liz picked Michael up off the kitchen floor, where he had entertained himself with pots and pans, an empty cereal container, and a collection of wooden spoons. She carried him back outside. This was their time together – for reading, playing, and talking – before the sun rose higher in the sky and the yard turned too hot. Michael didn't want to be carried, so she lowered him to the terrace and held his pudgy, little hand while he toddled down the steps to the lawn. Then she let him run free.

He ran to the glider swing and climbed onto one of the seats. "Swing, Mommy," he called.

Liz walked behind Michael to push the swing. She exulted in being a mother. Michael was her miracle.

Children's voices carried over the stone wall separating one side of their backyard from the elementary school grounds beyond. Liz turned and stepped onto a cinder block retaining wall enclosing a small, raised flower bed and stretched to look over the top at the school's blue and white Greek flag moving lazily in the slight morning breeze. She smiled at the trio of grade-school girls waving at her. Even on weekends, the school's playground attracted the neighborhood kids. Then the girls ran off toward the far side of the school grounds and all became quiet.

"Swing, Mommy," Michael said.

"Okay, sweetie," Liz said when she turned back. "Mommy's coming."

Liz had just stepped over the sleeping White Dog and taken a stride toward the swing set, when a whining sound came from the dog. Liz turned to look at White Dog and was surprised to hear the animal now growling low in her throat. The dog was usually calm, but now her brown-tipped ears were erect. She stood up and bared her fangs.

"What is it, girl," Liz said, "having a bad dream?"

The doorbell rang.

Amazing! Liz thought. Fast asleep and she hears someone at the front door before they ring the bell. Liz looked at Michael seated on the swing. "Come on, Mikey. Let's go see who's at the door."

"No-o, Mommy. I want to swing."

Liz glanced around the backyard. The five-foot-high, wrought iron street-side fences, along with the stone wall at the back and the school-side of the property, would keep her son safe inside the yard.

"Okay, Mikey. Mommy will be right back." White Dog preceded her up the steps from the yard to the terrace and through the open back door into the house, barking all the way.

When Liz reached the hall leading to the front entrance, she looked out through the glass panel of the locked front door. A dark-complected, black-haired woman of about thirty, dressed in an ankle-length red dress and a yellow headscarf, stood on the porch. A Gypsy.

White Dog was now growling, her nose pressed against the door handle.

Gypsies often came through Kifissia in horsedrawn wagons, stopping at houses to trade for clothing, blankets, and small appliances. A month ago, Liz had traded an old winter coat for a longhaired, white *flokati* rug.

"It's okay, girl," Liz told the dog. "Sit!"

White Dog sat but continued her low growling.

Liz unlocked and opened the front door.

"Hello, Missy. You vant buy nice rug?" the Gypsy said in a thick Slavic accent, fingering a long string of beads around her neck with one hand and pointing with the other hand at a fluffy orange *flokati* she had spread out on the porch. The woman gave Liz a warm smile.

Liz smiled back. The woman had bright, penetrating eyes, sparkling-white teeth, and was taller than most Gypsies Liz had seen in Greece.

"No, thank you; we already have more than we need." She felt bad about turning the woman down. She knew the Gypsies had a tough life, but she already had four of the rugs.

The Gypsy frowned. "I guess I get here too late," she said.

"Maybe next time you'll bring something other than rugs," Liz said.

The woman showed a bright, toothy smile. "You vont find good rug like this no vere. Ve got many more to show in vagon. You sure you don't vant?"

"I'm sure," Liz answered. "But not – "

White Dog suddenly rose up, her ears erect, her growling increasing in pitch and volume.

Liz grabbed the dog's collar, concerned that she might go after the Gypsy woman.

The Gypsy stared, stepped back, raised her hands as though to defend herself.

White Dog turned, twisting her collar in Liz's hand. She lunged toward the back of the house, now barking ferociously.

"I'm sorry," Liz said to the woman. "She never acts like this."

The Gypsy smiled, then shrugged, bent down, and slowly folded the rug, while Liz stood in the doorway and watched, tightly gripping White Dog's collar. With swaying skirts and a hand wave thrown over her shoulder at Liz, the woman walked down the stairs to the front gate and out to the street.

Liz shut the door and turned toward the rear of the house, releasing the dog. She was shocked at White Dog's behavior. The dog rushed toward the back door, snarling in a way Liz had never heard. Vicious rather than just protective. White Dog raced ahead, careening into the high chair in the breakfast room, her paws sliding on the marble floor.

Liz trailed, more puzzled than alarmed. By the time she reached the open back door, White Dog had already crossed the terrace, jumped the four-foot drop onto the lawn, then ran to the empty swing set. Michael wasn't on the glider. He was nowhere in sight.

"Michael! Michael!" Liz called.

No reply.

Liz watched White Dog, a speeding blur vault over the fence separating the yard from the side street. Liz dashed to the fence and looked down the street in the direction the dog had run. Nothing.

Panicked now, her heart racing and acid assaulting her stomach, Liz turned right at the back corner of the house and ran down the interior walk paralleling the street and leading around to the front porch. Where was Michael? She caught a glimpse of White Dog racing down the street in front of the house. Liz rushed to the front gate.

"Mommy!" she heard Michael cry. Liz could hear fear in his voice. "Mommy!" he screamed. But she couldn't see him anywhere.

Blood pounding in her throat, Liz slammed into the front gate, snapping its metal latch. She looked down the street to the right. A horse-drawn wagon moved quickly away. A young woman wearing bright-colored Gypsy attire briefly looked back in Liz's direction as she scurried after the wagon. The woman carried a squirming, screaming bundle – Michael. She looked back at the wagon and thrust Michael toward a man standing on a narrow platform at the back of the wagon.

"Michael!" Liz screamed.

The man passed Michael to another Gypsy woman standing at the wagon's curtained doorway. She turned and disappeared with Michael inside the wagon. The woman looked like the one who had come to Liz's door with the rug.

Liz chased after them, screeching, "Oh God, Michael!"

The man on the platform reached down and pulled the running Gypsy woman up by her arms into the wagon. White Dog leaped up after her.

Liz sprinted as fast as she could, but the wagon, gaining speed, pulled away from her. It turned a corner at the end of the street and disappeared with a receding clatter of horse's hooves. She heard White Dog's ferocious barking end with a yelp. By the time she reached the corner, the wagon had vanished and White Dog lay in the gutter, a knife handle protruding from her side, blood painting her snow-white hair a shockingly brilliant red.

CHAPTER THREE

"Thirty-seventh Detachment, Sergeant Carpenter speaking, sir."

"Sergeant Carpenter, it's Liz Danforth. Please, I need to talk to my husband now!"

"He's on the phone with the Colonel, Mrs. Danforth. How about I take a message and have him call you back in a minute?"

"No . . . No-o-o! I need to talk to Bob NOW!"

Carpenter carried a scrawled message into Bob's office: "Mrs. D on line two. Urgent!" He dropped the message in front of Bob and left, closing the door behind him.

Bob looked at the note, surprised at the interruption. Carpenter knew better than to disturb him when he was talking with Colonel Gray. When he saw the word "Urgent!" he asked the Colonel to hold for a moment. He realized Liz had a habit of reacting to little everyday problems as crises, but he also knew she'd never called before and said it was urgent. He pushed the button for line two.

"Liz, what's up? I was on the phone–"

"They took Michael," she sobbed. "The Gypsies took our baby!"

"Liz, what are you talking–?"

Bob heard Liz's voice suddenly change, from trembly to a brittle tenor akin to shattering glass. "He's gone, Bob. Michael's gone."

"Sergeant Carpenter!" Bob shouted loud enough to be heard through the solid oak office door.

Carpenter ran back into the office. "Yes, sir!"

"Get my driver. Call the Greek police and tell them to get to my house. My son's been kidnapped. Inform the security officer at the Embassy. And get on the line and explain to Colonel Gray."

15

Throughout the ride down the narrow, curving road from the nuclear missile site at Katsamidi, Bob begged his driver, Demetrius, to go faster. He tried to keep his imagination from cartwheeling out of control. What could have happened to his son? He'd held him in his arms less than an hour ago, nuzzling him, smelling his sweet baby skin. He'd kissed Liz and Michael and petted the dog and, as he did every morning, said, "Keep your head down."

He hadn't really worried about his family's safety – Athens was safer than his hometown of Pittsburgh. Their suburb of Kifissia was about as safe a place as anyone could find.

The pickup screeched around the corner, sliding on the gravel shoulder in front of the house, when Demetrius braked hard. Bob leaped from the truck before it completely stopped, then raced through the front gate. A trail of dark red spots led up the white, mottled terrazzo steps and onto the front porch. Flies buzzed around the spots. A smear of red led to a bone-handled knife with a bloodied six-inch blade lying in one corner of the porch. Bob's stomach seemed to somersault and the familiar tingling, breath-arresting signs of fear assailed his chest.

The droplets of blood continued past the threshold and down the marble entryway, back toward the bedrooms.

"Liz!" Bob called while he rushed toward the back of the house. No answer. He found her in Michael's room, kneeling next to White Dog, in the middle of a pure-white *flokati* rug, her arms, jeans, and tank top spotted, smeared with still-damp blotches of blood. A chill hit Bob's spine and nausea rose in his throat.

Liz looked up at him, her blue eyes glistening with tears, with an open-eyed, childlike expression. "She's dead, Bob. They took our baby and killed White Dog."

Bob dropped to his knees and pressed a hand against the dog's chest. Nothing. No pulse, no movement, no sound. He bent closer and leaned his head against White Dog's chest. He thought he heard a heartbeat but it could have been his imagination. No, there it was again.

CHAPTER FOUR

In a flurry of movement, Bob wrapped White Dog in the rug, carried her out to the pickup truck, and ordered his driver to take the dog to the veterinarian, three blocks away on Levidou Street. He then raced back into the house, back to Liz. He found her in the same spot, an open suitcase on the floor beside her, packing some of Michael's clothes.

"What happened?" Bob asked, forcing himself to remain calm. "Tell me what happened to Michael."

The look in Liz's eyes momentarily took Bob's breath away. They were dull, lifeless. "The Gypsies," she said. "They took my baby."

This made no sense to Bob. Gypsies kidnapped children only in old wives' tales. He'd never heard of Gypsies stealing children in Greece. He would have known about such crimes from the weekly intelligence briefings he received. Bob tried to get Liz to talk, but she appeared almost catatonic. He reached down for her and pulled her to her feet. He used a hand to brush her hair away from her face.

"Come on, sweetheart; let's get you cleaned up," he said, trying to keep the terror out of his voice while he moved her toward the bathroom.

She moved sluggishly and leaned heavily against him. Then, as though she'd suddenly been charged with electricity, she lashed out at him, beating his chest with her fists, screaming. "You weren't here, you weren't here! We needed you, but you weren't here!"

Then, just as suddenly as she had turned on him, she seemed to deflate, sagging into him.

Bob wrapped an arm around her waist and continued toward the bathroom.

"I carried White Dog home," she said in a little girl voice.

"I know, Liz." Bob felt as though his heart had been diced into a thousand pieces. Her words had penetrated his very soul. *We needed you, but you weren't here.*

Bob gently moved Liz to the shower. He removed her blood-saturated clothes, tossed them on the shower floor, and turned on the water. The pan ran red, then pink with blood. After shutting off the water and toweling Liz dry, he took her bathrobe off a hook on the back of the door and helped her to put it on.

He tried again to get her to talk. "What happened, honey?" he rasped. "Tell me what happened. Tell me about the Gypsies," he pleaded.

"We have to get Michael's clothes to him, Bob," she said, her voice barely audible, droning as though she were drugged. "What's he going to do without his clothes?"

CHAPTER FIVE

Bob jumped at the sound of the doorbell. He patted Liz's shoulder, rose from the couch, bent over, and kissed the top of her head. No reaction. He now understood what it meant to have a heavy heart. Liz just continued sitting there. She seemed to be lost in some emotional black hole. Bob sighed and walked to the front door.

A short, thin man who looked like an undertaker in his all-black outfit stood on the porch. Two average-sized, uniformed Greek police officers bracketed him, emphasizing just how short the man actually was. At six-feet-two-inches, Bob towered over the man.

"Inspector Petros Zavitsanos," the man said, offering his hand. Bob noticed there was no emotion on the Inspector's face. His features seemed to be made of stone, his eyes black marbles.

Bob took Zavitsanos' hand. "Bob Danforth. Please come in," he said. "Have you heard anything? Have you found Michael?"

The Inspector's face appeared to sag for a moment, then recovered its granite-like composure.

Zavitsanos shook his head. "Nothing yet, Captain Danforth." Then he turned toward one of the policemen and made a waving motion of his hand. In Greek, he ordered, "Look around the grounds, check with the neighbors, the school next door. Maybe someone saw or heard something."

"Wouldn't the neighbors have said something if they'd seen my son kidnapped?" Bob said in Greek.

"Oh, you speak my language," Zavitsanos said. While Bob nodded, the Inspector added, "Yes, they probably would have already come forward. But you never know."

Bob stepped aside and allowed Zavitsanos to enter the foyer. He watched the two policemen step around the blood spots on the porch.

He turned and led the Inspector to the living room. Bob tipped his head in Liz's direction and grimaced. "She's been like this since I got home an hour ago."

Liz sat on the couch with their son's yellow-headed Playskool hammer in her hands, staring vacantly across the room. Bob thought her skin looked gray, her eyes disconnected from the present.

Bob turned to Zavitsanos and shrugged. "I don't think she's going to be able to help you."

Zavitsanos walked over to a bookcase and pointed at a framed photograph.

"This is your son Michael?" the Inspector said.

Bob nodded.

Zavitsanos took the picture to the couch and sat next to Liz. "Your son is very handsome, Mrs. Danforth. Can you tell me something about him?" He held the photo in front of her face.

Liz grabbed it from him and clutched it to her breast. "Michael's not here," she said.

CHAPTER SIX

Stefan Radko sat behind the wheel of the gray Mercedes parked on an Athens residential street. He shifted his six-foot, four-inch frame, trying to release the tension in his back and legs. Vanja, his Bulgarian mistress, sat beside him. She was complaining in a high-pitched, fingernails-on-a-blackboard voice, but Stefan wasn't paying attention to what she said. He twisted one end of his thick, black mustache while he concentrated on his current predicament. He'd been the leader, the *bulibasha*, of both his clan and a great band of families – a *kumpania*. But now the members of his old *kumpania* considered him *mahrime* – unclean, polluted. Having a mistress was considered "illicit." Especially a *gadja* – a non-Gypsy. But he knew his people ostracized him for another reason. They believed he had secret wealth; that he was holding out on his clan. They weren't wrong.

Now he led only a five-member team composed of a few blood relatives and Vanja. His little group had also become pariahs to the Gypsy community – the *Rom* – because they'd found a way to make real the *gadjo* myth that Gypsies steal children. Kidnapping babies, for profit or otherwise, was abhorrent to the Gypsy community. But it didn't bother Stefan Radko and his crew. Even when the *puri daj*, the old matriarch, "gave him the eye," cursing him and his followers – *Te bisterdon tumare anava* (May your names be forgotten) – he had just laughed.

Radko felt a rush of adrenaline each time he snatched a child. But this one was different. This one was American. He tried to consider all the implications. Would he still be paid? Should he just dump the kid? He needed to think this through, but Vanja wasn't helping. He looked at her. No matter how mad she made him, he still felt a stirring in his loins. Twenty years his junior, blond and blue-eyed, voluptuous; she was the best looking woman he'd ever fucked. But he had to teach her who was boss.

"Shut up, woman," he yelled, shooting her an icy-blue-eyed, venomous look. "I can't think with you complaining in my ear!"

"I told you not to send that imbecile, Rumiah. Didn't I say she'd cause trouble?" Vanja shouted. "But, oh no, just because she's your sister. I'll put a curse on—"

He busted her lip with the back of his hand.

Silence.

CHAPTER SEVEN

Bob sat with Liz until the drugs the doctor gave her kicked in. Then he helped her to their bed and left her long enough to call the veterinarian to check on White Dog. He wasn't surprised but his heart still felt leaden when the vet told him he shouldn't get his hopes up. Bob looked across the room at White Dog's bed. "You were here," he whispered. "You tried to save Michael. That's more than I did."

Even after the sedatives knocked her out, Liz moaned in the bed, her arms and legs twitching spasmodically. She tossed her head from side to side. Bob paced. He passed the telephone a hundred times, each time silently praying for it to ring with news about his son. But the doorbell rang instead.

He couldn't keep disappointment from his face when he saw his commander, Colonel Geoffrey Gray, and Gray's wife, Susan, on his front porch.

"How's Liz?" Gray asked.

"Out cold," Bob said. "The doctor said she'd sleep until morning."

Gray shook his head. "And how are you doing?"

"Jeez, Geoffrey, how do you think he's doing?" Susan snapped at her husband.

Gray shot his wife a look. "Why don't you check on Liz?" he suggested between clenched teeth.

Susan stomped toward the bedroom.

"It's been over fourteen hours, and not a word," Bob said, his voice breaking. "I don't have a clue where to look for him. I'm a soldier, Colonel. I know how to fight. But *who* do I fight? I've never felt more lost in my life."

Gray put a hand on Bob's shoulder.

"I pulled some strings over at the Hellenic army headquarters," he said. "They're sending someone from the police to escort you to a roadblock up north on the National Highway. They can always use another set of eyes and ears. And who better than you when it comes to identifying Michael? I think–"

The doorbell interrupted Gray. He walked to the front door and opened it. "Yes, what is it?" Gray growled.

"Inspector Petros Zavitsanos," the man said, displaying an identification card.

"We've been waiting for someone from the police," Gray said. "But I didn't expect an inspector to be sent on escort duty."

"Just part of the job, Colonel," Zavitsanos said. "Especially when the Minister of Security orders it." There was a hint of reprimand in his tone, as though he knew it was Gray who had called the Minister. Zavitsanos looked at Bob. "Are you ready?" he asked. "We are going to a highway checkpoint."

"Yeah," Bob said. "But give me a minute." He left the room and tiptoed back to the bedroom. The buzz of heavy breathing came to him when he opened the door. Susan Gray sat in a chair next to the bed. She held Liz's hand.

"Thanks for coming," Bob whispered. Then he stepped to the opposite side of the bed and bent over, putting his mouth next to Liz's ear. "I'm going out to try to find Michael, Liz. You've got to get better. I need you."

Liz's breathing skipped a beat, then subsided into a regular pattern again. Bob kissed her cheek and straightened up.

"Don't worry about her," Susan Gray said. "I'll stay with her. You go find your son."

Zavitsanos led Bob down the front steps to the blue and white police cruiser parked in front of the house. They entered the vehicle and Zavitsanos drove away, north toward the entrance to the National Highway.

"There are two routes from Athens to the northern border– the old road going through villages and towns, and the highway, bypassing them all," Zavitsanos explained. "If the people who kidnapped your son took the old road, they'll ultimately probably go through Thiva. We're stopping all traffic just this side of Thiva. Wagons are not permitted on the National Highway, so we assume the Gypsies are on the old road, unless they transferred your son to a car."

"Why are you focusing to the north?" Bob asked.

"Because my instincts tell me the Gypsies who took your son will follow their normal, traditional route north into the Balkans."

"What if the kidnappers passed Thiva before the roadblocks were set?"

"We also alerted the guards all along our northern border," Zavitsanos said.

"But kidnappers could hide out in any one of a thousand villages, until the government gets tired of operating roadblocks."

Zavitsanos nodded. "Yes, that is possible."

The drive to Thiva took an hour. They approached the roadblock just shy of midnight. The flashing lights of a dozen police vehicles illuminated the night sky.

Zavitsanos flipped a dashboard switch to turn on his own roof flashers and drove on the shoulder of the road to bypass the line of more than two hundred cars and trucks waiting to get through.

CHAPTER EIGHT

Zavitsanos said a silent prayer that they would find the little boy. But the more time that passed, the more discouraged he became. He knew the odds were already in favor of the kidnappers.

"We've been here more than three hours, Captain Danforth," Zavitsanos said, tapping his watch. "Maybe I should take you home. You look like you need some rest."

"No, no. I'm fine," Bob responded. "Just a little while longer. Okay?"

Zavitsanos shrugged and walked over to a policeman pouring thick *café turkiko* from a thermos into a tin cup.

"How's the father doing?" the officer asked.

"He's tough – a lot tougher than I would be under similar circumstances. But being here must give him some hope." Zavitsanos turned to walk back to Danforth.

"You know we're wasting our time here, Inspector," the officer said to Zavitsanos' back.

Zavitsanos spun around. "*Kopane!* The last thing we need around here is that attitude."

The officer's face reddened. "Yes, sir."

The Inspector walked away. Bad attitude or not, he thought, the policeman was probably right.

CHAPTER NINE

Janos Milatko stirred. Something off in the distance wasn't right. Pounding. Loud. Insistent. He came awake. Three rapid knocks, followed by a pause and then two knocks spaced around a three-second pause told him all he needed to know – it was someone from his clan. Janos picked up his watch off the nightstand. Three a.m. He glanced at his wife. Still asleep.

Janos slipped out of bed and padded barefoot across the wood floor of his tiny Athens apartment. He opened the door a crack and saw his uncle, Stefan Radko, the last person he expected or wanted to see. Stefan started to push his way in but Janos put a finger to his lips and pointed out into the hall.

"What do you want, Uncle?" Janos asked, after stepping into the dimly lit hall and closing the door to a crack behind him.

"I need your help," Stefan said. "Vanja and I have to get out of Athens."

"I left the family life, Uncle," Janos said. He hated that his voice quavered. "You know that. I want nothing to do with you or your schemes."

Stefan's smile was like a knife. "I wonder what your sweet little Greek wife would do if she found out you were *Rom*."

Janos' shoulders drooped.

"All you have to do is drive Vanja and me up north, just across from Petrich. I know your delivery route takes you to Thessaloniki and Kavalla in northern Greece. So you take a little detour, drop us off near the Bulgarian border. Then you can be on your way. And I will never tell a soul about being a Gypsy." He clapped Janos on the arm so hard the young man fell back against the doorjamb.

Janos looked at Stefan's bushy eyebrows and full mustache. They made him appear almost diabolical. He remembered stories he'd heard while growing up about his uncle. Stefan was a legend and an outcast. Some called him a Gypsy hero; others thought him the most ruthless man in all of Romany.

"I have to drive a shipment of televisions north this morning. My truck is already loaded."

"Then let's leave now, nephew. No point in putting off the inevitable." Stefan raised his hand as though to slap his nephew again, but Janos flinched and ducked away.

Janos sighed. "Okay! Wait downstairs; I need to get dressed."

"Sure, whatever you say."

Stefan walked away down the hall, whistling softly, as though he didn't have a thing to be concerned about.

"*Malaka*," Janos cursed.

Stefan ordered his nephew to open the panel truck's overhead door. When Janos did so, Vanja stepped out of an alcove in the adjoining building, carrying a child bundled in her arms.

"What the hell is this?" Janos exclaimed. "You said it was just you and Vanja. Whose kid is that?"

Ignoring Janos' outburst, Stefan said to Vanja, "Take the boy into the back of the truck and lie down behind the boxes. Keep him quiet." Vanja complied, and Stefan pulled down the overhead door and latched it in place. Then he turned toward Janos, grabbed him by the front of his jacket, and pulled him to his chest. "Listen to me, you gutless prick. You are not to ask any questions."

"Ye . . . yes, Uncle Stefan."

"Good. Now put your ass behind the wheel and get on the road."

CHAPTER TEN

By sunrise, Bob had, to no avail, helped search hundreds of vehicles.

"We'll have a riot on our hands if we don't speed this up," Zavitsanos was saying to his men. "Traffic is increasing. There must be five hundred vehicles backed up now."

"The cars are easy to search," one of the policemen answered. "The trucks are the problem. What if we just inspect the cargo area of every third truck? That should move things along faster. Besides, who would be dumb enough to be on this road with a kidnapped child? The news of the roadblocks has been on radio and television for hours."

Zavitsanos glared at the man. He wasn't in the mood to make any concessions that might let the kidnappers slip through. But common sense told him the man was right. They couldn't slow down the country's economy. He kicked at a stone lying just off the road shoulder, propelling it against the side of one of the police cruisers. He saw despair on Bob's face but knew he had no choice. "All right, do it. Every third truck. But if you think a driver or passenger in any truck is acting suspiciously, I want the vehicle searched."

Zavitsanos stood off to the side, behind a police van, away from prying eyes, and feeling as though his whole body was dissolving. He watched Danforth scurry from vehicle to vehicle, a manic father wired with fear and adrenaline. Danforth was trying to look through the windows of every truck the Greek officers ignored. He frantically tried to make up the difference. What a terror! Zavitsanos thought. To lose a child. He set his jaw, narrowed his eyes, and stepped away from the vehicle. He'd help the young American as much as possible, even though every cell in his body told him the boy would never be found.

CHAPTER ELEVEN

"Don't you have a radio in this goddamn truck?" Stefan asked.

Janos pointed to a portable tape recorder on the seat between them. "I'm taking a night class in German. I listen to language tapes during my trips. I don't need a radio."

"Always trying to learn something new, eh, Janos? Trying to improve yourself. If you'd used your brains and worked with me, you wouldn't be driving a fucking truck."

Janos didn't respond.

Suddenly, Stefan sat up in his seat and stared ahead. "Slow down," he ordered.

Janos brought the truck's speed down to forty kilometers an hour. "Looks like a traffic backup," he said. "Maybe an accident."

"Turn this thing around," Stefan yelled.

"Where?" Janos said. "There's a chain-link fence in the middle of the highway, in case you haven't noticed. And there are vehicles right behind us." He paused to look in his sideview mirror. "Including a police car."

Stefan pulled a pistol from the inside pocket of his leather jacket and placed it on the seat under his right thigh. "Okay, here's what we'll do. If there has been an accident, no problem. If it's something else – like a roadblock–"

"They're after you, aren't they?" Janos interrupted. "They're looking for the little boy!"

In a calm, but menacing voice, Stefan said, "You are in this thing all the way now. If we get caught, I'll tell the police you were in on the kidnapping from the beginning. Do you really think they'll believe a Gypsy could be innocent of anything? Stay cool and keep your mouth shut. I'll do the talking."

Janos sat behind the wheel, sweating, inching his truck forward. It took forty-five minutes to reach a turn in the road that allowed them to see the police cars up ahead.

"Shit!" Janos exclaimed, "It *is* a roadblock." He drummed the steering wheel with his fingers and beat a tattoo against the floorboard with his left foot.

"We're dead."

As they neared the front of the line, Janos noticed the cops searched only some of the trucks – every third one. He counted back to his own truck. One-two-three, one-two-three, one-two-three. He was a number three.

CHAPTER TWELVE

Bob shielded his eyes against the light from the rising sun. He knew he couldn't keep this up much longer. Lack of sleep and the emotional strain of the last twenty hours had taken a toll. His eyes burned and his head felt as though a dagger was embedded in each temple. He continued to throw himself into the vehicle searches, crawling over and around the cargo in the back of every third truck. But it drove him mad to think his son could be hidden in the windowless cargo bays of one of the trucks not being searched.

"Where are you heading?" the officer asked Janos.

"Thessa . . ." Janos began. His voice broke and Stefan finished answering.

"Thessaloniki," Stefan said. "My nephew has lost his voice. Too much yelling at last weekend's match between *Panathenaikos* and AEK. You young men and your football."

Stefan laughed. The policeman just stared back.

The cop waved at Janos to get out of the truck's cab. "Open the cargo bay," he instructed.

Stefan gripped the pistol under his thigh, just when a second police officer, armed with an automatic rifle, stepped onto the passenger-side running board. Two other armed policemen stationed themselves in front of the vehicle.

Janos looked at his uncle for guidance. All he received in return was a granite look that sent chills up his spine. He opened the door and stepped down to the road. After walking to the rear of his truck, he unlatched the cargo door and began lifting it. We're doomed, he thought.

Zavitsanos sat sideways on the front seat of the borrowed police cruiser, his feet planted in the road, listening to the man from headquarters speak over the radio. When the man finished, Zavitsanos released the venom he felt. "I've already cut back to inspecting only every third truck. We search only every fifth one, we might as well close the damn thing down."

Then he listened for a while again.

A few seconds after headquarters stopped talking, he spat, "Yes, sir."

Zavitsanos dropped the radio microphone onto the car seat and stood up. He looked down the line of traffic, then concentrated on the first truck in line. "*Scata!*" he yelled. He slammed the car door shut and walked to the policeman standing on the truck's passenger-side running board.

"Spiro, let this one through. We search only every fifth truck."

"But, Inspector, we—"

"Just shut up and do what I tell you," Zavitsanos said, turning away.

The cop stared after Zavitsanos, then glared at Stefan and spread his arms out. "You can pass through." The cop jumped down to the street and walked to the rear of the truck where he repeated Zavitsanos' instructions.

"Spiro, the fucking door is already open. It will only take a minute to look inside."

"Fine," Spiro said, "I'll go tell Inspector Zavitsanos you disagree with his order."

"Goddammit!" the second cop cursed. He turned on Janos and barked, "Close the door and get this thing out of here."

Janos pulled the cargo door back down and locked it in place. He went around the side of the truck, stumbling on fear-weakened legs. He continued to the driver's door, sweat pouring off him. After climbing behind the wheel, he started the engine, feeling as though his heart would fail as the truck idled.

"You can't do that! We'll miss Michael for sure," Bob shouted. "It was bad enough to let two out of three trucks pass. We might as well go home now."

Zavitsanos took a moment to respond. "I'm sorry, Captain Danforth," he said.

"Goddammit, man!" Bob grabbed at the Inspector's lapels. "This is my son you're talking about. Michael!"

Michael rubbed his eyes with his bunched fists. He heard shouting. He looked for his mommy, but it was so dark. Someone in the corner . . . who is it? Is it Mommy? Oh, it's the lady with the red scarf. A thin ray of light came through a crack in a wall and shined on boxes stacked to the ceiling.

I don't like it here. I'm hungry.

Maybe the lady has something to eat.

"Michael!"

He heard his name clearly. That's my daddy.

Then the room he was in began moving.

"No bye-bye, Daddy!" he cried.

CHAPTER THIRTEEN

Bob woke bathed in sweat, barely able to get his breath. He looked at the alarm clock beside the bed. Four o'clock in the afternoon. He'd slept for less than three hours since Zavitsanos had dropped him off back at the house. He looked for Liz, but she wasn't there. His heart leaped against his rib cage. Panic sluiced through him as he rushed from the bedroom.

He found her in Michael's room, sitting in the rocking chair, illuminated by a ray of late afternoon sun sparkling with dust motes. Her hand moved Michael's favorite toy – a black rocking horse. Bob knelt in front of her. "Everything's going to be fine, Liz," he said, knowing his voice betrayed how little confidence he had in his own words. He took her hands in his. "We'll find Michael, I promise."

Liz didn't speak. She stared into space, no emotion showing, and began to hum *Rock-A-Bye Baby*.

He dropped his head into her lap. First his son, now his wife. Had he lost them both? There wasn't much that could make him cry, but since Michael's kidnapping he'd cried a lifetime of tears. His tears now dampened the cotton of Liz's gown. Then he felt her hand on his head, stroking his hair.

Bob's heart lurched with hope. She'd finally responded. He raised his head and looked at his wife.

"It's okay, baby," Liz said. "I'll take care of you. You don't need to cry. You never have to cry when Mommy's around. You know that, don't you, Michael?"

CHAPTER FOURTEEN

"Turn here," Stefan Radko told his nephew Janos two miles from the border, pointing at a dirt road leading into a forest. About a mile up the road, he ordered Janos to stop.

"This is where we get out, nephew. I'm sure you'll be sorry to see us go." Stefan laughed as though he had just heard the greatest joke in the world. He slapped Janos on the shoulder. "Quite an adventure, eh boy!"

Janos slumped over the steering wheel, staring at the dashboard.

Stefan laughed again, then violently poked a finger into Janos' arm. "You keep your fucking mouth shut, you understand?" When Janos did not respond, Stefan grabbed the young man's arm and squeezed until Janos grunted from the pain. "Did you hear what I said?" Stefan growled.

"Yes, Uncle Stefan," Janos whimpered.

"You'd better keep quiet. Or I'll track you down."

Stefan opened the truck door and jumped to the ground. He walked to the back of the vehicle, rolled up the rear door, and whispered hoarsely, "Let's go, woman."

A shuffling sound came from the front of the cargo area, and then Vanja peered out at him from between two rows of boxes.

"Where are we?" she asked.

"What do you care?" Stefan spat. "Let's go."

The sleeping boy in her arms, Vanja lowered herself to a sitting position on the back of the truck bed, then dropped carefully to the ground. Stefan made no attempt to assist her. He closed the back door and, without a word, set off on foot through the trees. The sun was now low in the sky. They would have to wait until after midnight to try to cross the border into Bulgaria.

Janos watched his passengers in the sideview mirror. He felt a chill go through him when they seemed to disappear in the dense forest. Oh, God, he thought. What have I done?

CHAPTER FIFTEEN

The drugs the doctor had prescribed for Liz kept her listless and mostly silent. They helped her construct a shell around herself that Bob couldn't penetrate. Nothing he said seemed to reach her. The blank, lifeless look in her eyes scared him.

He needed to feel his family around him. He went to the hall closet and pulled out a box of home movies and a movie projector. He selected a reel he'd taken a few Sundays before and threaded it through the projector. After closing the shutters to darken the room, he flipped on the machine, and looked at the images of Liz and Michael that popped up on the living room wall. His wife and son stood in the kitchen doorway, silhouetted against early-morning sun bathing the patio and the yard beyond. The weather had been perfect – warm, but not hot. He knew how much Liz loved her mornings with Michael.

"Swing, Mommy, swing," Michael said.

"Okay, baby," Liz responded. "As soon as Mommy finds her sunglasses, we'll go play on the swings."

The next scene showed Liz and Michael facing each other, lazily swinging back and forth on the glider. White Dog lounged on the terrace, basking in the sun.

"Look at the bird in the tree, Michael," Liz pointed. "It's a robin."

"Wobbin," Michael repeated and pointed with a pudgy finger.

"Do you know that one over there?" Liz said. She pointed out a bird perched on a bush.

Michael showed a confident smile and said, "Wenn."

"Good boy," Liz exclaimed.

Michael began singing some indecipherable tune, hamming it up. The sound of his voice coming from the projector filled the room and Bob's eyes brimmed with tears. He stared at his son's image and felt an ache penetrating his entire being.

Then movement in the hallway startled Bob. Liz suddenly stumbled into the living room, frantically looking around. He stood and moved toward her. She turned to Michael's image on the wall, staring, frozen in place. Then she rushed to the wall, her hand raised to touch Michael's face. But she blocked the projector's lens, obliterating her son's image. She backed away and stared at the wall.

"Michael, it's Mommy. I'm here, sweetheart." Then she began to sob.

Bob reached his wife and held her until she stopped crying. "Take it easy, Liz. We'll get our son back," he said, stroking her face. "But I can't do it without you."

Liz's eyes grew wide in the light from the projector. Bob thought he saw a brief hint of lucidity, but then she seemed to fade back to the demented vacuum she'd been occupying since Michael was kidnapped. She grabbed the front of his shirt. "What can we do?" she said, panic in her voice. "What can *I* do?"

Bob couldn't hold her gaze. The guilt he felt over not being with his family when they needed him was already like a bleeding wound. The lost look in Liz's eyes only made him feel worse.

"First, you have to eat something," he said. "I need you strong and well. Then we'll figure something out. No one's going to keep our baby from us."

Bob's words seemed to bring Liz all the way back for a moment. She turned to the wall. "Look at his face, so trusting. We've got to find Michael before it's too late." Then she devolved into sobs and sank to the floor.

Bob knelt and wrapped her in his arms. "We'll find him, honey. You can count on it," he said. He wanted to believe what he'd said with every fiber of his body and soul.

CHAPTER SIXTEEN

Stefan and Vanja took turns sleeping and watching the child. They twice gave the boy milk, but the sedative they'd given him kept him asleep most of the time. At midnight, they left their hiding place in the forest, carrying the child through the trees. When they approached the border, they squatted down behind a cluster of boulders. It was almost 1:00 a.m.

"It's cold, Stefan. How long do we have to stay here?"

"Until I damn well tell you to move," he rasped. "Now keep your mouth shut. If the border guards hear you, we're finished."

Stefan timed the guards. The Greek guards walked past from right to left at fifteen minutes before the hour and, ten minutes later, walked in the other direction. Because of the dark and the distance, he couldn't see the Bulgarian guards on the other side of the border wire. But he heard them. He saw the glow of their cigarettes. They patrolled on the half-hour, also reversing course ten minutes later.

Vanja tugged at Stefan's sleeve. "I don't know how much longer the boy will stay asleep," she whispered. "We have no more pills to give him."

"The Greeks should pass by again in fifteen minutes. We'll cross over after that. Calm down; you'll wake him."

Stefan studied the obstacles they'd have to cope with when they emerged from the trees. It would be a simple matter to slip through the barbwire fence running down the middle of the deforested strip of land. The trip wires on either side of that fence were another matter. He would have to use the flashlight even though its beam might give them away. If the guards on either side changed the interval of their inspections. . ..

Radko thought about the hundreds of times he'd hidden in forests, risking his life for profit. He remembered his days as a *haidouk*, a guerrilla – a fancy name for a bandit really – during World War II, fighting the Nazis.

He'd joined a Communist guerilla cell, not because of any affinity for the Communists, but because the Communist guerillas operated close to where he lived. They ambushed German military convoys and looted the vehicles and the bodies of the soldiers they killed. He'd first come in contact with the Bulgarian Intelligence Agency during that time. His relationship with the BIA had lasted ever since.

Ten minutes after the next Greek patrol passed, Stefan rose from the ground. Vanja stood and grunted with Michael's weight in her arms.

"Stay right behind me," Stefan ordered. He set out at a slow pace, bent over, with the flashlight beam pointed at the ground and his hand cupped around its lens. Fifteen paces, sixteen paces . . . twenty-nine paces. He froze. "See here," he whispered to Vanja. A trip wire in the short grass gleamed under the flashlight beam.

They stepped carefully over it and proceeded as before, slowly, quietly, encountering a second trip wire just before reaching the barbed wire fence marking the border.

Stefan lifted the top strand of barbed wire and put his foot on the middle strand. Vanja put the sleeping baby on the ground and slipped through the opening Stefan made for her. Stefan picked up Michael in Greece and handed him to Vanja in Bulgaria. Then he stepped through and joined her. They were fifteen minutes beyond the border before Michael woke and started to wail.

Stefan stepped out of the shadows and walked to the guard shack outside the People's Home for Orphans' entrance gate. He saw a man leaning against the shack suddenly come alert, drop his cigarette, and fumble with his rifle.

Quickly moving into the cone of light coming from a flood lamp attached to the shack's roof, Stefan raised his arms and said, "Take it easy. It's me, Radko, to see Headmistress Vulovich. I've got a delivery for her."

The man used the telephone in the guard shack to call the office in the massive stone building beyond the gate. After a short conversation on the telephone, he unlocked the tall wrought iron gate.

"She's expecting you. Go on up."

Stefan and Vanja followed the long gravel walkway to a stone staircase that climbed to a pair of huge double wooden doors. Michael started crying again.

"Can't you shut him up?" Stefan growled while lifting the iron knocker on the right door panel and letting it drop.

The door opened, creaking as it moved slowly, exposing the ornate marble-floored entryway under a massive five-tiered chandelier.

"Ah, Stefan," Katrina Vulovich said. "What have you and Vanja brought me this trip?"

"A little boy, Katrina. I brought you a little boy. I think you will be pleased."

"Come into the light," Katrina said. "Let me have a look at him."

Stefan and Vanja stepped through the doorway and into the brightly lit foyer.

Katrina gasped and clasped her hands together against her chest. "He's beautiful," she said.

"How can you tell," Stefan asked, "with him screaming like that?"

"You just don't know how to handle children, Stefan. Give him to me." Katrina took the boy from Vanja. His screams subsided into whimpers when she hugged him to her breast.

"Did you have any trouble?" Katrina asked.

"No, everything went smoothly," Stefan lied.

"Good." She walked over to a side table and picked up an envelope. "Here's your fee, Stefan. Ten American one hundred-dollar bills. Your little business is going to make you rich. How many has it been?"

"Twenty-seven with this one," Stefan said. "It's good doing business with you, Comrade Vulovich."

"When can I expect to see you again, Stefan?" Katrina asked.

"In less than a month."

CHAPTER SEVENTEEN

Few people would be able to tell from looking at Franklin Meers that he was the U.S. Embassy's Chief of Intelligence in Greece. He had wire-rimmed glasses, pale skin, and an Ichabod Crane-like Adam's apple. Tall and gawky, in a preppie way, he looked more like a thirty-five-year-old professor than a spook. His physical appearance lent credence to most people's opinion of him: Someone devoid of feeling, just another low-level bureaucrat doing grunt work for Uncle Sam. They didn't know the real Franklin Meers. Just because he had learned to hide his emotions well didn't mean he wasn't passionate or capable of acting out his passion. Now seated across a table from Bob and Liz Danforth, Meers was damned upset and having a tough time not showing it.

They sat at a corner table shielded from the hot afternoon sun by a blue canvas umbrella with *Campari* printed on it in big white letters. The tables near them were unoccupied. Thank God for the Greek siesta, Meers thought. Most of Athens is probably asleep.

"Captain Danforth, Mrs. Danforth, what I'm about to tell you is classified," he said, keeping his voice down. "Even with the kidnapping of your child, technically you don't have a need to know. Providing you with this information could get me in trouble."

The tortured look on Liz Danforth's face when she stared at him tugged at Meers' heart. She nodded.

"I want you to bear with me while I provide some history," Meers said, "then I'll explain what may have happened to Michael." At his mention of the boy's name, a grim look came over both of the young parents' faces.

"When the Germans invaded Greece during World War II, Greek partisans took to the mountains and forged a resistance movement. Allied governments – principally England and the United States – supported many of the resistance units. The U.S., for example, infiltrated OSS agents into Greece to facilitate the provision of supplies and equipment to the partisans and to gather intelligence on Nazi activities."

"What's the OSS?" Liz asked.

"The Office of Strategic Services," Meers said. "Effectively, the forerunner to the CIA. Its information gathering focused not only on Nazis, but also on Communist resistance groups. The U.S. and Greek governments were concerned about Stalin's plans for Greece once the war ended."

"But what has this to do with getting Michael back?" Bob interjected.

"Maybe a lot!" Meers said. "You need to let me finish. Then you'll understand." He removed his glasses and wiped them with his handkerchief. "The Soviets also supported resistance groups, whose members often murdered members of non-Communist guerrilla units who threatened their influence over an area. You can't imagine the atrocities the Greek Communists visited on their own countrymen."

Meers sketched a rough map of Greece and the Balkans on a paper napkin. "The Communists concentrated their activities in these areas," he said, jabbing at the map with his pen, "along Greece's border with Bulgaria, Yugoslavia, and Albania. The West suspected Stalin of planning to extend his control to the Balkan countries and beyond after the war ended. Once Soviet troops occupied all the Balkans, the only obstacle to their influence over the Aegean and the Ionian Seas would have been Greece.

"Anyway, after the war, a revolution began in Greece. The Soviets backed the Greek Communists. It was touch and go for awhile, but the Communists were finally run out of the country. Many escaped across the border and settled in Yugoslav and Bulgarian villages.

"This is where the story gets sinister . . . and where it might have touched you. Stalin ordered the fleeing Communists to take every child they could get their hands on to villages across the border. Most of the villagers who lived on the Greek side of the border were simple, uneducated farmers and craftsmen. The Communists told them, because they lived in what had been Communist-controlled territory that the Nationalists would sweep through their area and exact reprisals against them and their children. Even many who were anti-Communist believed the story. Hundreds of parents entrusted their children to the Communists. They assumed they'd eventually get their kids back when things cooled off. Instead, most never saw their sons and daughters again. Many of those who resisted were killed, their children kidnapped."

"What did Stalin want with those children?" Bob asked. "And what does this have to do with our son?"

"I'm getting there," Meers responded sympathetically. "The Communists have always impressed me in one aspect. Where we worry about the short-term – the next election or the next quarterly report – those Russian bastards think generations, even centuries ahead. Stalin wanted to indoctrinate thousands of Greek kids, to turn those kids into rabid Communists who could be integrated back into Greece years later as spies and, ultimately, as leaders of a Communist Greece." Meers shook his head as though to clear it of the distasteful information he had just conveyed and shrugged, spreading his hands in a palms-up gesture, adding, "Of course, taking the children also had a very effective psychological component."

Bob opened his mouth to ask a question, but Meers cut him off with another hand gesture.

"They took those kids to villages in Yugoslavia and Bulgaria, raised them as Greeks, and trained them as Communists. This program must have pleased Stalin. He ordered the Communist leadership in Yugoslavia and Bulgaria to continue kidnapping Greek children – infants and kids up to age two or three. Each year since the Greek Revolution, the Greek government has investigated reports from police departments across the country about mysterious child abductions. But no one could discover who took the children or why. Until five years ago.

"Greek Intelligence arrested a twenty-six-year-old man who offered to pay a Greek Air Force officer for information about U.S. nuclear missile sites in Greece. Under interrogation, he told of his training as an intelligence agent for Bulgaria and gave up an incredible amount of information about ties between the Soviet and Bulgarian Intelligence agencies. But he really shocked the interrogators when he said he'd been born in Greece and, at six years of age, after the revolution that followed World War II, had been kidnapped and taken to Bulgaria. He said babies were still being kidnapped at the time he was interrogated – often by Gypsies who delivered them to Bulgaria for cash payments."

"Why would they take an American child?" Liz asked.

Meers shrugged. "Think about it. You live in a Greek neighborhood. Your son is dark-haired and could pass for Greek."

Bob leaned back in his chair and ran his hands through his hair. He exhaled loudly. "I want to see all the files you've got at the Embassy on these kidnappings. And I want to read the file on this Greek who spied for the Bulgarians."

"I understand what you're going through. Change that. I can only imagine what you're going through," Meers said. "But there's no way I can give you the files. If anyone discovered I helped you, I'd be up the creek. Besides, what would you do with the information, even if I let you see it?"

"If we can figure out where these kids have been taken, I can go there and find Michael."

"Do you have any clue how dangerous that would be?" Meers said. "You don't speak Serbo-Croatian, Bulgarian, or Albanian, do you?"

Bob shook his head.

"Your position in the U.S. military means you'd be shot as a spy if you're captured in Bulgaria . . . after they interrogated you. The Bulgarians would love to get their hands on you. It's not like U.S. Army officers with Top Secret-Crypto security clearances show up in Bulgaria every day."

"You need to understand something, Mr. Meers," Liz said. "With or without your help, we're going to do whatever it takes to find our son."

"Including," Bob added, "talking to the press about these kidnappings that have been going on for years. The press will love the story."

Meers looked from Liz to Bob, deciding. The last thing the U.S. State Department would want was an international incident over these child abductions. Embarrassing the Soviets and their Eastern European vassal states would disrupt strategic arms talks then going on between Washington and Moscow. He stood and stared down at them. "Okay," he finally said. "Be at your home tomorrow morning at 9:00."

CHAPTER EIGHTEEN

Janos' wife, Demetria, helped him give his delivery truck its weekly cleaning. Demetria directed a steady spray of water from a hose into the corners of the cargo area, trying to wash out black, slimy remnants of lettuce leaves. The force of the water pushed aside a loose heap of them, revealing a small blue garment. She shut off the water, put down the hose, and lifted the filthy piece of clothing with her thumb and forefinger. A child's shirt. She turned toward Janos, holding it out to him. "What's this?" she asked.

The wide-eyed look on Janos' face made Demetria's heart leap to her throat. "What's wrong? What's going on?"

Janos turned his gaze away from her and took a broom from where it leaned against the side of the truck wall. Looking at the floor of the truck bed, he said, "How do I know? It's just trash."

Demetria walked over to Janos and grabbed his arm. "Don't lie to me, Janos. I always know when you're not telling the truth."

Still not making eye contact, Janos shook her hand off his arm. He yelled, "I told you, it's nothing!"

She grasped his arm again and spun him around. "Janos!" she screamed, her mouth so close spittle sprayed his face. "Tell me the truth! What's going on?" She held the shirt in front of his nose and shook it at him. "Why is a baby's shirt in your truck?" Then a horrid thought speared Demetria's brain and she felt her throat constrict as blood seemed to gush from her heart to her head. "Oh my God," she said. "It's the same color as the clothes the radio said that kidnapped American child wore."

Janos' Adam's apple bobbed as he tried to swallow his panic. "I don't know how it got in my truck, Deme," he said.

"Don't you *Deme* me! What have you gotten yourself into?"

Janos turned his back on his wife, jumped down from the back of the truck, and hurried into the apartment building. Demetria followed him, demanding an answer. She kept after him even after they entered their apartment. Still, he would not explain the presence of the shirt.

Stefan could hear a woman shouting. He climbed the apartment house staircase, turned the corner at the third floor, walked down the hall to Janos' door, and knocked. The shouts suddenly ceased. When a young woman opened the door, he pushed his way inside.

"Well, well," he said, sneering, "what do we have here? A lovers' spat?"

Janos sat on the sofa, appearing close to tears. He gave his uncle a dirty, squint-eyed look. "What are you doing here?" he said in a spiritless voice.

Demetria, too angry to be afraid, glared at Stefan and asked, "Who the hell are you?"

"Is that any way to greet your uncle, my dear? I'm shocked my nephew hasn't told you all about me," Stefan said.

"If you're related to this *kolokithas*, I don't want you here," she said. "Get out!"

Stefan stepped towards her, smiling. Demetria stood her ground. She pointed her finger at him and again ordered him to leave. He struck her in the face with his open hand. The force of the blow drove her backward against the wall. She slumped to the floor, her hand to her cheek. She stared at Stefan, tears flooding her eyes. A trickle of blood ran from the corner of her mouth.

Janos leaped from the couch, ran to Demetria, and reached down to help her to her feet. But she slapped his hand away. He then turned toward Stefan. "You sonofabitch!" he yelled. "I'll kill–" The sudden appearance of a knife in Stefan's hand cut off his threat.

"Janos, go sit on the sofa," Stefan growled. "You, woman, make some tea. We're going to have a nice chat."

CHAPTER NINETEEN

Katrina Vulovich couldn't calm the little boy. He didn't respond to her Greek words, and the more she spoke, the more he cried. She thought he must be ill and called for the orphanage's doctor. While she waited for the doctor to appear, she continued pacing her office floor, cradling the boy – her boy. Singing to him. Talking soothingly. She hugged him to her breast and remembered the baby she'd once had, so many years ago. The little boy she'd loved with all her heart. The child who'd died during the influenza epidemic because there wasn't enough medicine in Bulgaria to treat all the sick children.

The office door opened and Dr. Petrovic stepped inside. Katrina shuddered at the sight of the bald, gnome-like physician. His legs were too short, even for his abbreviated body. His black unruly eyebrows matched the long black hair protruding from his open shirt collar. Katrina was reminded of a wolf each time she looked into his amber eyes.

"Doctor," Katrina said, "look at him. He won't eat. Hardly sleeps. He just cries all the time."

"Comrade Vulovich," the doctor said, after touching the boy's face to see if he had a fever, "this child appears to be in excellent health. I suspect he misses his mother. That's all. Give him time. He's young; he will forget. Time will resolve your problem. A week and he will think you are his mother."

"He's just a baby, Comrade Petrovic," Katrina said. "Doesn't it bother you to see him crying?"

Dr. Petrovic shrugged and walked out of the room.

Katrina stuck a finger inside the high neck of her dress and extracted the jeweled cross she kept hidden there on a gold chain. She touched and kissed it, and said a silent prayer . . . for herself. So what if I know these children have been taken from their real mothers, she thought after she finished praying. I love them as much as their mothers could ever love them.

Katrina looked down at the sobbing boy in her arms and began walking around her office again. She softly sang a lullaby her mother used to sing. When he finally fell asleep, she put him on the office couch and covered him with her coat. And then her tears flowed. Taking a handkerchief from her dress pocket, she began to blot them away. The handkerchief was quickly soaked – and still her tears flowed.

CHAPTER TWENTY

Bob slammed a file down on the dining room table. "Most of this stuff is crap. There are dozens of kidnappings mentioned here, but few of them are tied to Communists or Gypsies. And those that are, are based on conjecture, not facts."

Liz came behind him and rubbed his neck and shoulders. "What about that Bulgarian agent the Greeks arrested? Let's try to find his file."

"It would be a lot easier if we knew the guy's name." Bob began checking the incident dates on the tab of each file. "Meers said the Greeks arrested him five years ago, 1966."

He spread Meers' files across the table until he found the ones from 1966. One file – the thickest of the 1966 group – caught Bob's eye. It was labeled: *George Makris.* Bob read a few sentences from an interrogation report in the file and said, "This is it." Then he read aloud. "Kidnapped by Communist guerrillas in 1946 at six years of age. Raised by an ethnic Greek family in southern Bulgaria. Trained as a Communist. Indoctrinated to believe his parents gave him up – that they sold him to the Communists. Taught to hate anything Western, non-Communist. Integrated back into Greece at twenty-six."

"Does it say anything about where he is now, what he's doing?"

Bob leafed through the pages. "Not that I can . . . wait a minute. Here's something. His parents live on the Island of Evoia. They reunited with him after the Greeks released him."

"Then we need to go to Evoia."

The doorbell interrupted them. Franklin Meers' voice carried through the locked front door to the dining room. "Anybody home?"

"He's come back for the files," Bob said. He went to the door and brought Meers back to the table. Before Meers had a chance to say anything, Liz shot him a hopeful look.

"We need you to do something for us," she said.

Meers closed his eyes and sighed. "Oh shit," he said. "What now?"

CHAPTER TWENTY-ONE

Katrina Vulovich's voice was shrill and seasoned with anger. "It's been over a week since that damned Gypsy brought the boy here. He hardly eats. He only sleeps when he's too tired to cry. Look at his face. You can see he's exhausted. Dr. Petrovic, if we don't do something soon he will starve."

"Comrade Vulovich, you are overreacting," Petrovic said, leaning forward on the plush, leather couch and placing his coffee cup on the table. He looked at his watch as though she were keeping him from something *really* important. "Children will not starve themselves. He will come around, you'll see. And why isn't he with the other children? You aren't supposed to be a babysitter." Before she could respond, Petrovic stood up. "I have to go. Call me if there are any *real* problems."

Katrina Vulovich scowled after Petrovic left the nursery. "Call him if there are any *real* problems," she said, mimicking the doctor. "He calls himself a doctor," she said under her breath. "He knows nothing. This child's heart is broken and he's terrified. He *will* starve to death if I don't figure out something soon."

She sat on the couch next to the boy and picked up the food tray on the coffee table. "Come on, my little boy, you must eat something. See, I made this just for you. At least drink the milk. Your Mama Katrina will make it better. You'll see. No one can love you the way Mama Katrina can."

The boy looked up at her, his blue eyes wet with tears and underscored with dark circles. He took in several stuttering breaths, stuck his thumb in his mouth, and rolled into a fetal position.

CHAPTER TWENTY-TWO

Liz sat in the front seat while Meers drove to the ferry dock. Bob sat in the back and read aloud from the George Makris file. Even on the ferryboat ride to the Island of Evoia, they remained in the car and listened to Bob quote excerpts from the file.

After the ferry docked on Evoia, Meers drove north. Just past a tiny village of a dozen or so white stuccoed homes with blue shutters and doors, he pulled the Volvo onto the dirt shoulder in front of a small house sitting between the road and the beach. Its back to the sea, the house faced the road. On the opposite side of the road, an olive grove covered a hillside.

"Are you sure Makris is here?" Liz asked.

"He agreed to talk with you after he learned about your son's kidnapping," Meers said. "I have no reason to believe he'd change his mind."

When they got out of the car, Bob put his arm around Liz. "Calm down," he whispered. "Let's not spook this guy, okay?"

She took Bob's hand and pressed it to her lips. They followed Meers down the gravel walk to the front door.

Before Meers could knock, a frail, sickly-looking man of medium height opened the door. His thick mustache was a black, glossy swath across his death-pale skin. High cheekbones and a prominent hooked nose gave him a dramatic, Middle Eastern appearance. His eyes were spiritless. In a whispery-soft voice, he said in English, "Mr. Meers? Mr. and Mrs. Danforth?"

"Yes," Meers said.

"Georgios Makris," the man said. "Call me George. Please come in."

They followed Makris through the small stone house, which was full of the sweet smell of lamb simmering in tomato broth, out to a back patio.

Makris directed them to chairs arranged around a table, on which sat a tray of fruit and olives, a carafe of white wine, and four glasses. A gnarled grapevine grew next to the table, its ancient arms extending up the side of a trellis, before spreading overhead on a lattice.

Liz looked closely at Makris. He seems terribly ill at ease, she thought. He won't make eye contact with any of us.

"Thank you for meeting with us," Meers said. "I'm sure this subject is not an easy one for you. But, as I explained on the telephone, we need all the assistance we can get to try to recover the Danforths' son."

Makris sat hunched over, looking down, his hands held together between his knees. He didn't respond.

"George, would you take a walk with me?" Liz finally said.

Makris gave her a slight, uncomfortable smile. "Yes, I'd be happy to, Mrs. Danforth."

Liz caught a look from Bob that seemed to say, What the hell are you doing? She barely shook her head in response.

"Do you live here alone, George?" Liz asked when they had walked the one hundred yards from the house to the shore.

"No, Mrs. Danforth. This is my parents' home. They are both working in the olive grove, where I would be if you weren't here. They should be returning to the house soon. I would like them to meet you."

"If I'm going to call you George, I expect you to call me Liz."

"Sorry, Mrs. Danforth . . . uh, Liz," Makris said.

"Meers makes you nervous, doesn't he?"

He hunched his shoulders and looked at her out of the corner of his eye. "How did you know?"

"A guess."

"I will never again trust anyone from any Intelligence agency. I was kidnapped on the orders of the Communist Intelligence types. Can you even imagine what it's like to be six years old and taken from your father and mother? I'm not discounting your own son's kidnapping. But there is a big difference between being six and two, like your son. I remembered everything about my parents, this home, my friends, my school. Everything. Even when the Bulgarian teachers – brainwashers, really – told me my parents gave me up, convinced me they didn't love me anymore, I still remembered everything about them. At your son's age, he won't remember you or his father after two or three months." He looked at Liz and gave her an apologetic look when her expression turned anguished.

"I'm an only child. My parents were in their early forties when I was born. I was the child they thought they'd never have. Now that I'm back, I spend nearly every waking hour with them – in the olive grove, in the house, at church every morning, at the market. I catch them staring at me as if they don't believe I'm here."

Makris stopped at the edge of the water and sat in the sand. Liz dropped down, too, and hugged her knees.

"And what Greek Intelligence put me through, after my arrest here, was just as cruel. I was the hated Communist, the spy who wanted to undermine Greek civilization. It got even worse when they found out I was born Greek. My abduction as a child, the brainwashing I endured, made no difference to them. They treated me like the worst sort of scum – a traitor. They beat me, told me my parents didn't want to see me. Tell me, Liz, is one side any better than the other?"

Makris didn't wait for Liz to answer. "I have nightmares nearly every night. I tried to tell people around here what happened to me, but no one believes me. Some sympathize, but most just think I'm crazy. I can't get a job. I have no future. No woman sees a future with a traitor who's also crazy." He suddenly stood up and walked ten yards down the beach. He stopped and turned back toward Liz. "How old do you think I am?" he called.

"I know how old you are," Liz said. "I've seen your file. You're thirty, almost thirty-one."

"How old do I look?" Makris demanded.

Liz knew she needed to answer truthfully. His prematurely gray hair and worry lines around his mouth and eyes were obvious. But it was what she saw in his eyes that told her his soul had aged at least as much as his body. "You look a lot older than that, George."

He just nodded his head.

Liz got up from the sand and brushed off her skirt. She caught up to Makris and continued walking with him. She sat next to him on a rock outcropping and stared at the sea. She listened to waves lapping against the shore, to a fisherman's oars slapping the water in the distance.

"Tell me about your kidnapping," she said.

"I remember that day like it was yesterday. My father had taken us to visit my grandparents in Drama, about halfway between Thessaloniki and the Turkish border. One afternoon, we drove to an ancient Byzantine site where we toured the ruins and picnicked. Afterward, I wandered alone into the forest and came upon a group of ten children being led by three men. Some of the children were crying. All of them were tied together by a rope that circled each of their waists. I hid behind a tree and watched for a while, believing I hadn't been noticed. But one of the men must have spotted me. He came around behind me and clapped a hand over my mouth and then dragged me over to the group. I tried to yell, but the man tied a cloth over my mouth.

"The next memory I have is of a large building, like a school. At the time, I didn't know I was only a few miles from the Greek border – not that it would have made a difference. It wasn't until later I found out I'd been dropped in a state orphanage near the town of Petrich. They never left me alone. They drummed thoughts into my brain. 'Your parents abandoned you. They sold you to the Gypsies. The Bulgarian People's Republic saved you from the Gypsies. Greece is a corrupt, westernized country that will collapse under the weight of the righteousness of the united Communist nations.' On and on, until I believed every word of it. They rewarded me with treats and hugs when I recited my lessons well. When I didn't do well, they locked me in a rat-and-cockroach-infested, unlit basement. After three years, they placed me with an ethnic Greek family. They wanted me to be Communist, but Greek in language, customs, and culture"

"You mentioned Petrich?" Liz asked. "Where's that?"

Using his hands, Makris placed the Balkan countries for Liz in the air between them. "Albania is here, then Yugoslavia, and Bulgaria. Petrich is just across the Greek border, in Bulgaria, not far from Yugoslavia."

"How long were you in Petrich? With the Greek family?"

"Until my fourteenth birthday. Then they moved me to a military school in Yugoslavia where I studied the usual academic subjects, along with military classes and more Communist propaganda. At nineteen, they sent me to Moscow where I was enrolled at Patrice Lumumba University. When not in university classes, I received espionage and language training at a KGB site outside Moscow."

"Did you learn English there? You speak like an American."

Makris nodded. "German, too."

"Is that what happened to all the children in the orphanage?"

"No! Training and education depended on your test scores and work habits. Some children became farmers or mechanics or teachers, never becoming part of the Intelligence system, but still lost in the Communist workers' utopia."

Makris' face had suddenly become beet-red and his eyes took on a fiery look she hadn't seen there before. This man may be free in a sense, Liz thought, but he's carrying an incredible amount of emotional baggage.

"Now, you tell me about your son," he said.

Liz smiled. "He's a beautiful two-year-old boy. He's got his father's black hair and dark blue eyes. He can already count to fifty. You should see him kick a ball." Liz looked away. "We wanted him always to be safe and to know we loved him. I don't want him growing up without us. I don't want him not knowing how much we love him. I . . .." She began crying.

Makris moved as though to put his arms around Liz; but, instead, just folded them across his chest. "Liz, I'll help you find your son."

Liz turned toward George and grasped his hands. "Thank you," she whispered. "Thank you so—" Then her crying devolved into sobs, and she collapsed to her knees on the sandy beach.

CHAPTER TWENTY-THREE

"Pay attention, Gregorie," Stefan hissed to his fourteen-year-old son. "Mornings are the best time for us. Mothers take their babies outside before it gets too hot, before they start their other chores."

Gregorie Radko, sitting in the backseat, peered through a side window of his father's Mercedes at his aunt, Rumiah, climbing down from the back of a horse-drawn wagon parked forty meters up the street. A man in the back of the wagon handed down several colorful fabrics to her. Gregorie's breath steamed the glass again, and he wiped it with his shirtsleeve.

"Are you looking?" Stefan demanded.

"Ye . . . yes, *O Babo*," Gregorie said.

Vanja, sitting in the front with Stefan, looked at the boy, then at Stefan. "Why get the boy involved with this business?" she said.

"Don't interfere. He's my son, not yours," Stefan growled, his face reddening.

Gregorie hated when his father got angry. It scared him. It always had. He wished his father had left him with Mama in Yugoslavia. He turned back to the window and watched the wagon roll around the corner toward the rear of a two-story, corner house. When the wagon disappeared from view, he turned his attention to Aunt Rumiah standing in front of the house, her arms draped with colorful scarves and shawls. She pushed the doorbell. A young woman opened the door. Gregorie stared open-mouthed at them, until his father's voice broke the silence in the car.

"The job's been done," Stefan said, while he started the Mercedes.

They drove to a point several blocks away and waited there in the idling Mercedes. Five minutes later, the Gypsy wagon drove up and stopped next to the car. A man stepped from the wagon, walked to the Mercedes' passenger side door, handed a small bundle wrapped in a pink blanket through the window to Vanja, and climbed back into the already moving wagon. Stefan hit the gas and sped away. Vanja inspected the bundle.

Gregorie leaned forward and looked over the front seat. Vanja turned and their eyes met. He saw what he thought was shame in hers.

"What is it?" Stefan demanded.

"A little girl."

Gregorie shrank back in the corner of the backseat. He felt frightened. This is a sin, he thought. Every part of his being ached with a tremendous desire to scream at his father, to curse him, to tell him how he felt. But the ache grew until he thought his head would explode. He knew he could never stand up to his father.

CHAPTER TWENTY-FOUR

"Are you crazy, Janos?" Demetria said, pacing the floor of the small apartment. "Your uncle will get us sent to prison."

"You don't understand, Demetria," Janos said, slumped on the couch, head in hands. "We have no choice. He'll kill us if we don't cooperate."

She took a deep breath and softened her voice. "What do you mean we have no choice? Of course we have a choice. We should go to the police now, before your uncle gets you in even deeper." She walked to the telephone and lifted the receiver. "Here," she said in a pleading tone, "call them."

Janos' head came up and his eyes shot open. He leaped off the couch, snatched the receiver from her hand, and slammed it onto the cradle. "Don't even think such a thing," he rasped, as though Stefan were within earshot. "You must not ask me any questions," Janos said, forlornly. His shoulders slumped and he turned away.

"How can you say that? I'm your wife."

Janos opened and closed his mouth three times, like a fish gasping for oxygen. He turned and walked out of the apartment.

CHAPTER TWENTY-FIVE

Franklin Meers was shocked when George Makris announced after returning from the beach with Liz that he was going to help the Danforths find their son. The man had seemed so emotionally beaten that Meers didn't think he had the fortitude to get involved. He was stunned when Makris said he would go along with them on the ride back to Kifissia.

On the drive from Evoia, George proved to be more vocal, more animated than he'd been at his parents' home. He told them all he could remember about his three years in the Petrich Orphanage. By the time he'd told his story in detail, Liz was quietly crying and Bob couldn't seem to stop cursing the Bulgarians and the Gypsy band that took Michael.

The trip back to Kifissia took nearly two hours. Meers parked the car in front of the Danforths' home and they all followed Liz into the house.

After Bob set out drinks for everyone in the dining room, he asked, "What do we do now? We can't just drive across the Bulgarian border to Petrich, knock on the door of some building, and ask if there are any two-year-old American boys there."

"Of course not," George said. "There are patrols all along the border and guards at the orphanage. We're not going anywhere near Bulgaria until we do some groundwork in Athens." George then focused on Meers. "And before we start, we need to know how much help we can expect to get from Mr. Meers here."

Both Bob and Liz snapped their heads toward Meers, wide-eyed expectant looks on their faces.

"Oh no. I've already stuck my neck out to here," Meers said, holding his hand two feet away from his face. "If you think I'm getting in any deeper, you're nuts. What do you want me to do, ruin my career, go to prison? I've already crossed the line. You can't even think about me helping anymore. You're on your own from here—"

Meers was already losing steam, but the look on Liz's face completely stopped him. He halted in mid-sentence, swallowed, and started again. "The risk is too great. Not just for me, but for all of you, too. You could get killed. And the odds against finding Michael are staggering. You've got to understand, if you—"

Liz was now staring at Meers with begging eyes.

"Goddammit!" he said. "Goddammit!" He couldn't fight the desperation he saw on her face.

CHAPTER TWENTY-SIX

Following Stefan's telephoned instructions, Janos drove his truck until he found the Mercedes parked on a narrow, deserted road just outside the Athenian suburb of Glyfada. Stefan sat behind the wheel. Vanja was in the front passenger seat. But Janos didn't know the person sitting in the back, a boy about fourteen years old.

Stefan got out of the Mercedes and walked to the cab of Janos' truck. "Show me what you've done," he ordered.

Janos stepped down and led Stefan to the rear of the truck. He rolled up the cargo door and hopped up into the empty bay. Stefan followed him to the front of the bay.

Janos used a crowbar to pry at a section of the front wall. It swung open on hinges to reveal a nine-meter-high, two-meter-deep compartment along the entire width of the truck. A thin mattress was on the floor of the compartment, next to an ice chest.

Stefan clapped his nephew on the back. "Good job, Janos. We're going to do a lot of business together."

Janos felt a lightning bolt of fear race down his spine.

Stefan jumped down into the street and waved toward the Mercedes.

Vanja got out of the car, holding a baby in her arms. She walked to the truck, followed by the boy from the backseat. Without a word, she handed the baby to Stefan, climbed up into the truck, reached down for the baby, and walked to the secret compartment. She sat down on the mattress. The boy stayed outside the truck.

"I think it's about time you cousins met," Stefan said, smiling, his eyes narrowed with humor. "Gregorie, say *'dobar dan'* to Janos, your Aunt Ismerelda's oldest son. Janos, this is my son, Gregorie. He's going to work with us. Radko and Son. Kind of catchy, don't you think?" He laughed uproariously.

The boy hung his head, seemingly cowed by his father. Sparse, silky hairs grew above his upper lip. He had his father's dark skin, but his hair was lighter.

Poor kid, Janos thought. He's probably as afraid of his father as I am.

"All right," Stefan said. "Enough formality! We go! After we have loaded the crates of wine from the warehouse, we'll be on our way north. Wine for Thessaloniki; a baby for the Bulgarian Communist Party. Capitalism at its best. Ha ha!"

With Vanja and the baby shut up in the compartment, Gregorie in the passenger seat beside him, and Stefan following in the Mercedes, Janos pulled the truck onto the pavement and drove back to Athens.

CHAPTER TWENTY-SEVEN

"What do you mean you want to meet one of my undercover agents?" Meers shouted, rising from his chair at the Danforth's dining room table. "I've helped all I can. I won't do that. If you compromise one of my operatives, I'll be useless here. You're asking too—"

"Please, Franklin," Liz pleaded.

Meers turned to Liz. "Listen, I'm sick about what's happened to you and Bob, but I can't do this."

In the sudden silence that came over the room, George said, icily, "You don't have much choice." He put his hands on the table and leaned toward Meers. "I could see to it your superiors find out you've already allowed unauthorized persons access to classified intelligence files."

Meers stared at George. His eyes widened, then narrowed in a squint. "You play rough."

"That's the way the Communist Bloc trains its agents," George said, sitting back in his chair.

Meers stood and walked to a window. He looked out at the street. After a few seconds, he turned back to the others. Taking a small notebook from his jacket pocket, he wrote something on a sheet of paper. Passing the sheet to Makris, he said, "Be there at seven tomorrow morning."

CHAPTER TWENTY-EIGHT

After weeks at the Petrich Orphanage, Michael finally did more than pick at his food. He ate his first full meal. And he began playing with the other children and learned some of the funny language they spoke. He didn't really like his big new house. It was cold all the time and he kept getting lost. And there were no dogs in this house. At night, the house made him scared. He could hear some of the other children crying. Sometimes he had nightmares.

He liked the way Mommy Katrina took care of him – like he was special. But he wished she'd let him sleep with all the other children. She made loud noises when she slept and it made him wake up a lot. But, she's nice, Michael thought. She gives me candy and hugs me. I like her hugs. They're warm like Mommy's. But my other Mommy smells better. Mommy Katrina says Mommy and Daddy don't want me anymore. That makes me sad. I miss White Dog.

Michael saw Mommy Katrina smiling at him. She crossed the room and patted him on the head. She picked him up from his chair.

"Oh, what a good boy you are," she said. "You ate all your food. You have made your mommy so happy."

Michael stared at Mommy Katrina. He understood her words, even though she talked funny. I like when she's happy, he thought. I like to make my new mommy happy.

CHAPTER TWENTY-NINE

Janos tried to get Gregorie to talk during the drive north, but conversation seemed almost painful for the boy. He'd rub his hands on his trousers, stutter, and look straight ahead down the highway.

"Do you go to school?" Janos asked.

"No," the boy said, almost too quietly to be heard.

"Why not?"

The boy just shrugged.

Janos reached back and knocked on the wall between the truck's cab and the cargo bay. "Are you all right back there?" he shouted through the small screened air vent he'd installed in the partition.

"It's hot, but we're okay," Vanja answered. "You just woke up the baby."

For the next five miles Janos listened to the infant cry. Then the crying abruptly stopped.

Gregorie's voice suddenly broke the quiet. "He's a bastard," he said softly, his fists clenched on his thighs, his face red. The bitterness in his voice was unmistakable.

"He leaves my mother, his *romni*, alone while he parades around with his *pornee*. He has made all of us *mahrime*."

Janos reflected on the superstitious Gypsy life. Stefan has a mistress, therefore his family must be unclean—*mahrime*.

"Have you been living with your mother?" Janos asked. "Is that why I've never seen you before?"

"Yes, in Gevgelija, in Yugoslavia. My father visits there maybe twice a year." The boy paused. "It's disgusting. My mother treats him like a king when he shows up. Then he disappears again. He spends more time with his whore than he does with his own family."

Janos heard hatred as well as disgust in Gregorie's voice. And he also heard fear.

CHAPTER THIRTY

Meers had written the name of a beach – *Kaki Thalassa* – on the piece of paper he'd given them. They arrived there early, at 6:45 a.m. The beach was deserted. Bob and George got out of the car and looked around. A strong wind blowing off the water whipped the sand into a stinging frenzy. They retreated to the car and wiped the sand from their eyes.

"Damn! The wind must be blowing forty miles an hour," Bob said. "My face feels like it got hit by a cactus."

The ticking of the car's clock sounded louder and louder with each passing minute.

"Do you think he'll show?" Liz asked.

"He'll be here," George answered. "He's got too much to lose if he doesn't."

Meers finally drove up, twenty minutes late, with a passenger seated in the back of his black Volvo.

"Wait here," George ordered.

Using his hand to shield his eyes from the blowing sand, George walked to Meers' car. He opened the right rear door and slid onto the backseat, pulling the door shut behind him. Meers looked back at George. "I'll leave you guys alone," he said. Meers then turned and left the car.

The stranger across from him looked straight ahead, not acknowledging George in any way.

"Thank you for coming," George said, extending his right hand.

The man didn't take the hand, but did finally turn his head to look at George.

George withdrew his hand and brushed his windblown hair off his forehead while taking the measure of the other man. He could tell from his features the man was a Gypsy. He had a curved white scar running down the left side of his face, from his cheekbone to the rim of his jaw. The scar seemed to shine against his mahogany skin. The man's eyes were ebony-colored.

"I take it you don't like being here," George said in Greek.

Leering at George with a "you must be stupid" look on his face, the man said, "If it ever gets back to the *Rom* I helped you, my own clan will kill me. Let's get this over with."

"All right. Who's behind the kidnappings of children in Greece?"

"Why the fuck should I tell you?" the Gypsy said, his mouth twisting into a cruel slash.

He wants money, George thought. He glared at the Gypsy, who leaned back against the car seat and smiled smugly. George leaped at the man and grabbed his throat. "You're going to tell me everything," he said in a dead-calm voice. "If you hesitate once, if you lie to me, I will rip your throat out."

Croaking through compressed vocal chords, the man raised a hand in submission. "Okay! Ease up."

George released him, all the while watching his eyes. They seemed to have turned even blacker. He watched the man massage his throat. "We know Gypsies have done at least some of the kidnappings," George said. "Who are they?"

"It's not *Gypsies*. You say it as if all of *Rom* is behind the kidnappings. It's only a small band of renegades."

"Who's their leader?"

"A mean sonofabitch," the man answered. "Guy named Radko, Stefan Radko. His own *kumpania* won't have anything to do with him. Been working with the Bulgarians, kidnapping kids for over twenty years. He's in his forties now. In tight with the Bulgarian Secret Police."

"How do you know so much about Radko?"

"Radko's a *Rom* legend. Gypsy mothers tell their children he's the bogeyman. The clan leaders are afraid if it ever gets out that a Gypsy has been kidnapping Greek children, there'll be a massacre of Gypsies all over the country."

George rubbed his face with his hands and focused on the sound of the sand blowing against the car. After a moment, he looked over at the Gypsy and asked, "Where can I find Radko?"

"I don't know. I heard he has a cousin or nephew, last name Milatko, living in Athens. I can't remember his first name."

"Where are the kidnapped children being taken?" George asked.

"Somewhere in Bulgaria."

"Does Petrich sound familiar?"

"That's it!" the Gypsy exclaimed. "How did you know?"

Nothing's changed, George thought.

"Okay, one last question," George said, while he pulled the handle to open the door. "Since you're working for the Americans, why didn't you give them this information before?"

"No one asked," the Gypsy replied, laughing.

That drove George over the edge. The years of bottled-up anger and sadness overflowed. He leaned toward the Gypsy. "If Meers hadn't brought you here, I'd slit your throat. You're slime of the worst kind." Then he spat at the man's feet and turned to open the car door.

The Gypsy lunged – something flashed in his hand. George felt a hot sensation just below his left armpit. He fell through the open door onto the sand. The Gypsy scrambled across the seat after him. "You bastard!" he screamed. "You fucking put your filthy hands on me! You call me slime!"

George rolled on his back and kicked at the door, slamming it against the man's knife arm. The knife fell to the sand. The Gypsy pushed the door open, tumbled out of the car, and lunged for the weapon. George grabbed the Gypsy's wrist as the man wrapped his fingers around the knife handle. They wrestled in the sand, rolling over and over, gouging and hitting each other with their free hands, fighting for control of the knife. George felt blood running from the wound in his side. The Gypsy managed to roll on top of him and press his weight behind the knife – the blade quivering just inches above George's heart.

George got both hands on the man's wrist and pushed up, fighting to raise the point of the blade higher. The two men matched one another's strength, George pushing upward, the Gypsy pressing down. George suddenly changed tactics. Instead of pushing upward, he turned his wrists outward, twisting the other man's hands and the knife back at the man's chest. George pushed, driving the blade into the other man's chest. The Gypsy groaned and then cursed George.

George rolled the man off him at the moment Meers ran up.

"Sonofabitch!" Meers shouted. "What the hell happened?"

"He pulled a knife."

Meers knelt next to the now-still Gypsy. He pressed two fingers against the side of the man's throat. "Damn!," he said.

"We've got to get rid of the body," George said, as Bob and Liz ran up.

"Oh my God," Liz said breathlessly. "George, what happened?"

George ignored her.

Meers looked down at the Gypsy again. "Shit, shit, shit. How the hell am I going to explain this to my boss?"

"It seems to me," George said in a weakening voice, "that you'd be better off not explaining anything to your boss. Just dump the body and claim you never heard from him again."

Bob glanced at George who was pale and perspiring profusely.

Meers suddenly blurted, "Help me put the body in my car. Then I want you all out of here."

Bob and Meers lifted the Gypsy's body into the trunk of Meer's car. Meers ran around the car and opened the driver side door. He yelled across the car roof, shielding his eyes from the blowing sand. "What are you waiting for? Get the hell out of here. I'll call you at your house later." He then got behind the wheel and drove off the beach toward the road.

Bob started for his car when George groaned and sagged to the sand.

"My God, he's hurt," Liz said. "He's bleeding."

"Wait here; I'll get our car," Bob told her.

When Bob returned and got out of his car, he and Liz helped George get up and into the back seat. After telling Liz to get the first-aid kit from the trunk, Bob removed George's jacket. He tore a strip of cloth from George's shirt to wipe blood away from the upper left side of his chest.

"How bad is it?" George asked weakly.

"Pretty clean wound," Bob said. "I think we'll be able to stop the bleeding with a pressure bandage."

Liz opened the other rear door and got in next to George. She opened the first-aid kit and went to work on him.

Bob watched Liz patch up George. "Are you okay?" he asked George.

"I'll be fine if you can find me a couple of pain killers and a bottle of Ouzo as a chaser."

"It sounds like he'll live," Liz said, smiling at George.

"We'd better get him back to our place," Bob said.

"He should see a doctor," Liz suggested.

"Call Meers when we get to your place," George said. "He's sure to know a doctor who will keep his mouth shut."

While Liz sat with George in the backseat, Bob got behind the wheel and floored the accelerator, sending sand shooting off the spinning rear tires. He glanced at Liz in the rearview mirror. She was sitting quietly next to George. My innocent little wife is getting tougher by the minute, Bob thought. It gave him no pleasure.

CHAPTER THIRTY-ONE

Katrina Vulovich sat in a rocking chair in a corner of the nursery, the sleeping American child in her arms. Her heart felt as though it would leap from her chest. She loved this boy with every fiber of her being. He was the son she always wanted.

"Andreas, my little boy," she whispered, "how beautiful you are." She brushed the hair away from his forehead and lightly kissed him. "You are different from all the others. They will become workers in the Communist system. Drones to operate the machines, work the fields. Maybe one or two will go into the Intelligence Service or the Army and become heroes of the State. But you shall become greater than them all. Yes, you will, my son."

Katrina wiped a tear from the corner of her eye. She felt disoriented – as though she was moving in her mind from one place to another. Children stolen from their families surround me, she thought. And now I'm taking this boy with me to visit my parents in Sofia. If I'm found out, I'll be sent back to the fields – or executed. But I can't help it. This is my son. How could I leave him behind with these orphans? He isn't an orphan. He's my flesh and blood, my son.

CHAPTER THIRTY-TWO

"When are we going after this guy Radko?" Liz asked, spitting out the Gypsy's name as though it was a curse. She stared at George, seated across the dining room table, surgical tape around his chest, holding a clean pressure bandage in place under his arm. Bob stood behind her with his hands on her shoulders. The remnants of lunch lay on plates scattered around the table.

"We're not," George said. "At least, not yet."

"Why not?" she said, her eyes wide, her hands flexing with impatience. "He's the best lead we've got."

"I agree," George said. "But even if we track him down, do you think he'll admit to taking your son, or any other children for that matter? And if we question Radko, the first chance he gets he'll contact the Bulgarians. If that happens, they'll close down Petrich and move all the children to another location. We'll never find Michael."

"Then we go to Petrich," Bob said.

"As soon as Meers briefs us on everything your Embassy knows about the area around Petrich. God forbid, the Bulgarians are planning military maneuvers along their southern border just when we decide to cross over. If we can meet with Meers tomorrow, you and I might try to cross the border the day after tomorrow – late at night."

Liz leaped to her feet, forcing Bob to jump back. "You're not going without me," she snapped.

Bob put his arm around her. "Liz, it makes no–"

She shrugged away. "You macho idiots get one thing straight. If my son's in that damn orphanage in Bulgaria, I'm going there with or without you!"

In the sudden silence after her outburst, George said, "Then it's without me."

"What's the matter?" Liz demanded, her fingers drumming nervously against the sides of her legs. "You don't think I can keep up with you?"

"That's not the problem," George said. "Do you know how to use a weapon?"

"What the hell does that . . ." After a beat she shook her head. "No, I've never held a gun."

"We may have to kill people," George said. "At the border, or getting into the orphanage . . . and getting out. There were always guards there."

Liz's face seemed to sag, but the anger was still there. Her eyes blazed at George.

"And what happens if Bob and I are captured or killed in Bulgaria?" George said. "It'll then be up to you alone to work to find Michael."

CHAPTER THIRTY-THREE

Janos dropped off the crates of wine in Thessaloniki and drove northeast toward Seres. The only cargo left in the back of the truck were several empty boxes, Vanja, and the kidnapped baby girl. Just south of Seres, the truck's fuel pump failed. While Janos and Gregorie waited with the truck – Vanja and the infant still locked in the cargo bay – Stefan drove the Mercedes into Seres and arranged for a tow truck. When he returned an hour later, beating the tow truck, he transferred Vanja and the infant to the sedan.

After eight hours cooped up in the back of the truck, Vanja had a deer-in-the-headlights look. Perspiration plastered her hair to her face and her dress stuck to her body. Her skin looked two shades redder than normal. The baby girl squalled in her arms. It smelled like she'd soiled her diapers.

"You sonofabitch," Vanja screamed over the baby's cries from the backseat of the car.

Stefan twisted in his seat and raised his arm. Vanja shrank out of reach.

"Go ahead, hit me," she yelled. "I'll walk away from here and leave you alone with this baby."

She rocked the infant in her arms, trying to quiet it. "You left us in the truck for hours. We could have died in there. It's bad enough you get me involved in this baby stealing; must you try to kill me, too?"

Stefan shot her a hateful look and opened his mouth as though to say something. Instead, he just stepped from the car and walked over to the stranded truck.

CHAPTER THIRTY-FOUR

Bob sat with George under the Campari umbrella at the same table where he and Liz had first met Franklin Meers. They'd left Liz at home. This time when Meers arrived, he stood by the table, barely acknowledging their greetings. Bob assumed from Meers' rigid posture and clipped speech that he was still pissed off about the death of his informant on the beach at Kaki Thalassa.

"Please sit down, Franklin," Bob said.

After a second's pause, Meers took a seat. He had barely settled into the chair when George peppered him with one question after another.

Bob could tell George was not making the intelligence officer any happier.

"Did you find out if the Bulgarians are planning any military exercises along the border near Petrich?"

"There's nothing going on – at least in the next week."

"What about trip wires, security lights, or alarms along the border?" Bob asked.

"Mostly concertina wire and intermittent patrols on the Bulgarian side. Some alarm trip wires. Not very sophisticated. After all, how many people want to sneak into Bulgaria? There are two sets of trip wires on the Greek side, though."

George nodded.

Meers looked at Bob. "Have you thought this through? You get caught and they'll shoot your ass as a spy. And if you don't get caught and actually make it back – which I seriously doubt – you'll probably be courts-martialled. Your Army career will be over."

"What's my alternative, to let those bastards keep my son? Screw my Army career." Bob knew he had his priorities right, but he also knew giving up his Army commission would be painful.

Meers nodded, then said, "When are you going across?"

"I think it would be best if you didn't know our schedule," George interjected.

"Look," Meers said. "I want to help you. If you tell me when you plan to cross the border, I can arrange to get a message to the Bulgarian Secret Police through one of our double agents. Tell them a saboteur will try to cross into Bulgaria – at some entry point far away from Petrich. It would distract, maybe draw away some guards from your area."

"We'll reconnoiter the crossing point while it's still light," Bob said. "We're leaving–"

But George cut him off. "We're starting out early in the morning, the day after tomorrow," he said.

"I'll set things in motion," Meers replied. He stood and looked down at Bob and George. "You guys don't have a hope and prayer, you know?" Then he walked away from the table and disappeared around the corner.

"Why'd you lie to Meers about when we're going across?" Bob asked. "Don't you trust him?"

"I believe he's on our side. But what he doesn't know can't hurt us."

They found Liz sitting on the living room floor surrounded by backpacks and an assortment of gear.

"Did you get everything?" George asked.

Liz picked up a sheet of yellow notepaper and read off the list. "The camouflaged clothing is over there," she said, pointing toward the couch. "Black grease paint, ropes, a grappling hook, flashlights, a first-aid kit, and two .45 caliber pistols – all this stuff on the floor will go in the packs. One of the pistols is yours, Bob. Will Spence dropped the other one off about an hour ago. He never asked one question about why you wanted it. "

Bob knelt down next to Liz and kissed the top of her head. "Thank you," he said.

She gave him a quick smile. "I'll fill the canteens and make sandwiches in the morning. I put the money Mom and Dad sent in your backpack – ten thousand in large bills. My father said to tell you something." She dropped her voice to a lower register: " 'You tell Bob that good, hard American currency can sway the mind of even the most dogmatic Communist.' "

"What's this?" Bob asked, lifting a small, soft-sided bag from the top of one of the open backpacks.

"That's for Michael," she said.

Bob unzipped the bag and saw one of Michael's shirts, a pair of shorts, underwear, sandals, two cans of juice, and a teddy bear.

That night, Bob dreamed he heard Michael: "Daddy, Daddy!" But he couldn't find his son. Gone! Gone! "Michael, where are you?" Bob called in his dream. A strange woman held his son and Michael called her "Mama." Then he saw wave after wave of young men – Soviet soldiers – marching in Red Square, wearing high-brimmed Russian Army hats and carrying AK-47 assault rifles. They yelled in cadence, "Down with the American dogs; death to Robert Danforth." Michael, now a tall young man, marched in the middle of the front row of soldiers, yelling the loudest.

CHAPTER THIRTY-FIVE

Katrina Vulovich tried to force from her memory the obligatory visit to her fat boss' Sofia apartment – his lying on top of her, sweating and grunting. She owed him for giving her the job at the orphanage. If she didn't service him on demand, she'd find herself back in the fields of a government collective farm.

As she walked back to her parents' apartment in the center of the Bulgarian capital to pick up her little Andreas, she talked to herself, her hands moving as though she were gesturing while talking to another person. She ignored the stares of passersby. "What choice do I have? I have to let him fuck me. It only lasted thirty minutes, but it seemed like an eternity." She shivered. "That fat, stinking body!" she said. "Things will be better as soon as I have Andreas in my arms."

Her mother answered her knock on the apartment door.

"Ah, Katrina, it's you."

"Hello, Mama. And how is Andreas?"

"No problems. Papa has been playing with him on the floor. I don't think I've ever seen Papa happier."

Katrina followed her mother from the doorway to the living room, where her father watched Andreas draw circles in a coloring book.

"So, when are you going to get married, Katrina?" her mother said. "You need to give us a real grandchild. We're not getting any younger." Katrina's father looked over at her, waiting for her answer.

Katrina stared at her little Andreas. "Mama," she said, "Andreas *is* my son. He *is* your grandson."

Her parents glanced at each other, worry and shock etching their features.

Katrina ignored the looks. They couldn't understand how she felt. She walked over to Andreas. "Today's Saturday," she said. "The carousel in Lenin Park will be running. Do you want to go to the park?"

Andreas jumped up, a gleeful smile on his face. "*Da, Momi,*" he said.

His position as cultural attaché at the U.S. Embassy in Sofia provided Andrew Morton with cover. He was, plainly and simply, a spy. Pausing in signing the last few letters due to go out in the diplomatic pouch, he looked at his eight-year-old daughter, Erica, leafing through a stack of papers on his secretary's desk in the adjoining room.

Morton leaned back in his chair, stretched his arms over his head, and groaned. So much work left to do. But he had promised Erica he would take her to ride on the merry-go-round. He stood and reached for his jacket. Erica skipped into the room, a piece of paper in her outstretched hand.

"What's this, Daddy?" Erica said. "What's 'abducted' mean?"

Morton took the sheet of paper from Erica, looked at the photo on the flyer, and glanced at the information printed above and below the photo. He feigned interest, wanting his daughter to think he found her discovery exciting.

Pointing at the photo on the flyer, he said, "It means someone took this little boy away from his parents." He saw the sudden look of fear in Erica's eyes. "I'll tell you what," he said, "let's take this with us." He winked. "We'll run our own investigation. Maybe we can find this little American boy and return him to his family."

"Okay," Erica said. "Can I hold the picture?" she exclaimed, clapping her hands.

Morton laughed. Kids and their fantasies. "Sure, honey," he said.

Katrina watched little Andreas try to chase down the soccer ball some older boys were playing with in the park. He would get right back on his feet whenever one of the bigger boys knocked him down, but still Katrina began to fear he might get hurt. She rushed into the melee on the field to rescue him. After brushing dirt from his clothes and face, she took his hand and set off toward the carousel.

She bought a ticket from the operator. "My horsey, my horsey," Andreas said. He ran to the black horse with a red saddle. The carousel horse stood frozen in a half-rearing pose; its painted eyes seemed wild with rage. It was just like her little boy to pick the fiercest of all the carousel animals. Katrina lifted Andreas onto the horse's back.

"I can get on myself, Daddy. Here, you hold the picture," Erica Morton said, passing the kidnapping bulletin to her father.

Morton nodded to Erica and stood next to a group of other parents while she ran to the merry-go-round. He watched her mount one of the horses.

The merry-go-round began to turn, slowly at first, its calliope music chiming loudly. It picked up speed and Erica's long brown hair streamed behind her while she exhorted her horse to go ever faster. Lost in the pleasure of the moment, Morton almost didn't notice something picking at his consciousness. Words shouted by a child other than Erica. English words. Out of place in Sofia.

"Giddyup, horsey." The carousel spun around and the words came again. "Giddyup, horsey."

There! A little black-haired boy, three horses behind Erica, called over and over, "Giddyup, horsey."

Morton looked around, trying to locate the boy's parents. He thought he knew all the few Americans in Sofia. After scanning the crowd and finding no familiar faces, he turned back to the carousel. Something about the child seemed familiar. Erica flashed by him again on her own wooden horse. Seeing her reminded him. He reached into his jacket pocket and pulled out the bulletin with the picture of the kidnapped American boy.

CHAPTER THIRTY-SIX

Liz hadn't been able to sleep since Bob and George took off for Bulgaria. She'd cleaned the house twice, washed dishes that didn't need washing, and was now weeding the garden. She'd just taken a break, to go into the house to get some iced tea, when a car pulled up in front of the house. She recognized Franklin Meers' Volvo. Liz's pulse elevated. Oh God, she thought, something's happened to Bob.

Her knees wobbled as she watched Meers leave his car and approach the gate. She rested an arm on the rail next to the steps going up to the porch.

"I need to talk with you and Bob," Meers said while opening the wrought iron gate.

Liz swallowed. She wasn't sure she could trust her voice. She swallowed again and said, "You'll have to settle for talking to me. Bob and George took off early this morning. Didn't you know?"

"Oh, Jesus!" Meers ran both hands through his hair and seemed suddenly terribly upset. "They told me they weren't going until tomorrow."

Liz squinted her eyes at the change in Meers' face. "What's going on?"

Then Meers smiled. "We've found Michael. He's safe."

"Oh, my God." Liz's eyes filled with tears. She collapsed onto the flowerbed.

Meers helped her up and into the house, into a chair.

"Where's Michael?" she asked. "When can I see him?"

"He's in Sofia, in Bulgaria. Apparently, the female director of the Petrich orphanage had him. They were in an amusement park. She tried to run away with Michael, but an American assigned to our Embassy there caught her and called the police. Michael's at police headquarters in Sofia now."

"Michael's okay?"

"He's in perfect health. We can catch a flight to Sofia this afternoon. Can you get word to Bob?"

"He said he'd call tonight before crossing the border."

"We'll already be on our way to Sofia. I can put a man here in the house. If Bob calls, then everything's fine. But if he doesn't, he and George could be in bigger trouble than they ever imagined. The Bulgarians will surely send a team to Petrich to close down that orphanage. We're trying to get the United Nations to intervene, to conduct an investigation. You can bet the Bulgarians won't leave any evidence there. If Bob and George show up in Petrich while the Commies are still clearing out the place . . .."

Liz's chin trembled. "What can we do? How can we stop them before they cross the border?"

"I'd better call my office. Maybe we can put some of our people near the border to intercept them."

While Meers used the phone, Liz packed a bag. Her hands wouldn't stop shaking.

Meers waited for Liz by the front door. He looked deep in thought.

"Franklin, I've been meaning to ask you something," Liz said. "You and the Greek government have obviously known for some time about the Bulgarians' kidnapping scheme. Why did George get treated so poorly by his own people after he was arrested here? And why hasn't the government put out word of the kidnappings to the Greek people?"

Meers looked surprised by her questions. His face flushed.

"Liz, if the word had spread that the Bulgarians were behind these kidnappings all these years, we could've had a war. Every Greek would've screamed for revenge. If Greece provoked Bulgaria, the rest of the Iron Curtain countries would've gotten involved. The U.S. and NATO would've helped Greece. The next thing you know, we'd've had World War III. We had to keep George quiet. We had no choice."

"You people make me sick," Liz said, poking a finger into Meers' chest. "You could've put a stop to these kidnappings a long time ago. Instead, you did nothing."

"Liz, there are bigger issues involved than you can understand," Meers said.

Liz zeroed in on Meers' face and gave him her most hateful look. "Bullshit!" she said.

Meers drove to the airport. The silence in the car felt oppressive. Liz wouldn't even look at him. He parked the car and Liz walked ahead toward the Olympic Terminal. She suddenly stopped and turned around.

"How did you and the Greek government keep George silent about the Petrich Orphanage and the kidnappings?"

Meers blushed. "We didn't," he said. "George talked about it every chance he got, to anyone who'd listen. The government just spread the word around – to the press, even to the people in his own village – that he was insane. His parents, too. We said he'd been living with relatives in Athens all these years. People only listened to him because they felt sorry for him. No one believed a word he, or his parents, said about Bulgarians and Gypsy kidnappings."

Liz, turned away from him again.

CHAPTER THIRTY-SEVEN

People stuck their heads out the windows of houses in Petrich to see a caravan of two buses and five trucks rumble through the small town. But they quickly pulled their heads back inside and closed the shutters. The citizens of the Bulgarian People's Republic had learned that curiosity killed more than just cats.

The vehicles sped over the cobblestone streets, and at the end of town turned uphill. A guard at the orphanage threw open the gates. The vehicles moved up the semicircular gravel drive and stopped in front of the ornate, two-story stone structure.

Four female staff members immediately came through the orphanage's oversized front door carrying infants, dodging the men from the trucks who ran into the building. After three round trips by the staffers, all the infants were on board the first bus, and the women began to herd out the other children.

One woman yelled at two little boys who wandered away, then chased them down and dragged them back to the second bus. The sounds of children crying joined the shouts of a man barking orders to his workers moving furniture from the building to the trucks. After only fifteen minutes, the buses loaded with children drove away.

The truck crews remained, removing furniture, files, pictures – anything of value, anything that could be considered evidence. Finally, the senior man shut the orphanage's front door, looked around the grounds, and then boarded the lead truck.

As the truck turned onto the road in front of the orphanage, the driver said, "Not bad! We cleaned the place out in pretty good time. But why the rush?"

The senior man continued to stare at the road ahead and said, "Shut up! It's none of your business."

CHAPTER THIRTY-EIGHT

Liz paced the tile floor of the Olympic Airlines terminal, looking up at the flight schedule board every thirty seconds. Meers was standing in front of the concession stand. She walked over and tapped him on the arm. "Where's the plane? We should have boarded fifteen minutes ago."

"Calm down, Liz," Meers said in a soft voice. "Remember, this is Greece. Things go along at their own pace. It'll be–" An announcement over the terminal's loudspeaker system interrupted him.

A stream of Greek filled the room. Then the announcement was made in English.

"Olympic Flight 131 to Sofia will be delayed for mechanical reasons," the bass voice boomed.

Every minute of delay seemed like a lifetime to Liz. How wonderful it would be to hold her baby again! She resumed her pacing. Meers found a seat in the crowded waiting area.

Momentarily stopping her pacing, Liz stood in front of Meers and asked, raising her voice to compensate for the din of Greek conversations all around them, "Have you called my house? Has your man heard from Bob?"

"I checked in just a little bit ago. Bob hasn't called."

She began wandering around the terminal, her mind filled with terrible thoughts of Bob being captured by the Bulgarians – or worse. Finding a relatively quiet corner, she turned her face away from the people in the waiting area and cried.

CHAPTER THIRTY-NINE

The trip from Athens to the Bulgarian border took Bob and George four hours. They parked Bob's car in a grocery store parking lot, walked five miles to the border, and waited in a wooded area for night to fall. They watched the Greek Army border units for hours, timing their patrols, and then at 3:20 a.m., George came out of the dense woods in a crouch and scooted from tree to tree in the buffer area leading up to the empty, moonlit, hundred-yard slash of the border. Bob followed closely behind him. About to break from the tree cover, George dropped to the ground and signaled Bob to do the same. A Greek Army patrol, breaking the usual patrol time routine, appeared from behind a large rock outcropping on their right. The soldiers were talking and smoking cigarettes while they slowly strolled along.

After the patrol passed, George and Bob rose and ran for the barbed-wire fence separating Greece and Bulgaria.

It was 4 a.m., a mile west of where Bob and George crossed the Bulgarian border, when Stefan Radko and his son Gregorie waited for a Greek patrol to pass by. Stefan turned toward his son. Moonlight highlighted the boy's pale features, his wide-open eyes, and the grim set to his mouth. Gregorie would be able to move faster than Vanja – an advantage. But the boy had never been part of this before and might make a mistake.

The baby girl slept in Gregorie's arms. Stefan hoped she would remain asleep at least until they had crossed to the Bulgarian side. "Keep your eyes open and your mouth shut," Stefan hissed at Gregorie.

Gregorie nodded his head several times.

The Petrich Orphanage's massive wrought iron gates in the high, white, moonlit wall gaped open. Without lights, the building behind the wall appeared foreboding, a looming dark-gray presence.

"Something's wrong," George said. "Those gates were never left open during my time here. And there was always a light on at the front. And now there's no guard. There was *always* a guard."

Bob followed George across the road that paralleled the wall. Imitating George, he pressed himself against the wall's stuccoed surface and edged to the gate to peer into the grounds. Still no one. They sprinted up the gravel drive, between tall evergreens lining both sides.

"Stay close," George ordered, while they climbed the front steps.

When George pushed on the heavy front door, it slowly swung open. They stepped inside and, after Bob had shut the door, both men switched on their hooded flashlights.

George ran a hand over his face as though to wipe away the memory of his past here. Then he led the way into a high-ceilinged lobby. "I don't get it," he said. "Even at night, this place always felt alive, like the building was breathing. It scared the hell out of me when I was a kid. Now it feels dead."

Bob pointed his flashlight upward, staring at the twenty-foot-high ceilings and the ornate-carved crown moldings running around the lobby. A design had been sculpted in the ceiling and a mosaic he couldn't quite determine in the muted light from his flashlight had been laid in the marble floor.

George moved out of the lobby and down a hallway leading off to the right.

The first room on the right was empty. Discolored squares on the walls showed where pictures had hung. A file cabinet stood in a corner, its empty drawers gaping open. All the bookshelves were bare. Vagrant pieces of paper lay scattered around the room. Velvet drapes covered the windows.

"This was the director's office," George said.

Bob ran his hand over the top of the file cabinet. "There's barely any dust here," he said. "They evacuated this building very recently. Like yesterday, or even today."

All the other rooms along the hallway had been stripped. The last room was the size of a basketball court.

"We ate all our meals here in the dining room," George said, circling the room. "Three times a day we sat here like good little soldiers." His voice echoed off the walls of the cavernous room. "Sit up straight! No talking! Clean your plates!"

Let's check the second floor," Bob said.

"Okay, but let's be quick," George answered.

They raced up the curving, marble stairway two steps at a time and began poking into rooms on either side of the stairs.

Bob found nothing but almost empty rooms. He kicked at a mattress rolled up in a corner of the last room. "Dammit!" he muttered. "This can't be happening!"

George was waiting for him at the head of the staircase.

"Come on, Bob," he said. "It's time to get out of here."

Gregorie stood in the dark, first-floor hallway, cradling the baby. The only light was the faint glow of moonlight coming through the windows of the rooms on the right side of the hallway. Through the open door, he watched his father sweep a flashlight beam around a room that must have been an office – a dented file cabinet with empty drawers askew, a few papers scattered on the floor, a broken desk chair lying on its side. Stefan kicked the chair.

"The bastards have deserted the place," Radko growled. "I won't make a dime off that brat."

Gregorie felt the baby begin to stir in his arms. Without warning, she wailed.

"Keep her quiet," Stefan growled.

"She's probably hungry," Gregorie said. "What do you want me to do, nurse her?"

Stefan shot him a vicious look, making him shrink back a step. "You shut your mouth!" he snarled. "You ever talk to me like that again and I'll rip your balls off! No one talks to Stefan Radko like that."

George's heart seemed to stop. He couldn't believe what he'd just heard: Stefan Radko, the name of the Gypsy Meers' agent gave him in the car on the beach. Stefan Radko: the ringleader of the kidnappings, the man responsible for so much anguish and suffering. A man just like Radko had taken him from his own parents twenty-five years earlier. Maybe it had been Radko himself.

Bob was hunkered down near the bottom of the staircase, a few feet below where George knelt on a step and pointed his gun between the railing posts toward the voices. George heard footsteps growing louder on the hall's marble floor. When the footsteps began reverberating off the walls and ceiling of the lobby, he clicked on his flashlight, lighting up a man and a teenaged boy. Yelling in Bulgarian, he ordered them to stop and put up their hands.

Bob shouted, "Watch out, George, he's got a gun."

"Drop the gun or I'll shoot," George yelled.

The man raised his left hand to shield his eyes against the flashlight beam. He seemed disoriented by the sudden bright light. Dropping his pistol on the floor, he said something to the teenager in a strange language.

George saw a swaddled infant in the teenager's arms. The baby squealed. The boy took a step toward the older man, and then suddenly turned and bolted out of sight down the corridor.

Bob and George started down the stairs to the lobby when the boy suddenly returned, no baby in his arms but a pistol in his hand.

"Gregorie, No!" the man shouted from where he stood in the middle of the lobby, highlighted in George's flashlight beam, his hands over his head. Then the man wheeled and ran out the open front door. "Gregorie, run!" the man called before vanishing through the doorway.

But the boy began shooting at Bob and George. Bob returned fire. In the flashlight's funnel beam Bob saw the boy pitch backwards, hit the wall, and slide to the floor.

Bob ran the rest of the way down the staircase to where the boy lay spread-eagled on the floor.

George ran down to the lobby to the front door. "Bob, let's go! We've got to get out of here."

"Hold on," Bob hissed. He checked the boy's body. One round from Bob's .45 had impacted the kid's chest; another round had torn his throat. He pocketed the boy's pistol. Stupid kid, Bob thought.

Bob ran from the lobby into the hallway. On the floor in the first empty room on the left, he found the infant the boy had been holding. He stuck his .45 in his jacket pocket, scooped her up, and moved back toward the lobby. But, after just four steps, he heard a door opening at the end of the corridor. He turned at the moment muzzle flashes sparked from a weapon.

Bob dove to the marble floor, landing on his side to protect the baby. There was a sharp, prickling feeling in his right calf. He reached down, touched the spot, and jerked his hand away when shards of pain shot through his lower leg. He touched his fingers to his tongue and tasted the sweetness of blood. He crawled to the covering shadows of the side wall. He adjusted his hold on the baby and fumbled for his pistol. It was wedged inside his jacket pocket. Two more shots came from the end of the hall. Then he heard approaching footsteps.

Bob knew time was running out. He could make out the outline of the man down the hall – now only a few yards away. Then shots exploded from the lobby.

"Get out of there," George yelled.

Bob scrambled to his feet and, in a crouching run, made it to the lobby. He leaped behind the side wall and ripped the pistol from his jacket pocket.

George moved sideways toward him. But the whining echo of a gunshot filled the lobby and George grunted and dropped to the floor.

Bob fired two shots down the hall and heard the clatter of what sounded like a pistol hitting the marble floor. Then the man there said something sounding like a curse. Bob laid the baby on the floor and reached out with his free hand for the neck of George's jacket. He pulled him toward him, out of the line of fire.

"Shit!" George groaned.

Bob unsnapped George's jacket. Blood already saturated the lower left side of George's shirt and dripped onto the floor, pooling and moving in a slow, inexorable flow toward the screaming baby.

Bob sloughed off his pack and opened it. He searched blindly with his hand for the first-aid kit, while peeking around the corner. He could hear someone moving around, but couldn't see a thing.

"Go!" George whispered. "If you don't get away quickly, either that guy's going to shoot you or the local police are going to show up. Either way, you'll be finished. You'll never have the chance to find your son."

"Shut up, George," Bob replied.

"Think of Michael," George gasped.

Bob knew his odds of getting out of this building and out of Bulgaria, and of ever seeing his wife and son again, were worsening by the second. But he wouldn't abandon George. He hadn't left his dead and wounded behind in Vietnam – no matter the risk, no matter the consequences – and he wouldn't do it now. Despite the pain he felt in his heart as he conjured up images of Liz and Michael.

Bob removed George's pack and found the first aid kit Liz had packed there.

"You've got to stop exposing your chest," he said. "First a knife wound and now a gun shot."

George groaned. "I'll try to remember that."

Bob dressed the wound in George's side with wads of cotton and then pressed an adhesive dressing over the wound. Pulling up George's shirt in back, he saw an exit wound and hoped the bullet hadn't passed through any organs. He guessed it had not based on the little amount of blood seeping from the wound. He glanced once more around the corner. For good measure, he picked up the .45 from the floor and fired a shot into the dark corridor. He heard running footsteps recede down the corridor and a door slam shut. Then he stuck the pistol in his jacket pocket and patched up the exit wound in George's side.

Bob swung George's pack over a shoulder and helped George to his feet, leaning him against the wall. He then picked up the squalling baby, holding her against his chest, letting her suck on his little finger, something he'd done with Michael. She quieted down. Then Bob wrapped his other arm around George and struggled to the front entrance. After descending the steps, keeping to the trees along the driveway, he slowly made his way to the main gate.

Before reaching the road beyond the gate, Bob heard the sickening sounds of sirens coming from somewhere across the valley.

Five minutes passed and then flashing strobe lights on the roofs of police cars illuminated the night sky as they raced up the road toward the orphanage gate. Bob helped George into the cover of bushes one hundred yards up the road from the gate. Two white police cars, followed by an unmarked black sedan, careened off the road onto the orphanage's drive.

Having tucked the infant inside his zippered jacket, Bob said, "Come on, George." He took George's arm and helped him to stand. They weaved down the side of the road like two drunks, Bob's leg wound causing him to limp. George was barely able to support himself, and Bob was bearing much of his weight, staggering under the combined burden of the two packs, the baby, and George. They moved deeper into the forest and rested behind the dense screen of the trees. The baby had dropped off into a fitful sleep. Probably so exhausted she's past the point of hunger, Bob thought. He placed her on a bed of pine needles and then pulled up his right pant leg to check his leg wound. The bullet had entered his lower left calf, thankfully missing bone and artery. The calf muscle was cramping and the wound was seeping blood. He quickly ripped off a strip of cloth from the bottom of his shirt and wrapped it tightly around his calf. Then he stuffed everything from the two backpacks he thought he wouldn't need into one of the packs. He used a flat stone to dig a depression in the earth beneath the low branches of a fir tree and buried the pack.

Bob checked his calf wound again and knew he had to keep moving or it would seize up on him. He hefted the remaining pack onto his back.

Even in the muted moonlight barely filtering through the treetops, Bob could see George's face was terribly pale. He checked the bandages on George's side and back and found the exit wound in George's back bleeding again. While he fixed the dressing, he realized George hadn't made a sound since they'd stopped to rest. After propping him up against a tree trunk, Bob pushed up one of George's eyelids and shined a flashlight into his eye. George moaned and slapped at Bob's hand.

CHAPTER FORTY

Early on the morning after Liz and Meers arrived in Sofia, an American Embassy Chevrolet sedan sped down Sofia's rain-dampened, time-worn cobblestones. Franklin Meers sat in the front seat, across from the driver. Liz sat in the backseat with Andrew Morton, staring at the depressingly-gray buildings lining the streets. She felt numb, drained of emotion. Until I have Michael in my arms, none of this will be real, she thought.

"We're going to the Bulgarian Premier's office," Morton said. "After your papers are checked, you'll be reunited with your son Michael. Then the Premier will make a speech at a press conference you will attend. His people have notified the press agencies. They've nicely orchestrated the whole thing to make themselves look good."

"I don't care, as long as I get Michael back."

"I want you to understand," Meers added, "the Bulgarian government will use this press conference for propaganda purposes. And they'll condemn the people who kidnapped Michael."

"Nice twist," Liz said, exhaling a stream of air. "The Bulgarian Government was behind my son's kidnapping all along."

"Probably right, Mrs. Danforth," Morton said. "But I warn you, say nothing about that. It won't do the other kidnapped children any good for you to attack the Premier. Just say how happy you are to have your son back and how grateful you are to the Premier for his assistance."

Keeping quiet about the Bulgarian Government's involvement in kidnappings didn't seem to Liz to be the way to protect other kidnapped children, but she had one priority at the moment. She'd keep her mouth shut until she had Michael back in her arms.

"I understand, Mr. Morton," she said. "I'll behave." Liz shrank into the corner of the backseat and looked out the car window again. The morning sun was just beginning to light up the city. She visualized Michael's face and conjured up the sweet smell of his skin. *What have the Bulgarians done to him?*

Then she snapped her head forward, looking at the back of Meers' head. "Franklin, how are we going to know if Bob called?" She tightened her hands into fists and pressed them against her thighs.

Meers twisted in his seat to face her. "When we get to the government building, I'll call our Embassy here. I left instructions for my messages to be forwarded."

Liz nodded. She pressed her forehead against the cool glass of the car window, feeling a terrible emptiness. She felt suddenly chilled. An image of Bob came to her. She imagined him running through a dense forest, being chased by armed men shooting at him. Liz blinked her eyes and tried to erase this nightmarish image from her mind. *What if I get my son back and then lose my husband?*

"Ah, Mee-ster Mor-ton," Premier Mimovich said in heavily accented English, "it is always good to see you. And this most be tha mother of our bright leetle boy."

Liz cringed at the Premier's use of the word, "our."

"Mee-sus Dan-forth, I am huppy to meet you and to place you together vith your son. I understand all the formalities haf been taken care of, so let us not put off tha reunion any lunger."

Mimovich gave an almost imperceptible nod to a barrel-chested man standing in a far corner of the spacious office. The man took two steps to a door, twisted an ornate brass doorknob, and opened it.

Michael stood there next to a heavyset matronly woman who was dressed in a long gray dress and *From Russia with Love's* Elsa Clinch shoes, dwarfing the little boy, making him seem especially small and vulnerable. Liz took a step toward her son, but stopped when she saw him shrink back against the woman. Liz saw Michael's fear – his eyes round, his little fists clenching the woman's skirt.

Liz knelt on the floor, arms extended, and softly said, "Michael, it's Mommy."

Michael peeked from behind the woman. Liz's voice seemed to have lit a spark in his eyes. He took a tentative step toward her. Then another. And another. Then he began running.

Liz burst into tears when Michael cried, "Mommy! Mommy!"

Morton stood in the back of the briefing room, no expression on his face, listening to Premier Mimovich feed the international press a line of bullshit about the Danforth kidnapping and the "tremendous satisfaction the Bulgarian people and our government have received from playing a vital role in the recovery of this little American boy." Morton surveyed the room and saw Anatoly Bruskoff, a member of the Bulgarian Intelligence Agency, eyeing him. Bruskoff motioned with his head toward the door leading to the outside hallway. Morton watched the Bulgarian leave the room. He followed him.

"So, Andrew," Bruskoff said, shaking Morton's hand, "isn't it wonderful about the little boy being found and returned to his mother?"

"Anatoly, I hope you're not going to give me the same load of crap your premier is shoveling to the press. You and I know better."

Bruskoff looked offended for a second, then laughed the dry, hacking laugh of a chain smoker. "Ah, Andrew, of course not. For a moment I forgot who I was talking to."

"Tell me, Anatoly," Morton said, "what's going to happen to the woman who had the Danforth boy?"

Bruskoff frowned at Morton. "There's nothing more we can do to the woman. One of the prison guards found her hanging from a pipe in her cell. Committed suicide before we could even question her."

"How convenient," Morton said. "Would have been nice to find out who she worked for. Who was bringing the kidnapped children to her."

"Of course, I agree," Bruskoff replied. He slapped Morton on the back and walked away.

CHAPTER FORTY-ONE

Sveta Vulovich sat by the window in her fourth-floor apartment and looked out at the darkening sky. The window gave her an unobstructed view of the street down to the park four blocks away, where her daughter had taken the little boy two days earlier. She rubbed her eyeglasses on her apron, put them back on, and watched the street, hoping to see Katrina. She'd been gone for over thirty-six hours. Sveta's calls to the police had been a waste of time. They said they would look into it, but Sveta could tell from their tone they would do nothing.

A black, official-looking sedan coming around the corner caught her eye. It stopped in front of her building. Four men dressed in suits and wearing fedoras got out. While the driver stayed next to the car, the other three marched into her building. Some poor idiot probably got caught dealing in the black market, Sveta thought. More than likely the good-for-nothing Katanach boy. She turned her attention back to the park in the distance.

Then a knock sounded on her door. Sveta stood, groaned, and stretched her arthritic limbs. What now? She patted her hair back and closed the top button on her dress, smoothing her apron with her hands. Opening the door, she found the three brawny men who'd gotten out of the car. She gasped when they pushed their way inside. Two of them rushed through the apartment to her husband's bedroom.

"What is it? What do you want?" she asked, her words squeaking out of her tightened throat.

"We're taking you and your husband in for questioning. Get your coat and your papers."

Sveta looked at her husband, Butros. The men had dragged him into the living room. "Wh. . . . what is it, Butros?"

Butros stared at his wife and Sveta saw the fear in his eyes. He seemed to be trying to smile at her, to reassure her, but he couldn't quite suppress his fear. Finally, he said, "A mistake, Sveta. These things happen. You will see; it is all a mistake."

The three men herded the Vulovichs to the street and pushed them into the back of the black sedan. Two of the men got into the car. One stayed on the sidewalk in front of the apartment house.

A moment after the car pulled away, a large truck drove up and took its place at the curb. Two men in coveralls stepped from the truck's cab. The driver walked up to the man in the suit and hat. The other man from the truck walked to the rear of the vehicle and opened the cargo door. He stepped aside when four more men in coveralls jumped from the cargo bay onto the street.

The driver said to the man in the suit, "Which floor, comrade?"

"Fourth."

"Shit! What else? They're never on the first floor!"

The man in the suit ignored the complaint, his face expressionless.

"What did these people do, comrade?" the driver said. "They must be real criminals to be sent to the Gulags, to forfeit all their possessions."

The suit, his face still blank, looked at the driver. "They are being sent away because they asked too many questions," he said.

The driver's mouth dropped open and then slammed shut; his face turned pale. He walked over to join the rest of his crew.

CHAPTER FORTY-TWO

Morton took Liz, Michael, and Meers to his house on the outskirts of Sofia. Their flight to Athens wasn't until six that night, nine hours away. The atmosphere was jubilant in Morton's living room. They all knew Michael's return was a miracle.

Meers read a book from Morton's library, while Morton sat on a couch, hugging his daughter, Erica. Liz sat in a chair opposite Morton, staring at her son asleep in her lap. The ringing phone interrupted the quiet. Morton snatched up the receiver. After listening for a few seconds, he replaced it in its cradle and settled back against the couch.

Morton's lips were compressed into a slash. He looked as though he wanted to say something, but seemed to be going through internal conflict about what to say and how to go about it.

Liz sensed his discomfort. "Who was on the telephone?" she asked.

Morton ran his hands through his hair and blew out a gush of air. He sat forward on the edge of the couch and said, "A man who provides information to me."

Liz stared into Morton's eyes and said, "An intelligence agent." After spending time with Franklin Meers, she was becoming adept at interpreting the euphemisms used in the intelligence community.

Morton smiled at her. Then he said. "He tells me the Bulgarians evacuated the orphanage. Our finding Michael in Sofia has caused the government to cover its tracks."

"Where did they take the other children?" Liz asked.

Morton shrugged. "We don't know." He paused for several seconds. "My man also told me there was police and Bulgarian Secret Service activity around the orphanage before dawn this morning. Gunshots were reported coming from the property."

"Is there any news about my husband?"

Morton shook his head.

Tears brimmed in Liz's eyes. She inadvertently shifted, waking Michael.

The boy looked up at his mother, rubbing his eyes.

"Where's Daddy?" Michael asked.

"We're going to see Daddy soon," Liz told him, with more confidence than she felt.

Michael brightened for a moment. "Daddy no bye-bye," he said. Then he laid his head against her breast and fell back to sleep.

Liz hugged Michael. Then she broke down; great shaking sobs racked her body. Please God, she silently prayed, Daddy no bye-bye.

CHAPTER FORTY-THREE

Liz's emotions surged like the tide – elation over the return of Michael, and then an unrelenting fear she had lost Bob.

The time on the flight from Sofia to Athens had seemed like an eternity. The only good thing she could say about it was it left on schedule.

An Embassy car waited outside the terminal in Athens for Meers, Liz, and Michael. After leaving the airport, the driver announced, "Mrs. Danforth, I was told to pass on to you that your dog's going to make it." He added, "The entire Embassy staff has been holding their collective breaths waiting to hear about White Dog. She's a real American hero."

At her house in Kifissia, Liz, holding Michael in her arms, started to get out of the car's backseat, but changed her mind and looked back at Meers.

"Franklin, I apologize for getting so angry with you," she said. "I'll never be able to thank you enough for what you've done for my family. Getting Michael back."

Meers smiled and patted her arm. "Liz, I don't believe for a second you're sorry about being angry with me. But I accept your thanks." Then, after a beat, he added, "He'll make it, Liz; he's got too much to live for."

Liz leaned sideways and kissed Meers on the cheek. She didn't know what to say, and she didn't trust herself not to break down.

Inside her home, she put Michael in bed and then made sure all the doors and windows were locked. She knew she was being paranoid but even paranoid people had enemies. She sat down in the rocking chair next to Michael's bed and listened to the soft sounds of his breathing. Not for the first time did she contemplate what life would have been like without her son. And not for the first time did she wonder how she would go on if Bob didn't return to her.

Then she thought about the man who kidnapped Michael. The Gypsy Meers brought to the Kaki Thalassa beach said the kidnapper's name might be Radko. She felt as though the name was indelibly tattooed on her brain. She couldn't remember ever hating another human being. There were few times when she'd even felt real anger toward a person, anger that didn't stem from annoyance. But these unfamiliar feelings of hatred and anger, seasoned by fear for Bob, stewed together in a fiery cauldron of emotion she knew had changed her forever.

CHAPTER FORTY-FOUR

Bob didn't care if the Bulgarians found their fence cut. Once inside Greece, they would be safe. He used the wire cutters Liz had packed for him and separated the strands of the barbwire fence. Pausing for only a moment to make sure there were no Bulgarian border guards in sight – the last patrol he'd seen had passed by just five minutes earlier, he adjusted the infant inside his jacket and lifted George off the damp night earth and hunched his back to shift his pack.

George was as gray as a ghost and the baby couldn't possibly sleep much longer. Bob figured she hadn't eaten in at least six hours. He'd run out of spare clothing to take the place of diapers. And, on top of all that, the wound in his calf had caused his right leg to cramp to the point he had to walk flat-footed. The pain was becoming almost intolerable.

They'd made it about fifty yards into the Greek zone when all hell broke loose. Floodlights and flashlights shone from several directions and a male voice ordered them to halt and lie down on the ground. The Greek the voice spoke made Bob want to laugh and cry at the same time. He let George sag to the bare earth. He dropped to his knees and raised his arms above his head just as the baby girl started screaming bloody murder.

CHAPTER FORTY-FIVE

It took the doctor at King George Hospital in Thessaloniki less than an hour to clean and dress Bob's wound and administer antibiotics. It took another four days for Bob to recover from an infection that could have cost him his leg. Liz and Michael barely left his side the entire time.

George Makris never made it out of the hospital alive. His wounds were too severe; he'd lost too much blood.

Bob exulted over the return of his son but, at the same time, agonized over George's death. The man had given his life to save Michael. He thought long and hard about what he could do for George's family, to rehabilitate George's reputation. He discussed it with Liz. She was the one who came up with the idea.

Bob and Liz stood on a raised platform next to George Makris' parents, before a phalanx of television cameras and reporters. They read from a prepared statement, telling about George's kidnapping years ago, his return to and arrest in Greece, the treatment he'd received by Greek authorities, his role in trying to find Michael and in rescuing the Greek infant they'd brought back from Bulgaria, and, finally, his death. Bob also revealed the Bulgarian Government's part in kidnapping Greek children. The story made headlines in the Greek papers and was highlighted on all the Greek television stations. It burst on the international press like a 10-megaton hydrogen bomb.

Bob had been ordered to keep his mouth shut about his and George's little excursion into Bulgaria, and about Bulgarian involvement in child kidnappings. The woman from the U.S. Embassy in Athens had explained that divulging what he knew would be politically naive and could be damaging to Bob's military career. The press conference had been in violation of that order.

CHAPTER FORTY-SIX

Stefan Radko sipped the *raki* from the glass in his hand. He stared at the television screen with an intensity that made his eyeballs ache and his brain fuzzy. The American Army officer read from a piece of paper and told the world about his son's kidnapping, about the death of a man named George Makris, and many other things. The words the American spoke barely made an impression on Stefan. The man's comments about how Makris was shot in an orphanage filtered through Stefan's anger. He knew he had shot and killed the man, and that made him feel good for a second or two.

He concentrated on the American's face, memorizing every feature. "Robert Danforth," he said over and over again. "Robert Danforth, the man who murdered my only child, Gregorie. Robert Danforth, you will die a horrible death." He pointed a finger at the television screen. "I will live to see you dead."

Stefan finished the remainder of his drink and poured another measure of the strong Turkish alcohol. He continued staring at the television.

Vanja entered the room. "Were you talking to someone?" she asked.

Stefan swallowed half his drink. His eyes still glued to the television screen, he said, "A dead man. I was talking to a dead man."

JOSEPH BADAL

CHAPTER FORTY-SEVEN

Two days after the press conference, Bob limped across the carpet, came to attention, and reported to Colonel Gray, who sat on the other side of a desk, bracketed by the American flag and the unit flag.

"Christ, Bob, take a seat," Gray said. He took a deep breath and grimaced as though he had a sudden pain. Exhaling slowly, he pulled open his desk drawer and removed a bottle of antacid tablets.

"Damn ulcer," he said. He poured water from a carafe into a glass, popped two tablets into his mouth, and washed them down with a swig of water. Bob waited while the Colonel took another deep breath.

"Well, your trip into Bulgaria ruffled a few feathers," Gray said. "But that press conference really did it." Gray looked uneasy, almost sick.

"Yes, Colonel," Bob said. "I hope I haven't caused *you* any trouble."

Gray waved a hand. "Nothing I can't take care of. But I've got orders for you." Gray paused and cleared his throat. An apologetic look crossed his face. "I'm damned pissed off about this, Bob." He reached across his desk and handed Bob a sheet of paper.

Bob read the document, then looked over at Colonel Gray. "This is a request from me to resign my commission and be discharged, Colonel, I–"

"That's right, Bob. The Army decided your trip to Bulgaria wasn't in the best interests of the military services. Disobeying the order to keep your mouth shut was a foolish thing to do. You've got forty-eight hours to pack up. You'll be honorably discharged at Fort Dix, New Jersey."

Bob realized his mouth was hanging open. He slammed it shut. He felt as though he would choke. When confident he could speak without his voice croaking, he said, "What if I refuse to sign, Colonel?"

"Then you'll be the oldest Captain in the U.S. Army. They'll never promote you. I've already tried to stop this, Bob. The decision's been made."

"This hurts, Colonel," Bob said, his face feeling flushed. "The Army was going to be my career." Bob clenched his jaw and lasered his eyes at Gray. "Colonel, I'd do the same thing all over again. Even knowing this would happen."

Gray smiled at Bob. "So would I, Bob."

"I guess I'd better go home and tell Liz," he said. "Am I excused, sir?"

Gray stood and came around his desk. Bob also got up and came to attention. "At ease," Gray said. "I want you to know I don't agree with the Pentagon's decision. The Army needs officers like you."

"Thank you, sir," Bob said. "Looks like I'd better start thinking about another career."

Gray reached into his shirt pocket and extracted a business card. "This man asked me a bunch of questions about you. He seemed impressed with what you did, going into Bulgaria, bringing back the little girl." He handed the card to Bob.

"Cultural attaché? What does he want?"

"He wants to talk to you about a job."

"Sir, if the Army doesn't want me, I doubt the State Department is going to feel I'm diplomatic material."

Gray smiled at Bob. "For your information, that cultural attaché business at the Embassy in Athens is nothing but a front. He's CIA."

PART II

1999

CHAPTER ONE

Liz lay next to Bob, one of her legs across his. She lightly rubbed his chest. "You made me feel wonderful," she said.

"Uh huh."

"There's a snake in the bed; it's about to bite you."

"Umm," Bob said.

Liz poked him. "You're not even listening to me. What's going on?"

"I'm sorry." He turned toward her, stroked her thigh. "You know, the Agency ought to hire you as an interrogator."

"Dammit, Bob. What's wrong?"

Bob sighed. "I'm worried about the situation in Kosovo."

"What do you have to do with that mess?"

"You know I can't say."

"What can you say?"

"That it's a mess."

"You're just full of useful information," Liz said, slipping out of bed.

CHAPTER TWO

Bob looked around Jack Cole's spacious office while he waited for the CIA's Special Operations Chief – and his long-time friend – to finish the phone call that had interrupted their conversation. He looked at the walls and thought about what could have been hanging there: the Silver Star Jack had earned in Vietnam, the Bronze Star with "V" device, the two Purple Hearts, the citations he'd won in his twenty-some years with the CIA. But there was only one "ego" item in sight: The photo of Jack's sailboat.

Bob noticed there were more lines in Jack's face and that his once sandy-blond hair had turned almost completely gray. Jack looked older than his fifty-two years. But the blue eyes were still alert, intelligent.

Jack replaced the telephone receiver in its cradle. "Bob, I don't have to tell you how important this is," he said. "You're the only man in the Agency with the knowledge and experience to pull this off. You speak Serbo-Croatian, you've got years of fieldwork, you recruited our agents in Yugoslavia. Besides, as my Covert Operations Chief, you have to do what I tell you to do."

Bob didn't reply. Jack was just stating facts.

"The wild card over there is the Serb President," Jack said. "His only concern is his own political survival. We're convinced he won't agree to any settlement involving Kosovo becoming an independent province. All our intelligence reports tell us the man is unstable, a megalomaniac with an insatiable appetite for power. If he isn't controlled, sooner rather than later, this thing in the Balkans could become a regional disaster."

"So you want to take out the Serb leader?" Bob asked.

"I wish it were that simple," Jack said. "Killing the leader of a foreign country is not an option anymore. Not since Congress, in its infinite wisdom, decided to handcuff the Agency."

"I can't believe any President would sign that legislation."

Jack nodded. "We've got to find a way to limit the Serbs' capacity to wage war, and maybe get the Serb President indicted for war crimes at the same time."

"Tall order," Bob said.

"I want you and your team to come up with a plan I can sell to the Director. I suggest you find a way to dilute the support the Serbs have in the international community. If we make it embarrassing enough for the Serbs' allies to associate with the Serb President and his henchmen, maybe we can politically and economically isolate the Serbs. Without the Russians, for example, the Serbs' supply lines will dry up."

"How much time do I have?"

"Three weeks at best. We've got to knock the Serb leadership down a peg. Maybe that will keep the President from having to commit American ground troops to a potentially very bloody war."

Bob reviewed agency files on the Serb President for hours, met with intelligence, diplomatic, and military experts on the Balkans, and even contemplated how – despite U.S. laws against it – an assassin might get close to the Serbian leader. He'd come to a dead-end. The Serb leader never stayed in one spot for very long. Never slept in the same building two nights in a row. According to a CIA informant within the Yugoslav People's Army, no one outside his inner circle knew the Serb President's plans more than four hours in advance. He never appeared in public without an impenetrable ring of bodyguards.

Bob had called his three top aides to a strategy session. They tossed ideas around, and then discarded them all. Bob checked his watch. They'd been at it for ten straight hours. While his people continued rehashing possible plans, Bob looked around the room and considered their skills.

Forty-five-year-old Frank Reynolds, a bookish, twenty-two-year employee of the CIA, with an IQ in the stratosphere, had spent most of his career with the Agency analyzing message traffic and news reports coming out of the Balkans, Turkey, and Greece. He'd studied Serbo-Croatian at the Defense Language Institute, West Coast, in Monterey, California, and received his doctorate in Balkan Studies at Georgetown. He knew more about the Serb leadership now ruling Yugoslavia than anyone in the free world. Frank's salt and pepper hair, as usual, looked as though it had never known a comb. The man was impatiently drumming the table with his fingers.

Thirty pounds overweight, Tanya Serkovic wore frumpy, grandmotherly dresses. She had thick, shoulder-length black hair, violet-colored eyes, and exotic Slavic features, with a trace of Oriental blood showing in the shape of her eyes. A Bosnian who was a former analyst with the Yugoslavian Intelligence Service, an expert in Eastern European Languages, and also fluent in Greek and Italian, she'd witnessed the genocide perpetrated by the Serbs against her people. She'd fought with the Bosnian resistance, and fled to the United States when Serb hit squads were sent to assassinate her.

Raymond Gallegos had the dark good-looks of a Latin moviestar and the intelligence of a brain surgeon. A highly decorated Army veteran, who got his Bachelor's and Master's degrees in geography after two tours in Vietnam, he'd spent years with the National Security Agency as a cartography consultant. He knew every foot of the Balkans the way most people knew their own homes or neighborhoods.

They all looked exhausted. "Okay, people," Bob said. "We've had a long day. Let's all go home and sleep on it."

They all groaned, as though disappointed about having to call it quits.

"I'll see you at 7 a.m.," Bob said. "We need to come up with something really soon."

CHAPTER THREE

Liz looked out the living room window and saw Bob's car pull into the driveway. She glanced at the grandfather clock in a corner of the room. Already half past ten. She went to the front door and watched through a glass panel while Bob slowly climbed out of his car and walked toward the house. He looks like a zombie, she thought. An old zombie. She opened the door and met him. She took his briefcase and topcoat, placing them on a chair in the entry. The dark circles under his eyes and the sallow cast to his skin were hard to miss. How can he continue working at this pace? she wondered. This was the third night in a row he'd come home after ten.

"How were your classes today?" he asked.

She smiled. She knew what an effort it must be for him to even ask, considering how tired he looked. "Actually, not bad," she said. "Thank God for graduate courses. My days of teaching Economics to freshmen are long over."

He appeared to try to laugh, but the sound he made came out more like a grunt.

"I've got a plate in the microwave. Why don't you go upstairs and change while I heat it up?"

Bob planted a kiss on Liz's cheek, trudged up the stairs, and plodded into the master bedroom. He turned on the television to catch the news. While he undressed, he listened to reports that yet another mass grave had been found in Kosovo. This one, just south of the Serbian border, held three hundred Kosovar Albanian bodies – men, women, and children – all executed with bullets to the back of the skull.

Bob felt a churning in his guts. I can't take three weeks to come up with a plan, he thought. The Serb hierarchy has got to be stopped *yesterday*.

The ringing of the telephone interrupted his thoughts. He jerked the receiver from its cradle. Who the hell's calling at this hour? "Hello!"

"Dad, it's Mike."

"Hey, Mike. How ya doin?"

"Great! How are things there?"

"Everything's fine. Sure you're okay? You usually don't call so late."

"No, no, I'm fine. Thought I'd better tell you before you heard it on the news. Part of the 82nd Airborne's been put on alert. My unit included. There's a good chance we'll be sent to the Balkans to join the part of the unit that's already there."

"When?" Bob asked.

"Probably within two to three weeks."

Bob slumped down on the bed, feeling what little energy he had left drain out of him. "Appreciate you letting me know, Mike," Bob said, keeping his true emotions from his voice. "Can we get together before you ship out?"

"Sure, Dad. Count on it. I'll arrange a couple days up there. But, listen, I've got to go now. Got a lot of work to do."

"Okay, Mike. We love you."

Michael didn't answer right away. There was a several-second pause before he finally said, "Give Mom a hug for me." Then he hung up.

"Will do, son!" Bob said to the dead phone line. He felt a tightening in his throat. He knew he'd surprised his son when he'd told him, "We love you." He balled his fists and told himself he was a shit and a coward. Why hadn't he said, *I love you*, instead of *We love you*. Bob stood up and continued undressing. There were a lot of things he wished he'd done over the last two decades. Not saying I love you was just one of many fuckups when it came to his relationship with his son. How many soccer games and wrestling matches had he said he was going to attend and didn't? How many birthdays had he missed? He'd put his work first and his family second. He'd been more attentive to Liz and Michael for a couple years after Michael had been kidnapped and found in Bulgaria. But then he reverted back to his old habits..

"Dammit!" he said aloud. Mike and his unit were going to be shipped out to the Balkans. This business with the Serb leader had just become personal.

CHAPTER FOUR

Bob rubbed his eyes. The glare from the overhead fluorescent lights in the Langley conference room were starting to get to him. "All right, where are we going wrong? We haven't come up with a thing."

Tanya Serkovic tapped her fingernails on the tabletop and swiveled back and forth in her chair. She gazed around the room at each of the others. "I think we're approaching the problem from the wrong angle," she said. "We're wasting our time talking about assassination squads. Besides, the Serb leader is impossible to isolate."

"Nothing's impossible," Frank Reynolds interjected. "But it sure as hell would be illegal."

"Yeah, right, Frank," Tanya shot back. "As I was saying, we need to change our approach."

"Well, we could catch him with an intern," Raymond Gallegos offered. "On second thought, forget it! Clinton's already done that, and it didn't hurt him a bit."

Groans and half-hearted laughs.

"Let's get serious, guys," Bob said. He got up from his chair and walked over to the blackboard. "Tanya's right. Let's look at the problem from a different angle. If we can figure out a way to destabilize the Serb regime . . .." He let the thought hang while he returned to his chair.

Deep in the bowels of the Central Intelligence Agency complex at Langley, Virginia, Photographic Intelligence Analyst Rosalie Stein inspected the contents of a file. News articles, agent-in-place photographs and reports, and satellite photographs were scattered on the table in front of her. She'd worked through the articles and reports first, but had come up with nothing new. The satellite photographs – hundreds of them – hadn't been touched. Like leaving dessert until last. She knew analyzing them would be tedious, but it was the part of her job she loved the most.

The National Reconnaissance Office had satellites passing over Serbia sixty times each twenty-four-hour period. Most of the pictures transmitted by the "eyes in the sky" were of scenery, rooftops, and traffic. The definition of the photographs was amazing. Anything that emitted a heat signature – living things, vehicle engines, and smokestacks – could be spotted in the dark by infrared ("IR") satellites. During daylight hours, the synthetic aperture radar ("SAR") satellites sent back shots that were so clear individuals could be identified.

Rosalie had to analyze each photo slowly and carefully. She never knew what she might find. After eleven hours, the images were starting to blur. She swept her dark red hair away from her face, while she leaned over and stared at the pictures, searching for something – a clue, an anomaly. Some of the photos revealed Serb military units in the field. But most, as usual, were of open space, or of one Serb town or another. Lots of scenic views. About to call it a day, she glanced again at one last picture, and suddenly shoved all the others aside. She reached for her magnifying lens.

The tension in the room was becoming thicker than the oppressive Washington humidity. Tanya and Frank had, off and on, been at each other's throats over the past two hours. Raymond sat slouched in his chair, his face in his hands. Bob glanced at his watch. "It's eight-fifteen. Let's wind this–." The telephone interrupted him.

Raymond answered it. "Who . . . Stein, you said?" He listened for several seconds, then covered the mouthpiece and looked across at Bob. "It's someone from Photographic Analysis. She claims she's got something to show us."

"Tell her to come right up," Bob said. "What do we have to lose?"

"Got lost!" Rosalie apologized when she rushed, blushing and breathing heavily, into the room fifteen minutes later. "Rosalie Stein, Photographic Analysis," she announced. "I'm new."

"Wonderful!" Frank murmured. "Tell me something I don't already know."

Rosalie's face reddened even more. She looked around the room, then focused on Bob at the head of the table. She walked to him and put six pictures on the table in front of him. "I looked at a bunch of photos today. Nothing stood out. Then, a little while ago, I noticed something in one photograph. I went back through the pile and discovered I'd missed the same thing in some of the others.

"Twelve of the satellite shots picked up one of the Serbs' top generals on several different days over a fifteen-month period. In three of these shots, the general is standing next to a woman. She's not his wife of record."

"Who's the general?" Tanya asked.

"Karadjic, Antonin Karadjic," Rosalie answered.

"Great! Karadjic!" Frank exclaimed. "The psycho has a girlfriend!" He shoved his chair away from the table and stood up.

"The guy's way up there," Frank continued. "He carries out the government's toughest assignments. He and the Serb President go way back. They were schoolmates and came up through the Yugoslav Communist Party system together. He's been involved in every major Serb battle since the breakup of Yugoslavia. Nearly every time there's been a massacre – of Croats, Bosnians, Slovenes, Gypsies, or Kosovar Albanians – Karadjic's troops are likely to have been involved. The guy's a master tactician, but he's a maniac. He enjoys the killing. The Serb leadership can't do without him."

Frank's words seemed to energize the others in the room. They all appeared suddenly alert, sitting up straighter, studying the photographs with renewed enthusiasm.

Frank returned to his seat at the table and pulled one of the pictures to him. He studied it for several moments. "Holy shit!" he suddenly exclaimed. "Why didn't we think of that?"

"Think of what?" Raymond asked.

"Karadjic could be the Serb leadership's Achilles' heel. If we're talking destabilization, Karadjic could be a terrible embarrassment to their regime."

"Good point," Raymond said. "But what's with these photographs?" Raymond switched his gaze toward Rosalie. The others in the room followed his example.

Rosalie's face reddened again. "Well, uh . . . I think the woman's a Gypsy."

Bob sat up straighter in his chair. Ever since Michael's kidnapping back in 1971, just the word "Gypsy" gave him a chill. "What about Gypsies?"

"So what if she's a Gypsy?" Frank said caustically. "We've got–." A sharp glare from Bob shut Frank up.

"She wears traditional, colorful Gypsy clothing. Her head's always covered with a bright shawl." Rosalie paused. She had their undivided attention. "Each time she shows up in a photo, a major Serb offensive occurs no more than one week later. I checked the dates of her visits against dates of Serb offensives."

"Are you saying before Karadjic goes to war, he has sex with this Gypsy?" Raymond interjected.

Rosalie shrugged.

Tanya said, "From what I know about the Serbs' feelings about Gypsies, I doubt Karadjic would have a Gypsy mistress. But maybe it's not about sex. She could be a . . . fortune-teller."

"Jee-z-z!" Bob blurted out. Heads snapped around. The members of Bob's team shot incredulous looks at one another. "Thank you, Ms. Stein," Bob said. "We'll look into this. Tanya, why don't you escort Ms. Stein back to her office. I wouldn't want someone as important as she is to get lost again." Bob smiled at Rosalie to make sure she knew he was teasing her. "And while you're there, Tanya, go over all her photos. Maybe you two will come up with something else."

As Tanya and Rosalie left, Bob turned to Frank. "Call the Serb desk. Get a message to Bessie, our agent in the Balkans. I want to know if she knows anything about Karadjic meeting with a Gypsy woman. If so, what's their relationship? Who is she?"

CHAPTER FIVE

"I've tried to reach you for two days, General," Olga Madanovic said, leaning toward the man standing in front of her. She put her hands on her hips and gave him a challenging look, as though demanding an apology. "I chalkmarked the fire hydrant, just as I always do. What happened?"

General Darius Alexandrovic took a seat and smiled at the blond American agent. "You Americans are so damned impatient. What do you think? I wait all day for you to leave me a signal?"

Olga turned away and looked around the bungalow she rented in the Yugoslav capital. She reached over and pulled the curtains aside a couple inches and peered out the living room window at the General's staff car parked out front, and then at the Belgrade skyline in the distance. She inhaled deeply and brought her anger under control. "Things are getting critical. I need you to respond to my signals as quickly as possible."

"I'm managing logistics for the whole Serb Army. NATO's bombing us every day and blowing up our supplies. It just makes my job more impossible. On top of everything else, I'm helping you, but only so this civil war doesn't escalate into a worldwide conflict."

"Yeah, General. Do you think your assistance might also have something to do with the million dollars we put in a Swiss account for you over the last eighteen months?"

Alexandrovic leaned back and stared, grimfaced, at the CIA field agent. Finally, a smile creased his features. "Well, you've got me there, Olga, darling. So why did you want to see me? I can't stay much longer. Have you finally decided to go to bed with me?"

Olga frowned at the Serb general, keeping the disgust she felt from showing. Their cover was that they were having an affair. In reality, that would never happen.

"You know, my dear," he said, "it would be better if we *did* fuck once in awhile. There's nothing better than authenticity in a cover story."

Olga smiled at him. "Tell you what. I'll do it if you sign over your Swiss bank account to me."

"You've an inflated opinion of yourself. But it's helpful to know you have a price."

Olga dropped her smile. "What do you know about Antonin Karadjic meeting with a Gypsy woman?" she said.

"That's what this is all about?" Alexandrovic laughed. "You wanted to see me about Karadjic and his Gypsy fortune-teller? What Washington idiot sent you on this mission? So what if the great Karadjic is superstitious – he likes to get his fortune told. If I recall correctly, Nancy Reagan consulted with a fortune-teller."

"You're telling me it's common knowledge Karadjic consults a fortune-teller?"

Alexandrovic laughed. "No, not common knowledge. No general wants people to think he's sharing secret battle plans with an ignorant Gypsy woman who rides around in a horse-drawn wagon. Only a few members of the senior command know about this. Whatever the woman tells him seems to make him happy. It's harmless, Olga. Nothing to get excited about."

"Tell me when he meets with the fortune-teller," Olga said.

"Before he goes into action," Alexandrovic quickly responded. "You know, before a battle, or . . .." He stopped. "Oh, now I understand. You think there's a connection."

"I want to talk with the Gypsy woman. Can you make it happen?"

Alexandrovic stared at her. "What a shame!" he said. "That long, blond hair, those green eyes, those breasts bulging like cantaloupes beneath your sweater." He cupped his hands under his chest. "Someone should be making love to you. Instead, you're risking your life for madmen." He sighed.

Olga let her anger get the best of her. "Thank you for the inventory of my physical attributes. But don't worry about whether or not I'm getting laid. And get it out of your head once and for all that you'll ever have a chance. This is a purely business relationship."

"All right, Miss Olga. Be in Dusan Park tomorrow at sunset. If I can arrange it, the Gypsy woman will be there. Don't approach her. She'll act like she's peddling something and will come to you."

"How will I know which Gypsy woman she'll be? That park's always full of Gypsies hawking their goods or begging and stealing."

Alexandrovic rose from his chair and walked across the room. Turning back to Olga, he said, "She'll ask if you want to look at some jewelry. You say yes. Her name's Miriana. Miriana Georgadoff. Hot little number, that Gypsy girl." He paused and stared at Olga's breasts.

"Concentrate, General."

Alexandrovic smiled at Olga. "Tie a blue scarf around your neck. Oh, by the way, I'll tell the woman you've agreed to give her a thousand dollars."

Alexandrovic left the room, laughing.

CHAPTER SIX

"Mr. Danforth, Cooney here in the Ops Center. There's coded message traffic for you."

"Where's it from, Cooney?"

"Zone thirty-two. Field Agent Bessie."

"Be right down."

Bob rushed out of his office and quick-walked down the hall to the elevator. Bessie – Olga Madanovic's code-name – was one of the agents he'd personally recruited. *That gal's got bigger cajones than most men*, Bob thought. But the thought didn't make him worry any less about her safety.

He took the stairs down to the Cryptography Operations Center, punched his personal access code into the keypad by the center's entrance, and entered the long narrow room. An assortment of cryptographic machinery occupied tables on both sides. Bob shivered at the cool temperature in the room. A thirtyish, pimply-faced-man with spiked blond hair looked up from his chair when Bob opened the door.

"Hey, Cooney." Bob said.

"Good to see you, Mr. Danforth."

"How do you stand it?' Bob asked, staring at the man's short-sleeve shirt. You could hang meat in here."

Cooney patted the machine in front of him and said, "Gotta take care of my babies. Can't have them overheating." Cooney then reached for a sheet of paper on the table next to him. "I've got your message decoded." He handed the paper to Bob.

Bob scanned it, then went over it again.

Gypsy fortune-teller to K. stop. Relationship known to only a few in military hierarchy. stop. Connection between K meeting with Gypsy and

Serb military campaign. stop. Meeting set with Gypsy sunset tomorrow. stop. Bessie. End Message.

CHAPTER SEVEN

Raymond Gallegos breezed into Bob's office. "What's up, Bob?"

Bob pointed at a carafe sitting in the middle of the table. "Help yourself to some coffee. We'll wait 'til the others get here."

Tanya and Frank arrived together just when Raymond settled into a chair. "We got information on the Gypsy woman Stein picked out in the photographs," Bob told them. "She *is* a fortune-teller. Bessie meets with her at sunset tomorrow — about noon our time. Let's make some assumptions based on what we know and develop contingency plans."

"This fortune-teller business is intriguing," Frank said. "Stein told us each time Karadjic met with the Gypsy a Serb military action followed within a week. I checked it out. She's right."

"And Bessie confirmed that," Bob added.

Frank paused, got up from his chair and walked over to the window. Hands in his pants' pockets, he rocked back and forth, heel to toe to heel.

"Let's assume Karadjic uses this fortune-teller like the ancient Greeks used the Oracle at Delphi," Frank said. "He asks her questions about the timing of major offenses; schedules attacks based on her answers. Let's also assume he's not crazy enough to give her details about his plans. How can these assumptions help us?"

As Tanya and Raymond mulled over Frank's question, Bob sat back and waited. They worked best when they brainstormed without interruptions from him.

"We don't want Karadjic dead," Tanya said after a thirty-second pause. "There would just be another psychopath in the wings waiting for his chance to take over. But we have to make an example of the general. And interrogate him."

"So?" Raymond asked. "What do you have in mind?"

Tanya massaged her forehead. "I think we need to expose the bastard."

"And how the hell are we going to do that?" Raymond asked.

"Hold on," said Bob. "Maybe we can do more than expose him." He chewed on his lower lip and steepled his hands in front of his face. What he was about to propose would be difficult to execute. "Maybe we can use the fortune-teller to put him in the hands of the War Crimes Tribunal at The Hague. Karadjic on trial would be a perfect way to show the world what sorts of people make up the Serb leadership."

"Aren't you getting ahead of yourself?" Raymond said. "The last I knew, Karadjic was safe and sound in Yugoslavia."

Bob put his hands flat on the table and leaned forward. "We're just going to have to kidnap General Karadjic and deliver him to The Hague."

CHAPTER EIGHT

Jack Cole gaped at Bob Danforth. "Let me get this straight. You want to snatch Karadjic. Then, you want to mount a massive information campaign against the Serb leadership based on testimony you *think* Karadjic will give. This is supposed to embarrass the Serb hierarchy and dissolve international support for the Serbs. You want this campaign coordinated among the Pentagon, the State Department, Congress, and the White House over here, and among NATO, the European Union, The Hague, and God knows who else overseas. All to convict one lousy Serb general. Does that about summarize what came out of days and days of meetings with your resident group of geniuses?"

Bob smiled and nodded. "That was a damn good summation."

"Why don't we just send in a Special Forces team and blow the sonofabitch away?" Jack shouted.

Bob smirked and said, "I can't believe you'd even suggest such a thing. You know the answer to that, Jack."

Jack caught the look on Bob's face and groaned. "Yeah, I know the answer to that. We'd be violating U.S. and international law. Demonstrations would start up outside every one of our embassies. Some other cowboy would replace Karadjic – maybe someone worse than him. And the ethnic cleansing would just keep on happening. Does that about cover it?"

Bob sighed and dipped his head.

"How do you propose grabbing him?" Jack asked.

Bob looked at his watch. "I'll give you my answer in three hours, after our agent in Belgrade reports in."

CHAPTER NINE

For one thousand American dollars Miriana would have agreed to meet with Dracula. The message she had received from an aide to General Alexandrovic described the woman she was to meet in the park and told her how to approach her. Miriana scanned the tiny park until she spotted a woman who seemed to match the description she'd been given seated on a bench. She walked along a meandering path in the woman's direction.

"Would the pretty lady like a nice ring?" Miriana asked in Serbo-Croatian, stopping in front of a blond, thirty-year-old woman wearing a blue scarf around her neck. She noticed the woman's deep blue eyes, straight nose, and prominent cheekbones.

The woman stared at Miriana, as though she was scrutinizing every aspect of Miriana's appearance: Her age – nineteen, her long black hair and pale blue eyes, her red and black shawl, bulky blouse, and ankle-length, and heavy skirt that Miriana knew failed to conceal her voluptuous figure.

"You have rings to show me?" the woman finally responded.

Miriana sat next to the woman. "Miriana has the best jewelry in Belgrade," she said, setting a leather pouch on the bench between them and opening it to spread out an assortment of cheap rings and bracelets.

They stared at the jewelry rather than at each other.

"I expected someone older," the woman finally said, still looking down. "Every fortune-teller I've ever seen was old and could pass for a witch."

"I will take that as compliment," Miriana said, unable to resist smiling. "What do you want from me?"

"What were you told?"

"That you would pay me one thousand American dollars if I met you here. Is this about sex? I am no whore."

The woman laughed out loud. Several people passing by on the path stared. "No!" she said in a whisper. "This isn't about sex. Why don't you pick up one of your rings and show it to me."

"First, I want the money."

The woman took a white envelope from her purse and slid it across to Miriana, who snatched it off the bench in a lightning-quick motion and slipped it into the bodice of her dress. Then she picked up a gold ring and made a show of trying to get the woman's interest.

The woman took the ring, slipping it on a finger as she said, "You know a Serb general named Karadjic?"

Miriana's mouth dropped open. "Did General Alexandrovic tell you that?"

"It's not important. What I want to know is when you are scheduled to see him again?"

"I'm not going to tell you shit," Miriana said. She pulled the ring off the woman's finger, rolled up her package of jewelry, stood, and began walking away.

"Miriana!" The woman called. The girl paused. The woman got up and went over to her. "Do you know how many Gypsies have died because of your friend Karadjic?"

Miriana stared defiantly at the woman. "What are you talking about?"

The woman walked to the bench, sat down, and patted it with her hand.

Miriana returned to the bench and sat.

The woman slipped three photographs from her large purse and laid them upside-down on the Gypsy's lap.

Miriana turned them over. When she looked at the first one she gasped, jerked a hand to her mouth, and kept it there while she scanned the other two. Each photo showed piles of bodies – men, women, and children. A giant mass grave yawned behind them. Most of the dead women wore traditional Gypsy clothing. Several yards away from the piles of bodies in one photograph, eight women were tied to stakes stuck in the ground. Their hair had been shorn and their breasts mutilated. General Antonin Karadjic stood proudly posing in each picture.

"Serb troops rounded up all the Gypsies within fifty kilometers of Mitrovica," the woman said. "They tossed babies, alive, into the pit. They raped the girls and women and made the men and boys watch. After the soldiers finished with the women and girls, they shot them. Then they shot the men and boys. According to a boy who escaped and hid in the woods nearby, the women who were stripped, tied to the posts and mutilated had resisted their rapists."

"Why would the Serbs do this to Gypsies? We have helped them by giving them information. We are their allies. The Kosovars hate us for this."

"You sleep with dogs, you come away with fleas."

"How did you get these photographs?"

"Your friend Karadjic had one of his own soldiers take these pictures. He keeps them so he can relive his greatest moments. How I got my hands on them is none of your business."

Miriana bent over and put her head in her hands.

"Are you crying?' the woman asked.

Miriana dropped her hands, raised her head, and turned toward the woman. "What do you want to know?"

CHAPTER TEN

The six men sat on the worn sofa and three chairs in the cramped space of the living room. The fireplace provided less than satisfactory warmth. Several of the men held their full tea glasses in their two hands to help cut the chill in their fingers.

"This damn war is ruining business," a wire-thin, middle-aged man announced to the group of men who'd assembled at Stefan Radko's house. "There's nothing to steal. Kosovars leave all their possessions behind when they flee their homes, but before we have a chance to grab anything, the Serb Army sweeps through. They steal or burn everything. Worse, American bombs scare Serb civilians into staying inside their homes, so even pickpocketing is poor."

Stefan forced himself to suppress his disgust for this group of men. A bunch of whiners, he thought. Seventy years old and I have more nerve than all of them put together. But he needed them to do his dirty work.

"Okay, have we heard from everyone?" Stefan said, sarcasm heavy in his voice. He looked around the room to make sure he had each person's attention. "We will shut down our operations for awhile. We cannot take the chance the Serbs will catch – and execute – our people on the street."

"But Stefan," one of the men protested, "how do we feed our families?"

"Try honest work!" Stefan snapped. "Or spend some of the money you've been hoarding."

The man's face went red, but he said nothing.

Stefan stood.

The other men began to leave. He walked them to the front door, giving each one a reassuring pat on the back. After they left, he sat in a chair and rested his head in his hands.

"What's wrong, *O Babo?*"

Stefan looked up when his daughter came into the room. "I worried about you, my beautiful, little *papusza*. How did it go?"

"I am not your little doll anymore, Papa, I am a grown woman," Miriana said, blushing. She pulled an envelope from inside her blouse and dropped it on the table.

Stefan slit the seal on the envelope and peered inside. "One thousand dollars?"

"As promised."

"Good job, Miriana. Now tell me what this woman wanted."

"She wants to know about my work as a *drabarni,* about my fortune-telling sessions with General Karadjic."

Stefan nodded encouragingly at his daughter.

Miriana's voice suddenly broke. "*O Babo*, she showed me photographs of Gypsies massacred by Karadjic's soldiers. There were dead bodies everywhere, and Karadjic just stood there by the bodies. *O Babo*, Karadjic has murdered our people. His men raped our women, killed our children."

"You listen to me, Miriana," Stefan said. "Your people, as you put it, are not the sheep Karadjic slaughtered. Your people include your brother Attila, your mother Vanja, and me. No one else counts."

"But, *O Babo—*"

"No buts, Miriana. You start worrying about Gypsies who don't have the sense to run away from the Serb Army and you will wind up dead. You worry only about yourself and your family. Now, tell me about this woman in the park. Who was she?"

"She wasn't *Rom*. She looked Serbian, but at the same time there was . . . something about her that made me think she was a western *gadji*. She had a Belgrade accent, but she was too confident, too aggressive to be from Serbia. I thought about it all the way back from Belgrade. If I had to guess, I would say *Amerikanka*."

"*Amerikanka?* Hmm."

"What are you thinking, *O Babo?*"

"What did this woman promise you if you helped her?"

"Ten thousand dollars!"

Stefan thought for a minute.

"If she is European – British or German – we cannot expect to get any more money than what she offered," he said. "But if she is with the Americans, and the information they want from you is important enough to them, we may be able to squeeze them for a whole lot more. When do you see her next?"

"The day after tomorrow – Thursday. Same time, in the park."

"Good, Miriana. By the way, you got a call. The General wants to see you on Sunday."

"*O Babo*, when can I stop meeting him? He scares me. There's evil in him. The *mulo* is on him."

"Don't start that superstitious junk. The spirit of the dead is no more on Karadjic than it is on you or me. As long as Karadjic needs you, we're safe."

CHAPTER ELEVEN

The Serb Army force left Surdulica and crossed the Morava River into Kosovo. It was a relatively small unit – really more of a raiding party: Forty-three men packed into two armored personnel carriers, two Jeeps, and a two-and-a-half ton truck. The soldiers were tense, but excited. Whenever General Karadjic joined a patrol, they could anticipate mayhem and looting.

The patrol moved northwest and arrived at the staging area at dusk. The men got out of the vehicles and lounged around, smoking cigarettes and talking in excited, but muted voices. They waited an hour until the sun dropped below the horizon, and then reboarded the trucks and moved at speed to the twenty-house village of Prizla. When the trucks skidded to a stop in the center of the village, the soldiers jumped to the ground and fanned out, forming a perimeter around the village.

Thirteen-year-old Nuradin Osmani, late as usual returning from the high pasture with his two dozen sheep, heard the sounds of vehicles racing into Prizla. Several hundred meters away from his village, he hid, terrified, behind a rock outcropping and looked down on the cluster of one-story homes. He strained to see what was happening, but it was too dark. Only dim candlelight showed through the house windows in the distance.

Suddenly, the glare of floodlights filled the night. Nuradin saw men dressed in Serb Army uniforms kick in the doors of houses. They shouted at the people and forced them onto the dirt road that ran through the village. Some people cried and begged for mercy. But most seemed dumb-struck with terror.

Nuradin watched a giant soldier drag his little brother, Sultan, by his collar, out into the center of the road. Then other soldiers pushed his father, mother, and sister, Salima, into the circle of villagers huddling under guard.

An officer walked over to a Jeep and saluted. A man with gold braid on the shoulders of his uniform blouse got out of the Jeep, walked with the officer to the frightened captives, and marched on short legs around the group. He strutted arrogantly, his large belly protruding over his belt. Then he suddenly stopped and pointed. One of the soldiers pulled Salima over to him. The fat man grabbed Salima's wrist and dragged her into one of the houses.

Salima's screams carried up to Nuradin's hiding place. He covered his ears, but he could not silence his sister's screams. He wanted to run away, but he seemed paralyzed. Then he heard a gunshot. Nuradin peeked around the rock and saw the fat man come out of the house alone, stand in the road, and shout, "*Uradite to!*"

Do it? Nuradin wondered. Do what?

He felt cold. He began to shake. Tears poured down his cheeks. He saw his father in the crowd of villagers. *Baba*, you must do something, Nuradin silently pleaded.

The soldiers were quickly separating the men and boys of Prizla from the women and girls. They lined up the men and boys and forced them to kneel. A soldier stood behind each of them and, on the command of the fat man, fired a bullet into the back of each male's head.

Nuradin felt a wetness pour from him, but he still couldn't seem to move. His piss steamed in the cold night air and made him shiver even more.

The soldiers shot all the old women, too, before taking the remaining girls and women, including Nuradin's mother, into the houses. Nuradin listened to the screams for over an hour. Then more gunshots.

In the eerie silence that followed, there were flashes of strobe lights. Someone was taking photographs of the massacre.

CHAPTER TWELVE

The satellite messaged information, including a dozen photographs, back to the National Reconnaissance Office. Copies were immediately wired to the White House, State Department, Pentagon, National Security Agency, and CIA. The information ultimately landed on CIA Analyst Rosalie Stein's desk. Rosalie scanned the dozen satellite photos on her desk, and then, shaking with rage, called Bob Danforth's office. Danforth's assistant transferred her call to one of the conference rooms at Langley.

Discussion in the conference room stopped when the telephone rang. Bob picked up the receiver, listened for a moment, and then said, "Bring them right up." He replaced the receiver, rubbed his hands over his face and sat back in his chair.

"What's up, Bob?" Frank asked.

"Another slaughter in Kosovo. It looks bad. We've received photographs from the NRO. That was Stein down in Analysis. She's bringing them up here."

"How many dead?" Tanya Serkovic asked.

"Don't know," Bob said. "We'll find out soon enough."

Rosalie Stein burst into the room, red-faced and out of breath. She dropped a stack of photographs on the table in front of Bob.

After studying each picture, Bob passed it around the table. "This thing's escalating," he said. "The Serbs aren't satisfied with just driving the ethnic Albanians out of Kosovo. Now they're slaughtering them, too. It's ultimate ethnic cleansing."

Bob felt anger building inside. Stay cool, he told himself. Stay cool.

After the meeting broke up, Bob took an elevator down to the Crypto vault.

"What can I do for you, Mr. Danforth?" the Crypto Clerk asked.

"I want this message sent on a Flash Traffic basis."

"Yes, sir," the Clerk said, taking the paper from Bob's hand. After inputting the message text into his computer, the Clerk punched in encryption instructions and tapped the transmit key. Bob's message sped across space at the speed of light in a burst of code toward the radio-fax receiver of Agent Olga Madanovic, code name: Bessie.

CHAPTER THIRTEEN

Olga found the message on the machine she kept hidden under a floorboard in her apartment:

The Butcher Is To Be Extracted. stop. Code Name: Operation Oracle. stop. Advise Earliest If Gypsy Is On Board. stop. Instructions To Follow. End Of Message

The Gypsy girl looked nervous, Olga thought, when, later that day, she approached Miriana sitting on the park bench. The girl kept glancing around the park as though she was afraid someone had followed her.

"Good evening, Miriana," Olga said. She took a seat next to the girl. "It's good to see you again."

"What more do you want of me?" the girl asked.

"You know, Miriana. I'm going to give you ten thousand American dollars for telling General Karadjic's fortune."

Olga waited for the girl's response. None came.

"Do like I tell you and you'll have the cash in twenty-four hours."

Olga paused. When the girl finally nodded, Olga continued.

"First, do you have another appointment set with Karadjic?"

"Why?"

"That's none of your business," Olga snapped, then quickly softened her tone. "It's for your own safety. The less you know, the better."

"I don't think I want to play this game by your rules," Miriana said, sudden confidence in her voice. "I want a million dollars put in a numbered account in Switzerland."

"What?" Olga exclaimed. "You've got to be kidding."

Miriana gave her a slip of paper. "This is the name of the bank. I also want safe passage out of Serbia for my parents, my brother, and me."

Olga sat stunned. "What makes you think you're worth that much money, that much trouble?"

"Why else would you want to know when Karadjic's going to meet me? It must be very important."

"A million dollars is out of the question. It's ten thousand or nothing."

Miriana stood. "Fine, then it's nothing." She walked away.

"Wait!" Olga said. She rose and hurried after Miriana, not caring about the curious stares from people on nearby benches. Gripping Miriana's arm, she whispered, "Maybe I can get you a little more than ten thousand."

"All or nothing," Miriana insisted. "And you better get it quick. I'm meeting with Karadjic three days from now. On Sunday."

Miriana felt the sweat trickle from under her arms and down her sides. What is O Babo thinking? she thought. Why would he risk losing ten thousand dollars? They will never agree to one million.

CHAPTER FOURTEEN

"A million bucks!" Jack Cole yelled.

"Hell, Jack, it's a whole lot less than the cost of one Cruise missile," Bob said. "If this operation works, we'll save twice that for every minute we can shorten the war. And think of the lives we can save."

"Jee-zus, Bob! This is absurd."

Bob didn't respond, waiting for Jack's anger to burn off.

Finally, Jack said, "Okay, Bob, I'll sign off on it. But I want you there on the ground, to make sure everything goes as planned. As an observer only."

"Right!" Bob said, wondering whether he'd be able to remain an observer during the operation.

Bob could always tell when Tanya was worried: She had two vertical creases in her forehead, just above her nose, which looked deeper than usual. "All right, out with it, Serkovic. What's on your mind?"

"No insult intended, Boss, but you're fifty-three years old," she said. "What the hell is Jack Cole thinking, sending you into the field?"

"Don't think I can handle it?" Bob asked, barely suppressing a smile.

Tanya shrugged.

"I won't be in on the actual snatch. The Marines will handle that. I'm just going to observe."

"Until something goes wrong." Tanya said.

"What could possibly go wrong?" Bob said, with a wry smile – knowing all too well the Peter Principle was alive and well anytime an agent went into the field. If something can go wrong, it will. He waved Tanya out of his office. Then he sat back in his chair, hands behind his neck, and stared at the ceiling. The hardest part would be telling Liz.

Late that afternoon, Bob found Stan Bartell at a corner workbench in the Special Operations Section. Everyone called Bartell "Q" after the character in Ian Fleming's James Bond series.

"Hey, Bob, long time no see," he said. "I hear you're going out."

"That's right, Q. Got my paperwork done?"

"You bet! Look here."

Documents were spread out on the workbench. Each featured Bob's photo.

"You're going into Serbia with press credentials," Bartell said. "This one says you're a freelance writer for a Canadian newspaper. Next, here's your Canadian passport. And your visa to enter Serbia."

Bob examined the papers and nodded his approval. He put them in a leather briefcase Bartell provided. Stacks of cash were already in the case. "Where do I pick up a weapon?"

"There'll be a Sig Sauer 9mm, along with two spare clips, under the mattress in your hotel room in Belgrade."

Bartell slid a receipt for the cash – fifty thousand dollars in U.S. currency – and handed over a pen. Bob signed the receipt and pushed it back to Bartell.

"Thanks, Q," Bob said. "I'll see you when I return . . . assuming your documents pass the test."

CHAPTER FIFTEEN

At sunset on Sunday, Olga again sat next to the Gypsy girl on their usual park bench. She briefly wondered if the girl really understood the risk, but quickly forced the thought from her head. That wasn't her business. The mission was all that counted.

"Here's the deal," Olga said. "No negotiations, no changes. Take it or leave it. You understand?"

The Gypsy girl nodded.

"The money will be placed in your Swiss account after you do as you're told," she said.

"That was not our deal," Miriana exclaimed, her voice rising. She kneaded her hands in her lap, scrunching the fabric of her dress between her fingers. "We want the money up front. We—"

Olga saw fear in the girl's eyes. "Tough shit," she said. "You do the job, first." It was time the girl understood who was boss in this matter.

Miriana visibly gulped. "What do you want of me?" she asked. "What must I do to earn this money?"

"I'm going to tell you slowly, and I want you to repeat it – word for word. I want no misunderstandings or screwups. Your life . . . and mine . . . could depend on it."

Miriana leaned forward and stared raptly at Olga. She listened to the blond woman's whispered instructions. Her eyes grew bigger and bigger while Olga talked.

CHAPTER SIXTEEN

"One of these days you're going to knock the door right off its hinges," Liz said when Bob walked into the kitchen. Her voice displayed mock irritation. It was just part of their normal daily routine.

Bob paused. "Sorry. I can't seem to close it softly. I'll try to remember next time."

"No you won't," she said, feigning anger. Then she turned from emptying the dishwasher, a glass in each hand, and gave Bob a kiss. "What are you doing home so early? The last time you came home unannounced was two years ago, when you were being sent off on some cockamamie mission to some godawful third world country in Africa." Liz laughed at the absurdity of her comment. But then she noticed the frown on Bob's suddenly reddening face.

"Bob, don't tell me you're going into the field," she said. Her heart lurched. "That's crazy! You promised that wouldn't happen again."

He hunched his shoulders and spread his arms. "It can't be helped."

She scowled.

"Calm down, honey. Getting upset isn't going to change anything."

She put the two glasses down on the kitchen counter. "Goddamit! What's wrong with the Agency?" She stared at him, stepped into his arms, and began to cry. "Oh, Bob," she said. "Not after all these years. Not now."

CHAPTER SEVENTEEN

Two days later, Bob arrived in Belgrade on a commercial flight from Toronto, Canada. He took a cab from the airport to the Hotel Belgrade. After doing a quick inspection of his room, checking for listening devices and cameras, he reached between the bed's mattress and box springs and found the 9mm and two fully loaded magazines Stan "Q" Bartell had arranged to be put there. After removing another magazine from the pistol and checking to make sure the chamber was empty, he tested the trigger pull. Satisfied, he replaced the magazine and put the weapon back under the mattress.

Deciding to reconnoiter the hotel, and to establish his cover as a reporter, he went down to the hotel bar, figuring that's where he'd find members of the press contingent. He chose a guy sitting by himself at the bar, a laminated ID badge on his vest, sipping a drink.

"Excuse me," Bob said.

The man looked up. "Can I help you, mate?" the man said. He shook Bob's hand. "Henry McCourt, Adelaide Times."

"Greg Davis, freelance out of Toronto," Bob said.

"Take a seat," McCourt said, dropping back into his own chair. "Had ya pegged for a Yank."

"Canadian, American. How do you tell the difference?" Bob said, sitting down next to McCourt.

"Just so, mate," McCourt answered, laughing.

"So, what's happening around here that will interest my editor?"

"With NATO planes bombing Belgrade, you won't have to go too far from the hotel to find a story. Milan Bozic, deputy mayor, is holding a press conference at noon today. He's going to make another speech about how it is NATO bombs – not the poor, misunderstood Serbs – that are driving the ethnic Albanians out of Kosovo."

"Interesting."

"Why don't you tag along with me," McCourt said. "I've got a car. I'll meet you in the lobby at eleven." McCourt shoved away from the bar. "Gotta file my story," he explained. "Bloody fuckin' deadlines."

After McCourt went off to file his story, Bob moved to the hotel restaurant and ordered breakfast – coffee, hard-boiled eggs, and hard, dark bread. Afterward, he ventured onto Belgrade's streets. He had to walk only three blocks before he saw the results of NATO's precision bombing: Pockets of government buildings and factories destroyed with no damage to the buildings around them. He jotted details of what he saw in a small notebook and took photos. He would turn these over to CIA analysts when he returned to Langley.

When Bob returned to the hotel lobby, he found Henry McCourt waiting. The Australian led Bob back out on the street and around a corner to a beat-up Lada sedan parked half on the sidewalk.

"Our limousine awaits," McCourt said.

It took fifteen minutes to get to the Belgrade Municipal Building and another thirty minutes to get through security and credentials check. Bob and McCourt took their seats in the pressroom, a large, high-ceilinged room with windows on one wall. Bob looked around, recognizing many of the television correspondents from FOX, CNN, and the broadcast networks. He began to ask McCourt a question when Deputy Mayor Bozic entered. The cameras started rolling.

"Thank you, ladies and gentlemen, for coming today," the said. "Before I take your questions, I am going to make a statement about the grievous wrong being perpetrated on the Serb people. Many of you have personally seen the damage NATO bombs have done to my city. Nine more people were killed last night, and many more injured." Raising a fist in the air, Bozic appeared to lose his professional calm. "We will never surrender," he yelled.

McCourt jabbed Bob in the side. "Here comes the bullshit."

"We are trying to make peace with the Albanians in Kosovo. We would be happy for them to live in Kosovo and become productive citizens of our country. But not as long as the KLA – the Kosovo Liberation Army – continues attacking innocent Serbs. Now, for no good reason, NATO is attacking us. NATO claims Serbs are committing atrocities against the Bosnian Muslims, the Kosovars, the Albanians. I assure you these claims are lies. Their bombs kill people in Kosovo and Bosnia, and NATO claims we are responsible for the deaths."

He shook his head and shuffled the papers on the podium. "I will now take your questions."

McCourt shot out of his chair, waving his arm. "The Serb government is now holding NATO soldiers prisoner –English, German, American. You've threatened to put these men on trial, in violation of the Geneva Convention. Are they being well treated? Are you going ahead with the trials?"

CHAPTER EIGHTEEN

"Geneva Convention, my ass," Stefan Radko spat while he watched the press conference on CNN International. "They bombed Serbia. They will be treated like criminals."

"I think you are wrong, Stefan," Vanja said. "Even the President isn't that crazy."

"What the hell do you know about these things, woman?" Stefan shouted. The CNN camera moved from the reporter who'd asked the question, to the deputy mayor, and back to the reporter. At first, Stefan concentrated only on the reporter. Then his gaze settled on the man seated next to the reporter. He rubbed his eyes. The man seemed familiar. Had he seen him before? But where? When?

And then, as though a flashbulb had gone off in his brain, he shouted, "It can't be." He moved closer to the television set. "It can't be," he repeated. Stefan knelt on the floor. His mind washed the gray from the man's hair. It erased the wrinkles in his face. Despite his natural doubts of not having seen the man for almost thirty years, Stefan recognized Bob Danforth. How could he ever forget the face of the man who murdered his son Gregorie? Bob Danforth, the man who had stood at another press conference twenty-eight years earlier and disclosed the role the Bulgarian government played in child kidnappings in Greece. And now Danforth was in Serbia, delivered up like a lamb to the slaughter.

"What is it, Stefan?" Vanja asked.

Stefan waved away her question and continued staring at the screen until the camera settled again on the deputy mayor. He stood, flexed his fists, and picked up the telephone.

CHAPTER NINETEEN

Just as Stefan had instructed, Niko Papolu sat in his car across and down the street from the municipal building entrance and watched people stream out. He still fumed over Stefan's calling him at home and ordering him around like some young pup. But he was too afraid of the old man to defy him.

The man Stefan had described suddenly appeared on the steps of the building. Dark-blue sport coat. Wavy salt-and-pepper hair. Mustache. About fifty-five years old. Another man walked with him. The two got into a Lada and drove off.

After following them to the Hotel Belgrade, Niko parked his own car and ran into the hotel lobby. He frantically jerked his head left and right, searching, and sighed with relief when he caught sight of both men entering an elevator.

Niko found a bank of pay phones and called Stefan.

"*Halo*," Vanja answered.

"Daj da govorim ti Stefan," Niko said.

"He's right here–"

Stefan was suddenly on the line, shouting into the mouthpiece, "I'm listening. Did you see him?"

"He's at the Hotel Belgrade. He just went up in the elevator."

"What room?" Stefan demanded.

"How am I supposed to know that?"

Stefan breathed loudly into the phone. "Watch the lobby," he ordered. "If he goes out, follow him. I'll be there in about eight hours."

"But, Stefan, my family is visiting. We are having a–"

"I don't care if the Pope is visiting you. Stay there and keep your eyes open." Stefan broke the connection with a bang.

Niko held the receiver away from his ear and stared at it.

Bob woke up shortly after eleven-thirty p.m. feeling drugged. Jet lag still lay over him like a wet wool blanket. He forced himself out of bed. He stripped down and stepped into the shower. The cold sting of the spray helped to dissipate his doped-up feeling. By the time he finished brushing his teeth, he felt almost human again. He'd just finished dressing when the telephone rang.

"Mr. Davis?" queried a rough male voice before Bob could even say hello.

"Right," Bob said.

"Mother told me to contact you."

"I've been expecting your call," Bob said, smiling at the use of Jack Cole's code name. "Are you all set?"

"Ready to go."

"Almost. How will I know you?"

"Dark-brown Range Rover. Green anorak. I'm parked across the street from the hotel entrance. I'll stand on the sidewalk by the car. And wear a warm coat. It's cold and rainy out here."

"Okay," Bob said. "Give me five minutes."

He put on a dark-blue ski jacket and then pulled the pistol and extra magazines from under the mattress. He stuck the pistol in one outside pocket of the jacket and the magazines in the other pocket. He made sure he had his papers – press badge, visa, and passport – and put them in an inside jacket pocket. After grabbing the briefcase with the currency, he left his room.

Stefan walked through the Belgrade Hotel's wide, brass-trimmed doors while nearby church bells tolled midnight. He spotted Niko dozing in a lobby chair. Stefan walked over to his so-called lookout, kicked his foot, and growled, "*Idiota!*"

"Wha . . . who the hell!" Niko said, a startled look on his face. He jumped out of his chair, ran his fingers through his hair, and mumbled something unintelligible. Stefan saw the fear in the man's eyes.

"If he's left the hotel," Stefan hissed, "I'll cut your throat."

Niko's fearful look suddenly changed. "Nothing to worry about," he whispered. "He's just come out of the elevator."

Stefan turned to look just as Danforth hurried past him. It took huge will power to not pull his dagger and stab the man right there in the crowded lobby. He watched Danforth leave the hotel. Pushing Niko away, Stefan rushed after Danforth. He reached the street in time to see Gregorie's murderer enter a brown Range Rover that immediately pulled away from the curb.

Stefan waved in the opposite direction. A Fiat pulled out from a parking place half-a-block away and slid to a stop in front of him. In addition to the driver, there were two men in the backseat.

"Stay with the Range Rover," Stefan ordered as he got into the front passenger seat.

CHAPTER TWENTY

"Greg Davis," Bob said, introducing himself to the driver, using his code name. "What do I call you?"

"Yanni will do."

Bob hefted the briefcase over the seat onto the floor in back and slid the case partway under the back seat. Then he looked closely at Yanni, who had one of those nondescript faces that would allow him to hide in a crowd. His dark hair and olive complexion would help him to pass as a native in almost any of the Balkan or Mediterranean countries.

"What's our destination?" Yanni asked.

"The Kosovo border with Albania."

"Don't lose them, Zoran," Stefan growled at the driver, a Buddha-shaped thirty-year-old with a shaved head, large belly, and powerful arms and legs. He'd been a member of Stefan's gang for ten years. Like all of the members of the gang, Zoran was *Rom*, a Gypsy.

Zulkar, seated behind forty-five-year-old Zoran, was Stefan's assassin — the man Stefan had counted on for nearly two decades to do his dirty work. He had murdered a dozen men on Stefan's orders. He had jet-black hair, mustache and goatee. He looked like a Tartar, with chiseled cheekbones and narrow, slanted, angry gray eyes.

Kukoch, next to Zulkar in the back seat, wore his trademark beret, which covered his unruly straw-like blond hair. Tall and lanky, twenty-four-year-old Kukoch was fundamentally a non-violent thief who ran Stefan's black market operations.

"Where are these guys going?" Kukoch said in his grating high-pitched voice, sounding like fingernails screeching on a blackboard. The son of an old Gypsy confederate of Stefan's, Kukoch had the body of a weightlifter

152

and a head that was too small for his body. His nickname was Peahead, but no one outside the gang had the nerve to call him that. "What's the plan, Stefan?" Kukoch asked.

Stefan hesitated a moment before answering. Finally, he said, under his breath, *"Koke per koke."*

"What do you mean, 'a head for a head'?" Zoran asked. "Is this about revenge?"

Stefan glared at Zoran's profile. "It will be my only reward in this matter. Whatever the men in that Range Rover might have on them is yours. You can split up the spoils. But the passenger is mine."

Bob and Yanni's documents – and a hundred dollar bill – got them through each of the six checkpoints they encountered on the way to the Albanian border.

They continued south, the rain finally letting up when they approached a checkpoint near Pec.

Yanni pulled the car onto the road shoulder one hundred yards short of the checkpoint. He peered through the windshield at the four armed men standing in the middle of the road, in front of a barrier. They were highlighted by the Range Rover's headlights and two floodlights mounted on the guard shack behind the barrier. "I don't like the looks of this," Yanni said. "These men look more like bandits than Serb Army regulars."

Bob patted the bulge of currency in his jacket. "They're all bandits. Hopefully, our cash will make the difference."

"You're the boss," Yanni answered. He pulled off the shoulder, drove up to the checkpoint, and rolled down his window. Two men armed with automatic weapons approached, one on each side of the car.

The man on the driver's side spoke to Yanni in Serbo-Croatian.

"Where are you going?"

"My friend here is a Canadian reporter. We're driving into Kosovo. He wants to follow up on reports the KLA is killing Serb residents there."

While the guard considered Yanni's answer, the second one tapped on Bob's window with the muzzle of his weapon, then made a downward motion with it to indicate he should roll down the window.

Stefan and his crew had been having an easier time of it at the checkpoints. He carried a VIP pass General Karadjic had given Miriana. The bearer could travel anywhere in Yugoslavia.

When Stefan saw the sign announcing the guard station just ahead at Pec, then saw the Range Rover stopped at the checkpoint, he told Zoran to pull off the road. He got out and walked ahead, staying close to the trees bordering the rutted pavement. The Range Rover's taillights glowed brightly in the night. Two armed guards bracketed the car. Another two guards stood ten yards away, in front of the vehicle. Then Stefan saw those two split up and go to the sides of the pull the driver and Danforth out of the vehicle. They paired up with the two other guards and began manhandling Danforth and his companion.

Stefan cursed under his breath. "Shit! They'll kill him."

CHAPTER TWENTY-ONE

By the time Bob was dragged from the Range Rover, he knew he and Yanni were in real trouble. The guards wore a motley assortment of clothing – Serb Army fatigue jackets over a variety of shirts and sweaters and jeans. Two had military campaign caps; the other two wore blue NATO forces baseball caps. They apparently wore whatever they found or stole. They were nothing but bandits.

"Who's your leader?" Bob asked in English as the bandits dragged him off to the side of the road.

One of the bandits shouted something that Bob thought might be Serbo-Croatian and the other man released Bob's arm and jabbed the butt of his rifle into Bob's side. Bob sagged to the ground and groaned, despite his resolve to not show any weakness to these hoodlums.

The bandits then dragged him along the ground and into the trees. He heard the other two bandits laughing and Yanni crying out. The bandits were obviously beating him.

Bob tried to relax, to breathe normally. He offered no resistance while the two men hauled him into the woods. They stood him up against a tree. One man aimed his rifle at Bob while the other one leaned his rifle against another tree and searched Bob. He found the money belt and stripped it from around Bob's waist, and then, laughing, waved it at his partner. He tossed the money belt by his rifle and grabbed a length of rope hanging over a branch.

The bandit looped the rope around Bob's chest and then around the tree, but suddenly stopped when a voice from the road yelled something, and then Bob heard the sound of a car engine.

The man with the rifle looked over a shoulder toward the road. In that instant, Bob leaped forward, jerking the rope from the hands of one bandit, and lashing out with his foot kicking him in the crotch. The Serb bandit screamed and fell, dropping his weapon and holding his private parts. The other guard came around the tree at him, but Bob snatched the first guard's rifle from the ground and swung the weapon at the second man's head. Then he used the rifle to club the other one.

Bob snatched up the money belt and stuffed it inside his jacket, and then ran in a crouch back toward the Range Rover. Over the vehicle's hood, he saw the other two bandits dragging Yanni into heavy brush on the far side of the road. Fifty yards up the road, a car rolled slowly toward the checkpoint.

Bob saw the bandits dump Yanni in the brush and then move back to the barrier blocking the road. They leveled their rifles at the approaching vehicle, which stopped just feet behind the Range Rover, and moved forward, one on each side, as they had before. Suddenly, the sound of automatic weapons firing shattered the night; muzzle flashes lit up the second car's interior. The bandits were blown backward and fell to the ground.

The occupants of the car got out and quickly inspected the bodies. They fired bursts from their automatic weapons into the bandits. They then emptied the dead men's pockets and dragged their bodies into the woods.

Bob gripped the bandit's rifle and felt the comforting weight of the pistol in his jacket pocket. He had the option of melting back into the forest. But he couldn't abandon Yanni. He stepped out from behind the Range Rover and shouted, "Do you speak English?"

Three men from the second vehicle pointed their weapons at Bob. He dropped the rifle and raised his arms in the air. "Hold it! I'm a Canadian reporter."

An elderly man with sharp, hawk-like features stepped forward. "Your papers," he demanded in English tinged with a mild Slavic accent..

Bob slowly lowered one hand, reached inside his jacket for his Greg Davis passport, and handed it over to the man, who scanned the document in the light from the second car's headlights and looked back at Bob.

"Greg Davis?" the man said.

"Right!" Bob said.

"What are you doing here?" the man asked.

Despite the man's accent, his English was flawless. "I'll answer your questions. But, first, I need help for my friend," Bob said. "They beat him badly." He squinted against the glare of the Fiat sedan's headlights, trying to get a better look at his saviors, while pointing toward where Yanni had been dumped.

The old man nodded and waved at two of his men. He shouted something at them.

They followed Bob into tall grass near the edge of the forest. Bob knelt next to Yanni's still form. He checked his pulse. "He's alive," he said, "but his breathing is shallow. Let's get him to the car."

The two men carried Yanni to the back of the Range Rover. Bob climbed in first and helped pull Yanni into the vehicle's cargo area. Cuts and abrasions showed on Yanni's face. Blood oozed from his scalp. When Bob touched Yanni's chest, the man moaned.

"I think he's got broken ribs," Bob said. "Maybe internal injuries, too." He looked over his shoulder out through the open tailgate. "He needs a doctor."

"There are no doctors around here," said the hawk-faced man. "We need to get moving. These Serbs will be missed when they fail to report in. Where are the other two guards?"

"Over there, unconscious," Bob said.

Hawkface looked at Bob and said, "Unconscious? I'm glad to see you reporters know how to defend yourselves." Then he blurted an order in a language Bob didn't recognize.

Two of the men moved swiftly in the direction Bob had indicated, where the two unconscious bandits were. Two shots rang out a moment later. Then the men returned.

Bob turned to Hawkface. "Was that necessary?"

The man shrugged and turned away without a word.

Bob's stomach knotted. He moved back to the Range Rover and covered Yanni with a blanket from the cargo bay. Then he climbed out of the car and closed the tailgate. "What now?" he asked.

"Where are you going?" the leader said in English.

"The Albanian border."

"We are, too. We can join forces until we get there."

Bob shrugged. "Okay by me."

"I'll ride with you," the leader said.

"What the hell is Stefan up to?" Kukoch asked Zoran and Zulkar while they followed the Range Rover. "I thought he wanted to kill that guy."

"How do I know?" Zoran growled. "How can anyone understand what Stefan's up to?"

CHAPTER TWENTY-TWO

The USS *Nassau* plowed through high seas at the northern end of the Ionian Sea. Lightning streaked while thunderheads rolled overhead. The decks had been awash with heavy rain for hours.

The *Nassau* ran due north toward the Strait of Otranto on a course that would put her halfway between the Albanian coast and the boot heel of the Italian peninsula. From there she would turn forty-five degrees toward Albania. As part of a three-ship Amphibious Ready Group from Amphibious Squadron 4 (PHIBRON 4), she carried, in addition to her regular crew, the 24th Marine Expeditionary Unit (SOC), Special Operations Capable, under the command of Colonel Dell Taylor.

Commodore Frank Petty, gray-haired commander of PHIBRON 4, paced in front of two men seated in the briefing room – Taylor and Lieutenant Commander Ernest Crowley, Operations Officer (N-3) for PHIBRON 4. The *Nassau's* 30-by-15-foot briefing room resembled a miniature movie theater, with twenty-four plush chairs in six rows facing a raised platform. A podium was fastened securely in the middle of the platform. Maps and a blackboard hung on the wall behind the podium.

Petty, as thin and hard as an iron rail, stepped behind the podium and placed his palms on it. He glared at the other men. "I have to tell you both, I don't think much of this cowboy mission. It stinks of CIA."

Taylor and Crowley nodded, but remained silent.

"We're putting those young men in harm's way with inadequate intelligence," Petty continued. "Any captured Marines will be executed as spies – after a show trial. If this thing turns into a clusterfuck, you can bet the spooks won't be anywhere around to share the blame."

Taylor shrugged. "What the hell choice do we have, Frank?" he asked.

"I know, I know."

Petty walked over to a corner table and pressed a buzzer. An ensign entered the room almost immediately.

"Williams, find Lieutenant Garcia," Petty barked at the young officer. "Bring him here ASAP."

"Aye, aye, sir," Ensign Williams replied. He turned sharply on his heels and left the room.

Taylor got up from his chair to study the map hanging on the wall behind Petty. Acid began to flow in his stomach and backed up into his throat. He opened the bottle of antacid he always kept in reach and took a swig. He hated to think what the combination of after-dinner stomach acid and pre-action adrenaline was doing to his insides.

There was a knock on the door. A Marine lieutenant entered the room and came to attention.

"Lieutenant Garcia reporting as ordered, sir." His face was a stone mask.

Taylor strode over to Garcia. "At ease, Lieutenant Garcia. Take a seat" He pointed at a chair in the front row, then sat next to Garcia.

"It's time for you to earn the big bucks Uncle Sam pays you," Commodore Petty said, his gaze directed to Garcia. "As the Force Recon Direct Action Platoon Leader, you're about to find out why your platoon is assigned to this Marine Expeditionary Unit."

"Yes, sir," Garcia said.

"Major Crowley, why don't you get started?" Taylor said, leaning against the podium.

"Aye, aye, sir."

Crowley got up and walked briskly to the wall map. He grabbed a pointer propped in a corner of the room and tapped at the map. "This shows the land mass defined by the Adriatic, Black, Aegean, and Ionian Seas. Lieutenant, this mission has interest at the highest levels. You're going to do grunt work for some very important people. Our information is that there will be a CIA observer near the target area."

Crowley tapped at the map again. "Here's where your platoon's going. You and your fourteen Marines will take off at 0200 hours tomorrow in an MV-22 Osprey we have had deployed just for this mission. You'll be inserted into Albania at its border with Kosovo, near the Drin River. You'll have two AH-1W Super Cobras to provide fire support for the insertion."

"Yes, sir," Garcia said. "Glad to have those bad boys along."

"At 0330 hours," Taylor continued, "you will cross the border into Kosovo and take up positions on this ridgeline, just southwest of the city of Djakovica. A Serb general by the name of Antonin Karadjic will be on that ridge. Right here, on hill 652. At 0500, your team will move to capture Karadjic. You'll take Karadjic five miles west to your extraction point –

here." Another rap with the pointer. "You must be at this point by 0800 hours. Sharp."

Garcia sat as though frozen, studying the map. "A lot of distance to cover in a short time, Colonel," he said. "Over pretty rough, steep terrain. And this rain will slow us down."

"It's the best we can do, Lieutenant."

"Yes, sir."

CHAPTER TWENTY-THREE

Miriana hurried through the maze of narrow streets on the outskirts of Belgrade. She carried a large straw bag against her chest and scurried along as fast as the slippery pavement allowed. Rain had been falling for hours.

Damn Karadjic for continually changing the location of their meetings, she thought. Following his directions, she turned a corner onto Kondraki Lane. A black sedan sat at the corner. A man jumped out from behind the wheel, opened the back door, and waited for Miriana to slide inside. He then slammed the door shut, got back in the car, and drove for fifteen minutes, continually checking his rearview mirror. The last few minutes of the drive took them down narrow residential lanes with three-story row houses facing each other. The space between the facing houses was so narrow cars had to park on the sidewalks to leave a single lane clear.

Finally, the man eased to a stop in front of a row house. "He's inside," the driver barked. He let Miriana deal with her door.

She got out of the car and looked first left, then right. The street seemed deserted, except for a man seated in a car a couple doors down the street. She would never have noticed the man if she hadn't seen the red glow of a cigarette inside the car. Karadjic's bodyguard, she thought. She climbed the steps to the front door and knocked.

"Ah, my little Gypsy is here," Karadjic exclaimed after opening the door. He rubbed his hands together. The General was grossly overweight, with beady eyes and a bloated face. Miriana thought again that he looked like an apple with pencils stuck in it for arms and legs. The musty odor of the place told her the building had not been occupied in awhile. Even the strong smell of Karadjic's cigar couldn't hide that fact. There was no furniture in the front room.

Karadjic led her through the front room to a first-floor room furnished with nothing but a small, square table and four straight-backed chairs. Just another safe house the General would use once or twice, then abandon for another. He sat in one of the chairs and propped one of his legs on another. A cigar smoldered in an ashtray on the table. Karadjic lifted a tea glass filled with a cloudy, off-white liquid. "Would you like to join me, little Miriana? This is very fine *raki*."

"No thank you, General," Miriana said primly. "Alcohol and telling the future are not good companions." Her father drank the stuff. She couldn't stand the taste or odor.

"Ah, of course," the General said. "We mustn't do anything to taint the spirits."

Miriana put her bag on one of the empty chairs. She took a bottle of water, a shawl, a candle and candleholder, and matches from the bag. She set the candle in the holder and lit it. When enough wax had dripped from the candle to fix it in place, she walked to the wall near the door and turned off the room's overhead light. Moving across the room to the front room's single window, she gripped the two curtains. She hesitated a moment, stared out at the grim row of houses across the street – now partially obscured by the pouring rain – and closed the curtains. She moved back to the room with the table and took a seat opposite Karadjic.

The General picked up his cigar and tamped out the embers in the ashtray. He put the four inches remaining in his shirt pocket. Then he put down his glass and laid his sausage-fingered hands on the table. His eyes bored into hers.

Without turning her gaze away, Miriana lifted the shawl from the table and draped it over her head and across her shoulders. Then she lifted the water bottle, sipped from it, and sprayed a fine mist at the candle flame through her teeth. The flame sputtered, then revived. Miriana prayed aloud for the protection of the Virgin Mother through the use of Holy Water.

Miriana laid her hands on Karadjic's and closed her eyes. She fought to hide the revulsion she felt touching the man. They sat silently, without moving for several minutes, just as in all previous sessions.

Then Miriana held up both her hands and threw her head back as though jolted by an electric shock. Her mouth fell wide open and her pupils rolled back so her eyes showed white.

In an eerie, half-howling, half-wailing voice, she droned, "Antonin Karadjic, I see an ebony-black sky." She paused. Then she shook as though suffering convulsions. The shaking stopped as quickly as it had started. Taking exaggerated breaths, her breasts lifting and falling with the effort, Miriana moaned, "The stars and the moon are dead." Pause. "I hear the sounds of a million drummers."

She shuddered, then continued in a quivering voice, "The blackness is coming at me . . . it has a million eyes. Help me! I'm afraid! I see bodies in the dirt." A moan escaped her lips.

She clutched his hands with all her strength, digging her nails into his flesh. He yelled and jerked his hands away. Miriana shrieked, fell sideways onto the floor, and lay there as though unconscious. Karadjic knocked his chair over, jumping straight up.

Miriana sneaked a look at him with one slitted eye. The brave Serb general, victorious leader of a hundred battles, murderer of tens of thousands, is afraid. What a joke!

Finally, Karadjic reached for his glass of *raki* and knelt next to her. He held the glass under her nose. The strong whiff of alcohol made her cough, but she opened her eyes slowly. Shaking her head as though to clear it of confusion, she sat up on the floor. Karadjic took her arm, helping her off the floor and back into the chair.

"Te . . . tell me, Miriana," Karadjic said. "Wh . . . what did you see?"

"I have to go, General. I must go home." She stood and began hurriedly packing her things.

Karadjic shoved her back into the chair. "You'll tell me what you saw!"

Miriana sighed and clasped her hands to her breast. "I saw nothing but blackness and heard a loud thrumming sound. The blackness came closer and closer, as though it would swallow me. And the closer it came, the louder the noise became. Then the blackness showed itself for what it really was – a mass of flying blackbirds. The sound of their wings became a roar."

"What happened next?" Karadjic asked, his voice tremulous . . . respectful.

"I saw you being carried across the sky on the blackbirds' wings. And behind you were thousands of corpses floating on air. Each one carried a sign reading: *Prizla*. They cried out your name. Oh, General! It was awful. Please, let me go."

Karadjic's eyes looked ready to pop from his head. White spittle had formed at the corners of his mouth. "Oh my God!" he cried.

"What does it mean, General?" Miriana asked.

Karadjic just waved her question away. He commanded her to continue.

She swept her hair back from her face, looking at him. "The birds flew with you over the land – nothing but burned out buildings, scorched fields, dead forests."

"What about the bodies you saw?" Karadjic interrupted.

"They floated along after you." She let this sink in. "You, the birds, and the corpses moved across the sky like storm clouds. Then the birds stopped. You asked the birds, 'Why have we stopped?' "

Karadjic's eyes were saucers.

"What happened next?"

Miriana paused, lowered her head for effect, then looked back at Karadjic. His lips quivered. His face had gone white. "Then the birds fell on you and consumed your flesh."

The General shook his head and rubbed his temples with the tips of his fingers.

"This is bad, Miriana! You have to help me! What can I do to prevent my death? How can I save myself?"

CHAPTER TWENTY-FOUR

The recon platoon members went silent at 2015 hours when Lieutenant Emil Garcia entered the USS *Nassau*'s briefing room. Garcia looked around, meeting each man's gaze in turn. "I've got orders to take a team on a special mission. In addition to Sergeants Messina and Sackett, I'll need twelve men. Any volunteers?"

As one, all twenty-five men in the room stood and yelled, "Aruugahh!"

Garcia suppressed a smile and picked his team, trying not to let the disappointment of the men not selected affect him. He then directed the men selected to prepare their weapons and equipment and then return to the briefing room in three hours to receive the Formal Patrol Order.

At 2315 hours, after Garcia had fused the available intelligence into a cohesive operations plan for his team, he briefed the entire unit on the mission – they all needed to know the assignment in case an alternate was necessary. He answered their questions and directed Sergeant Messina to supervise the inspection of the men's equipment.

Corporal Joseph Yaurie hung back when the others left the briefing room.

"Something on your mind, Corporal?" Garcia asked.

Yaurie came to attention. "Yes, sir!" Yaurie's face turned crimson. His eyes were fixed on the center of Garcia's fatigue blouse.

"Well, Corporal."

"Well, sir, you know . . . I'm single. Got no . . . wife or kids," Yaurie stammered. "At least . . . no kids I . . . know of." He smiled, but got no reaction from Garcia. His face got even redder. "I was . . . just thinking . . . what with Hawkins' . . . situation, maybe—"

"What do you mean 'Hawkins' situation?' "

"He got a letter today. Found out . . . his girlfriend's, well, you know, pregnant. She said he had . . . to marry her. He's kinda got his mind on . . . other things right now."

"Okay, Corporal Yaurie, I got it. Anything else?"

"No, sir," Yaurie said. "Thank you, sir."

Garcia watched the Marine walk out of the room. Dammit, he thought, Hawkins is my best radioman. But I can't have a guy along who might have his head somewhere else.

CHAPTER TWENTY-FIVE

The two-car caravan bounced over Kosovo's rutted roads. Most of the paving had worn away, leaving muddy rainwater-filled depressions. Soon the pavement disappeared altogether and the road was nothing more than washboarded, potholed dirt. Worried about jostling Yanni, Bob slowed down and avoided the potholes as best he could.

Bob's attempts at conversation with the hawk-faced man, Stefan, had met with limited success. So far he'd learned only that he and his men were KLA members, fleeing to Albania to avoid Serb arrest warrants.

"We murdered a Serb general and his aide last week," Stefan boasted.

Bob had studied piles of intelligence before leaving Langley. There'd been no report of a Serb general being assassinated.

Two miles north of Djakovica, Bob turned to the west and followed another dirt road through dense forest. After five minutes, he stopped the car. The Fiat pulled up behind him. He checked his GPS. They were slightly more than a mile from the Albanian border.

"End of the line," Bob said, more to himself than to his passenger.

Stefan looked confused at Bob's use of American slang. "This is as far as I can take the car," Bob explained. "I'll have to leave it here."

"We will go along with you," Stefan said.

"That's not necessary," Bob answered.

The leader shrugged. "You are going in the same direction as we are."

Bob threat sensors were all on high alert. Stefan and his crew gave him the creeps. "Maybe one of you could stay with my friend," he said. "I don't want to leave him alone in the car."

"Fine," Stefan said. "But we should move him into the forest, out of sight of any patrol that might come this way.

"Good idea," Bob said.

Bob grabbed the strap of an infrared night-vision scope from the back of the car and draped it around his neck. Then he and the man named Zulkar carefully pulled Yanni, partially conscious now, from the car. They each shouldered one of Yanni's arms and began walking toward the treeline. Yanni groaned with each step. Stefan, Zoran, and Kukoch followed.

"Stefan," Zoran whispered. "Why are we following this man? We can kill him and his friend right here, take their car, and go back home."

Stefan glared at the man, then ran a hand through his thick white hair. He took Zoran's arm and pulled him to him. "This guy is no reporter. Yes, I can kill him, but he's up to something. I want to find out what. Maybe there's money involved." He shrugged and let go of Zoran's arm.

The group moved forty yards into the trees, with Bob and Zulkar half-carrying, half-dragging Yanni. Suddenly, from a clump of trees ahead, came the sound of voices. They all dove to the ground. But the voices did not come any nearer.

"Doesn't sound like Serbo-Croatian," Bob said in a hushed voice to Zoran, who lay next to him.

"Albanian. Maybe KLA. They vill shoot us just like the Serbs vould."

"I thought *you* were KLA," Bob said.

Zoran snorted. "What gives you such crazy idea?"

Bob's pulse rate accelerated. His instincts had already told him these men were "wrong." He didn't yet know what he'd gotten himself into, but he knew it was nothing good.

Then the voices stopped. No sounds of movement from the trees. Stefan and Kukoch crawled closer to Bob.

"We need to get away from here," Stefan said. "We'll leave your friend here. He'd just slow us down."

"You're mad if you think I'll leave him," Bob whispered.

Stefan rose from his prone position and knelt next to Yanni. He pressed one hand over Yanni's mouth and nose. With a knife in his other hand, he slit Yanni's throat before Bob could react. Arterial blood sprayed.

Bob reached for the pistol in his jacket, but Zoran brought a piece of dead wood down on his gunhand, knocking the pistol from his grip. "You sonofabitch," he rasped at Stefan.

Stefan's black eyes narrowed. "Had you fired your weapon, that patrol out there would have found us. We'd all be dead."

A gurgling sound erupted from Yanni's throat and his body convulsed. Bob jerked around to look and swore to himself he'd find a way to take revenge for Yanni's death.

"Now," Stefan said, "you will do exactly as I order . . . Mr. Robert Danforth."

CHAPTER TWENTY-SIX

Lieutenant Emil Garcia watched the helicopter disappear while he and his men moved from a clearing to a stand of trees. He had no idea where the aircraft was headed – and didn't care, as long as it came back to pick up his team at 0800 hours, four hours and forty-five minutes from now. He said a silent prayer of thanks the rain had finally stopped. He knew they could now make better time. Faces streaked with black and green grease paint and camouflaged clothing blending into the vegetation, the Marines were nearly invisible in the moonless night.

There were no buildings or people in sight. The little valley was narrow – about three hundred yards across and a couple miles long. It ended to the west at a steep incline that rose straight up for several hundred feet. To the east, the floor of the valley meandered along the course of a stream and disappeared into the forest. This was the direction Garcia and his men were headed.

Garcia sent two men to the east side of the stand of trees to reconnoiter the open area between their present position and the forest ahead. When the men radioed the all clear, Garcia and his men moved out.

The Marines maintained a steady pace in the dark. They moved cross-country through fields and around a couple of small Albanian villages. They scaled rocky, forested hills, and scrabbled down shale slopes – not a word spoken. After forty-five minutes, they came to a barbwire fence near the Albania/Kosovo border. One Marine held up the top wire strand and put his foot on the second strand while the rest of the team passed through the gap. The last man opened the wire for the lone Marine still on the other side of the fence. Garcia signaled his men to take cover among the trees. They would rest for ten minutes.

Garcia positioned two men to provide security – one to cover their backs, the other to watch the path ahead. While his men rested and drank water, he pulled a GPS receiver from his pack and a flashlight with a red lens from his web belt.

"Right on target," he said to Sergeant Jimmy Messina, after using it. The hooded flashlight illuminated his map, and he pointed toward two hills with a higher elevation than the others in the area. "The smaller of those two hills is 652," Garcia told Messina, pointing at the map.

Messina nodded, then circulated among the squad, getting the men ready to move again.

An hour and twenty minutes later, they reached the base of Hill 652. They used goat trails to climb through thick foliage until the natural cover gave out fifty yards below the flat top of the hill. Garcia donned night vision goggles. Seeing no movement ahead, he ordered Sackett and Messina to position the men on the western slope of the hill – just inside the line of foliage.

CHAPTER TWENTY-SEVEN

Miriana sat frozen with fear in a backseat of the Russian-made helicopter.

Karadjic looked over his shoulder from the co-pilot's seat and caught her eye. He winked. "What's wrong, my little Gypsy? You don't like flying?"

Miriana shook her head and scrunched even deeper into her seat. It wasn't the flying she was afraid of. It was dying a cruel death. If Olga's plan worked, she was finished. She wasn't supposed to be on this damned helicopter. That had been Karadjic's doing at the last minute. She and her family were supposed to be spirited out of the country while Karadjic was being kidnapped.

Karadjic laughed – more like a bark – then lapsed back into the sullen mood he'd been in since they left Belgrade.

"General, the hill you want is straight ahead," the pilot reported.

"I can't see a damned thing," Karadjic said.

"Take my word for it, General. The instruments on this aircraft are the most advanced the Russians have."

"Fuck the Russians," Karadjic growled. "Set us down on the crest of the hill and be ready to take off again in a few minutes. I don't like being out here with only a squad of soldiers. Too damned close to Albania."

"Yes, sir," the pilot answered. He put the helicopter down near the center of the hilltop. The rotors continued to rotate while the Russian-trained members of a Serb Army Special Forces Team – SPETSNAZ – leaped out of the cargo bay behind the seats to establish a protective perimeter around the helicopter.

Karadjic awkwardly climbed out of the helicopter on his stubby legs. He reached in and released Miriana's seat belt. Then he pulled her from the jump seat into the brisk, predawn air. He then lifted a small wire cage from the helicopter.

"Okay, Miriana, tell me again how I can defeat the bad omen you saw in your vision," Karadjic said. But before she could answer, he added, "You'd better be right about this omen. Dragging me out here in the middle of nowhere is not my idea of a good time."

Miriana's voice quavered. "I don't know why you suddenly doubt me, General. Haven't I given you good advice in the past?"

Karadjic grabbed the front of Miriana's sweater and slammed her against his chest. "You're only as good as your last act, my little Gypsy." He released her. "Now, what must I do?"

"You have to walk alone down to the edge of the hilltop, where the bare rock stops and the bushes start. You must shout as loudly as you can, 'I curse the Turks and all Muslim heretics. I have slaughtered and raped tens of thousands of Kosovars. Beware, Albania, I come for you next.' Do this five times. Then release the bird."

"And this will save me?" he asked again, incredulity and hope in his voice. "This will void the prophecy you saw?"

"Yes, General," Miriana said, as she glanced over the general's shoulder. She looked for movement in the bushes. Nothing. Then she added, "But only if the bird flies towards Albania. If it flies toward Kosovo, there is no hope."

Karadjic took a step toward the end of the clearing, one hundred yards from the helicopter and the SPETZNAZ team. But he stopped abruptly and turned around. He grabbed Miriana's wrist and yanked her down the hill.

When they were half-a-step from the end of the clearing, up against the dense field of chest-high bushes and shrubs, Karadjic pulled Miriana against his chest again. He stood nose-to-nose with her. "If this goddamn blackbird flies toward Kosovo, I'll cut your throat," he said. Then he faced west and began mumbling what she'd told him to say. "I curse the Turks and all Muslim heretics. I—"

"No, no, General Karadjic," Miriana interrupted. "You have to yell." That's what Olga had told her. She looked again into the brush line, trying to spy movement there. Olga had explained there would be men who would snatch the general. She breathed out a slow, steady breath.

Karadjic looked at her, then turned and shouted.

Crouched in the bushes a few steps away from Karadjic, Marine Sergeant Eric Sackett listened to Karadjic yell against the backdrop of the noise coming from the helicopter's engine and rotors. He didn't understand a word the man said; but he thought the General must be nuts to be screaming into the night. Sackett waited for the Serb to stop yelling, as he'd been ordered to do, then turned off the miniature tape recorder he had been issued before leaving the ship. Sackett knew the tape was to be used as evidence against the General. He hoped it would pick up the general's words with all of the aircraft noise.

Karadjic bent to lift a container at his feet. The Serb unlatched a door at one end, reached inside, and pull out a black bird. He put the box down and held the bird in both hands. Then he threw his hands into the air and the bird flapped away.

That's when Sackett leaped. He struck Karadjic on the side of the head with a lead-filled sap, knocking him to the ground with a thud. He dragged Karadjic into the cover of the bushes and covered the Serb's face with a chloroform-soaked cloth. Then, to Sackett's surprise, the young woman who'd stood next to Karadjic sprinted past him down the hill – away from the helicopter and the Serb troops.

Garcia and Messina ran over to Sackett's position, staying behind the cover provided by the bushes along the side of the hill. Messina gagged the General. Garcia stuck a syringe into Karadjic's arm, sedating him.

They carried Karadjic down the hill to where the rest of the team now waited. Sackett heard the caw of a bird overhead. The bird's cries carried to him more faintly while it appeared to fly eastward – deeper into Kosovo.

CHAPTER TWENTY-EIGHT

The Serb Special Forces team leader was getting nervous. Captain Slobodan Bromidivic had heard much about General Karadjic from other army officers. Eccentric and brutal, they said. Egotistical. Even depraved. The General's shouts in the darkness only reinforced what Bromidivic had heard about the man. At first, he hadn't the nerve to interrupt the General in whatever he was doing down the hill with the Gypsy woman. But after there had been no shouts or other sounds for several minutes, Bromidivic took one of his men and descended the hill. He focused his flashlight ahead, but saw no sign of General Karadjic or the woman.

"Here," his man suddenly yelled. "Over here."

The beams of their flashlights shone on a syringe lying on the ground and the General's campaign cap. Several sets of fresh bootprints in damp earth led down a path through the bushes. The general and the Gypsy had disappeared.

Lieutenant Garcia moved his team as fast as possible toward the extraction point back across the Albania border. Four men at a time carried the limp Serb general.

They retraced the route they'd taken into Kosovo. Garcia breathed a little easier when they recrossed the fence line, putting them back inside Albania.

"We should be safer here in Albania," he told Messina. "I'm hoping the Serbs – If they're following us – won't want to risk capture in Albania."

Miriana had never been more frightened. She'd run down the hillside and crawled under a bush at the bottom. When the soldiers ran past, carrying Karadjic, she'd followed them as fast as she could, blood pounding in her throat, her lungs burning. She knew her only hope was getting away from the Serbs. Once they realized the general was missing, they would suspect her of being involved. After all, it was she who told the general where he needed to go to void the prophecy. The sudden lightening of the sky, with the moon escaping from behind clouds, allowed her to catch periodic glimpses of the men from a distance, so even though she couldn't match their pace, she could at least follow their route.

The Serb team, unencumbered by the dead weight of General Karadjic, raced down through the thick bushes at breakneck speed. At the bottom of the hill, Bromidivic led them into a meadow a foot deep in lush grass and wildflowers. His flashlight revealed a trail trampled in the grass. The Serbs followed it to the apparent crossing point at the fence. A sign was attached to one of the barbwire strands: Albania. Bromidivic and his men didn't hesitate; they crossed into foreign territory.

Bromidivic knew his career — and perhaps his survival — depended on rescuing the General.

CHAPTER TWENTY-NINE

Zoran tied Bob's arms behind his back while Kukoch tied a gag around his mouth. Zoran then searched Bob, removing his wallet and the money belt, and handed both to Stefan.

Bob wondered how Stefan knew his real name. Had he been compromised? But by whom? A double agent?

They walked through the forest, Stefan and Kukoch ahead of Bob, Zoran and Zulkar behind. They reached the barbwire fence marking the Albanian border. The fence had been knocked down; dirt covered the wire strands. Stefan led the way, marching purposefully into Albania. When they were a hundred meters past the border, Stefan called a halt.

Bob sat on the ground and stared at him, trying to figure out who the man was. He appeared to be about seventy, with snow-white hair and dark skin like thick parchment. Too old, Bob thought, to be traipsing through the forests of Serbia and Albania – or any forests. The man's eyes seemed to burn like pieces of black coal. When he looked at him, Bob felt as though he'd seen the face of something evil.

"What the fuck are you looking at?" Stefan hissed in English.

Bob averted his eyes. There was no point in antagonizing the man.

Stefan walked to where Bob sat and planted a boot in Bob's chest, forcing him backwards. Then he stomped him in the stomach. Bob writhed on the damp, spongy earth and gasped for breath, a wave of nausea hitting him. Stefan knelt, straddling Bob, and ripped the gag from Bob's mouth. He leaned forward, just inches from Bob's face. Bob could smell the man's sour breath.

"You don't recognize me, do you, Danforth?" Stefan said. "Well, I never forgot you. You have been branded in my memory all these years. You and Georgios Makris." Stefan exhaled a growl. "I never would have known who you were if you hadn't done that press conference after you returned to Greece."

Memories of George Makris, his friendship and his death, were never far from Bob's thoughts. His mind whirled back in time and raced through the short time he had spent with George: their journey into Bulgaria to rescue Michael, the gun battle in the Bulgarian orphanage . . ..

"Figured it out yet?" Stefan asked, raising his voice. "No? That night in the orphanage in Bulgaria? You killed a young man that night. You—"

"Radko!" Bob gasped. "Stefan Radko!"

"Right, Danforth. Stefan Radko. You killed my only son, Gregorie. You're a dead man," Stefan said, his spittle striking Bob's face. "I could have killed you a hundred times tonight, but I waited. I wanted to find out what you were up to. But I don't care anymore. I'm going to enjoy making your death slow and painful." He pulled a knife from his boot – the knife he'd used to kill Yanni – and drove it into Bob's left shoulder.

Bob screamed and reflexively brought his knees up into Radko's back, sending him sprawling. Bob struggled to his feet, his hands still tied behind his back, the knife blade imbedded in his shoulder. Blood ran warm from his shoulder down his chest.

SPETZNAZ team leader Bromidivic heard a man scream followed by men shouting. He raised his hand in the air, bringing his team to an immediate halt, and then waved them to the ground while listening for more sounds.

"What the hell!" Corporal Yaurie whispered to Sergeant Messina. "Sounded like somebody got killed."

"Get him!" Stefan yelled to Zoran and Zulkar, who were standing ten yards away, seemingly fascinated by the conversation between Radko and Bob.

Bob ran for the nearby trees. He stumbled, nearly falling, but regained his balance and ran on. But he'd gone only fifty yards when Kukoch stepped from behind a tree in front of him. Bob charged, lowering his good shoulder to hit Kukoch in the middle of the chest and drive him back against the tree. Kukoch's head cracked against the tree trunk. Bob ran deeper into the woods.

Sergeant Messina pointed at Corporals Yaurie and Wright and motioned for them to follow him. They went along a narrow path toward where they thought the scream and shouts had come from.

After several hundred yards, Messina heard the sounds of several people crashing through the undergrowth. He placed Yaurie along the trail and whispered, "First one through is yours." Then he turned to Wright with a silencing finger at his lips. "You've got the second one through." Pointing, he directed the young Marine to take cover in the bushes twenty yards down the path, then hid opposite Wright, behind a Volkswagen-sized boulder. He would take down any and all people who might be with the first two that passed his position.

Zoran and Zulkar were gaining on Danforth. But then their quarry disappeared around a boulder. They rushed after the man. As they moved around the boulder, two uniformed men confronted them. Before they knew what had happened, they were disarmed. Then all went dark.

Messina and Wright searched the two men's pockets, taking their wallets and weapons. Then they moved back up the path to where Yaurie had taken down the first man through.

"Jeez," Messina said. "This guy's a mess." He pointed at the knife hilt protruding from the man's shoulder. Then he noticed the man's hands were tied at his back. Messina pulled a wallet from the man's pocket and found photo identification. He took out a flashlight and pointed it at the ID: Gregory Davis. "Sonofabitch!" he said in a barely audible voice after checking all the credentials, "This guy's Canadian. A reporter."

"Where'd *he* come from?" Wright whispered.

Messina pulled a plastic packet from a pocket, tore off the edge with his teeth and shook out a large, sterile bandage. While Wright clamped a hand over the man's mouth to stifle the moan he knew would come, Messina pulled the knife out of the man's shoulder. Then he spread open the man's jacket and shirt and pressed the bandage over the wound. Then he put the torn and bloody shirt and jacket back into place, and hefted the wounded man over his shoulder. He headed back toward the rest of the team, Wright and Yaurie following.

CHAPTER THIRTY

Stefan, leading a wobbly Kukoch in a search for Zoran, Zulkar, and Danforth, stopped for a moment to get his bearings.

"Zoran! Zulkar! Where are you?" Kukoch yelled.

Stefan grabbed Kukoch's throat and hoarsely whispered, "Shut up, you damned fool."

Then several men seemed to explode out of the ground. They were covered with brush and wore camouflage clothing. One man pulled Stefan away from Kukoch and threw him face-down to the ground. Damp earth clogged Stefan's nostrils and mouth. He found it difficult to breathe. He felt a rifle muzzle jabbed against the back of his head.

"*Ko si ti sa jebani?* (Who the fuck are you?)" a voice asked in Serbo-Croatian.

Stefan recognized the Belgrade accent. They'd fallen into the hands of a Serb Army or militia unit. Think! he told himself. He turned his head slightly to look at the man standing over him.

"We're Serb citizens following an American spy."

The man jerked his rifle back as though to smash it into Stefan's back. "You're fucking Gypsies," he said.

"Yes, yes," Stefan said, spitting pieces of dirt from his mouth. "But it's true about the spy."

"Where is this spy?" the Serb said.

"He was headed in this direction," Stefan said, pointing his arm straight ahead.

"How do you know he was a spy?"

"If you'll let me up, I'll explain it to you."

The man grunted and stepped back a pace.

Stefan took that as permission to sit up. He again spit dirt from his mouth and quickly picked more out of his nostrils. He looked around and saw he was ringed by a group of Serb soldiers. Kukoch was sprawled on the ground, apparently unconscious.

Stefan adjusted his ski jacket, as though to straighten it after being tossed to the ground. He was really making sure Danforth's money belt was secure. Then he said, "The spy claimed to be a Canadian reporter. But he had night-vision goggles and a GPS. Pretty fancy stuff for a reporter. There was another man with him, but he died."

"What do you mean 'died'?"

"We killed him when he tried to run away. But we couldn't stop the other one. The spy."

The uniformed man bit his own thumbnail while staring at Stefan. "Who appointed you Spy Catcher?"

Stefan now saw the man wore Serb Army officer insignia. Stefan gave him his most innocent look. "Captain, we are all citizens of Yugoslavia. We consider it our duty to protect the motherland."

The officer hawked phlegm from his throat and spat at Stefan's feet. He turned away. "Sergeant, take six men. Go around this clearing. See if you can find a sign anyone else has been through here." Then he took the Gypsies' wallets and pulled out their IDs, reading them in the light of the first rays of the rising sun.

Lying in high meadow grass, Lieutenant Garcia turned his wrist toward the slivers of light provided by the sunrise: 0738. He checked his GPS and confirmed they were at the extraction point – with time to spare. He crawled over to General Karadjic. The sedative had begun to wear off and the man was stirring. "Knock him out," Garcia ordered.

The Marine guarding Karadjic opened a plastic bag, removed a chloroform-soaked cloth, and covered the Serb general's face with it.

Garcia crawled over to the now conscious Canadian reporter. "How ya feeling?"

"A lot better than when those Gypsies were about to slice and dice me."

"I'd love to hear your story, Mr. Davis, but I don't have the time right now."

"Listen, Lieutenant, my name isn't Davis, it's Danforth. Bob Danforth. I'm CIA. Those damn Gypsies messed up my plan to act as an observer of your mission. I was supposed to watch your snatching of Karadjic from a hilltop in Kosovo, just across from the Albanian border. I hope you've got room for one more passenger on the helicopter I know you're waiting for."

Garcia smiled and patted Bob's good shoulder. "Hang in there. We'll be out of here in a couple of minutes."

Miriana laid flat on top of a knoll and looked down at the Americans. They'd stopped, hidden in tall grass, in a mist-shrouded meadow about one hundred meters away. Then movement far off to the right suddenly caught her eye. In the glare of the rising sun, she saw a line of men in Serb Army uniforms filing into the edge of the meadow. At first, Miriana thought they were all soldiers, but the way one of them moved caused her to look more closely. Yes, one of the men walked stiffly – like an old man. Only four men wore uniforms. She guessed they were some of the soldiers from Karadjic's helicopter. But they were too far off and the mist too thick for her to see them clearly. She wondered where the rest of the Serb squad had gone.

CHAPTER THIRTY-ONE

Sergeant Bruto Drobac and six of the soldiers from Bromidivic's unit stayed just inside the treeline around the clearing. A layer of morning mist, like a low-lying cloud, moved by a slight breeze just over the tops of the tall grass. About to radio an "all clear" message to Captain Bromidivic, Drobac saw a flash of light in the grass near the middle of the clearing. He signaled his men to drop to the ground and took a pair of binoculars from a pouch hanging on his web belt. Slowly, patiently, he swept the binoculars across the clearing where he'd seen the light.

There! While the breeze played with the mist, he saw movement in the grass. He focused on the spot but nothing moved for two minutes. Then Drobac's breath caught in his chest. A greasepainted face filled his vision. More motion. Two more men shifted in the mist.

Garcia adjusted the tiny radio receiver in his ear. He stared at his watch. The choppers were two minutes late. Then he jerked toward a harsh whisper from one of his men. The man hissed: "Armed men at three o'clock."

Garcia spoke into his radio mic. The Marines reacted as they'd been trained to do – positioning themselves to lay down a devastating field of fire against the intruders.

A deadly stillness covered the valley. Garcia felt his heart pound. He'd seen where the intruders had dropped behind the valley's natural cover. What he wasn't sure of was how many men were out there, or what sort of support they had. Were the men across the field Serbs or Albanians? He searched the sky again for the extraction choppers. But he knew they weren't there. He'd hear them before he saw them.

Then a voice from the opposite side of the field broke the quiet. "You Americans, we have you surrounded," a man somewhere in front of them said in broken English. "Stand up. Throw down your weapons and put your hands on your heads."

"If we stay here, Lieutenant, we're dead," Bob said. "They've got us pinned down."

"No shit, sir."

Bob pointed behind their position. "If we can get into those rocks, at least we'd have some cover. The morning haze will help hide us a bit as we move. In another fifteen minutes, though, the sun will burn it off."

"How do you propose we get over there without getting shot?"

"Do any of your men speak Serbo-Croatian?"

"Yes, I do."

"Let's confuse these guys a bit." Bob told Garcia to shout *What do you want?* pretending to be Serbian.

"What if those men aren't Serbs?" Garcia asked.

Bob shrugged and said, "Then we're up the creek."

Garcia frowned at Bob, shook his head, and then yelled, "*Shto trebash sa nama?*"

Garcia's use of Serbo-Croatian seemed to surprise the man to the left of the Marine's position. After several seconds, the man said, "*Trazimo Generala Antonin Karadjic. Ko zi se?*"

"Oh, shit," Garcia whispered to Bob. "Serbs. They're after Karadjic." He yelled back at the voice, again in Serbo-Croatian, "We're a Serb militia unit that's been raiding in Albania."

The voice came again, loud, angry. "Surrender then! You have nothing to fear from us. We're Serb soldiers."

Bob asked Garcia, "What did he say?"

"He wants us to surrender."

Garcia look back at the rock formation Bob had pointed out to him. "Get ready to back up into those rocks behind our position," he radioed his men. Then Garcia shouted at the Serbs, "We left our equipment behind us in those rocks. Give us a minute to gather it."

Then Garcia spoke into his radio mic: "In fifteen seconds we break for the rocks. Sackett, you and your team cover our 3 o'clock; Messina cover our 9 o'clock. Start firing at will as soon as we begin moving."

The Marines backed up toward the rocks while firing their weapons in semi-automatic mode. The Serbs didn't immediately return fire, apparently surprised by the vicious firing against them. But they didn't hesitate for more than a few seconds. The Serbs unleashed their weapons on the Americans. Their firing came from the left and right of the Marines' position. The sounds of the shots echoed off nearby hillsides, seemingly trebling the noise of the firing in the narrow valley.

The back of the head of the Marine nearest Garcia erupted in an explosion of blood, bone, and brains. Garcia's tense expression turned to an open-mouthed look of shock.

"Yaurie's been hit," Messina shouted.

"Goddammit," Garcia said under his breath. Then he shouted to Sergeants Sackett and Messina, "Get the men behind those rocks."

Dragging Yaurie's body and Karadjic, the Marines moved out of their positions toward the rock formation. They fired at the Serbs, but Garcia ordered his men to cease firing when he realized they were shooting at ghosts. The Serbs were so well hidden the Marines were just wasting their limited ammunition. Once the Marines reached the rocks, the Serbs had also stopped firing.

The Marines dropped low behind the cluster of boulders and granite slabs. Garcia quickly took inventory of his men. They'd suffered only one casualty – Yaurie – but General Karadjic, screaming like a banshee, had taken a round in his right thigh, shattering bone. Garcia had just ordered one of his Marines to take the radio from Yaurie's body and try to raise the helicopter pilots, when the Serbs started firing again. Bullets ricocheted off the rocks and whistled around Garcia and his men. Rock splinters were flying like explosive shrapnel.

The team's Navy corpsman went to work on the General's leg, while the Marines repositioned themselves to take advantage of the terrain's natural cover. Garcia made sure his men were positioned to cover the two Serb positions and ordered them to fire at targets of opportunity.

"I'm hit! Corpsman, Corpsman!" one of the Marines yelled.

The sounds of firing weapons nearly obscured the man's shouts. Then another Marine shouted that he'd been hit, and still another man screamed. Garcia said a silent prayer the helicopters would show while jerking a grenade from his web belt. He launched the grenade at the Serbs on the right. The explosion was followed by the sounds of men voicing the terrible agony of hot metal wounds. Wounded men's screams from both sides vied with the clamor of weapons releasing their horrible missiles.

Garcia looked at his watch again. The helicopters were now nine minutes behind schedule.

Into the rat-a-tat confusion of automatic weapons fire, a different sound suddenly imposed itself – the sound of helicopter rotors heavily beating the morning air. The thrumming of the rotors seemed to vibrate Garcia's breastbone. Garcia stared in the direction of the noise, but when the aircraft came into view, it was not an American gunship. It was a Russian-made helicopter with Serb Army markings.

Garcia realized it must be the one that had carried the General and the Serb team to Hill 652. He watched the hovering helicopter descend to about two hundred feet above the clearing. Two bursts of flame shot from the helicopter toward Garcia. Rockets! The air in the valley seemed to shudder, and then the boulders around him shattered, rending the air with sharp-edged, granite shrapnel.

CHAPTER THIRTY-TWO

"Cease fire! Cease fire!" Bromidivic shouted into his radio to the helicopter pilot. "They have General Karadjic."

The pilot sharply veered away from the clearing and settled in a hover about three hundred feet above the clearing.

Bromidivic looked over his shoulder. "Where are those fucking Gypsies?" he shouted.

His men looked back where the two Gypsies had been lying in the grass a moment earlier. None of them had an answer for their Captain.

"Sir, the corpsman's down," Messina shouted. "Sluter's dead. Frantz, Kelly, and Koury are wounded."

"How bad?" Garcia demanded, ducking down when small arms fire erupted from the Serb position to his left, behind a stand of trees.

"Frantz and Koury can fight. Kelly's bad. You're bleeding, Lieutenant."

"I'll live; it's just rock splinters."

The voice again from the Serb position on the left: "You men are finished! Throw down your weapons! Come out!"

Garcia gritted his teeth. Things did not look good at all.

A blast of static from Garcia's radio, then words: "Homing Pigeon to Bird Dog, pickup in one minute."

Garcia shouted into his radio, "Homing Pigeon, this is Bird Dog. Homing Pigeon, we got enemy soldiers north and south of us. And a Serb chopper on top of us. We're pinned down. Got casualties."

"Hear you loud and clear, Bird Dog. I got the aircraft on my scope. Pop smoke so I can see your position. Keep your head down."

Garcia jerked a yellow smoke grenade from his belt, pulled the pin, and tossed the grenade twenty yards to the front of their position. "Homing Pigeon, I've just popped smoke; advise what color you see."

Two AH-1W Super Cobra helicopters peeked above the western treeline. Like a spectator at a sporting event, Garcia watched the Super Cobras emerge above the tops of the trees – from main rotor to windscreen to fuselage to skids.

"I got yellow smoke, Bird Dog. Over."

"That's us," Garcia replied.

One helicopter loosed a Sidewinder missile, which streaked to its target, sounding like a giant hissing cobra. The Serb helicopter exploded. The shock wave crashed onto the meadow, followed by fiery rubble.

The two Super Cobras swooped down on the Serb positions. Their pilots softened the opposition by first firing 2.75" rockets. Then they fired their turreted cannons and spewed 20mm rounds. In ten seconds, the giant chain guns each fired more than half their 750-round magazines. The Serb soldiers were left bleeding into the Albanian turf.

The Super Cobras rose above the extraction point and a troop-carrying MV-22 helicopter swooped in.

The Marines moved quickly, carrying their dead and helping the wounded to the aircraft.

The last few Marines were boarding the MV-22 when Bob pointed out the door and said, "What's that?"

A young woman, skirts flying and arms pumping, ran toward them. Lying just inside the helicopter's open door, Karadjic shrieked, "Miriana, you bitch!"

Bob realized this must be the girl, the fortune-teller, who'd helped snare the general.

"Let's get out of here," the pilot shouted.

"Hold it!" Bob said. "Wait for the girl."

The pilot looked over his shoulder at Bob, then turned his head back toward the aircraft's instrument panel and waited.

Stefan and Kukoch stood behind large trees. Stefan patted the front of his jacket and smiled at the thought of the money in the belt he'd taken off Danforth. He and Kukoch watched the carnage created by the American helicopters and watched the third, bigger helicopter drop into the grassy meadow. They'd observed the Americans clamber aboard. Then a flash of color moved from the left, diverting Stefan's attention. A young woman in Gypsy dress raced toward the American aircraft. He recognized her clothing and the way she ran: Miriana.

"My God," Kukoch said, "it's your daughter. What's she doing here?"

Stefan could not believe his eyes. He never knew exactly what would happen to Karadjic, but he had not for a moment thought Miriana would be anywhere near the action. She was supposed to be back in Belgrade, from where they were all supposed to be flown out of the Balkans. That bastard Karadjic! He'd obviously dragged her along with him to the Albanian border on the helicopter.

Then another movement distracted Stefan. A man rose in the clearing. He held a rifle. Stefan screamed, "No!" and ran toward him, willing his old legs to stretch to their limit, to run faster. It was the Serb officer, wounded – bloodstains on the back of his uniform. Stefan felt as though he was moving in slow motion. Everything seemed so clear – the bloodstained uniform, the man's broad back, the rifle pointed in the direction of the Americans. Again Stefan screamed, "No!" He launched himself at the man just when the crack of the Serb officer's rifle reverberated through the clearing.

Stefan ripped the knife from the scabbard on the man's belt and sliced the Serb's throat. He got to his feet and looked for Miriana. He saw the Americans lift her into the helicopter. She appeared limp . . . lifeless. His wail was washed away by the helicopter's revving motor and whining rotors.

CHAPTER THIRTY-THREE

"How are you, Mr. Danforth?" Colonel Taylor asked, lack of sleep showing in the droop of his mouth and his knitted eyebrows. He pulled a wheeled metal stool over to the bed in the USS *Nassau*'s infirmary.

"Not so bad, considering I'm on a damned ship," Bob said.

Taylor chuckled. "Don't care for the sea?"

"I was Army, Colonel. I like good old terra firma."

"How's the shoulder?"

"A little stiff, but otherwise okay. The pain killers your corpsman gave me aren't half bad."

"Good! Glad to hear it," Colonel Taylor said. "We'll pull into Piraeus at 0600 tomorrow. From there you'll go to the airport and fly to Landstuhl Army Hospital in Germany. You'll be in D.C. before the week is out."

"Thanks, Colonel," Bob said. "What's the story with Karadjic?"

"He's getting medical attention. But I gotta tell you, if we pull into Piraeus with him on board, the Greeks will take him from us."

Bob smiled at Taylor and said, "You'll be receiving instructions shortly. A pilot will land a chopper on board your ship and take Karadjic for a little side trip. He's going to be interrogated before being taken to The Hague. Next stop for General Karadjic – the War Crimes Tribunal."

"Any word out of Belgrade?" Bob asked.

"A spokesman from NATO has asked for a private conversation with the Serb President. Once he finds out Karadjic is in our hands . . . well, we'll see."

"What will you do with the Gypsy girl's body? She was an important part of our getting Karadjic."

Taylor smiled. "I'm a married man; I'm not going to do anything with her body."

Bob's puzzled look made Taylor laugh out loud. "She's alive. The bullet just grazed her head."

"There was so much blood," Bob said.

"She'll live," Taylor said with a smile. "By the way, do you know anything about a million dollars? She keeps rambling on about us owing her a million dollars."

CHAPTER THIRTY-FOUR

On his third day back in D.C., Bob and Liz were sitting down to dinner when the telephone rang.

"Bob, it's Jack. Am I interrupting anything?"

"Like that would make a difference, Jack."

Silence.

"What's up?" Bob asked.

"I thought you'd better hear this from me before CNN picks it up. Karadjic hung himself in his cell."

"Damn!" Bob cursed. "We got absolutely nothing out of the sonofabitch."

"And more of the 82nd has been called up, including Michael's battalion," Jack said. "They've been ordered to Macedonia."

"Sweet Jesus!" Bob whispered.

"What is it?" Liz asked.

Bob waved to shush her. "When's the unit ship out?"

"The President just made the announcement. They'll leave in two weeks. NATO will mobilize all its resources to provide refugee relief. But you can read between the lines as well as I can. Ground troops are going in."

"But I thought Congress voted against funding troops in the Balkans."

"They did!" Jack said. "The President's pulling a Teddy Roosevelt. He's sending troops to the Balkans and daring Congress to withhold the money he needs to support them."

"Assholes! The President and Congress are playing a game of chess, and a bunch of kids in uniform are the pawns."

"Mike will be fine, Bob."

"Thanks for calling, Jack." Bob replaced the receiver, all the while looking at Liz.

"Michael's unit is being sent to the Balkans."

CHAPTER THIRTY-FIVE

The Serb President looked at the man seated across his desk. Artyan Vitas had worked for him for decades. But, even though the man had been loyal to him for all that time, Vitas made him uncomfortable. The milky-white of his dead eye contrasted eerily with the dark blue of his good eye. His sharp features were evidence the Turks had conquered Serbia centuries earlier. Vitas, at fifty years of age, had been a hired killer for twenty-six years – first for the Yugoslav Communists, and now for Serbia. The leader collected his thoughts before speaking.

"Antonin Karadjic and I grew up together," he finally said, anger in his voice. "He was more responsible for carrying out my programs than any other person. And he was my friend. His death is a personal tragedy to me. *Razumijes ti, Artyan?*"

Vitas nodded. "I understand."

The leader continued. "General Karadjic died a great Serb patriot. He killed himself rather than give information to our enemies and cause our country embarrassment. I want the people responsible for his kidnapping to pay for his death. I want you to track them down no matter where they are. I want them to suffer a thousand deaths." The leader's tone increased in volume as his words came faster and faster. "I want the enemies of the Serb people to know that no one dares violate our land. No one abducts a hero of the people."

Vitas displayed his stained smile. A gold incisor caught the sun streaming through the office window and glinted. A smile creased his lips and his nostrils seemed to flare.

The leader felt suddenly chilled.

PART III

1999

CHAPTER ONE

Olga Madanovic's eyelids fluttered while she slowly regained consciousness with an onslaught of pain that took her breath away. She came fully alert with a long, low moan. Her face felt burnt – she remembered the punches the rat-faced man had inflicted. Olga's stomach cramped and a wave of nausea hit her. She retched and tried to lean over the floor, but the ropes held her too tightly and she soiled her clothes. Something wet ran from her nose and onto her split lips. She touched her tongue to it. Blood.

Olga was bound hands and feet to a chair. She cocked her head to look with her left eye at the metal-barred window set high in the wall of her cell. She couldn't open her right eye; it seemed to be swollen. There was no light outside. Only darkness.

The man. Where was the rat-faced man? The beatings had been terrible, but somehow she'd endured. She tried to slow her breathing, to remain calm. Maybe he's finished with me, she thought, a shred of hope fluttering in her brain.

Olga started at the sound of footsteps. Someone approached her cell. The metal cell door squealed open and then the rat-faced man appeared in the doorway. He stepped into the tiny room, the door creaking as he slowly closed it behind him. Leering at her with his gap-toothed smile, he took a pair of pliers from a canvas bag sitting in a corner of the cell. He licked his lips as though he were about to eat his favorite meal. He moved to Olga and took hold of the little finger on her strapped-down right hand, then placed the jaws of the pliers on the finger's first joint.

Olga stared down at her hand. She tried to shake her head, but the tape securing her head to the high-backed chair allowed minimal mobility. She groaned through the gag in her mouth. She knew what was about to happen, but felt a sense of disbelief.

The man ripped the gag from Olga's mouth. "I want to hear you yell, my pretty," he said in Serbo-Croatian, licking his thin, purplish lips. He squeezed the handles of the pliers and the tool's jaws bit into Olga's flesh, then into bone.

Her screams reverberated off the damp stone cell walls. The pain shot through her, seeming to explode in every nerve ending of her body. She writhed helplessly against her bonds.

"Are you going to confess now, my pretty?"

"I don't know what you're talking about," Olga moaned. "Plea-a-a-se! Why are you doing this to me? I've done nothing wrong."

The man answered her by moving the pliers and crushing her thumb, a smile creasing his face. His eyes seemed to sparkle with pleasure. "Lying *puta*. Who are you working for? You are a spy. I know it! I can smell it on you. Tell me!"

"No-o-o-o!" Olga screeched when the pliers bit through the flesh of yet another finger, crunching bone, splattering blood – a crescendo of pain. She felt her heartbeat accelerate higher and higher. She wanted to live but knew the rule: Hang on as long as possible.

The cell door creaked open and the rat-faced man turned abruptly toward it. A shadowy figure entered. Ratface walked into the shadows next to the door. Olga heard him whispering. Ratface came back to her, stepped behind her chair, and freed her from the too-tight ropes that bound her wrists and head. Then he bent down in front of Olga and untied her ankles.

She groaned when blood rushed to her hands and feet, bringing more pain to her body. Olga looked down at her mangled fingers and suddenly felt faint. She toppled from the chair to the floor, fighting to remain conscious.

"She stinks," Olga heard the newcomer say. "Clean her up."

Ratface picked up a bucket of water from a corner of the cell and threw its contents over her.

The shock of the frigid water washed away her dizziness. She felt a hand grab her upper arm and lift her back into the chair. Maybe they believe me, she thought. Maybe they're going to let me go. I didn't tell them a thing – about General Alexandrovic being a spy, about General Antonin Karadjic's kidnapping, about the Gypsy girl. I made it! I held out.

She raised her face a few painful inches. Ratface stood in the hall just outside the cell, bathed in the light from a naked bulb hanging on a cord. He faced toward Olga and gave her a toothy smile. She could see no one else. Ratface slammed the cell door shut. She heard his hoarse laughter and footsteps recede down the hall.

Olga sighed. I made it, she thought again. Then she heard a click and bright overhead lights flooded the cell. She raised an arm to shield her eyes. The other man was still inside with her.

He stepped around the chair and stood in front of her. He bent slightly. His face made Olga shudder. One of his eyes, milky-white dead, seemed to zero in on her like the eye of a hunting shark. His thick eyebrows met over the bridge of his crooked nose and a jungle of long hairs matted his ears. His jet-black hair was slicked back. Light flashed off a gold upper tooth. Olga turned her head aside to avoid his rancid breath.

The man grabbed her chin and twisted her face back toward him. He slowly scrutinized her face, touching places that made her wince and moan with pain. Turning her head from side to side, he said, "Not too bad, my dear. Not nearly as bad as it's going to be." He took his hand away. Then he punched her in the mouth, knocking her off the chair. Olga tried to make her mind detach from her body, to pretend this was just a bad dream. The pain told her otherwise. She spit out tooth fragments through busted lips. Blood streamed from her nose and mouth. The man grabbed her hair and yanked her up off the floor. He shoved her onto a cot in a corner of the cell and slammed his fist into her stomach.

"Come on, my little spy, fight me. I like it so much better that way."

Olga rolled into a fetal position and gasped for breath. She heard the man's roaring laughter echo off the moldy cell walls. His hands ripped away her blouse, her skirt, her panties. He forced her to lie on her back again. She looked up and saw light reflect off the blade of a dagger.

He put the knife blade between the cups of her bra, her last piece of clothing, and sliced it away. Then he placed the knife on her stomach, its cold steel sending a shiver through her.

Olga tried to will herself to reach for the knife, but her body seemed frozen in place. The man reached down, lifted a length of rope from the floor, and dragged it slowly over her legs, her pubic area, her stomach and breasts. Then he tied her wrists to the cot's top rail.

Olga watched him undo his belt and unzip his pants. He kicked off his shoes and stepped out of his trousers. Then he took the knife off her stomach. He climbed on the cot, straddling her. He ran the point of the cold steel blade over her breasts, down the center of her chest, and down the insides of her arms to the tips of her mangled fingers.

Olga stiffened, panic coursing through her, while the man moved the knife over her body.

Then he spoke, icily, dead calmly. "Now, my beautiful American bird, you will find out about pain." He drove the dagger blade into the mattress, just above her head and mounted her.

"I wonder how long you will remain silent, my dear," the man said between grunts. "Will you finally talk after I am finished with you?" He laughed between thrusts. "Maybe I should have Drago return with his pliers."

A wail escaped her lips. "I'll talk, I'll talk," she cried.

The man grinned. "Oh, I know you will. But, not just yet. I can't have you ruining my fun."

Olga prayed for a quick death. Pain exploded inside her like a pane of glass shattering into a thousand shards. She prayed he would finish. Maybe then he would be too exhausted to continue. Maybe then he'd kill her. But the rape seemed to go on forever. His sweat dripped on her; he grunted like a pig.

Olga tried again to find the safe place inside herself, but it had disappeared. Now demons had taken control of her mind. She heard herself babbling, but none of the words made sense. She tried to tell everything about the plot to kidnap General Karadjic – about Alexandrovic, the Gypsy girl, the CIA, her boss, Bob Danforth. But her words sounded like gibberish. Her pain-crazed mind could no longer make sense of anything.

Finally, the man rose from her. He extracted the knife from the mattress and slit the ropes binding her wrists. Despite the pain and degradation she'd endured, Olga felt momentary relief wash over her. She heard the man open the cell door and leave. Her mind had become fuzzy with pain. She wanted to pray, but felt God had abandoned her.

My clothes, she thought. I have to find my clothes. She moved in stuporous slow motion, finally getting into a sitting position before rolling off the cot onto the chilled floor. Supporting herself on her knees and elbows – her hands useless – she crawled across the damp, uneven, cobblestone floor toward her ripped and bloodstained blouse. Just when she touched its fabric, Ratface reentered the cell. He dragged her back to the cot and took his turn with her.

There were others, too. But she soon lost count.

CHAPTER TWO

The Serb leader looked out his third floor office window. He stood with his hands clasped behind his back and stared in the direction of the snowcapped mountains in the distance. "Did the woman give you the answers we needed, Artyan?" he asked in a level, unemotional tone. "Was she cooperative?"

"Yes, Mr. President," said the man seated on the far side of the room. "She was most cooperative."

"Did you interrogate her personally? There is no doubt in your mind she gave you accurate information? We know who the responsible parties were?"

"Of course, Mr. President. I would never leave something so important to underlings. I made sure she did not lie to me. It was Americans. The CIA."

A shudder chilled the leader. "When do you leave for the United States?"

"Tonight."

"I will expect to hear good news from you."

"Yes, Mr. President," Vitas said quietly. "I will take care of everything."

The Serb leader just stood there, facing the window. Vitas sat in silence for fifteen seconds, then, without a sound, rose from his chair and departed.

CHAPTER THREE

Bob Danforth walked down Connecticut Avenue beside Jack Cole. He was grateful for the light breeze cutting Washington D.C.'s summer humidity and rustling leaves on the trees bordering the sidewalk. The leaves made a whispery sound that was barely discernible above the engine noise of traffic and the voices of the noontime pedestrians crowding the sidewalks.

"I can't believe the sonofabitch hung himself," Jack said.

"Jack, Karadjic was a zealot. We knew that. That's why we had him under a 24-hour-a-day suicide watch. We suspected he wouldn't sit calmly in his cell and wait to be interrogated and then shipped off to The Hague for the War Crimes Tribunal. One guard looked away for a few minutes."

"I figured the bastard would want one more chance to tell the world how misunderstood the Serb government is," Jack said.

"That's what we all hoped for."

Bob bent his head back and massaged his neck. The thought of the dead Marines who gave their lives to capture Karadjic — all for nothing — made him sick. He and Jack walked in silence past the next cross street.

Jack intruded on Bob's thoughts and asked, "How's your shoulder?"

"It's sore, but healing nicely. Thank God for antibiotics. The doctors were more concerned about infection than the knife wound itself."

The packed sidewalks gave Artyan Vitas all the cover he needed. He carried an umbrella tilted toward the sidewalk, its six-inch metal tip gleaming in D.C.'s sunlight. Vitas followed the two CIA men, gaining on them with each step. A young woman with a skirt so short it left little to the imagination strutted on stiletto heels between him and his target.

Danforth! Vitas thought. The President will kiss my ass when he hears I killed him.

He stayed behind the young woman, using her as a screen, while she got closer to the two strolling men. He matched her pace step-for-step, his footfalls synchronized with the clack-clack-clack of her high heels. When she started to move to pass Danforth and the other man on top of the left, Vitas moved slightly to the woman's right. Still a foot back from her right shoulder, now close to Danforth, he lifted the tip of the umbrella higher in preparation for the forward thrust.

Then Danforth and the other man suddenly moved left, stopping in the middle of the sidewalk, outside the entrance of an office building. The young woman abruptly slowed and shifted right to avoid bumping into Danforth, just as Vitas jabbed the umbrella forward, its tip injecting a pin-sized iridium pellet into the back of her thigh.

A scream. Bob turned. A woman collapsed into his arms. Before he could lower the woman to the sidewalk, he met the stare of a tall, thickly-built man with one dead eye who rushed past him. As Bob gently lay the young woman on the sidewalk, she began to convulse violently, white foamy saliva oozing from her mouth. Then she went rigid, her jaws locked.

"What the hell!" Jack said.

Without looking at Jack, Bob said, "Better get an ambulance." He tried to pry open the woman's jaws. He thought she might be having an epileptic seizure.

CHAPTER FOUR

Jack put down the telephone and swiveled around in his chair. He looked at Bob standing at the office window, hands in his pockets, shoulders drooping. The silence in the room was oppressive.

"Finally," Jack said. "That was the lab. Someone poisoned that girl with a cholinesterase inhibitor. Shut down her nervous system. They found a poison pellet under the skin on the back of her thigh. That's an old Bulgarian trick. Remember how they killed both a double agent and a Bulgarian defector in London in the early eighties that way?"

"Who's the woman?" Bob asked, still staring out the window, his voice etched with a somber tone.

Jack picked up a slip of paper he'd made notes on during the phone conversation with the lab technician. "Elyse Vanderpool. A staffer over at the FCC. Just some gal in her twenties. Apparently in the wrong place at the wrong time. Nobody you'd expect an assassin would go after. And there's no question it was a professional hitman. I mean, you don't find street thugs running around with poisoned-tip umbrellas. Whoever killed her screwed up. But who the hell was the sonofabitch after?"

Bob blew out a loud stream of air, then turned, anger showing in the set of his jaw, the tightness of his lips. His hands were still shoved deep into his pants pockets, his gaze down at the carpet. He lifted his head, opened his mouth, and bit his lower lip. Then he said, a catch in his throat, "I was the target," he said. "Whoever killed that young woman was after me."

CHAPTER FIVE

Liz Danforth scrubbed at the hardened remnants of last season's barbecues. She wanted Michael's going-away party on Saturday – two days away – to be perfect. It would be the last day she'd see her son before he shipped out to the Balkans with his unit. Damn! she thought. Why couldn't he pick a safe career – like plumbing?

She heard the front door slam. Married thirty years and I still haven't trained him to close doors so the whole house doesn't vibrate. "I'm out back, Bob," she yelled.

He came out from the kitchen through the open patio door.

"Hard at it I see," Bob said.

She brushed a few unruly strands of hair away from her face with her forearm. "I wouldn't have to do this if you'd cleaned the damn thing last year, instead of letting this gunk set all winter and spring."

Bob smiled. "I appreciate you doing the dirty work," he said. "You're so much better at it than I am."

She laughed and tossed the filthy Brillo pad at his smile. Bob ducked. The pad sailed over his head and through the open door into the kitchen.

"Dammit!" Liz groaned. She ran inside and found the greasy pad on a white-cushioned stool at the kitchen counter. "See what you made me do?" she accused, while he came up behind her.

"Me! I was just standing there."

Liz gingerly picked up the pad in her rubber glove-clad hands and looked at the dark, wet stain on the cushion. She glared at him.

"You know, you're damn cute when you're pissed off," he said. He brushed the hair away from her face and kissed her lips. She let him sweep her into the air, her grease-stained gloves stretched out away from his suit.

"You're just as cute as the day we met," Bob said. "Why don't you come upstairs and I'll show you how cute I really think you are.'

She scowled and said, "Promises, promises. Put me down, you big oaf."

Bob set her down and walked toward the staircase to the second floor. Liz heard him climb the stairs. She went to the kitchen sink and shed the gloves. Walking back to the barstool, she once again looked at the dark spot on the cushion. I'd better let it dry before I try to clean it, she thought. Bob's footsteps sounded on the floor above. What the hell, she thought. She walked to the staircase, leaving a trail of clothes on the steps behind her.

CHAPTER SIX

Artyan Vitas had been seething with anger for three days, since he'd screwed up. He'd been sitting behind the wheel of his rental car for hours now, watching catering and flower vans make deliveries to the Danforth residence. It was six p.m.

A dark-blue Lincoln Towncar drove up and parked in front of the house. A middle-aged man and a young woman got out of the car and walked up the path toward the front door. Vitas recognized the man – he'd been with Danforth on Connecticut Avenue three days ago. He felt a bolus of anger rise inside him at the memory of his failure. Then he concentrated on the woman. Where have I seen her? The connection wouldn't come. He concentrated on her shapely body. She wore a black sheath and black high heels. Her long, thick, black hair cascaded over her shoulders and down the middle of her back.

He imagined getting his hands on her tight young body. His vision wavered momentarily, distorted as though under water. He forced himself to focus on his mission. Suddenly he recognized her. Karadjic's Gypsy fortune-teller! Miriana Georgadoff. That's it! Olga Madanovic had given him information about the Gypsy girl. Serb intelligence had given him the girl's photograph. But it can't be, Artyan thought. Here in Washington, D.C.? Dressed like that! How the hell did she get here?

Yet it all made sense. She had been in on the plot to kidnap Karadjic. She's working with the CIA. They brought her out of Yugoslavia. This is getting interesting, he thought, rubbing his crotch.

When the doorbell rang, Liz removed her apron and hung it on a hook by the refrigerator. The guests are arriving, she thought, glancing at the stove's digital clock. She hurried to the front door and saw Jack Cole through the glass, standing next to a woman of about twenty, with blue eyes, black hair, and olive skin. She looks swimsuit-model perfect in that dress, Liz thought. She opened the door.

"Jack, thanks for coming," Liz said with a sparkling smile. "And who's this?"

Jack gave a little bow. "Let me introduce you to Miriana Georgadoff, a visitor from Yugoslavia."

Liz shook the girl's hand. "Come in, my dear. Even though you're in the company of Mr. Cole, we won't hold it against you." She led them through the house to the backyard and pointed at a corner of the lawn. "Michael's messing with the barbecue."

"Where's Bob?" Jack asked.

Liz felt her face get hot. She didn't want to let Jack know how pissed off she was. Bob had promised to get home in time for Michael's party. Just one broken promise in a series of thousands of broken promises. With Bob, work always seemed to come first. "He'll be here any minute," she said.

"Hey Mike," Jack said when he came through the door onto the patio, "You look great."

"Thanks, Uncle Jack, it's good . . .." Michael inhaled an audible breath when Miriana stepped from behind Jack, then exhaled loudly. Unfortunately for him, the sound came out as a whistle. Jack laughed while Michael's face turned crimson.

"Michael, meet Miriana Georgadoff."

Michael put out his hand and shook Miriana's. "Nice to meet you," he said.

"You have a nice whistle," she laughed, a devilish grin showing on her face.

"Oh, jeez," Michael said, his complexion turning even redder than before.

"Why don't you take Miriana over to the bar, Mike? You look like you could use a cold drink."

Michael gave Jack an embarrassed look, then touched Miriana's elbow. "Would you like something to drink?" he asked.

"I would love a Coca-Cola," she answered, smiling radiantly.

As the two young people walked off, Bob came through the door onto the back patio and moved to where Jack stood on the lawn. He followed Jack's gaze and said, "Don't tell me that's the Georgadoff girl."

"Yep, that's her," Jack responded.

"She sure cleans up nice," Bob said.

"Yeah. I hope you don't mind my bringing her along. I told her she'd been invited. I thought she could use a change of scenery from her guarded room at Andrews Air Force Base. I had to sign a damn form taking responsibility for her custody. I didn't think they were going to let her come with me without a squad of armed guards."

"Of course she's welcome. And from the look on Michael's face she may be more welcome than we know."

Jack smiled. "I noticed."

Liz walked up to the two men. "She's a little young for you, Jack, don't you think?"

"I'm flattered you think she's my date."

Liz kissed Jack on the cheek. "Not such a big stretch, kiddo. You're still one of the best looking men in the District."

"Ah, Liz, you've got a bit of the blarney running through your veins."

"Now, go talk to Michael," she said. "Give him some good advice, like 'Keep your head down in the Balkans.'"

Two hours later, the party was in full swing. Bob finally found Miriana alone for a moment. "It's good to see you again, Miriana. How's the debriefing going?"

"Fine! Is supposed to be over in few weeks."

"I understand Jack has talked to you about a job."

"Mr. Cole arranged job with American State Department. But I do not know vhat to do. If desk job is right for me."

"What about the money the Agency gave you?"

"That is for family. For ven they get out of Serbia."

"That's a nice thought," Bob said, not believing for a minute her family would survive the purges the Serbs were executing. For some reason, Miriana's family never showed up at the Belgrade airstrip from which they were supposed to be evacuated.

Bob saw Liz waving at him to come to the house. He excused himself and started to walk away. He noticed Michael detach himself from a group of other young men and make a beeline for Miriana.

Looking through the kitchen window, Liz watched Michael cross the yard toward the young woman from Yugoslavia. She saw the expression on his face. It was the same one she'd seen on Bob's face thirty-one years ago – the first time they met.

CHAPTER SEVEN

Artyan Vitas had been in his rental car for hours, watching people come and go at the Danforths'. But none of them was his concern. He had come to exact revenge for the kidnapping of General Karadjic. He would kill Danforth. And maybe Danforth's wife as well. He'd caught a couple glimpses of her at the front door of the house. She was a bit old for his tastes – he liked them in their twenties – but she was damned good looking and had a great figure for a woman her age. Mrs. Danforth would be a fringe benefit. And then he'd go after the Gypsy girl.

He couldn't keep his thoughts off the Gypsy – that slinky dress hugging her tight young body. Those breasts. Those legs. He'd make her suffer, a thought he was relishing when the girl suddenly emerged with her escort, the older man who'd been with Danforth during the botched umbrella attack. When the two of them got into the Lincoln, Vitas started his car. He could come back for Danforth later. He knew where Danforth lived; now he needed to find the Gypsy girl's residence.

The Lincoln pulled away, and Vitas was about to follow, when a red Porsche shot out of the driveway.

Vitas fell in behind the Porsche, while it trailed the Lincoln toward Bethesda's business district. He memorized the Porsche's license plate number. Vitas had a contact at the Embassy who could get the owner's name.

The two cars pulled into a restaurant's parking lot. Vitas drifted past, went around the block, and came back to park in the lot. The Lincoln and the Porsche were now empty.

"You tell the CIA I had anything to do with getting you together here with Miriana and I'll see to it that you get assigned to Antarctica. I got plenty of contacts at the Pentagon."

Michael smiled and said, "I really appreciate you letting us spend some time together before you take Miriana back to Andrews Air Force Base, Uncle Jack."

Now Jack grinned and patted Michael on the shoulder. "You got one hour, kid. Whatever you want to say to her, you better get it done by midnight," he said, tapping the face of his watch.

"What are you two talking about?" Miriana asked, returning from the Women's Room, stepping next to Michael.

"Your curfew," Jack said.

She glared at Jack and said, "We would call you the bogeyman in Yugoslavia."

"I've been called worse," he said, then laughed and walked toward the bar near the front of the restaurant.

Michael put a hand on Miriana's back and guided her toward the dining room. Only two tables were occupied at this late hour. He asked the hostess to seat them at a corner table, pointing at one well away from the other diners.

"I just vant coffee," Miriana told a waitress.

"You sure you don't want something else?" Michael asked.

"No, no. Thank you very much. I am pretty full from the good foods your mother served."

Michael smiled, raised two fingers, and told the waitress, "Two coffees, please." He looked back at Miriana and felt butterflies erupt in his stomach. He loved looking at her. He loved her accent. It sounded like a mixture of French and Russian. He met her eyes and saw her blush but she held his gaze and smiled back.

"So, tell me what you're doing with the CIA," he asked, lowering his voice.

Miriana shook her finger at him and said, "You bad boy. You know I cannot tell you that. If I tell you, I must kill you."

Michael blurted a laugh. "It sounds like you've been around the CIA spooks too long already. Perhaps I should rescue you from that den of iniquity."

She furrowed her brow. "Den of vhat?" she asked.

He waved a hand in front of him, trying to come up with the right definition. "Evil, sinful," he said.

"Ah, yes," Miriana said, "like villains."

"Exactly!"

Miriana suddenly looked melancholy. Her face seemed to sag and her eyes shut. She bowed her head.

"What is it?" Michael asked, reaching across the table and taking her two hands in his.

Miriana's head jerked up and her eyes opened. "Oh, I am sorry. It is just that I miss family."

Michael moved his hands from hers when the waitress returned and placed two coffees on their table, along with a plate of biscotti.

The waitress said, "The biscotti are compliments of the house."

Miriana seemed to retreat within herself. Michael tried to get her to talk about her family, but she suddenly appeared withdrawn, worried.

Finally, Michael said, "I'd really like to see you again, Miriana. But with my unit shipping out next week, I don't see how it's possible. I'd like to write to you from Macedonia, though . . . if that would be all right."

Miriana met his eyes again and gave him a radiant smile. She took one of his hands in hers and said, "That would be nice, Michael."

Michael felt his pulse race. He hoped his unit wouldn't be in the Balkans very long.

Jack hated to break up the kids' conversation, but it was already past midnight and he had a long drive home after dropping the girl off at Andrews. And he couldn't help worrying about Michael starting off tonight on the long drive back to Ft. Bragg, North Carolina. He walked over to their table. "Sorry, guys," he said. "I hate to be a party-pooper, but it's time to go." He saw Michael nod his head and push his chair back. Jack walked out toward the front door. He felt a warm glow when he looked back and saw the two of them embrace by their table.

Vitas felt like his bladder would burst. But he didn't dare go inside to use the bathroom, in case the girl and the man with her chose that time to leave. He forced himself to ignore his need to piss – it was a self-imposed test. Only moments later, the Gypsy girl walked back outside with her escort and a tall, good-looking young man. Vitas felt an instant hatred for the young man. He had always felt that way around tall, handsome men. They had something he would never have. And this one looked extremely fit, as well. The parking lot lights set off the man's short, dark hair and chiseled features. The younger man got into the Porsche and drove off. Vitas followed the Lincoln.

The Lincoln went to a guarded gate of what appeared to be a military compound. A wooden guard shack with windows stood between a lighted monument sign and a chain-link fence topped with barbed wire. Vitas parked his car two hundred feet from the gate, took a pair of binoculars from the glove compartment, twisted in his seat, and looked at the monument sign, which read, "Andrews Air Force Base." He lit a cigarette and tried to get all the gears in his brain to mesh.

He waited for the Lincoln to pass through the gate, then he pulled away. Leaning over to pick up his cell phone, he punched in a Virginia number.

"Hello, who . . . who is this?"

Vitas stifled a laugh. Paulus Tomavic's sleep-thickened voice made him sound pathetic.

"Greetings from the President," Vitas said.

Paulus didn't respond.

"Why, Paulus, are you not happy to hear from me?"

Silence.

"Did you go back to sleep, Paulus?" Vitas asked.

"No, no, I'm here."

"Good boy. Get a pencil and paper. I want you to get some information for me." Vitas dictated the red Porsche's license plate number. "I want to know that car's owner's name.

"Artyan, please don't call me at home," Tomavic pleaded.

Vitas hung up.

CHAPTER EIGHT

"Great party, Liz," Bob said from the king-size bed. "I didn't think the Bensons would ever leave."

"Uh huh," Liz answered. She sat at her antique vanity.

He watched her reflection in the mirror. "What's on your mind?" he asked. "You still angry with me?"

She sighed heavily. Without turning to look at him, she said, "You'd think I'd have learned not to expect you to show up on time, after all these years."

"I lost track of the time," he said. "I really intended to—"

"Stop!" she blurted. "Don't go there. You always intend to be on time, but your actions never match your intentions." She turned around and glared at him. "This was your son's going-away-party before he ships out to a war zone. What sort of message do you think you send to Michael when you can't even show up for his party on time?" She turned back to the mirror.

"Come on, Liz, you know how much I love that boy."

"Yeah, I know how much you love him. But how about the old saying that actions speak louder than words?"

"The way Mike was looking at Miriana, I don't think he even knew I was here."

"Jeez," Liz said.

"What?"

"You just don't get it, do you?"

Bob knew Liz was right. He'd screwed up again. He loved Liz and Michael more than life itself. Liz had described his work as his mistress. She'd said often enough she'd been competing with his job since the day they got married. First the Army, and now the CIA, one mistress after the other. She was pissed off, but he knew she didn't want to go to bed with a storm cloud of anger hanging over them. They always tried to resolve their differences before going to bed. He decided to try to cut the tension.

"Hell, Michael didn't just look at her; he followed her around most of the night."

"We don't know anything about her. Where'd she come from? Who are her parents?" Liz met his eyes in the mirror. "I've never seen him moon over any girl that way."

"Come to bed, I'll tell you a story about her," Bob suggested.

Liz turned to look directly at him. Then she rose from her chair, went over to the bed, and slid under the covers.

"Miriana played a role in my Balkans mission," Bob told her. "Without her we would never have been successful. She got wounded. I thought she'd been killed. So much blood. Fortunately, the bullet only grazed her scalp. A little lower, it would have shattered her skull. Miriana risked her life for us – and nearly lost it."

Bob didn't mention the million dollars the CIA had put in a Swiss bank account in Miriana's name. Her motives hadn't been entirely altruistic.

"So, what do you think of Miriana now?" Bob asked as he closed his eyes and rolled over in bed. He knew he wouldn't be able to sleep, but, rather, would lie awake worrying about Michael going to the Balkans.

"I hope he'll write to her," Liz said.

CHAPTER NINE

Bob entered the conference room and searched his colleagues' faces. Their hangdog looks did not engender confidence in him. He sighed. "You haven't come up with a thing?" he asked.

"About right, boss," Tanya Serkovic said. "We followed up on the Bulgarian link, because of the poison pellet business, but we got zip. Our guy at the Bulgarian mission – Tetranoff – looked horrified when I told him what happened. I don't think he was acting. He swears it wasn't one of his people."

"What else?" Bob asked.

"I checked with my contact at the Russian Embassy. *Nada,*" Raymond Gallegos offered.

"How about you, Frank?"

"Nah . . . well, maybe. But it ain't much."

Bob had known Frank Reynolds for fifteen years. The man had a habit of understatement. Bob let him proceed at his own pace. Frank didn't like to be prodded.

"I called Cherkoseff at the electronics store. You remember him, Bob, the Bulgarian agent who defected just before the Iron Curtain fell?"

"Yeah, I remember," Bob responded, trying his best to contain his impatience.

"Right. Well, he told me that at the time he defected, the Bulgarian Intelligence Service was in turmoil. He said the most common question agents asked each other was 'If you had to leave Bulgaria, where would you go?' The hardcore guys said they'd go to Yugoslavia, and some of them did in fact flee there, taking their deadly toys with them, according to Cherkoseff."

"So our umbrella killer could have been working for the Serbs," Raymond offered.

"Yeah! Coulda, shoulda, woulda, but who the hell knows?" Frank said.

"Let's go to work on this," Bob said. "If—"

A loud knock on the conference room door interrupted him. Then Rosalie Stein entered the room. "Sorry, Mr. Danforth, but I thought you'd want to see these." She laid a file on the table.

"You look flushed, Ms. Stein. You run all the way up here?" Bob said, smiling, as he opened the file.

"Yes, sir."

"Shit!" Bob exclaimed, staring at a photograph he pulled from the file.

"What is it, boss?" Raymond asked.

Bob passed the photograph across the table to Raymond. Then he leafed through the rest of the file before skidding the whole thing over. Photographs spilled from it.

Raymond picked them up one at a time, scanned them, and passed them to Tanya.

"Now we know how the Serbs found out about my involvement in Karadjic's kidnapping," Bob said. "Even with the mutilation of her face, I'm sure it's Olga Madanovic hanging at the end of the rope. I personally recruited that poor woman."

Frank stood up, walked behind Tanya's chair, and looked over her shoulder. "Who's the guy hanging next to her?"

A small gasp escaped Tanya's throat when she looked at the third picture. She took a deep breath and looked at Bob.

"The man in the photograph is Darius Alexandrovic. Serb General Darius Alexandrovic. Olga's top informant. And the sign reads: *Blackbirds will pick at the flesh of Serbia's enemies – wherever they are.*"

CHAPTER TEN

The sun sliced through a gap in the motel room drapes, waking Vitas. He rolled to a sitting position on the edge of the bed, moving like a bear coming out of hibernation, hunching his shoulders, groaning from the stiffness he felt. He looked at the clock radio. Almost 7 a.m. He reached for the telephone on the bedside table and dialed a number. Paulus Tomavic answered the phone on the third ring.

"What did you find out?" Vitas barked.

"Why are you calling me at home?" Tomavic whispered. "I don't want my family involved in any of this. You should call me at the Embassy. I told—"

"The red Porsche, Paulus," Vitas shouted. "Who does it belong to?"

There was a rustle of paper before Tomavic answered. "It's registered to a U.S. Army officer, Captain Michael Andrew Danforth. Stationed at Ft. Bragg, North Carolina, with the 82nd Airborne Division. I heard on television the 82nd received orders to go to Macedonia as part of the NATO Peacekeeping Force."

"Any other information?"

"According to our intelligence records, Danforth's father works at the CIA."

"I know, Paulus," Vitas said to himself after hanging up the receiver. He rubbed his hands together.

An hour later, Vitas sat in his car down the block from the entrance to Andrews Air Force Base. He was out of the line of sight of the guards and trained his binoculars on the road just outside the gate. It was early morning. He rubbed his erection through the fabric of his pants, thinking about the Gypsy girl. She'd become an obsession. He couldn't help it.

It was a long shot he would see the girl, but he had to take the chance. Would her nipples become erect when he pinched them? How loud would she scream when he bit them? A chill ran up his spine. He shuddered.

All morning he waited, and half the afternoon. Then a bright red pickup truck came out through the gate. The Gypsy was at the wheel, and she was alone.

When she'd driven past him, he trailed her for nearly an hour. She seemed lost, doubling back several times, circling around several blocks. Finally, she pulled into a bus depot parking lot, got out of the pickup, and entered the terminal building. Vitas followed her inside, ducking behind a column. From a distance of ten meters, he watched her go to the ticket counter, hand over money to the ticket clerk, and walk to a bench. Thirty minutes later, she boarded a bus for Miami. He raced out to his car and pulled in behind the bus when it drove away.

CHAPTER ELEVEN

Michael jumped at the sound of the ringing telephone in his off-base apartment. He grabbed the receiver and sat up on the couch. "Hello," he said, clearing his throat, rubbing the sleep from his eyes. He searched for the remote to the television, found it on the floor in front of the couch, and pressed the power button, shutting off the set.

"Michael, is that you?"

Michael became immediately alert. "Miriana?"

Miriana giggled. "How are you?" she asked.

"I'd be a lot better if I was there . . . with you. But things are going well. The unit is ready to go."

"I . . . I vish you vere not leaving so soon. Is there chance you could get away for a day?"

Michael smiled to himself. He loved Miriana's accent. She sounded like Natasha in the old Rocky and Bullwinkle cartoon series. "No hope of that. I barely get time off at night. Besides, we're restricted to the Fayetteville area."

"I knew you vould say that," Miriana said, giggling again. "I am here in Fayetteville. Can you come to my motel?"

Michael felt a surge of heat go through him; his throat tightened with excitement. "You're kidding!"

"No, I am not kidding. I am in room 116 at Rebel Inn. I am tired from long bus ride. I am starved. I do not like being alone." She sounded as though she was scolding him, but then she laughed.

Michael checked his watch. "It's 9:30; I'll be there in fifteen minutes." He replaced the receiver and made a mad scramble for the bedroom. After changing into a clean shirt and brushing his teeth, he raced out the apartment door, took the steps three at a time to the first floor, ran to his car, and broke several traffic laws while he sped down Persons Avenue, Fayetteville's main drag. He goosed the Porsche to seventy miles an hour. The brassy lights of the strip joints and fast food restaurants seemed to be one continuous blur. He whipped into the Rebel Inn's gravel parking lot and skidded to a stop in front of room 116. She opened the door before he could knock.

When the Porsche roared into the parking lot, Vitas knew his hunch had been correct. Two birds instead of one. Killing Danforth's son would feel just right.

He glared at them while they embraced at the door of her room. When they shut the door, he banged the steering wheel and muttered, "She is mine!"

Vitas opened the car door and hesitated a moment before stepping out onto the loose gravel. He grunted a bear-like sound and stretched his tired frame. Lack of sleep had left him bone-tired. Clenching his hands, he took two paces toward the room, but the door suddenly opened again. He quickly turned his back and just stood there, hoping they wouldn't notice him. He heard them laugh, the sounds of their feet crunching on the gravel, then the Porsche's doors opening and closing. A moment later, he heard the throaty tone of the sports car's engine.

Vitas rushed back to his car and started the engine. The Porsche had turned left out of the parking lot, but by the time Vitas pulled out onto the street, it had disappeared. He exhaled a mighty sigh. He could only hope they would be back. The girl had not taken her suitcase.

He walked to the motel office and paid for a room of his own, purposefully requesting a room on the same side as the girl's. He would catch a nap while the lovebirds were gone.

CHAPTER TWELVE

The clock-radio alarm went off at eleven-thirty p.m. Fully clothed, except for his shoes, Vitas rolled out of bed and peeked through the purple curtains. The Porsche was not in the lot. He fell back onto his bed and used the remote control to turn on the television. He flipped through the channels until he found CNN, and waited patiently through sports and U.S. national news for coverage of the conflict between the Serbs and NATO. It gave him a rush to think about how the little Balkan country had the whole western world by the balls.

Vitas listened when the announcer finally updated her viewers on recent events in the Balkans. Then she said, "The United States is sending fourteen more Apache helicopters to Macedonia. The helicopters, along with twenty-four hundred members of the 82nd Airborne Division, will leave for Macedonia on Friday. This will beef up the American commitment of military personnel to well over . . . .."

What a joke! Vitas thought. These dumb-ass Americans never learn. He spat a disgusted curse. Then he chuckled. Idiots! The fucking President of Serbia and his generals must be thrilled to know they can turn on CNN, twenty-four hours a day, seven days a week, and learn about NATO's war plans. It's like having a spy in the Pentagon. But better. Vitas laughed out loud. Big belly laughs.

He rose from the bed and again peered out the window. Still no Porsche. He was getting impatient. What if the Danforth kid was screwing Miriana right this moment? His entire body went hot and sweat popped out on his face. He rubbed his crotch and felt the swelling in his pants. It would not be long now. He walked back to the bed, lay down, rubbed his cock, and imagined what he would do with the Gypsy. And, if the Army Captain had been playing with the Gypsy girl's sweet spot, he would make him pay.

CHAPTER THIRTEEN

A large mirrored globe turned slowly above the dance floor, reflecting multi-colored spotlights. Thousands of tiny lights spun around the floor and splashed off the couples moving to the sounds of the music. Miriana pressed against Michael and tried to follow his movements. She found the music strange, the dance steps incomprehensible. But she didn't care. Being held by Michael made her feel wonderful. The band played songs Michael said were "country and western." She didn't ask for an explanation.

"I'm going to have to teach you how to dance to American music," Michael said.

"A part of my American education I will look forward to," she answered. "You know my people would kill me for being seen in public with *gadjo*. And dancing! Oh my God! They would stone me."

"You say *gadjo* like it's a dirty word. What's it mean?"

"Anyone who is not Gypsy is considered *gadjo*. Our people consider all *gadji* unclean – *mahrime*. A Gypsy who goes with a non-Gypsy also becomes unclean. So, I guess it *is* 'dirty' word, as you say."

Miriana looked at Michael's face and thought, You could be the *gadjo* of all *gadjos* and I would not care a bit about what other Gypsies think.

"But my mother is Bulgarian – a *gadja*," she said, "so I am already soiled."

"Does your mother have blue eyes, too?"

"Yes."

"Tell me about her."

"Are you really interested?"

"Sure. I'm interested in anything to do with you."

Miriana felt herself blushing. She brought her head back to Michael's shoulder so he wouldn't notice. "My mother, with no support from my father, teached my brother, Attila, and me history, geography, foreign languages – English and German – and other things. She read articles from foreign newspapers and magazines to us. Made us read them back to her."

"She must be well-educated."

"Self-educated. She not want us to follow my father's Gypsy ways."

The band finished the song and took a break. Michael guided Miriana to their table.

"And your father?" Michael asked gently.

Miriana hesitated for only a moment. She decided it would be better to know now if her past offended him.

"My father is much older than mother. He was leader of big Gypsy clan at end of World War II. He led clan for years. Then something happened – I do not know what – and he went on his own. He was married before, but divorced after death of only son. In the sixties, he met my mother, Vanja. She had escaped to Greece from Communist Bulgaria with her parents when she was only twelve. My father was thirty-eight when they met; she was eighteen."

Michael whistled. "Big age difference," he said.

Miriana paused a moment. "I think my mother loved my father very much. He was good looking and – how you say it? – dashing. Still is handsome man. She found him exciting. She was oldest of seven children. I think Mama would have done anything to get away from her parents' home." Miriana laughed. "She was tired of raising younger brothers and sisters. Whether my father ever loved Mama" – she hunched her shoulders – "I cannot tell you. He never showed affection for her."

"What's your father's name?"

"Stefan. Stefan Radko. But for some reason my mother, brother and I have always gone by my mother's maiden name – Georgadoff."

"It sounds like your father has skeletons in his closet," Michael said.

Miriana's eyes rounded and her mouth dropped open in an "O."

Michael laughed. "That means he must have secrets from his past."

"Oh! I see. Kidding again. You are big kidder, no?"

Michael laughed again. "I am big kidder, yes," he said.

"I think Father has many skeletons in closet. Understand, I love my father. But he is what you Americans call big son-of-bitch."

CHAPTER FOURTEEN

R-r-r-ing.

Bob, instantly awake, jerked the receiver from its cradle on the nightstand. He looked at the clock by the phone: one-fifteen. "Danforth residence," he whispered hoarsely.

"Bob, it's Jack. Sorry to bother you at this hour."

Bob sat up against his pillow.

"Miriana's disappeared."

"What!" He said breathlessly. "How the hell is that possible? She was under guard on a secure airbase, behind a barbwire fence."

"All we know is she told a guard at the base she had an upset stomach. He went down the hall to use the telephone to call the base doctor. That's when she slipped out. She took his keys from the field jacket the guard had left hanging on the chair outside her room. She took his truck. The cops just found it at the bus terminal."

"Didn't the gate guard challenge her?"

"They don't challenge people leaving the base."

"Did she get on a bus? Did you talk to a ticket agent?"

"Yeah. She's a little hard to miss. The guy at the bus terminal remembers seeing her, but he couldn't remember which bus she took. She could have gone anywhere."

"So what are we doing?"

"We contacted Greyhound. They're cooperating."

"Good for them!" Bob said sarcastically.

"Listen, Bob. This young lady can place Karadjic at several locations on specific dates where atrocities occurred. The stuff she's given us will be one more nail in the Serb hierarchy's coffin – if we can get them in front of the War Crimes Tribunal – and if she's there to testify."

"I understand, Jack. What can I do?"

Jack didn't answer.

"What's up?" Bob asked.

"Would you do me a favor and call Mike?"

"What for?"

Jack didn't answer.

"Oh no," Bob said. "You can't really believe Mike had anything to do with her disappearance. There's no way he'd do something that stupid."

"Bob, if the other side picks her up, they'll kill her. And if Mike happens to be with her . . .."

"I'm telling you, he'd never help her run away."

"I'm sure you're right, Bob. But the bus to Miami left shortly after Miriana disappeared. And it stops in Fayetteville. Do me a favor and call Michael."

"I'll get back to you." Bob hung up the phone and swung his legs out of bed.

"Who was that?" Liz asked in a thick voice.

"I'll explain in a minute. I've got to make a call."

Bob went downstairs and dialed Michael's number. He got his answering machine.

CHAPTER FIFTEEN

The rumble of the Porsche's engine woke Vitas. He leaped from the bed and went to the window, pulling the curtain aside a couple of inches. Michael Danforth got out of the driver's side and ran around to help Miriana out of the low-slung vehicle. Vitas watched them walk to the motel room three doors down from his own. They embraced and kissed. Danforth then returned to the car and drove off. Vitas checked his watch: three-twenty.

He grew angry while he watched them. He had wanted to charge down to where they had stood and pound the young man into the concrete walk. But he would bide his time.

He waited nearly an hour, until long after the sliver of light coming from Miriana's window disappeared. Then he put on his jacket, stepped outside, tossed his bag in the rear seat of the rental car, and backed it into the slot in front of Miriana's room. He got out of the car, opened the trunk, listened for a moment, then kicked in her door.

The girl moved on the bed and Vitas pounced on her before she could throw off the covers. He swung his fist against the side of her head, heard her moan, and then watched her go still. He bound her ankles and wrists with strips of cloth he tore from the bed sheets, and gagged her with one of her own socks from the floor. He went to the light switch and turned on the room's overhead light. After hastily stuffing her things in her overnight bag, he walked outside, looked around to make sure no one else was around, and dumped the bag in the trunk. He went back into the room and made sure he'd packed up all of her things. He wadded up the sheets and tossed them into a corner. There would be no ready evidence she'd been abducted. He wanted it to look as though she'd packed up and left of her own free will.

The girl was moaning and her head moved from side to side. Vitas stared at her bare legs and the bulge of her breasts against her T-shirt. He licked his lips and felt a tension build in his groin. This one will be one of the best, he thought.

Miriana felt dizzy. Her head ached. She blinked her eyes and tried to figure out what was wrong. Her vision seemed blurred. Then she saw the man and it all came back to her. Miriana's breath caught. She tried to scream, but only a series of muffled grunts and whines came through the gag. He looked like the devil. She felt a wave of desperation overwhelm her while staring at the man's cruel features – the pink scar running down his right cheek, the thin slash his mouth made, the beak-like nose, and the one gold tooth. But his dead, milky-white eye frightened her most. She detected no humanity in the man's face. Miriana felt a chill grip her, like an icy hand squeezed her heart. Tears rolled from her eyes. She'd never been more afraid.

The man smiled.

Vitas bent down and roughly squeezed the girl's breasts. He stared at her silk bikini underpants. He lifted the front of her pants and stared at her pubic area. Smiling again, he said to her in Serbo-Croatian, "We are going to have much fun, my little bird."

Vitas walked away from the bed, opened the door, and peeked outside. He looked up and down the row of rooms. No lights had come on. No doors had opened. Returning to the bed, he whistled as though he was out on a Sunday stroll. No cares, no worries. He took a plastic bag from his pocket, extracted a chloroform-soaked cloth from the bag, and pressed it against her face, waiting until she stopped struggling and her breathing slowed. He lifted the girl and carried her out to the car trunk. He went back to the room, clicked off the overhead light, and closed the door. Then he got behind the wheel of the rental and drove away.

EVIL DEEDS

CHAPTER SIXTEEN

Michael tossed his keys on the table by the front door and walked into his apartment. The blinking light on his message machine seemed like a beacon in the dark living room.

What now? he thought, moving to the machine and punching the play button.

"Michael, it's Dad. I don't mean to alarm you, but Miriana Georgadoff is missing. Jack's worried about her; very worried. For reasons I can't explain on the phone, she could be in danger. I told Jack you wouldn't know anything about her whereabouts. But he insisted I call. I need you to get back to me immediately, regardless of the time."

What the hell! Miriana in danger? Michael pulled out the Fayetteville White Pages and found the number for the Rebel Inn. A man answered after ten rings. His slurred words told Michael the man had been fast asleep.

"Room 116, please." It seemed an eternity before Michael was connected to Miriana's room, but the phone went unanswered. Convinced the motel clerk had dialed the wrong room, Michael hung up and called again. The same voice answered.

"I just called for Room 116," Michael said. "It rang, but no one answered. Would you try again, and stay on the line this time?"

Michael heard the guy say "Jesus H. Christ" before the phone began ringing. Again nothing.

"You still on the line?" Michael asked, his voice rising.

"Yeah, pal, but not for long. I got better things to do than play games with you."

"Listen, mister. I'm worried about the woman in 116. Could you walk down there and check things out? I just dropped her off a little while ago."

227

"What do you think this is, buddy? The Waldorf fuckin' Astoria."

The sound of the receiver being slammed into its cradle hurt Michael's ear. He felt the heat in his face and growled, "Bastard!"

Michael speed-shifted through Fayetteville's streets. Once he reached Persons Avenue, he opened the throttle on the Porsche and raced down the four-lane avenue at one hundred miles an hour.

Traffic at 4 a.m. was nearly nonexistent. Just the cop who pulled in behind him a mile from the motel. Michael reflexively hit his brakes when he saw the cop's flashing roof lights, but then gunned the Porsche's engine again. He would deal with the cop when he got to the motel.

The sportscar's tires screeched when it turned off the avenue and careened into the motel parking lot. When he pulled up to Miriana's room, he saw the door was closed, the room was dark. The cop skidded to a stop at Michael's rear bumper, lights flashing and siren wailing. Michael ran toward Miriana's room, adrenaline rushing through his system. He tried the door knob on the room door and found it unlocked. He opened the door and flipped on the light switch. Empty. No Miriana. No luggage. Nothing visible, except the unmade bed, to prove anyone had been in the room.

"Hands over your head, asshole. You make a sudden move, I'll blow your head off."

Michael slowly raised his hands.

"Now turn around, nice and easy."

The cop crouched in the doorway. The bore of his .38 police special looked as big as a howitzer's.

CHAPTER SEVENTEEN

Vitas drove south on Route 1 until he found an isolated area. He pulled onto a dirt road bordered on both sides by tall stands of pines. The trees were so dense he couldn't see moonlight through them. He got out to check on the girl. She was beginning to stir in the trunk, though still sedated from the chloroform. She looked so tantalizing, he wanted to climb into the trunk and take her right then and there. He reached down and felt her breasts. Then he touched her pubic area with the tips of his fingers. The sense of anticipation coursing through him was like a fever that had taken control of his mind and body. He would have to find a place to hole up soon.

He straightened up and stood at the rear bumper for over a minute, just looking down at the girl. Her legs were exquisite. Long, smooth, finely muscled. Her skin was a golden brown – naturally tan. He removed a handkerchief from his pants pocket and mopped the sweat that had magically appeared on his forehead. This one would be the best ever. Not just one of the best. He knew that as a matter of fact. His instincts were never wrong.

He slammed the trunk lid in place, walked around and got back behind the wheel, started the car, and returned to the highway. There were numerous billboards along the highway advertising hotels and motels in and near the larger cities. Miles away. That wouldn't do. He would need an out-of-the-way motel, where he could be far from traffic and prying eyes . . . and ears, where he could play the game in seclusion. He felt his heart hammering in his chest. He loved this part of the game. The anticipation always made the realization even better.

"Mir-i-a-na," he sang.

CHAPTER EIGHTEEN

The deputy who'd followed Michael into the motel lot and drawn his pistol on him now stood just outside Miriana's room, talking with a very big man, dressed in the same kind of khaki uniform the deputy wore. Michael stared at the two men, but couldn't make out what they said. Finally, the large man entered the room and stood over Michael, squinting down at him sitting on the motel room bed.

"I'm Sheriff Collins," he said. "You know you got problems here, boy."

Michael looked up, blinked. The Sheriff stood six feet, four inches tall – at least – and had forearms as thick as cordwood. His accent was so thick his words drawled on forever. But his blue eyes said, I'm a mean bastard and I'd like nothing better than to prove it to you.

"Yes, sir," Michael said.

"My deputy here says you were driving on my streets at one hundred miles an hour. You didn't stop when he signaled you to. And when you got here, you ran away from your car and into this room. I suppose you got some smart-ass explanation for your behavior."

The Sheriff wiped his face with an already damp handkerchief and turned to his deputy. "Crank up that air conditioner, Del. I'm about to melt from this humidity."

Michael ignored the man's bluster. "I don't know exactly what's going on here, Sheriff Collins. But I'm really worried. I think a friend of mine's been kidnapped."

The Sheriff squinted. "Before we get into some bullshit discussion about kidnapping, suppose you tell me what you're doing down here in God's country." His eyebrows arched, as though he expected lies from Yankees.

"I'm stationed at Bragg. I'm with the 82nd Airborne."

Collins stared at Michael for a moment. "I hear they're sending some of you boys over to goddamn Serb-i-a pretty soon."

"Yes, sir. We're shipping out Friday."

The Sheriff pulled a straight-backed chair from a small table, dragged it over, and sat down. "Now, son, what's this horseshit about somebody being kidnapped?"

Michael felt like he'd overdosed on coffee. His legs jiggled up and down, and he had to put his hands on his knees to make them stop. He forced himself to try to breathe calmly. "I left my friend here about an hour ago. We'd gone out for dinner, then went dancing over at the Sackett Inn."

"What's your friend's name?" Collins asked.

"Miriana Georgadoff."

Collins looked over his shoulder at the deputy. "Didya get that, Delbert?" his voice heavy with sarcasm. The deputy fumbled at his shirt pocket and pulled out a pen and note pad.

"Yes, Sheriff," he replied.

Collins turned his attention back to Michael. "Don't the Sackett Inn close down about two a.m.?"

"That's right. We sat in the parking lot there talking for over an hour. Then I dropped her off here and went to my place."

"And what made you break a bunch of my traffic laws to rush back here?"

"There was a message from my father on my answering machine. He said Miriana might be in danger. I called Miriana's room and got no answer."

"Why would your daddy think your friend was in danger? What's he got to do with this?"

"He's with the Agency," Michael said.

"And what agency would that be, boy?"

"The Central Intelligence Agency, Sheriff," Michael said. "You've heard of the CIA, I presume?"

The Sheriff blinked.

CHAPTER NINETEEN

Bob Danforth hadn't been able to go back to sleep after calling Michael's apartment in Fayetteville and leaving a message. He was wired. The fact Michael hadn't called him back was causing all sorts of scenarios to reel through his mind – all of them bad. He'd been pacing the floor of his home office or trying Michael's phone number for the past hour. When the phone on the desk rang at 4:15 a.m., he rushed to the desk and snatched the cordless receiver from its cradle.

"Michael?" Bob shouted.

"Mr. Danforth? Mr. Robert Danforth?"

"Yes," Bob answered the unfamiliar voice.

"This is Sheriff Roy Collins calling from Fayetteville, North Carolina."

Bob's heart sank.

"I have an Army officer with me who claims to be your son, Michael. Would you kindly tell me his middle name and date of birth?"

Bob took a deep breath and exhaled. "Is Michael all right? Has there been an accident?"

"The young man is fine, Mr. Danforth. There haven't been any accidents. Now if you would answer my question."

"His middle name is Andrew. Date of birth, 28 April 1969."

"Okay, Mr. Danforth," Collins said. "I'm going to put your son on the phone."

"Hi, Dad."

"Michael, what the heck's going on?"

"Miriana's missing."

"I know. I called and left a message for you. She skipped out of Andrews Air Force Base."

"I mean she's missing from her room here in Fayetteville."

Bob's heart sank again, but for a different reason this time. Jack's instincts were right. Michael did have something to do with Miriana's escape from Andrews.

As though he knew what his father was thinking, Michael said, "Dad, I had nothing to do with Miriana running away from Andrews. I didn't know she'd follow me down here. She said she'd been given a pass."

"Jesus, Mary—"

"Whoa, Dad. You're the spook in the family. I'm just a soldier. What do I know about this stuff?"

Michael told him all about his evening with Miriana – what they'd done, if not what they felt – and ended with his finding her room empty. "I think she's been kidnapped," he said.

"Why do you think that?"

"The door looks like it was kicked in. The bed sheet has been ripped, like someone tore strips off it. Maybe to tie her up. Besides, she wouldn't have taken off without telling me."

"Michael, you barely know this girl. How can you say what she would or would not do?"

"You just have to take my word for it, Dad."

"Okay, son. Now put the Sheriff back on the line."

Michael handed the receiver to Collins.

"Sheriff Collins, I want to thank you for your kind treatment of my son. The young woman in question was in CIA custody. She took off without telling any of us. I'm going to need your help."

Mentioning *CIA* must have gotten the Sheriff's attention. "We'd be happy to cooperate with you in any way we can," he said.

"We need to find that young lady. Fast! I'm going to come down there with a few men. Do you have an office where we can set up a command post?"

"You bet," Collins said. "I assume you vouch for your son's moral character and law-abiding nature."

Bob said, "A day or two in the can might do him some good."

CHAPTER TWENTY

When Vitas found the Pineview Lodge in the late afternoon, he knew it was just what he'd been looking for. On a side road, a half-mile away from Route 1, it was a collection of run-down log cabins tucked among the trees.

"I vant quietest cabin you have," Vitas told the bespectacled clerk. "I do not want telephone calls. I vant quiet."

"Ain't no phones in our cabins, and you're the only customer I got, mister," the clerk said in a slow, bored drawl, scratching his three-day beard with a dirty finger. "Take your pick."

Vitas selected the cabin farthest from the road. He paid cash in advance for two nights, and then drove to the back of the property. As he parked in front of the eight-step staircase leading up to the cabin, a sudden banging came from the trunk of the rented Buick.

He ignored the noise, took his luggage from the car's rear seat, and climbed the cabin's porch steps. Before entering, however, he turned to survey the grounds. Good! Trees screened the other cabins from view. There was no one in sight. In the distance he saw the craggy tops of mountains. He unlocked the door and dumped his bags on the floor. Then he returned to the car, popped the trunk, put one arm under her legs, the other under her back, and lugged Miriana's bound and thrashing body into the cabin.

Vitas saw the girl's tears and the fear showing in her eyes. Wonderful, he thought, the destruction process begins. He smiled down at her in his arms and licked his lips. He could smell the onslaught of fear and panic in the girl. He'd sensed it many times before with other victims. His spine tingled with pleasure. This little one is going to be the best, he thought once again. Those perfect features. How much fun it will be to smash that nose, to blacken those eyes, to bust those teeth! He couldn't wait to watch her react to the fear and pain that would assault her brain and charge through her nervous system. Her whimpering only increased the thrill.

Vitas laughed, dropping her onto the thin, green spread covering the bed's sagging mattress. He ripped the spread off the bed, pulling it from underneath her as though she weighed nothing. Then he quickly untied the cloth strips from around her arms and legs and bound her with them, spread-eagled, to the bedposts.

He noticed her eyes followed his every movement, as though she was his audience, and he was an actor. He walked to the side of the bed and bent over, exaggeratedly sniffing the side of her neck. The combination of perfume, shampoo, sweat, and fear – a powerful, erotic potion – made Vitas' skin tingle. "Aah," he moaned. He licked the side of her face and felt her shiver.

CHAPTER TWENTY-ONE

Seventeen-year-old Danny Farrell, hiding in an out-of-control growth of scrub oak, tried to make sense of what he'd just seen. This was different from anything he'd ever seen since he began hanging around the cabins. He willed his brain to solve the puzzle. He'd watched the car drive up to the cabin, and seen the man get out and carry the girl inside. Why does he have her in the trunk? he wondered. It was all very confusing. He just couldn't figure it out. He removed his baseball cap and scratched his unruly blond hair.

What that man doin' wit dat girl? She was kickin' and got somethin' wrapped 'round her mouth – her arms and legs, too. Somethin' not right goin' on over dere.

Intrigued, he thought again about how the big man took the girl up the stairs into the cabin. His instincts told him the man was bad. He didn't know why he knew that.

Using the trees and brush for cover, Danny crept closer to the cabin. He was going to get a look inside – just like he always did. He could slip inside and watch the people when they were sleeping. They never even knew he was there.

Danny snuck around the back and hid in the trees. He settled his back against the trunk of a giant oak and closed his eyes. They'd be asleep real soon. Just like all the people who stayed in the cabins. Then he'd play a trick on them. He started giggling and covered his mouth with both hands.

CHAPTER TWENTY-TWO

"Listen to me," Vitas said in Serbo-Croatian. "I can make what is left of your life a misery. Cooperate, and I will go easy on you. Understand?" The lie was just part of the process. Of breaking the victim down to a babbling, incoherent sexual tool.

Miriana nodded.

"I am going to take off your gag. If you scream, I will knock your teeth out and put the gag back in your mouth. You can choke on your own blood."

Miriana nodded again.

The man jerked the gag roughly from her mouth.

"Wa . . . water," she stammered.

Vitas went to the bathroom and returned with a plastic cup of water. He lowered the cup to her mouth and let a few drops dribble between her lips.

"What . . . what do you want . . . with me? What have I done?" Her voice quavered.

"Ah, my little bird. You have been a very bad girl. Perhaps you will understand your predicament a little better if I tell you I had a very informative conversation with a friend of yours in Serbia. I found her very cooperative – and tasty." He kissed his fingertips as though praising a fine meal.

"Wh . . . what friend?"

"Olga Madanovic, my dear. You must remember Olga. She told me everything. She just babbled and babbled."

Miriana shuddered. She looked back at the man, the pistol in his shoulder holster gleaming ominously, his face a nightmarish vision. Then she quickly jerked her gaze away from the man's piercing, one-eyed stare, letting her eyes fall on a corner of the room.

The man showed his gold-toothed, yellow-stained smile. "Olga told me everything. Initially, she tried not to. But I have great powers of persuasion. Such a beautiful woman. And what a body. She had this golden-blond hair on her arms and on her pussy. But she looked quite hideous by the time I finished with her."

His face suddenly took on a faraway look, as though he recalled past events. Then he shouted, "Look at me when I talk to you!"

Miriana's body spasmed at the man's bullhorn of a voice. She moved her eyes to his face and saw his smile.

"I remember Olga's terror when she told me about your involvement in the kidnapping. She tried for so long to protect you. She didn't want to give me your name. But, you see, my dear, she had no choice. Olga was a very strong woman. Much stronger, I suspect, than you are. But, in the end, I destroyed her will. Then I destroyed her body."

Miriana shivered, noticing the glint of joy that seemed to be in the man's one good eye, in his smile. There appeared to be consummate pleasure showing on his face, in the way his eyebrows arched, and in the way his breathing had become faster. The plastic glass in his grip suddenly shattered. The noise sounded like a firecracker in the confined cabin space.

Vitas watched the girl's face and knew immediately her emotions were at the breaking point – especially when he calmly picked plastic shards from his bleeding palm and fingers. He saw the circle of wetness spread over her underpants and onto the bed sheet between her legs. The acrid odor of urine overwhelmed the musty cabin smell.

Vitas shivered. It took Herculean effort not to rip off his own clothes and jump on her. The smell of her fear was such a turn-on. The addition of the urine odor to Miriana's other scents only excited him further. He stuffed the sock back in her mouth. "I will be back in just a moment, and then we can get started."

Vitas checked the strips of cloth securing her to the wooden bedposts, then marched out of the cabin and drove eight miles to a pizza joint. He couldn't get his mind off the Gypsy girl during the drive. It had been tough to leave her lying there on the bed – so vulnerable, so available. But he knew the time would increase her fear. So much the better.

CHAPTER TWENTY-THREE

Danny Farrell heard heavy footfalls on the cabin's front steps and sneaked out from the stand of trees to the corner of the cabin. He peeked around at the front and saw the big man drive away. When he couldn't hear the car anymore, he returned to the back of the cabin and carefully removed two of the boards covering the crawlspace underneath the cabin floor. He scooted across the earth until he came under the trapdoor and reached up to remove the bolt holding the trapdoor shut. But a movement to his left caught his eye and he froze. It was a raccoon. Danny chittered at the animal, trying to reassure it. It moved back into deeper shadow.

Crouched under the floor, Danny reached up and released the bolt. Pineview Lodge was a bootlegger's place back during something called *Probishun* – at least that's what his daddy had called it. And Daddy told him how the trapdoors were bolted from the outside now to keep motel guests from opening them and falling through. Danny thought that was funny. People falling through the trapdoors.

Danny liked sneaking into the cabins when they were empty, and he liked sneaking into them when they weren't empty, too. He'd watch the people while they slept. And he almost always took something – a watch, a ring, a piece of clothing. Then he'd listen to the people yell at each other, "What'd you do with my watch? Where's my jacket?" Then he'd put the stuff back. That really confused them.

Danny quietly lowered the trapdoor and silently pulled himself into the cabin.

Miriana opened her eyes and saw a young man wearing a light blue work shirt, jeans, and a red baseball cap standing in the middle of the room. He peered down at her, tilting his head one way, then the other, as though he was trying to understand what he saw. He stared at her near-nakedness, seemingly more confused and intrigued than interested in a lascivious way.

He walked around the bed, inspecting the way her arms and legs were tied to the bedposts. He even pulled on the knots. He had the silky, immature growth of hair of a teenager on his cheeks and over his upper lip. His honey-blond hair stuck out of the cap on his forehead and hung several inches down his neck. The way he looked around the room, the expression on his face reminded her of a little boy. The only thing about him that contradicted the impression she'd formed was how he moved – like a stalking animal. Powerful, but light on his feet. Soundless.

Danny focused on Miriana's eyes – that pleading look – just like Mama's when Daddy got liquored up and beat on her. Danny went down on his knees next to the bed. He tugged again at the knot that tied her right hand to the bedpost.

"Wh . . . why you be tied up like that?" he asked.

Miriana groaned.

Danny reached for the gag, but then jerked his hand back. "Mama says I should mind ma own bizness," he said. "Don't be stickin' my nose where it don't belong."

But he couldn't help himself. Slowly, he moved his hand toward Miriana's face and touched her cheek. How soft her skin felt! Her eyes bored into him, pleading.

"You know you pissed yourself," he said, as matter-of-factly as though he was commenting on the weather.

Danny stood and padded over to the two suitcases lying open in a corner. One of them had girl's things in it. He lifted a blue-and-gold silk scarf to his face. He'd never smelled anything so good. It made him feel lightheaded. He went back to the bed, bent over, and smelled the girl's hair and face. The same wonderful smell.

A car came crunching up the crushed-shell driveway to the cabin. The engine stopped. A door slammed. Danny jerked erect and, in three strides, rushed to the opening in the floor, dropped through it, and closed and locked the trapdoor behind him.

Miriana wanted to scream. You can't leave me here. Please! Then she felt a twinge of hope. Someone else knew she was in this cabin. Please tell the police I am here, she prayed. Please tell someone.

CHAPTER TWENTY-FOUR

Sheriff Roy Collins, Richard Turner, the FBI Supervisory Special Agent from the Winston-Salem field office, and three of Turner's agents from the Fayetteville office met Bob Danforth and the two CIA agents who'd accompanied him to the Fayetteville municipal airport. While Bob, Collins, and Turner got in the Sheriff's SUV, the others piled into a van.

Sheriff Collins led the way to town. "I'm glad to see you boys working together," Collins said. Supervisory Special Agent Turner didn't pick up on the mischief in his voice.

"What's that supposed to mean, Sheriff?" Turner asked.

Uh oh, Bob thought. I can feel the turf battle starting already.

"Don't mean a thang," Collins said, heavily laying on the southern drawl. "I'm jes happy to be workin' with you all. We're proud to have sech distinguished visitors down here in little old Fayetteville."

Bob managed not to laugh. Turner harrumphed in the backseat while the Sheriff pulled onto the highway.

After going a couple of miles, Turner asked, "So what's so damn important I had to be called off the golf course?"

Bob turned in his seat and looked at the FBI man in the backseat. "Didn't you get briefed before flying in here?"

"Yeah, but it sounds like a wild goose chase. Some young woman gives you guys the slip and runs off with an Army officer. Probably fucking each other's brains out. Doesn't appear to be a national security matter."

Bob controlled his anger and said, "The Army officer you just referred to is my son." He saw Turner gulp, then avert his eyes. Bob faced forward again. Obviously, he thought, the briefing Turner received had been incomplete.

They all entered the Sheriff's office and took seats around a large, old, scarred wooden table set in the middle of the room. Chipped and stained tile covered the floor, and photographs of politicians and uniformed men adorned the walls. The room smelled like cigarettes and bad coffee. Behind a desk on the street side of the room, under a high bank of windows, were two flag stands – one with the Stars and Stripes, the other with the North Carolina State flag. A Confederate flag was mounted in a frame on the wall opposite the desk.

A primly dressed woman of fifty opened the office door and asked if they would care for anything to drink. She took their orders and left the room.

"Your son doesn't have a clue as to what happened to the young woman," Collins told Bob. "There was nothing of hers in the room – no toiletries, no clothes, no nothin. But he's damned insistent she didn't take off on her own."

"How can he be so sure?" Turner asked.

Bob frowned at Turner.

"Look, Danforth, we got two young kids here with raging hormones," Turner said. "Isn't there a possibility your son could be hiding Ms. Georgadoff to get her away from the CIA? Maybe he kicked in the door to make it look like someone broke in. She probably screwed your boy silly and now he's willing to do anything."

Bob jumped out of his chair, reached across the table and grabbed Turner by the knot of his necktie. The other men in the room, except Sheriff Collins, leaped to their feet. But no one tried to interfere between Bob and Turner. Bob pulled Turner forward until they were almost nose-to-nose. "Listen to me, you prick. First, Michael's no fifteen-year-old kid. He's a thirty-year-old Army Captain. Second, he signed an official statement under oath to Sheriff Collins. A lie would make him susceptible to a perjury charge. And lastly, he gave me his word. You challenge my son's character, or call his or Ms. Georgadoff's honor into question again, and I'll shove your badge so far up your ass you'll need a proctoscope to find it."

Bob shoved Turner. Turner and his wheeled chair slid three feet and slammed into the wall. Two framed photographs – the North Carolina Governor and the U. S. President – fell from the wall and crashed to the floor.

Red-faced, Turner stood and straightened his tie. He scowled at Bob, then at Collins. "You'll pay for that," he hissed, and marched out of the room, followed by his three fellow agents. The last agent slammed the door behind him.

"Normally, I would have stepped between you two. I don't like people messing up my office. But I sure enjoyed watching you knock that banty rooster down a peg or two," Collins said.

"I must be getting cranky in my old age."

Collins shrugged. "Ain't no big thang."

Turner and his agents left the Sheriff's office and waited on the sidewalk in front of the Fayetteville Municipal Building. He pointed at two of the agents and said, "You go back in that room and listen closely. I want to know everything that CIA asshole says and does." When the two men hesitated, he shouted, "Go! Now!"

As the agents climbed back up the stairs, he turned to the remaining agent, Geoffrey Fricke. "I want you to go out to Ft. Bragg," he told him. "Locate Michael Danforth's commanding officer. Leave the impression the young Captain fucked up in a very big way. He's hiding something, and I want to know what it is." He ignored the sour look Fricke gave him. He didn't give a shit what the agent thought.

CHAPTER TWENTY-FIVE

"Jack Cole!"

"Jack, it's Bob."

"How's it going down there?"

"I'm in Sheriff Collins' office in Fayetteville, North Carolina," Bob said, catching the Sheriff's eye. "So far, we got zip. Just the information Michael gave us."

"Hmm. What did Mike—"

"Michael had *nothing* to do with her going to Fayetteville," Bob interrupted.

"I'm glad to hear it. Just raising the issue with you wasn't easy for me."

"I understand, Jack. Miriana got tired of confinement at Andrews and Michael was the only person she'd met outside the CIA. She took off on her own."

"What do you think happened to the girl?"

"It's pretty obvious. Someone snatched her. Too many things have happened recently. You connect the dots and a picture starts to take shape. The incident with the umbrella on Connecticut Avenue; the murders of Olga Madanovic and Darius Alexandrovic. Now Miriana's disappearance. If we assume the attack with the poisoned umbrella was directed at me, then every one of the targets or victims was directly or indirectly connected to Karadjic's kidnapping. The Serbs are bent on revenge. They've put a killer on the ground here in the States."

"How are things working out with the FBI?"

"Don't ask. The head guy here is a royal ass."

"Bob, you know we didn't have a choice. A kidnapping on American soil is FBI turf."

"I know, Jack. But this bastard down here – guy named Turner – thinks Michael and Miriana set up a scam to get her away from protective custody."

"Jesus! He can't be that stupid. We were going to turn her loose in a few weeks anyway."

When Bob didn't reply, Jack said, "*That* stupid?"

"Yep," Bob said. "And arrogant. A bad combination."

After Bob and Jack finished their conversation, Bob dialed his home number. Liz answered, obvious hesitation in her voice.

"Liz, it's me," Bob said. "Everything all right?"

"Fine, honey. How are things down there? How's Michael?"

"Miriana's disappeared and Michael's sick about it. The FBI agent-in-charge is pissed off at me. And there's a hired killer on the loose. Other than that, everything's great."

"Try to keep an eye on Michael, Bob. Our son's in love. He's got to be hurting."

"Christ, Liz. They just met. How in the world do you know he's in love with Miriana?"

"Take my word for it. I just know."

Bob scratched his head after replacing the receiver.

CHAPTER TWENTY-SIX

"I understand Colonel Dennis Sweeney is commanding officer here," FBI Special Agent Geoffrey Fricke said, presenting his ID to the Sergeant Major seated at the desk nearest the entry. "I'd like to speak with him."

The Sergeant Major looked up under bushy eyebrows at the man standing in front of his desk. He sized him up. Five feet, ten inches tall, short blond hair, ruddy complexion, powerfully built, aviator sunglasses, dark suit and spit-shined shoes. Suit! FEEB. I hate suits, he thought. I hate FEEB suits even worse.

"So you want to talk with Colonel Sweeney, sir," Jewell said, running a hand over his shaved head. "What can I tell the Colonel about the nature of your business?"

"That's all you can tell him, Sergeant, that it's my business," Fricke said in an authoritative, self-important tone – just as he'd been taught at the academy. Just as he'd done hundreds of times before, intimidating people.

Jewell slowly rose from his chair, pushing himself up on massive arms, and glared with cobalt blue eyes at the FBI agent. His tailored, short-sleeved uniform shirt fit his body in a way that accentuated his muscular build. Standing and looking down at the man from his six-foot-five-inch vantage point only heightened the effect. The veins in his neck bulged and his head reddened. It was the same purposeful, intimidating tactic he'd used many times with recalcitrant soldiers.

"Sir," he said in a steely voice, "I'll ask you once more, and only once more. If you choose to continue to be discourteous, I will have your ass thrown off my base. Do we understand one another?" He paused, then again asked, "What . . . is . . . the . . . nature . . . of . . . your . . . business?"

Fricke visibly swallowed and gave Jewell an apologetic look – as though he'd come to the conclusion he'd misjudged the NCO. "Sergeant, I need to talk with Colonel Sweeney about one of the officers in his command," he said, in a much more cooperative tone. "We have reason to believe he has broken the law."

"It's Sergeant Major, not Sergeant, sir. And what officer are we talking about?"

"Captain Michael Andrew Danforth," Fricke said, adding "Sergeant Major," as an afterthought.

"Bullshit!" Jewell said, the word tumbling off his tongue before he knew it. He wheeled around and knocked on the Colonel's door, then entered, closing it behind him. "I got a FEEB out here demanding to see you. He claims Captain Danforth's in some kind of trouble."

"FEEB? You mean FBI? Looking for Mike Danforth? Danforth's in trouble? What kind of trouble?"

"The guy says he broke the law."

"Bullshit!" the Colonel spat.

"That's what I said, Colonel."

"Well, send him in. And then find Captain Danforth. Have him wait down the hall until I tell you to bring him here. I want to find out what this is all about before I put his neck on the line."

"Yes, sir!" Jewell returned to his desk, escorted the agent into Colonel Sweeney's office, then returned to his desk. "Corporal Cunningham," he yelled to the clerk sitting in the office directly across the hall from his, "get on the radio and track down Captain Danforth. According to the training schedule, his unit's out on the grenade range. The Colonel wants to see him NOW."

"What's going on, Sergeant Major?" Cunningham asked while he reached for his telephone.

Jewell's voice suddenly changed, dropping several octaves, his words rumbling as though spoken inside a fifty-five-gallon drum. "Corporal Cunningham, unless you can show me a typewritten, military order, signed by at least a full Colonel, saying you have a right to know the reason behind my orders, I expect you to do as I tell you – without hesitation and without any goddam questions. Got it?"

"Yes, Sergeant Major," Cunningham said meekly.

"Now explain this to me one more time," Colonel Sweeney said to Special Agent Fricke in a reasonable, quiet tone, while he leaned forward in his chair, hands folded together on his desk blotter. "You say Captain Danforth, *Captain Michael Danforth*, conspired with a CIA-protected witness – some gal named Georgadoff – to fake her kidnapping. She's a foreign national and he's got her holed up somewhere. And he's risking national security. Is that about it?"

Fricke nodded.

"Before I call Captain Danforth in here, would you care to share with me what proof you have to substantiate these accusations?"

"I don't need to, Colonel. This is government business involving national security," Fricke said.

"You're right, Mr. Fricke. You don't have to tell me squat. But in case you haven't noticed, I'm also involved with national security."

Fricke opened his mouth as though to interject, but Sweeney's raised hand cut him off. "You're going to hear me out. Don't try to interrupt me. Captain Danforth is the finest company-grade officer in my command. He's got generals' stars waiting for him down the road – unless some bullshit allegation like this gets into his record. I'm going to have Danforth brought in here. But I'm going to sit in on your meeting with him. You fuck with this young man without good reason and I'll call my cousin, the esteemed senior United States Senator from my home state of Tennessee." He punched a button on his intercom and said, "Sergeant Major Jewell, send Captain Danforth in here."

Sweeney and Fricke stared at one another, neither saying a word, until Michael entered. Ignoring Fricke, Michael came to attention in front of the Colonel's desk and saluted. "Captain Danforth reporting as ordered, sir."

"At ease, Captain," Sweeney said. "Take a seat." He waited for Michael to sit down and then said, "This gentleman is Special Agent Fricke with the Federal Bureau of Investigation. He's investigating the disappearance of a Ms. Georgadoff and is going to ask you a few questions. If you don't fully understand a question, make him repeat it until you do understand it."

"Yes, sir," Michael said. Then turning to the FBI agent, he asked, "Have you found Miriana? Is she all right?"

Fricke grilled Michael for forty-five minutes. Michael told him the same things he'd told Sheriff Collins and his father.

"Well, that should just about do it, Colonel Sweeney, Captain Danforth," Fricke said at the end of it. "I appreciate your time."

"You're quite welcome," Colonel Sweeney said in a honey-sweet tone, all the while thinking, Asshole. "Always glad to assist the FBI." The Colonel then called Jewell on his intercom and told him to come to his office. When the NCO entered the office, Sweeney said, "Sergeant Major Jewell, would you show our guest out?"

"Yes, sir. Be happy to." The agent followed the Sergeant Major through the building and out the front door to the parking lot. Jewell started to go back into the building, then suddenly turned and said, "Agent Fricke, it may not be my place to say anything; but I want you to know there's no way in hell Captain Danforth would ever do anything illegal – except maybe drive his Porsche faster than the speed limit. He's one fine officer."

248

For a moment, Fricke looked as though he was considering what he'd just heard. Then he said, "Thanks for your input, Sergeant Major."

CHAPTER TWENTY-SEVEN

Vitas dumped the pizza box on the kitchen table and walked into the bedroom. "Hungry?" he asked.

Miriana grunted into her gag.

"You promise to behave and I'll let you eat."

She nodded.

Vitas removed the gag and undid the cloth knots of her restraints. But then he tied her ankles together. He led her to the table, watching her breasts bounce while she hopped on bound feet. "You have nice breasts," he said. He reached over and squeezed one until she screamed in pain. Laughing, he shoved her into a chair and slid the pizza box over to her.

Miriana wolfed the food, aware the man never took his eye off her. She felt her skin crawl under his gaze. But it had been over twenty hours since her last meal – dinner with Michael – so she ignored him and ate. The thought of Michael made her eyes fill with tears. She couldn't stop herself.

She finished two slices of pizza and three glasses of water, then sat back in her chair and brushed her hair away from her face. "Can I put some clothes on?"

"No!"

"What do you want with me?" she asked.

Vitas half rose in his chair and swung his arm across the table. He hit Miriana across the cheek with his open hand and knocked her to the floor. "You don't ask questions!" he yelled. "I ask, you answer."

Miriana touched her cheek. A sob escaped her lips. Tears now flowed freely.

Vitas came around the table and sniffed the air. "My God, you smell like piss! You stink!" He grabbed her arm and lifted her up.

"Get undressed."

"I can't take off my clothes with my ankles tied," Miriana whimpered.

Vitas took a bone-handled knife from a pants pocket and flipped open the five-inch blade. He sliced through the cloth binding her ankles. He shoved her toward the bathroom door. "Get your ass in there and clean up. And wash your clothes while you're at it."

When Miriana started to close the bathroom door behind her, Vitas kicked it open. He pulled a chair over and sat down.

Miriana hesitated.

"Get in the shower," Vitas shouted, jabbing the knife toward her.

His voice echoed off the walls of the tiny bathroom, making Miriana jump. She stepped into the shower and reached for the handle on the glass shower door; but then she jerked her hand back, seemingly afraid to do anything without the man's permission.

Vitas smiled. Things were going so well.

Miriana felt her lower lip begin to tremble. The man's dead eye seemed to stare alternately at her face, her breasts, her crotch. In his good eye, she saw no sign of . . . anything. Nothing. Not even lust. She felt icy-cold splinters of fear. She hugged herself when she stepped into the shower. Turning her back to the man, she pulled the shower knob and tensed when the cold water hit her. Her breath caught in her lungs and she backed away from the icy spray. She heard the man chuckling. It took all the strength she had not to void her bladder again.

"Now take off your T-shirt and panties," the man growled.

Miriana shook. Fear and cold water combined to make her feel as though she was losing control of her body. She whimpered while stripping off her T-shirt and panties.

"Wash your clothes," the man yelled.

She did as she was ordered.

"Now your body," he said. "Use the soap."

Again, she followed his instructions.

"No, no," he screamed, "slower. First your hair. Yes, that's it. Now your neck. Good, good. Now your breasts."

His voice now seemed strained, higher pitched. Miriana mechanically did what he told her to do, washing every part of herself while he continued to stare.

After washing herself, he ordered her to pick up her clothes off the shower floor and squeeze the water from them. She hung them over the shower door and reached for a towel. But the man was too fast. He snatched the towel off the towel bar and dangled it out in front of her. Then he dropped it to the floor. A smirk showed on his face.

He crooked a finger at her, beckoned her toward him. Miriana couldn't move. She stood frozen in place, her arms wrapped around herself. He reached out, grasped her hair, and jerked her forward, crushing her body against his.

"Dry yourself," he ordered, sitting back in the chair, "and get in bed. It's time."

Miriana bent and snatched up the towel. While she wrapped it around herself, she noticed the daylight that made it past the bathroom curtain was fading. It would be dark soon. That thought made her feel even more frightened. The man had returned to the chair in the bathroom door opening. He just sat there, staring. She tried to tighten the towel around her. He stood up and calmly ripped it away. He grabbed her by the hair again, jerked her head back, and slowly ran the tip of his knife over her face, neck, breasts, stomach, crotch. She stiffened, then began shaking uncontrollably.

Vitas felt ecstatic – her fear, her smell, the texture and color of her skin, her supple body, all made him delirious. He lifted her and carried her almost tenderly to the bed.

He took one of Miriana's nipples between two fingers and squeezed it, hard. She slashed at him with her nails, raking the side of his face. She kicked him in the gut.

He was exhilarated. That's more like it, he thought. But he had to teach her who was boss. He swung his fist and struck her head. "Uh," she moaned, then crumpled on the bed.

Vitas tried to rouse her, but she didn't move. He'd hit her too hard. "Shit, shit, shit!" he cursed. He gagged and retied her to the bedposts and tossed the bedspread over her.

CHAPTER TWENTY-EIGHT

In his hiding place under the cabin floor, Danny heard the door slammed, the sound of the car engine starting, and the noise of tires on the shell driveway. When all was quiet, he opened the trapdoor and climbed back up into the cabin.

The woman still lay on the bed, gagged, with her hands and feet tied to the bedposts. Danny noticed new cuts and swellings on her face.

He gently touched her shoulder. "You awake?" he asked.

The woman groaned; her eyelids flickered.

"Hey, lady, you awake?"

The woman's eyelids snapped open – round with fear.

"That man hurt ya?" he said.

She slowly nodded her head.

"What for?"

No answer.

Danny untied the gag.

"Water," the woman rasped.

Danny went to the bathroom and filled a cup. He put it to the woman's lips and let her sip. Water sloshed down her chin. He took the cup away when she started to cough.

"Please help me," the woman croaked.

Danny laughed. "You talk funny," he said.

"He is going to kill me," she said. "You must help me."

"I better be goin'," he said. "Don't want no trouble."

The woman yelled, "No, please," she begged. "Untie me."

He shook his head. "Oh no. My mama, she tell me not to go messin' in other people's bizness. I always listen to my mama."

"Your mama must be good woman. She must tell you, always do right thing."

"That's Mama!"

"Vould your mama want you to help person in trouble?"

Danny appeared to think about the question for a moment. He removed the baseball cap and tousled his hair. "I guess. Maybe."

"What if she knew you had chance to help someone in trouble and did not help?"

"Oh, she be mad at me."

"If you do not help me now, your mama will find out. You get in big trouble."

Danny scrunched up his eyes and wrinkled his nose. He put his cap back on and stared down at his shoes. Then he suddenly looked up. "If I help you, will you go home with me?"

"Absolutely," the woman said on a gush of air. "I tell your mama vhat big hero you are. How you save Miriana's life."

"That yo' name?" he asked. "Miriana."

"Yes," she said. "Miriana."

Danny smiled. "What do I gotta do?"

CHAPTER TWENTY-NINE

"Mr. Cole's office, may I help you?"

"This is Joe Callahan in Signal Intelligence at NSA. I have information for Jack Cole. Priority Red."

"Hold please."

Jack's secretary transferred the call to her boss.

"Hey, Joe," Jack said. "What d'ya got?"

"Jack, we've been listening to telephone traffic into and out of the Yugoslav Embassy. One of my people just heard a conversation between Paulus Tomavic, an Embassy employee, and someone named Artyan. The call came in from some backwater town – Pineview – in South Carolina."

"Yeah . . .."

"The guy named Artyan said he had the Gypsy girl."

"Damn! Joe, were you able to pinpoint his location? How close can you put us to the caller?"

"He called from a pay phone about a mile east of Route 1, two-and-a-half miles into South Carolina. We're pulling up maps now. That close enough for you?"

"You bet! Anything else?"

"Yeah. This Artyan said he will have avenged the Karadjic kidnapping by Saturday. He also said something about punishing the son for the sins of the father. We haven't figured that one out yet. Make any sense to you?"

CHAPTER THIRTY

Danny sliced through the cloth strips tied around Miriana's ankles. His face lit up as though a happy thought had suddenly struck him. He knelt on the floor and stared at her. "I'm real good with locks. I opens locks on cabin doors when I want to. Then I locks the doors. Nobody knows I been there."

"Good for you, Danny," Miriana said. "Now, please cut my arms loose, Danny."

"You wanna hear how I sneak into these cabins and watch people sleepin'?"

Miriana inhaled a great rush of air into her lungs and held it. "I would love to hear all about it, Danny. But not right now."

Danny frowned.

"Come on, Danny. We have to get out of here. We can go tell your mama you are big hero."

The smile returned to Danny's face. "Yeah!"

He cut through the strips of material that bound her wrists to the bedposts, then stepped back and wiped the knife blade on his dungarees.

Miriana threw off the bedspread and rolled naked onto the floor. She had lost circulation in her feet while they were tied. She used the side of the bed to pull herself up from the floor and sat on the bed, rubbing her feet until they no longer felt prickly.

Danny gaped at her nakedness. She realized he'd probably never seen a naked woman. She scrambled over to her suitcase and grabbed underwear, a pair of jeans, a lightweight sweatshirt, and a pair of athletic shoes. After dressing quickly, she'd started for the door when the sound of an arriving car sent a burning spike of fear through her. She froze where she stood.

She didn't know what to do, unable to take any action. Fear engulfed her and her body shook. It took all her self-control to keep from screaming.

Danny calmly took her hand and led her to the trapdoor.

Vitas figured he'd spend a couple of hours with the girl before killing her. He looked at his watch. It was now 7 p.m. He could be gone by midnight. "Miriana, honey," he sang out after unlocking the cabin's door, "your lover is home." He laughed while he walked toward the bedroom. He felt his blood rushing, his body hot with excitement.

Vitas roared when he saw the empty bed. He hadn't been gone more than twenty minutes. One goddamed phone call to that asshole, Paulus Tomavic. How could she have gotten away? Then he saw the cleanly sliced strips of cloth on the bed. In a rage, he pulled the mattress off the bed and threw it against the wall.

He took a flashlight from his bag, ran outside, and searched around the cabin. Two sets of footprints in the dirt led away from the back of the cabin.

Then he noticed the loose boards. He kicked at the boards, sending them flying into the crawlspace. He peered into the darkness but saw only empty space. He moved the flashlight's beam and saw the dirt had been disturbed under the cabin. After crawling through the opening, he shone the beam up at the cabin floor. A trapdoor! With a quick jerk, he pulled back the bolt on the latch and opened the door. Vitas stood up in the opening and looked around the inside of the cabin. How could she have gotten to the latch? Someone else must have opened it from below. Someone else now knows I'm here.

"*Dupa!*" he shouted. "How could I be so stupid?"

Vitas started to climb into the cabin when something snarled under him. He felt a sudden pain in his right calf. He leaped up and onto the cabin floor with a yell. A huge raccoon clung to his leg, its teeth imbedded in the meaty part of his calf, its claws hooked around his leg.

Vitas pulled a 9mm Smith & Wesson from his shoulder holster, shot the beast, splattering gore around it. He kicked it back into the crawlspace.

He rolled up his ripped pantleg to examine the wound. Then he cleaned it with soap and water and tore a strip of bedsheet to wrap around his leg as a bandage. He went outside and tried to follow the footprints at the back of the cabin, but they disappeared at the edge of the woods.

I've got to get out of here, he thought. The girl could be anywhere. If she gets to a phone, I'm dead. He hopped into the car and sped out of the Pineview Lodge. While driving north, the image of her naked body in the shower returned to him. He slammed his fist against the car seat over and over, all the while screaming her name.

CHAPTER THIRTY-ONE

When the CIA plane landed at the Pineview Airfield late that night, Bob took his attention from the file on his lap.

The Pineview Sheriff, Don Mechem, met Bob when he climbed down the steps from the plane, followed by two CIA agents and three FBI men, including Agent Fricke. Bob was pleased that Supervisory Agent Turner had elected to skip the trip. He was apparently still pissed off with Bob over the incident at the Fayetteville Sheriff's office.

Short, wiry, and intelligent-looking, Mechem showed no sign of being impressed by the big-city Feds.

"I got two four-wheel drive Tahoes waiting," Mechem said. "Ready to hit the road?"

Mechem drove one of the Tahoes, Bob sat in the front seat beside him, and FBI Special Agent Fricke sat in the backseat. Bob took a map from his inside jacket pocket and spread it out on the center console. He pointed out a circle drawn in with the words PAY PHONE next to the circle.

"This is the location where the man named Artyan used a pay phone to call the Yugoslav Embassy. Sheriff, what's located at the intersection of Dogwood and State Highway 176?" Bob asked.

"Gas station on one corner, convenience store, pizza joint on another," Mechem said. "The other two corners are undeveloped."

"Okay," Bob said. "Let's assume he used a phone relatively close to where he's holding the girl – say no more than five miles. How many motels would be within that distance?"

"Two . . . no, three," Mechem said.

"We'll check out the closest one first."

Mechem pulled over to the side of the road and studied the map.

Bob watched the Sheriff "X" motel locations on the map.

"The closest one to the pay phone is Lori's Bungalows. Then the Sunshine Inn. Lastly, the Pineview Lodge. These three are all on this side of the highway. If your theory's correct, the guy is probably staying at one of them. There are two other motels in the area, but they're clear on the other side of town. A lot farther away than five miles."

"Okay!" Bob said. "Let's do it. We'll check out the motels. If we come up with nothing, we can go over to the pizza joint. Maybe someone there saw our man."

Mechem gunned the engine, sending stones flying off the spinning rear tires. The rubber gripped the road surface and the truck shot forward with a lurch. After only a few minutes, the Sheriff called out, "Lori's is right around the bend."

The motel looked like any of a thousand others spread across rural America. A neon sign flashed "VACA_ CY." The overall ambience of the place, Bob thought, recommended against stopping there – faded and cracked yellow-painted exterior walls, a shingle-covered portico with numerous shingles missing supported by white posts between the rooms, and a gravel parking lot. Only one car was parked in the lot.

"This place barely makes it," Mechem said. "It gets the occasional tourist or the bored housewife shacking up with her equally bored neighbor."

When the other Tahoe pulled in, Bob told the CIA agents to take two of the FBI guys and watch the building's rear. He, Mechem, and Fricke went into the motel office.

A fifty-something, fat woman in an enormous flowered muumuu sat behind the counter. Her garish red hair, done up in pink curlers, looked as though it had been fried by way too many permanent waves. A lipstick-stained cigarette dangled from her tobacco-yellowed fingers. When she offered a grimace of a smile, Bob saw that lipstick also marked her teeth. The place smelled like cheap perfume and body odor.

"Well, well, well. If it ain't ma old *Cher* Donny Mechem," she said in a Cajun accent. "I ain't seen you out here in a coon's age, boy. You must be behavin' yoself fo a change."

"Now, now, Ms. Lori, you be nice," Mechem said, a genuinely friendly smile showing on his face for the first time since he'd met Bob at the airfield. "I got important visitors here from outta town. We wouldn't want to give them the wrong impression, you hear?"

Lori batted her eyelashes at Bob, then at Fricke. "What you bring me here, Donny Boy. Dese men look like some kinda *federales*. Dat right?"

"Something like that," Mechem said.

"What can I do for you gentlemen?" Lori said, giving Fricke a gap-toothed leer full of lascivious intent. "Never let it be said Lori Pontchartrain don't treat visitors like *impotant* people."

"Lori, we're looking for a man; he had a young woman with him. Seen anyone like that?"

"You jes described 'bout half my clientele," Lori said with a chuckle. "This guy you lookin' fo, he local?"

"No way," Mechem said.

"No one here for over a week what wasn't local."

"That's all we need to know. Thanks, Lori." Mechem half-turned toward the door, then stopped. "Whose car is that out there?"

Lori smiled. "I give you my word, Sheriff, it ain't whoever you lookin' fo."

The Sunshine Inn looked like a carbon copy of Lori's place – even down to its yellow paint. But the Sunshine Inn appeared to be doing a better business. There were eight cars – all with Virginia plates.

Bob followed Mechem into the motel's office and was introduced to the owner, Johnny Roy Pulsever, a pencil-thin, crane-necked guy with pallid, acne-scarred skin. Cross-stitched, framed religious messages hung on two of the walls. A brass sign with black lettering sat in a small tripod on the counter. The words read BORN AGAIN.

"Looks like business is picking up, Johnny Roy," Mechem said.

"Just some people down for the prayer meeting tomorrow night."

"Can't never get enough prayer, huh, Johnny Roy?" Mechem asked.

The motel owner gave Mechem a sour look and said, "Something I can do for you?"

"Looking for a guy with a foreign accent. Had a young woman with him. Seen anybody like that in the last twenty-four hours?"

"Sheriff, you know I won't allow no adulterous fornicating here."

Mechem stepped closer to the counter. "I didn't say these two were messing around. Just answer my question, Johnny Roy."

"Nope. Haven't had anyone like that stay here."

Mechem tipped his hat at the man and walked out.

When Bob caught up with Mechem, he asked, "He's strung a little tight, isn't he?"

Mechem sighed and shook his head. "More than you know. For all that asshole's religious bullshit, he's the worst racist in the area. I've been trying to pin a murder on him for two years. No luck."

Bob noticed Fricke react to Mechem's words. The man hadn't said a word so far, but it was obvious he was listening, taking everything in.

The Pineview Lodge spread out over several acres, with individual cabins scattered among dense stands of brush and enormous pine trees that stood like rigid sentinels behind the office. It was too dark to see how far back the motel's land went, or how many cabins there were. Like the previous two motels, the Pineview Lodge was rustic, but, unlike the other properties, it was better maintained.

"I wanta warn you, the owner of this place is one of the meanest sumbitches in these parts," Mechem told Bob and Fricke. "He's an old bootlegger. Doesn't like cops. Hates Feds with a passion. Claims he can smell a Fed a mile away. He ain't gonna go out of his way to make us feel welcome."

Bob and Fricke nodded their understanding and followed Mechem into the motel office, which smelled like booze and tobacco.

"What kinda company you keepin' now, Sheriff?" Buford Nolan asked, looking over glasses perched on the end of his nose. He spat brown, viscous liquid into a paper cup he held in his left hand. Then he smiled, showing tobacco-stained teeth.

"Buford, I don't take kindly to visitors to our city being treated with disrespect. Do I make myself clear?"

Buford didn't say a thing. He just scowled at Mechem, then at Bob and Fricke with a wrinkled nose and turned down lips. Then he displayed a sneering smile, again spitting brown juice into the cup.

"This gentleman here," Mechem said, "has a couple of questions to ask you, Buford."

Bob took his cue. "We're looking for a man who might have checked into your motel last night with a young woman. He probably had a Slavic accent. Do you remember anyone like that?"

"Only a couple guests here since last weekend," Nolan said. "But there weren't no woman with any of them that I could see."

"Can you describe these men?" Fricke asked. "Are any of them still here?"

Nolan shrugged. "Just men," he said. He rubbed one eye and spit once more into the cup. "The last guy was kinda strange, though," he said. "I think he *was* a foreigner. Like you said, he had an accent of some kind. Sounded like a Rooskie to me."

Bells went off in Bob's head. His heart raced. "Can you describe him?"

"Tall – 'round six foot two. 'Bout two hundred pounds. He *looked* kinda Rooskie, too. You know, sorta like one of them guys you see in the news. One scary lookin' sumbitch, too. And, oh yeah, he was blind in one eye. Goddam eye was white. Gave me chills just lookin' at it. He drove outta here a couple times, but came right back. 'Bout an hour ago he hauled ass down the road again like he had a bear chasin' him. If I had to guess, I'd say he ain't comin' back this time."

"Which way did he go?"

"North."

"Can you give us a description of the car? Did you get his license plate number?" Fricke asked, his voice now tinged with a bit of excitement.

Buford looked at Fricke, then at Bob. He smiled. "You bet your ass," he said, and just stood there staring at them.

Time passed, but Buford said nothing more until Mechem said, "You still hosting that high-stakes poker game here every other weekend, Buford?"

Nolan visibly swallowed. "Well, now, I think I can help you with that license number."

CHAPTER THIRTY-TWO

The motel owner got in the back of the Sheriff's vehicle with Fricke and rode with them to the cabin at the back of the property. Mechem radioed an APB on the car Nolan told them he'd seen drive away from the property. When they arrived at the cabin, Buford cursed, "Sumbitch left the gol-darn door open! Probably got critters running all over the place by now. Bastard left all the lights on, too."

Fricke and the men in the second vehicle encircled the cabin, while Bob and Mechem, guns drawn, carefully entered it.

Bob spotted the open trapdoor and the still-damp blood next to it on the floor.

"Who's the guy you're looking for?" Buford Nolan asked one of the FBI agents while they examined the back of the cabin.

The agent narrowed his eyes and scowled. Then his face relaxed slightly and he said, "He abducted a woman in CIA protective custody."

Nolan snickered. "Don't give you much confidence in the CIA, does it?"

The agent gave him a dirty look, but then smiled, as though to give the impression he'd thought the same thing earlier.

"Now who da hell busted up dese boards?" Buford said. "Gol-darn vandals!"

The FBI man inspected the broken planks. "What's in there, Nolan?"

"Just the crawlspace. Unless . . .." Nolan got down on his hands and knees. "Let me have your flashlight." He crawled inside. "Somebody been in here," he shouted. "The dirt's all rucked up. Jee-sus! Got a big ole dead raccoon lying in a pool of blood. Got some kits, too. They hissing up a storm. Gonna have to get rid of these varmints." He grabbed the dead raccoon's tail and tossed it back toward the broken planks. The agent, who'd been peering into the crawlspace, jumped back when it landed near his face.

Directing the flashlight beam at the trapdoor, Nolan called out, "The trapdoor's open. Someone's definitely been under here recently." He looked up through the opening in the floor and saw Bob looking down at him.

"What are you doing down there, Nolan?"

Nolan pulled himself up through the trapdoor into the cabin. "Somebody put a great big bullet hole in a raccoon down there. And somebody must have gone into the cabin through the trapdoor. It had to be opened from underneath."

Bob took the flashlight from Nolan and directed it back into the crawlspace. Something caught his eye. He lowered himself through the trapdoor to the dirt below and pointed the flashlight beam at something shimmery lying in the dirt. Bob picked up what looked like a piece of cloth. After shaking the dirt off it, he stood in the open trapdoor and, in the cabin's light, looked at the object: A blue and gold silk scarf.

Bob climbed back into the cabin and said, "Nolan, what's with the trapdoor?"

"Used to be an escape hatch for moonshiners," Nolan said. "So they could get away from the fuckin' Treasury agents comin' to arrest them." He laughed as though he'd just told the funniest joke in the world. When he got no reaction from Bob or Mechem, he continued by saying, "The stills were out there in the woods. All these cabins got trapdoors. I put throw rugs over them and bolted the trapdoors from underneath. Only way they can be opened is from below the cabins."

One of Bob's CIA men suddenly entered the cabin through the front door. "I found three sets of fresh footprints leading from the back of the cabin to the edge of the trees. Two sets continued into the woods."

"Did you follow them?" Bob asked.

"Yes, sir, but they petered out after ten yards or so."

Bob raised the plastic bag containing the scarf to eye level. He noticed a tag sewn into the lining of the material: Jan's Accessories, Washington, D.C.

Bob opened the bag and put it to his nose. The scarf carried the scent of perfume.

"Sheriff, we're going to need to bring in a forensics team," he said. He looked at Nolan and said, "I don't want anyone cleaning up in here until we've finished."

"You bet," Mechem said. Then he gave Bob an almost sorrowful look and said, "I probably ought to put some men in the woods behind the cabin. If he killed the girl, he may have dumped her body back there."

Bob just nodded. Then he pulled his cell phone from a pocket and called his son.

"Hello, hello," Michael shouted, as though he'd been startled. His voice was thick with sleep.

"Michael," he said, "we found a scarf that could be Miriana's. I'd like you to look at it, see if you recognize it."

"What else, Dad?" Michael asked.

"That's it."

CHAPTER THIRTY-THREE

Michael drove to meet his father at the Fayetteville airport later that night. The forty-five minute wait in the terminal for the CIA plane seemed interminable. When the aircraft finally landed, Michael rushed out of the terminal to the tarmac, meeting his father halfway.

Bob hugged his son and then said, "I can't tell you much, Mike. We found where we think she'd been, but we don't know where she is now. The man who kidnapped her was gone by the time we arrived. Do you recognize this scarf?"

Bob held up the plastic evidence bag, thinking the scarf lying crumpled inside was a pathetic way to try to bring hope to his son.

Michael stared at it. His shoulders suddenly slumped. "I've never seen it before, Dad. I can't tell you if it's Miriana's. Maybe if I took it out and looked at it."

"It's evidence," Bob said, "so only touch the edge." He popped the seal on the bag and watched Michael slowly and partially lift the silky material from inside with the tips of his thumb and forefinger. He put his nose by the opening and inhaled.

"It's Miriana's. I recognize her perfume. It's hers, Dad," he said in a slightly hoarse, quiet tone. "The night she came down, we had dinner and went dancing. I was half drunk from the scent of that perfume. I'll never forget it." A smile started to crease Michael's face, but it quickly dissolved. "What are we going to do, Dad? I'm nuts about her. You've got to find her."

"Yeah, I know, son." Bob said. "I'm doing all I can." He patted Michael on the arm, turned, and ran back to the waiting plane.

CHAPTER THIRTY-FOUR

Miriana followed Danny in the dark, through the dense woods, along a winding animal trail skirting the edge of moss-covered, granite cliffs. The moss and decomposing leaves made her footing on the rocky surface unsteady. She could hear a stream trickling below them, but couldn't tell how far below it was. She struggled to keep up, all the while frightened about what would happen if she fell off the path. Her chest heaved from the effort of trying to stay close to the boy. Once, when she could no longer see or hear him, she stopped and called out his name in a low, frightened voice.

Other than the thumping of her heart, her labored breathing, and the noise of her footfalls, the woods were silent. Even the animals and insects seemed to have taken the night off. She couldn't see or hear Danny. Then, as though he was a wraith, Danny appeared and took her hand to pull her along.

"Da . . . Danny, could ve . . . rest for minute? I need to . . . catch breath," she said, panting.

He moved around impatiently while Miriana bent over gasping for breath.

"Sure," he said, "but we gotta hurry home so you can tell Mama how I helped you get away from the bad man. Remember, you promised." He seemed to be agitated.

Miriana straightened up, her chest still heaving, and laid a calming hand on the side of his face. "You do not worry. I vill say to your mama you are bravest boy in all vorld. You saved Miriana's life. You are big hero."

A satisfied "Humm" came from Danny. Then a cloud moved away, revealing the golden surface of the moon, lighting up his face. He wore a jack-o-lantern smile.

CHAPTER THIRTY-FIVE

"Change of plan, Paulus," Vitas said, a hint of malicious humor in his voice, as though he loved jerking around the Embassy employee. He imagined Paulus' complexion turning red and the man's stomach lurching. Vitas knew the effect he had on people and thrived on it.

"I asked you not to call me here at the house," Paulus said in a hushed, pleading voice. "What is it, Artyan?"

"I will be in D.C. in about four hours. I need a place to stay until my plane leaves on Saturday. And I need another car. I've had this one too long."

Paulus sighed. "I thought you didn't plan to arrive until tomorrow night."

"Are you telling me you can't make arrangements?" Vitas growled.

"No, no, Artyan. I've already arranged for a safe house here. The key is under a flowerpot on the front step."

"What about the car?"

"Where did you rent yours from?"

"Handy-Rent-A-Car at the airport. I used forged papers and a credit card that I don't want to use again."

"Let me think . . . .. Okay, here's what you do. Go to the airport and drop the car in the public parking lot. Take the shuttle to the Airport Hotel. There will be another car waiting for you in the parking lot on the north side of the hotel. I'll put both visors down and an apple on the dashboard so you will know the car. The keys will be on top of the right rear tire."

"Good!" Vitas said. "I'll be there by 5 a.m."

CHAPTER THIRTY-SIX

Flying back to D.C. in the agency jet, Bob dialed Jack Cole's number at Langley. It was three in the morning, but he knew Jack was in his office.

"Bob, how're things going?" Jack asked.

"So far, I've got conjecture, hypotheticals, and speculation, but no hard evidence. We think we just missed the guy who took Miriana. We don't know if he's still got her with him, if she's dead, or what. I'd sure like to get at least a full name on the kidnapper."

"Ask and ye shall receive," Jack said. "I just got a response on that license plate. It's a rental from Baltimore-Washington Airport. Rented by a Johann Schmidt. The guy used a VISA card."

"Johann Schmidt – John Smith. Sounds like an alias."

"I called the rental people and told them to contact us the minute the car shows up. And I told them not to clean it." Jack paused, then added, "I was hoping you'd found the girl."

Bob sighed. "Common sense says she's dead. But . . . I don't know."

"I've got my fingers crossed," Jack said.

"We are scheduled to land in D.C. in thirty minutes. I'm going home to get some sleep, but I'll be in the office by noon."

"Okay, Bob, see you then."

Bob extinguished the overhead light and lowered his seat back. Maybe I can grab a few winks before we land, he thought. But sleep wouldn't come. He'd seen the pictures of what the Serbs had done to Olga Madanovic. He didn't want to find Miriana in the same condition. But his instincts told him this whole thing could end badly.

CHAPTER THIRTY-SEVEN

Danny Farrell's mother, Emily, sat in a dilapidated wicker chair on her log cabin's front porch, kneading her hands in her aproned lap while looking at her husband in the glow of a kerosene lamp. Jefferson Farrell, a scrawny, scarecrow—man sat on the steps below her, nursing a beer. Her fingers combed back the loose gray strands of hair hanging near her face. I hope he don't drink more than a six-pack tonight, she thought. The craziness always seems to start with the seventh bottle.

Jefferson suddenly belched. Trying to move the fear away, she looked away from Jefferson, out at the dark woods. Where was Danny? She hated it when he disappeared like this. He'd been gone almost twenty-four hours this time. Here it was the middle of the night and he still wasn't home. She could never sleep when Danny was out at night.

She imagined peaceful sights – deer foraging on the sweet new growth at the ends of tree branches, raccoons hunting for food. She smiled at the chirping sounds coming from the trees. Probably a possum, she thought.

"Where's that damn fool son of yours, off playing Daniel Boone again?"

Emily merely sighed. She didn't have a clue. Wherever Danny is, it's gotta be a sight better than on this porch with a drunken stepfather and a dried out old woman. Danny was a wonder at woodsmanship. He knew the names of every plant in the forest, could imitate the calls of nearly every bird and mammal, and could move so quietly no man or animal could detect him.

"I asked you a question, woman," Jefferson grunted. "Say something, you old sow."

Emily hated him. She buried her disdain for her husband where she stored all her other emotions, in the knot at the bottom of her stomach.

Sonofabitch, she thought. I gotta go clean other people's houses so we can have some cash income, and the only thing he ever brings in is a Budweiser six-pack. Idiot! Goddam idiot! Emily rose to go into the cabin.

Jefferson suddenly pointed with his beer bottle, "Well, speak of the devil. Look who's finally come home. Who the hell's that with him?"

Sure enough, it was Danny with his loping walk. And just behind him . . . a girl?

"Who the fuck you got with you, boy?" Jefferson called, while Danny and the girl came nearer. "You gettin' laid out there in the woods?" He laughed his husky cigarette laugh.

Emily rose and hitched up the worn jeans that had been too big for her for too many years now. She stepped off the porch and hugged Danny, then held him at arm's length to look him over.

"Where you been, Danny? You been gone a whole day. You okay?"

"I'm fine, Mama. I been bein' a hero," Danny said. He tilted his head at Miriana, his thumbs hooked in his jeans pockets. "Ask her, Mama, ask her."

"Hero, my ass," Jefferson snorted. "Damn retard!."

Emily ignored Jefferson. The young woman standing beside her son seemed scared to death. "Come here, sweetie," Emily said. "Let me get a good look at you. My Lord, what happened to your face?"

"It is long story. I . . .."

Then the girl's legs seemed to turn to rubber. She staggered and grabbed Emily's arm. Emily put her other arm around the girl's waist and guided her toward the cabin door. When they climbed the steps past Jefferson, Emily noticed him look the girl up and down with an interest he hadn't shown in her in years. Dumb old fool, she thought.

Emily helped the girl into the cabin's front room, furnished with a couch, a large chair, and a small table. A potbelly stove sat in a corner. The chair and couch were scarred and their cushions sagged with age and use. A woolen blanket covered the back of the couch. The small table had been branded with cigarette burns and wet beer can rings.

Emily lowered the girl onto the couch and rushed into the kitchen. She moved the pump handle up and down until a trickle of water came from the spout. She filled a glass and returned to the girl.

After Miriana downed the glass of water, she asked, "Could I use telephone?"

"Honey," Emily said, "there ain't a telephone line within two miles of this place. And we can't afford no cell phone."

Miriana gave an enormous, exasperated sigh. "I must have telephone. Please, I must have telephone."

CHAPTER THIRTY-EIGHT

Vitas pushed the button on the parking lot machine and took the card that slid out of the slot. He tossed the card on the floor of the rental car and drove down one lane, then another, until he found a space in the nearly full Baltimore-Washington Airport public parking lot. He looked around to make sure no one else was around. It was only 4:30 a.m., but no harm in being cautious. He grabbed his bag from the backseat, and got out of the car. After locking the doors, he threw the keys as far as he could, hearing them clang against some car a couple lanes away. He limped to the American Airlines terminal – his leg aching badly – and got into the backseat of the solitary cab parked by the curb.

"Where to, buddy?" the driver asked, turning down the flag on his meter.

"Airport Hotel," Vitas commanded.

"You got to be kidding me, pal. You could walk there in five minutes. I'm not tak–"

Vitas dropped a twenty-dollar bill onto the front seat. The man shut up and put the cab in gear.

The ride lasted two minutes. After getting out of the cab, Vitas waited until the cabbie drove away from the hotel parking lot. Then he wandered the lot until he found the car Paulus had left for him.

On the drive to the Alexandria safehouse, Vitas worked out a plan to handle Bob Danforth. It took an hour and a half to find the safehouse. By the time he'd parked the car and carried his bag inside, he was exhausted. Between the wound in his leg, too little sleep, the long drive, and the frustration of the day, he was spent. He collapsed on the bed and slept as though he had nothing on his mind.

CHAPTER THIRTY-NINE

Liz saw the glare of headlights flash across the front windows. She rubbed her eyes and rose wearily from the chair at her built-in desk in the kitchen. The clock on the wall said it was five in the morning. She'd sat up all night, working on paying bills and thinking about Bob, Michael, and Miriana.

She retied her bathrobe belt and brushed her hair back with her hands. Then she hurried down the hall from the kitchen to the entry and opened the front door. Her heart felt heavy while she watched Bob shuffle up the front walk, his posture bent.

"Hey, good-looking," she said, forcing off her own fatigue, trying to lift his obviously low spirits.

Bob looked up and immediately stood straighter. "Hey yourself," he said, stepping through the entry and putting an arm around her, kissing her forehead.

Liz took his briefcase and set it down on the floor. Despite her exhaustion, she was brimming with curiosity, wanting to ask Bob about progress he'd made. But they had an agreement. She asked no questions about Agency business; he told her whatever he felt he could.

She followed him up the stairs to their bedroom and sat on the side of the bed while he removed his clothes. Stripped down to his undershorts, Bob sat next to her. He took her hand and, in painful detail, went through the events of the last two days. She knew he needed to do it slowly and methodically to check his recollections for missing links. He always said the links solved every case.

CHAPTER FORTY

Miriana made good on her promise and told Emily how Danny had saved her life. She was so exhausted, she could barely get out the words. But the ecstatic expression on Danny's face made the effort worthwhile.

After being given corn bread and beans, Miriana put on one of Emily's flannel nightgowns and put to bed on a cot with a rough, woolen blanket pulled up to her chin. She sighed, rolled over on her side, closed her eyes, and drifted off to sleep.

The wind blew her hair. Michael sat beside her, at the wheel of a red convertible parked beside a sparkling lake. The radio played country and western music. In her dream, she was happy.

But that image faded into blackness. Something heavy pressed on her chest. She fought for air and smelled rank alcohol and rotten breath. She was no longer dreaming.

There was a man on top of her. He was squeezing her breast, pushing himself against her crotch. Oh, my God! It's the one-eyed man again! He found me!

She clawed at his face with her nails. He grabbed her wrists and put his mouth on hers. She struggled to throw him off, kicking at him, but he was too strong.

"Go ahead, girl," the man slurred huskily. "Squirm all you want. I like it better that way."

He released one of her wrists and clamped his hand over her mouth. Miriana tried to bite him, but only tasted the dirt and sweat on his hand.

Suddenly, the man yelled, "Goddammit!" He removed his hand from her mouth. She gasped for air. But she was still crushed by his weight.

She heard the man groan and then heard Danny's voice and remembered where she was. It wasn't the one-eyed man lying on top of her;

274

it was Jefferson Farrell. Danny seemed frightened. He murmured, "Bad daddy, bad daddy." He repeated it over and over again. "Bad daddy."

Farrell groaned again but didn't move. Something wet and sticky seeped onto Miriana's chest. She shoved with all her strength and rolled Farrell off her. He landed on the floor with a thud. Then Danny's mother entered the room, carrying a flashlight.

"What's going on out . . ..?" Then Emily shrieked. She looked down at her husband lying in a spreading pool of blood. Danny stood over him with a carving knife in his hand.

Danny backed against the wall, still holding the knife. His eyes were saucers; his chin trembled.

"Daddy was hurtin' my friend," he cried, tears rolling down his cheeks. "Why did Daddy do that?" Danny stepped forward and dropped to his knees next to his father. Sobbing, he laid the knife on Farrell's chest and began rocking back and forth, hugging himself.

Emily rushed over to Jefferson's still form and put her ear near his mouth. Dammit, he's breathing, she thought. For a moment she had considered how her life would change with her reprobate husband dead. "He's still alive," she said to Miriana, "we've got to get him into the pickup, take him to the hospital." She grabbed his feet while Miriana took his arms. They dragged him across the floor and out onto the porch. Emily ran to the truck and backed it over to the edge of the porch. Half-dragging, half-lifting Farrell, they put him in the truck bed.

"Danny," Emily called. No answer. She called again and again. Miriana looked around, but didn't see the boy. "Let's go!" Emily yelled. "Get in the cab. You drive. We've got to hurry."

Miriana moved as though in a stupor. She felt like nothing was real. Reacting mechanically, she pushed the shifter into DRIVE on the old, dilapidated pickup. The vehicle lurched forward, snapping her head back. The engine died. She turned the key again, starting the motor. The truck rolled forward, then gathered speed when she pressed down on the accelerator. The wheels spewed dirt clouds in the truck's wake, obscuring the front of the Farrell cabin. Miriana eased up on the accelerator where the dirt road met the highway. She glanced over her shoulder through the empty glass panel space behind her head and saw Emily cradling her husband in the truck bed. The truck bounced off the old rutted road onto the highway paving.

Emily shouted directions at Miriana through the window space. The trip took twenty-five minutes. At the hospital, Miriana saw that Jefferson Farrell's blood had soaked Emily's bathrobe and covered her arms and legs. While two men in white shirts and pants put Danny's father on a gurney and wheeled him away, Miriana noticed for the first time she was still wearing one of Emily Farrell's nightgowns – now stained with Jefferson Farrell's blood.

Miriana and Emily had sat silently in adjoining chairs in the hospital waiting room for fifteen minutes before Emily finally spoke. "What'd the sonofabitch do, try to rape you?" Emily asked.

Miriana nodded, head bowed, shoulders slumped, hands pressed together between her knees.

"Boy, I picked a winner when I married that asshole."

Miriana looked over at Emily. "Sorry," she said.

Emily patted Miriana's hand. "For what, sweetie? For being beautiful? For being young? For being desirable? Ain't your fault."

Silence again. Emily gripped Miriana's hand and gave it a squeeze, then she released it, stood up, and walked over to the bank of windows at the end of the room. The first rays of the morning sun showed over the green hills in the distance. She heard Miriana say, in a small, defeated voice, "I must use telephone," when the waiting room door suddenly flew open.

Don Mechem and one of his deputies burst into the waiting room.

"My God, Emily! What the hell happened?" Mechem said, rushing over to where she stood. "The hospital called and said Jefferson's here with a knife wound. They say he's in a bad way."

Emily turned and faced the Sheriff, a man she'd dated in high school. She noted the concerned look on Mechem's face, the sympathy showing in his eyes. All Emily could do was shake her head. She didn't dare speak at that moment, not trusting her ability to control her emotions.

"You're covered with blood," Mechem said, looking down at her clothes. "Are you hurt?" He knelt in front of her and took her hands in his.

Emily steeled herself, forcing her fragile emotions deeper under the surface. "I'm fine, Don. But you'd better sit down," she said, taking his arm and leading him to a bank of chairs a few feet away. "It's a long story."

Mechem told his deputy to check on Jefferson Farrell's condition, and then sat down next to Emily, again holding her hand. "Why don't you go ahead and tell me, Emily. I got all night." He glanced over at Miriana, then turned back to Emily.

"It was that old fool's fault," she said. "He got liquored up and tried to jump on that girl over there." Emily pointed a finger at Miriana who still sat in the same chair, bent over, her long black hair hanging over her face, staring down at the floor.

Mechem looked at Miriana again. "Who is she?"

"Friend of Danny's. He brought her home late last night. She'd been beat up. Poor thing was all tuckered out."

Mechem looked askew at Emily, wondering what kind of young woman would be hanging out with Emily's son. But he let the moment pass. He'd question the girl next.

Emily told the Sheriff how Danny protected the girl from Jefferson. After she finished, Mechem patted Emily's shoulder and asked, "Is that it?"

"No, there's more." Emily then recounted the story Miriana told her about being kidnapped and how Danny rescued her from the cabin at the Pineview Lodge.

Sheriff Mechem felt his breath catch in his throat. Leaping to his feet, he cut Emily off. "Hold it right there, Emily. I need to go over and ask the young lady a question."

Mechem crossed the waiting room and sat next to Miriana, who raised her head and looked up at him expectantly.

"Would you please tell me your full name, miss?" Mechem said in a slightly tremulous voice, unable to contain the sudden and urgent excitement he felt.

Miriana slowly nodded, sitting upright in the chair. "Miriana Georgadoff. I am—"

Sheriff Mechem's jaw sagged. His "Oh, my God!" startled Miriana and she jerked in her chair, bringing her hands to her chest. She pursed her lips and wrinkled her forehead. "What is it?" she asked.

"Stay right there and don't move," Mechem ordered. He rose from his chair and walked across the room to the courtesy phone sitting on an end table. He punched the zero button and, when the hospital operator came on the line, said, "This is Sheriff Don Mechem. I want you—"

"Hey, Donny, it's Claire. I got the night—"

"Not now, Claire. I want you to listen real close." He read a number to her from a card he'd taken from his shirt pocket. "Connect me to that number. This is an emergency."

CHAPTER FORTY-ONE

The phone startled Bob awake. It was six-thirty in the morning. He'd barely slept two hours.

"Mr. Danforth, this is the duty officer. I've got a Sheriff Donald Mechem calling for you from South Carolina. Do you–?"

"Put him through," Bob said, his breath catching in his chest. Please let it be good news. "Sheriff Mechem, can you hear me?"

"Loud and clear. You're not going to believe it. I found the girl. She's sitting across the room from me at Pineview General Hospital."

Bob's heart skipped a couple of beats. "Thank God! Is she hurt? Why is she in the hospital?"

"Long story. A guy tried to rape her, but not the one you're looking for. She's fine, except for some cuts and bruises."

"I'm going to send a plane down there for her. Don't let her out of your sight."

"You can count on it," Mechem said.

"Can you put her on the line?"

"You bet," Mechem said and handed the receiver to Miriana.

"Hello," Miriana said, sounding timid, afraid.

"Miriana, it's Bob Danforth." Bob felt Liz's hand against his side. He reached around and patted her arm.

"Mr. Danforth! Is really you? It has been . . . .."

Bob heard her voice crack. "It's okay now, Miriana. You're safe. I'm sending a plane for you."

"I'm so sorry. I should never have . . . .." Her voice cracked again and she began to cry.

"It's okay, Miriana. Everything will be fine."

Her voice steadied. "He is going to kill you. He told me his job here vould be finished after you were dead."

"Who, Miriana?"

"The man. The man who took me. He said he vould kill me and then kill you."

Bob felt a rush of anger course through him. "He's not going to kill either one of us," he assured her.

CHAPTER FORTY-TWO

Vitas woke up, surprised to see the sun streaming through the bedroom window. He checked his wristwatch: 10 a.m. His throat was parched; his T-shirt drenched. His leg throbbed with pain. He touched his calf where the raccoon had bit him and jerked his hand away when incredible pain shot through his leg.

He limped down the hall to the bathroom, tossed his shorts and T-shirt on the floor, and stepped into the shower. He let the cold spray bathe his body until his teeth started chattering.

In the kitchen, he took a quart of orange juice out of an ancient Frigidaire, plus some pastries Paulus had provided. He carried the food into the living room, set it on the coffee table, eased down into a worn, brocaded easy chair that might have been considered elegant fifty years earlier, and used the remote to turn on the television. He gulped down half of the juice and ate one of the pastries in three bites. Scrolling through the cable television channels, he settled on the Style Channel, rubbing his crotch while one long-legged, flat-chested fashion waif after another paraded down a runway. He imagined that each of them was Miriana.

CHAPTER FORTY-THREE

The C-5 transport plane rumbled over the Atlantic. Michael sat by a tiny window in an uncomfortable seat among two hundred and fifty other members of the 82nd Airborne, all in full combat gear. The temperature in the cabin couldn't have been over sixty degrees. Pallets loaded with vehicles, ammunition, and other supplies filled the space not taken up by soldiers.

He tried to concentrate on his mission, on what awaited him and his men when they landed in Macedonia. But his mind wandered to Miriana. He pressed his hands against his face and tried to force away thoughts of what might have happened to her.

"Captain Danforth, Captain Michael Danforth, I've got a message for Captain Michael Danforth," a voice suddenly intruded.

Michael raised his hand. "Here," he said.

"We just got this message radioed in from the Pentagon," a man in a flight suit said. He handed Michael a slip of paper. "Hope it's good news." Then he walked back toward the cockpit.

Michael unfolded the note: "We've got Miriana. Safe and sound under Agency protection. Says she misses you and to take care of yourself. Godspeed! J. Cole.

Michael wanted to yell his lungs out. He felt the tension flood from his body. She's okay. She's okay. If he could only hold her in his arms. Then his thoughts returned to the man who'd abducted her. He'd kill the sonofabitch.

CHAPTER FORTY-FOUR

Jack stepped out of his office at Langley and saw Bob opening the conference room door twenty yards down the corridor.

"Bob," he shouted. "Got a minute?"

"Sure, Jack."

Jack strided down the hall and took Bob's arm. "I've put a man outside your house," he said. He saw the frown on Bob's face and immediately said, "I don't want to hear any objections. If you're not afraid, I am. Think about Liz. That maniac who took Miriana could come after you."

"Okay, Jack. You're right. Thanks."

"What's going on? Any progress on finding the kidnapper?"

"I was just about to start a meeting on the subject. Want to join us?"

Jack looked at his watch. "Maybe for a couple of minutes. I've got a meeting with the Director in fifteen minutes."

When Jack and Bob entered the conference room, Tanya, Raymond, and Frank were already seated around the table.

"How's Miriana doing?" Jack asked.

"She's fine, Mr. Cole, considering the ordeal she's been through," Tanya said. "The doctor checked her out."

"How about the guy who snatched her?" Bob asked.

"Airport Security found the guy's car in the overnight parking lot. They called us right away," Raymond replied. "The lab boys took hair and fabric samples from the trunk and the front seat. The samples from the trunk matched Miriana's hair and clothing. We found four sets of fingerprints. Miriana's. Two sets belonging to car agency employees. And one that matches no one in any U.S. files."

"We have Miriana's description of the guy," Frank told them. "He mostly spoke Serbo-Croatian to her. About fifty-years-old, over six feet tall, powerful build, scar on one cheek, one gold tooth, and blind in one eye. She said he had the scariest face she's ever seen."

"Has a sketch been done?" Jack asked.

"In process," Frank responded.

"Maybe he's already left the country," Raymond suggested.

"I don't think so," Tanya countered. "He told Miriana he intended to kill Bob, so he's got unfinished business. And remember that comment picked up on the wiretap on the Yugoslav Embassy? Something about the sins of the father." She stared at Bob and gave him a worried look. "He's got Michael on his hit list, as well."

"Anything else?" Jack asked.

Frank looked at Jack and then at Bob. "Miriana told us the guy bragged about torturing and killing Olga Madanovic."

Bob clenched his hands into fists and had to force himself to breathe evenly. He looked around the table. "Okay, people, let's identify this guy. Call your informants. I assume you've already checked our records for anyone named Vitas."

"Yep, nothing," Raymond said.

Bob gave each of them detailed assignments. After they'd left, Jack smiled at him and said, "It seems to me you've got everything covered. I want you to go home now. Start the weekend a little early. You and Liz spend some time together. I'll send another couple of people out to watch your place. It'll be a whole lot easier protecting both of you if you're in one location."

CHAPTER FORTY-FIVE

Vitas woke with a start at a few minutes past three in the afternoon, astonished he'd fallen asleep. He felt groggy, agitated. His throat was as dry as he could ever remember it being. Maybe I'm catching something, he thought. I need to get up, get moving, try to shake this thing. His face felt warm and the wounds on his leg began to burn.

I'll drive out to Bethesda and get another look at the Danforth place while it's light. Sitting around here is not getting the job done.

Vitas didn't spot the man slouching in the car parked in front of the Danforth's house until it was too late. He turned his face away while he drove past.

Damn, I should have known they'd put a guard on Danforth. The girl probably told them I was after him. Should have killed her when I had the chance. But she looked so good. I really wanted to see her face twisting in pain. I love to fuck them when they're hurting . . . when they're screaming.

Vitas waved his hand in the air. Have to chase away thoughts of the Gypsy girl, he told himself. Concentrate. But he found it difficult with the vision of Miriana Georgadoff in his mind, the sudden fire in his groin, and the throbbing pain in his calf.

He turned left at the next corner and parked a half-block away.

The CIA agent parked in front of the Danforth home spoke into his cell phone. "A white Buick Le Sabre just cruised the street," he reported. "Male driver, late forties, early fifties. No passenger. Virginia tag." He read off the number.

"I'll contact DMV and call you with the results. By the way, Jack Cole sent two more men out there. He's not taking any chances."

"When are they due?" Bart asked.

"Should have been there already but they called about ten minutes ago and reported tie-ups on 95 because of a wreck."

Liz looked at the kitchen clock: 3:30 p.m. I've got time to take a nice leisurely bath, she thought. Bob probably won't be home for hours. The roast's in the oven, the champagne's in the refrigerator, and my negligee's all laid out. I'm going to do a little stress relief tonight. She smiled while she climbed the stairs to the second floor.

Vitas drove to the street paralleling the Danforths' street. He found the house directly behind their residence – the second one in from the corner.

He got out of the rental car and casually walked down the side of the second house and across the backyard. He gripped the top of the five-foot high cedar fence separating the backs of this property and the Danforth residence and pulled himself up. He rolled over the top of the fence, grunting loudly when he scraped his injured leg on the top of the boards, and landed on the Danforths' lawn. He cursed at the pain and quick-limped across the grass to the patio. He found the French doors open, but the inside screen door locked.

With a switchblade, he easily pried open the simple lock. The knife put back into his pocket, he drew his 9mm pistol, and stepped into the empty kitchen. There was no one in the first floor rooms. Then he noticed the sound of water coursing through the house's pipes. He slowly climbed the thickly carpeted steps to the second floor. At the top of the staircase, he heard the faint sound of splashing. After checking the other rooms on the second floor and finding no one there, he turned back toward the bathroom.

Water ran from the hot water spigot into the tub. The bath was beginning to ease the knotted muscles in Liz's back. The soreness accumulated in a day of gardening, and the tension of the past few days, was ebbing away. Eyes closed, she luxuriated in the sensation, in the peace of the moment.

Then a creaking sound came from the hall outside the bathroom. Her eyes popped open. She shook her head as though questioning her fearful reaction – the sudden thumping of her heart and the tightness in her throat. After all, the old frame house tended to creak and groan. But she sat up when another creaking noise sounded. She was now alarmed. If it were Bob, she would have heard the front door slam.

A man stepped into the bathroom, a smile on his face. He was pointing a pistol at her, but she couldn't look away from his face. The scar, the sick smile, the white eye, the gold tooth.

Liz's stomach contracted into a tight ball. She started to scream while she scrambled to get out of the tub, but only managed a squeak before the man's hand clamped over her mouth. He pushed her down, pressing her head under water.

She clawed his arm while her feet thrashed in the water. But he was too strong. She couldn't get away. Then he pulled her up by the hair.

"Are you going to be good little girl?" he asked, mockingly, his accent heavily Slavic.

Liz drew in one breath, then retched.

"I asked you question," he said, his hand clutching her hair, shaking her.

"Answer or I will see how long you can hold breath."

Liz lashed out at him with her hand, her nails extended.

The man sidestepped and slammed his free hand down on her shoulder, forcing her underwater again. This time, she was sure he would drown her. She felt faint, disoriented when he finally pulled her up. She gasped for breath. Nausea assaulted her and she coughed up soapy water.

"Get out of tub," he ordered, dragging her up by her hair.

Liz staggered out of the tub and groped for a towel. But he reached it first, stepped back two paces, and held it out at arm's length. When she hesitated, he waved the pistol at her, motioning her to come toward him. Liz covered herself as best she could with her arms. The man stepped back farther, holding the towel just out of reach.

"You must be Mrs. Danforth," he said. "Stay vhere you are. Let's see vhat kind of toy Mr. Danforth plays with."

Liz turned sideways, hunching over, covering herself again with both arms and hands.

"No, no," he said, wagging his finger at her as though she were a naughty child. "No cheating; drop arms."

Liz stifled a sob and bit her lip to keep it from trembling. "Who are you? How do you know my name?"

"Here are rules," he said. "I ask questions; you answer questions. Now drop arms, or I vill put bullet in you."

Her whole body shook with anger and fear. "Go to hell!" she said.

Still smiling, the man took two steps forward and struck her left shoulder with the gun barrel. An electric shiver of pain coursed down the length of her arm. Then it went numb and dangled uselessly by her side, exposing her breasts

"You see, I can make you do vhat I vant. You must decide how much pain you can stand. Now drop other arm."

Liz obeyed.

He placed the muzzle of the gun on her breastbone and slid it down between her breasts, then moved it lower, to her stomach, to her crotch. He rested the muzzle there for several seconds, then moved it up again and poked it into the underside of her chin.

"Where is husband?"

That accent. He sounds Russian, or . . .. "He's on his way home right now," Liz said. She thought Bob would be late as usual, but hoped the lie would scare the man away.

He surprised her by saying, "Good. Ve vill give him great velcome." He dropped the towel on the floor and lifted Liz's bathrobe off a hook on the wall. "Put it on," he said. "Ve vill have nice little chat until husband gets here."

Feeling just beginning to return to her arm, Liz snatched her robe and slipped into it with her back to him, tying it tighter than necessary, as though to protect herself. Then she remembered Bob's pistol in his bedroom wardrobe. If she could only get to that pistol.

Vitas grasped her arm and shoved her roughly from the bathroom, through the hall, and into the bedroom. She jerked out of his grasp and moved toward the wardrobe, but the man was too fast. He tripped her and snatched her off the floor with one hand as though she weighed nothing. He tossed her onto the antique four-poster bed, pulled a chair to the side of the bed, stared at her, and then glanced around the room. He returned his gaze to the bed and the nightstand. He lifted a Lladro figurine from the stand and ran his thumb over its smooth surface. He smiled at Liz, then threw the figure at the far wall.

Liz whimpered at the sound of the shattering porcelain.

"I like vhat I saw back in bathroom," he said. "You must exercise. Not bad for woman your age. I bet husband loves your body. How about it, does husband love to fuck you?"

Liz felt a wave of revulsion. Bile hit her throat.

"Remember rules, Mrs. Danforth. I ask questions; you answer questions. Does husband like fucking you?"

"Go to hell!"

"Ah, a fighter! I love woman who fights back. It makes everything much more . . . rewarding."

"What do you want?"

"There you go again, asking questions. But I guess telling vhy I am here vill not do any harm. But first, tell me your name. If I am going to tell you my deepest secrets, I must know your name."

Liz refused to answer.

"Do not make me angry, Mrs. Danforth."

"Elizabeth."

"Elizabeth. A good name. Okay, Elizabeth. Vhy am I here? The answer is very simple. I am here to kill husband."

Liz's hand flew to her mouth.

"It is not that I *vant* to kill husband," he continued calmly. "It makes no difference to me who I kill. It is just job. Mr. Danforth offended my employer, who is not man who takes offenses lightly."

"Who's your employer?" Liz asked, an icy feeling spreading through her.

Vitas blurted a laugh. "Very important man in Yugoslavia."

Liz's mouth dropped open. "What? That makes no sense," she protested.

"But it does, dear Elizabeth," Vitas said. "It makes all sense in vorld."

She saw the man look at the photographs hanging on the bedroom wall and walk over to one of Michael in his Army uniform. "Your son is quite handsome, Elizabeth. I recognize him. How old is he? Twenty-five, twenty-six?"

Liz's throat muscles and tendons constricted. A bilious taste invaded her throat again. Nausea overwhelmed her. "My son?" she said, a plaintive anguish etching the two words. "What do you mean, you recognize him?"

The man shot her a cockeyed look, as though he might hit her for asking another question. But then he said, "I have seen your son, Elizabeth. Vith Miriana Georgadoff. They seem friendly."

"How do you know?" Liz asked.

"Oh, I have vatched their little romance blossom. First, here, night of your party. Then in restaurant in Georgetown. And then at motel in Fayetteville. They do make handsome couple. But it vould be big mistake to get hopes up for grandchildren. I vill see that never happens." Vitas laughed heartily, scratching the side of his head with the pistol barrel.

"My goodness, do you run out of questions, my dear?" Vitas laughed again. "Ve are having such nice conversation, I think I vill tell you whole story. Vould you like that, Elizabeth?"

Liz couldn't control her trembling. A sense of evil seemed to envelope her.

"I follow Gypsy girl to Fayetteville," Vitas said, "vhere I see your son. You know, Gypsy girl was my guest for few days."

"You're the one who took Miriana."

"Right," Vitas said. "But I make mistake. The bitch escaped, just vhen I vas about to enjoy myself. Such a tight body. And those breasts . . . gorgeous. I am very upset about losing her. It is no fun just beating and torturing voman unless I get to fuck her, too. And then kill her, of course. You vill see vhat I mean after I take care of your husband. You and I vill have some fun. You vill have to make up for my loss of the Gypsy. Afterwards, I vill return to Balkans and find your son. I know his Army unit went to Macedonia."

Liz's trembling escalated. But it wasn't just her own fear of what this maniac would do to her driving it now. It was also visceral hatred and anger. Like hell you'll hurt Michael, you maniac, she thought. She looked away from the man for an instant, hoping to divert his attention, and then grabbed the alarm clock off the nightstand and threw it at him. When he ducked, she jumped off the bed and flung herself at him.

The man leaped out of the chair and easily evaded Liz's charge. She crashed into the dresser, but turned on him again. He slammed the pistol against the side of her head.

CHAPTER FORTY-SIX

Bob drove the winding streets of his neighborhood, feeling exhausted after fighting traffic and taking a longer route home because of an accident on I-95. When he turned onto his own street, he saw the parked car and recognized Bart Newcombe, the CIA employee Jack had assigned to watch his house. He stopped in the middle of the street next to the car, lowered his passenger side window, and said, "How ya doin'?"

"Everything's fine, Mr. Danforth. Coupla cars came by. I'm waiting for a callback on the most recent one. The DMV's computers are down, so I haven't heard anything yet. I checked on your wife about an hour ago."

"Thanks! I'll bring something out for you to drink."

"I'd appreciate it."

Bob pulled into his driveway and parked next to Liz's Tahoe, and for the thousandth time told himself to clean out the garage so they could park the cars inside.

The sound of a door slamming brought her partially alert. The room spun around her. She tried to scream but something was stuffed in her mouth. Her hands and feet were bound to the bedposts with Bob's neckties. She lay naked, spread-eagled and helpless.

"Honey, I'm home," Bob yelled.

Oh, God! Don't come up, she wanted to scream. Go outside. Get the man guarding the house. Call the police. Do anything, but don't come up here!

Bob went through the rooms at the back of the house. He looked out at the fenced backyard. No Liz. Her car was in the driveway, so she must be upstairs. Passing through the living room, something glistening caught his eye. Water ran across the ceiling in a beaded procession and streamed down one of the walls, soaking the carpeting.

"Liz!" he yelled, racing up the stairs. Maybe she'd fallen in the tub. His shoes squished on the water-soaked carpeting outside the bathroom. He threw open the bathroom door. The water was running, the tub overflowing, but Liz wasn't in it. He turned off the spigot and stepped out of the bathroom. The door to their bedroom was almost completely closed. Liz never closed that door, unless they had houseguests.

Bob felt a surge of adrenaline. There was a gun in the house, but it was in his dresser on the other side of the bedroom door. He turned around and went to Michael's old room at the other end of the hall and grabbed a baseball bat that had been leaning in a corner there for years.

He ran to the master bedroom and threw himself against the door. It slammed back, but hit something softer than the wall, something that went "oof." He swung around the door, holding the bat above his head.

Vitas bent to pick up the 9mm the door had knocked from his hand. Just when his fingers touched the pistol grip, a bat smashed into his left arm with incredible force. Despite the shock, he grabbed the weapon with his right hand and rolled with it, at the same moment ducking another swing of the bat. He came up on his knees and aimed the gun.

"Drop it," he said through clenched teeth, his left arm hanging at his side.

Danforth hesitated, then dropped the bat on the carpet and backed away. His wife moaned and Danforth turned to look at her. Vitas loved the way Danforth's face turned gray at the sight of his bound, gagged, and naked wife.

"Sit down," Vitas ordered. "On floor. Now!"

When Danforth hesitated, Vitas stepped forward and kicked him in the groin. While Danforth fell, groaning, Vitas shook his injured arm to get feeling back into it. When he felt his hand tingle, he flexed the fingers and placed the pistol on the foot of the bed. He needed to tie up Danforth while the man was still incapacitated. He jerked Bob's arms back and tied them with the belt from the woman's bathrobe. Then he retrieved the pistol.

"All right, Danforth," he said. "I vant to know about General Karadjic's abduction. Who gave order for mission? Who carried it out? Your sweet little Olga could tell me only so much."

"I don't know what you're talking about," Danforth protested.

"Answer me or I vill cut your lovely little Elizabeth." Vitas put the gun on the nearby dresser and took the switchblade from a pocket. He pressed a button to open the blade and laughed at the look of desperation in Danforth's eyes.

"I came up with the plan to kidnap Karadjic," Danforth said. "The people who grabbed him were military. I don't have a clue who they were."

"Now, now, Danforth, I know better. I spent hours vith Olga Madanovic. You remember Olga, don't you? What a luscious creature she was. But her heart gave out. Spoiled my fun."

"You bastard!" Danforth growled. The words rushed out like air escaping from a balloon.

"This is not really time for compliments, Mr. Danforth. I vant name of man who led Marine unit into Kosovo. Olga told me you vere along on mission. You must know Marine leader's name. Answer me now, or I start cutting Elizabeth."

"How am I supposed to remember the name of some kid I ran into in the middle of Albania?" Danforth said.

"You are fucking vith me!" Vitas dragged Danforth by the back of his jacket around to the side of the bed, so he could see his wife. He used his knife to cut a strip from the woman's robe and bound Danforth's ankles. Then Vitas bent over the bed and ripped the gag from the woman's mouth. With just the tip of his knife, he cut her skin-deep from her navel to her pubic area.

At first, the woman didn't react. Then the pain and the sight of her blood seeping along the fine incision must have hit her. She screamed.

Danforth struggled against his restraints and yelled, "Don't!"

Vitas smiled while looking at the blood leaking onto Liz's abdomen and dripping down her side. He reached over and slid a finger along the blood trail, then sucked on the finger, smacking his lips. "Isn't this fun?" he asked.

A feral sound came from Danforth, making Vitas laugh. He tossed the knife on the bed between Elizabeth's legs, walked over to where Bob lay on the floor, and said, "I am going to enjoy your wife, and you vill have the pleasure of vatching. Then I vill kill you. And, when I get back to the Balkans, I vill find a way to murder your precious son." He punched Danforth in the face and watched him fall backwards. He kicked Danforth's leg but got no response. The man was unconscious. Vitas then stuffed the gag back into Liz's mouth and walked down the hall to the front bedroom. He stepped to the window and parted the curtains a few inches. The man in the car was still parked out front.

Liz desperately pulled on the ties around her wrists and ankles while the man was out of the room. One of the ties around her wrist began to rip. Straining again, she felt the fabric tear some more. Scrunching her fingers together to make her hand as small as possible, she tried to yank it free. It wouldn't come. She raised her head. Bob lay motionless on the floor.

292

Come on Liz, she thought, you can do it. Try harder! She jerked her arm with all her strength and felt her hand pull free. She reached over with her now-free hand and loosened the knot to free her other arm. Once again she glanced in Bob's direction. His eyelids were fluttering.

Liz sat up and grabbed the knife. She sliced through the ties holding her ankles. Squishing sounds came from the hall. The man was returning.

She rolled off the side of the bed and crouched against the wall. When the man stepped into the room, she launched herself at him and plunged the knife into his thigh until it hit bone, then wrapped her arms around his leg and sank her teeth through his pants into his calf.

The man bent, grabbed her hair, and violently yanked her head back. "You bitch! You will pay for that."

He lifted her off the floor, one hand clutching her hair, the other around her neck, and threw her at the bed. She landed facedown on the mattress.

He wrapped his hands around her ankles and pulled her back off the bed. She felt her nose break when her face hit the floor.

JOSEPH BADAL

CHAPTER FORTY-SEVEN

In the car outside, the cell phone squawked. Agent Bart Newcombe pushed a button on the hands-free console and a frantic voice filled the inside of the vehicle. "Bart, are you there?" the voice shouted.

He turned down the volume on his radio. "What's up?"

"The license plate you called in. We finally got a response from DMV. It's a rental. An employee at the Yugoslav Embassy rented the car. He called in an hour ago and reported it stolen. Something's wrong."

Newcombe launched himself out of the car. As he raced to the front door, he used his cell phone to call the Danforth's telephone number. No response. He tried the front door handle. Locked. If he had to pay for a new front door, so be it. He kicked it in, jumped inside in a crouch, Glock semi-automatic extended. No one in sight. Water dripping from the ceiling, down one wall. He heard a thud upstairs and bolted for the stairs.

The sound of footsteps on the stairs seemed to distract for a split second the man holding her ankles. Liz twisted around, kicking her legs free of the man's grasp. She saw the knife handle sticking out of his thigh. Leaping again at the man, she slammed the palm of her hand into the knife's handle.

Vitas howled in pain and fury. He pulled his arm back and struck Liz a powerful blow to the side of her head. She crumpled to the floor. He looked for his pistol and remembered placing it on the dresser. Blood running down his leg, pain shooting into every synapse of his brain, the heavy sounds of footsteps on the staircase causing him to ignore the Danforths, he swept the pistol off the dresser, hobbled to the French doors at the far end of the bedroom, and pushed them open. He jumped from the

294

narrow balcony toward a hedge below just when he heard someone burst into the bedroom behind him.

Newcombe ran to the open French doors and fired at the man limping across the backyard. Too many trees prevented him from fixing on his target. He turned back to the room and saw what the fleeing man had left behind. Quickly ripping the spread off the bed, he covered Liz's naked body. Then he untied Bob. "I'm going after that guy," Newcombe said. "Are you all right?"

"Just get the bastard," Bob said.

As Bart started for the balcony, he said, "You'd better call an ambulance. Your wife looks bad."

Vitas backtracked along the same route he'd used to get onto the Danforth property. He could feel the knife blade shift when the muscles in his leg contracted with each step. He didn't dare pull it out, for fear it might be the only thing keeping the wound from bleeding out. He neared the place where he'd parked his car and saw a dark green Chevrolet Suburban backing out of a driveway a few meters away. He limped up to the open driver's side window and grabbed the female driver by the throat.

The woman hit the brakes, hard. "Put the gearshift in park," Vitas shouted. "Move to the other seat," he ordered.

She slammed the shifter into park, scrambled over the console, and shrank whimpering against the far door.

Vitas opened the door and pulled himself into the vehicle. He moved the gearshift, gunned the engine, and backed the rest of the way out to the street. He raced out of the neighborhood. He'd driven five miles from Bethesda before the woman finally spoke: "Please don't hurt me."

Vitas ignored her.

"You have . . . a knife stick . . . sticking in your leg?" she said in a trembling voice.

Vitas sneered at the woman. "No shit!"

CHAPTER FORTY-EIGHT

Jack rushed from the elevator at Bethesda Memorial Hospital. He entered the all-white, sterile atmosphere of the Intensive Care Unit and stopped at the reception counter. Over the top of the reception nurse's head, he spied Bob standing next to the bed in one of the window-fronted rooms facing toward a row of wall-mounted heart monitors. The asynchronous beeping of the machines grated on Jack's already overly-stimulated nerves.

"How's Mrs. Danforth?" he asked the nurse.

"Are you a member of the family?" the nurse asked, her face rigid. "We can't give out information—"

"Look, miss, I'm not in the mood for any bureaucratic bullshit. Answer my question, or I'll get the hospital administrator up here."

The nurse's mouth opened in a big "O," then shut. She looked at Jack, as though trying to determine if he had the influence he threatened her with. Expelling a stream of air, she took a file from a rack next to her chair and opened it on her desk. After consulting the handwritten notes on the first sheet in the file, she looked up at Jack and said, "She has a very serious concussion. Keeps slipping in and out of consciousness."

"Thanks," he said and turned toward Liz's room. He caught Bob's eye when he happened to turn away from Liz's bed.

Jack pressed his lips together and barely shook his head when he noticed Bob's haggard appearance. His friend's face looked transfixed with grief while he crossed the floor toward him. Bob's eyes were blackened and swollen and bandages had been placed on his forehead, both cheeks and chin. He seems to have aged ten years since I saw him a few hours ago, Jack thought. He looks sick and old.

Jack put his hands on Bob's shoulders. "Liz is strong, Bob. She'll recover."

"She took a hell of a blow to the head, Jack. I watched her drop when he hit her. I couldn't do a thing to help. Did we get the guy?"

"No! So far we got *nada*. Every law enforcement agency within a hundred miles is looking for him, but we haven't turned up a clue beyond what you already know."

"Any word about my neighbor, Doris Fineberg?" Bob asked.

"No, not yet. We assume the guy snatched her. The local cops found his rental car outside her house, and she's hours overdue for an appointment."

"From what I saw of that guy," Bob said, "Doris doesn't have a prayer."

Jack nodded, flexing his hands into fists.

CHAPTER FORTY-NINE

Vitas knew he had to do something about stopping the blood trickling from the knife wound in his leg. He knew if he lost much more blood he might pass out. He already felt woozy. The pain was the only thing keeping him conscious. The Danforth bitch had bitten him right where the raccoon had wounded him. He reached for the pistol in his holster and pulled onto the shoulder of the highway.

"Take off your scarf," Vitas growled at his passenger.

"My . . . why?" she asked, fingering the silk scarf draped around her neck.

Vitas narrowed his eyes and, for the first time, got a good look at her. She was moderately plump, but damned good looking, with green eyes and auburn-colored hair. Her clothes were expensive-looking. Her hair was coifed to perfection, and he figured she had fifty thousand dollars in jewelry on her hands and around her neck. Nice little bonus, he thought.

"Dammit! What is it with you American women?" Vitas shrieked. "You have more damn questions than sense. Ask one more fucking question and I will pull out this knife and stick it in your heart."

She shrank even further away from him, her eyes a window to the terror he knew she felt. But she did as she was told and, with shaking hands, slipped the scarf from her neck. The fabric danced in her trembling hand.

"Now reach over here and tie it around my leg, above the knife. Tight!"

She knelt on the passenger seat to loop it around his thigh and tied it as tightly as she could. Then she backed away again, cowering like an abused dog.

The flow of blood immediately began to slow. Vitas waited a minute before he put his hand on the knife handle. Then, taking a deep breath and clenching his jaws, he jerked it free. White-hot pain surged through his leg. Even with the tourniquet tied above the wound, blood spurted across the console, spraying the woman and the window behind her with a fine red mist. She screeched like a banshee.

Vitas gasped. He suddenly felt even dizzier than before, his eye losing focus. He knew he was about to lose consciousness. Balling his fist, he struck the spot from where he'd just removed the knife, sending new shock waves of pain into his brain. The pain jarred him alert.

He glanced at the woman. Her eyes looked as though they might pop out of their sockets, and her high-pitched voice made the inside of Vitas' brain feel as though it was full of broken glass. When she grabbed for the door handle, he smashed the back of his hand into her face. He felt the crunch of bone and cartilage. "Shut your damn mouth," he yelled. But she kept screaming. Vitas leaned over the console and cold-cocked her with his closed fist. Her head bounced off the window and she slumped down in her seat. He looked at the blood on his knuckles and licked his hand, enjoying the sweet taste.

Vitas put the Suburban in gear and, at the first break in traffic, floored the accelerator. Horns blared and brakes screeched while he veered from lane to lane. At the first exit, he cut across three lanes and made it to the off-ramp. Nearly passing out from the pain in his leg, he sideswiped a black Cadillac limousine and sent it careening off the ramp and into some trees. He barreled into the intersection at the bottom of the off-ramp, and took a left turn on two wheels through the red light.

He found a pay phone in the parking lot of a closed-down convenience store. No one was around. When he opened the car door and put weight on his injured leg, the pain nearly killed him. The few feet to the phone seemed like a mile.

"Hello."

"Paulus, it's me."

"I told you not to call me here. I–"

"I don't give a damn what you told me, you stupid fuck. Shut up! I need your help."

"The cops put your description all over the news," Paulus said. "They say you tried to kill two people in Bethesda and kidnapped one of their neighbors."

"Forget all that! You'll help me get out of the country – or I'll find a way to make you very sorry."

"Okay, okay, what do you want me to do?"

Vitas arranged to meet Paulus at the safehouse in Alexandria after dark. He told him to bring a first-aid kit, painkillers, and some cash.

"Where the hell am I going to get cash on Friday night?"

"You have three hours to figure it out, Tomavic. I'm sure the Embassy has a slush fund."

"What are you going to do until I meet you?"

"I need to dump some garbage."

CHAPTER FIFTY

Jack paid the cashier in the hospital cafeteria for his and Bob's coffees, then led the way toward a table. His cell phone rang just when they took their seats.

"Cole here."

"Mr. Cole, this is Tim Rutherford, the night duty officer at Langley. I've got a call here for Mr. Danforth from a Sheriff Don Mechem in Pineview, South Carolina. Do you know where I can–?"

"Hold on, Rutherford. Bob Danforth's sitting right here." Jack handed the phone to Bob. "Sheriff Mechem holding for you."

"Hello, is that you Don?"

"Hey, Bob. How's tricks?"

"Everything's fine," Bob lied.

"Good news here! We found Danny Farrell. He returned to his parents' place. One of my deputies found him."

"Was he all right?" Bob asked.

"Physically, he's fine. But he's scared shitless. He didn't seem to understand he could be arrested for assault and attempted murder. He's more frightened about what his stepfather's going to do to him."

"You said attempted murder. Did the boy's father make it?"

"Yeah! Unfortunately. He had so much alcohol in his system, he probably didn't feel any pain."

"What's going to happen to the boy?" Bob asked.

"Oh, the DA wanted me to arrest the kid. Dumbass politician! But I think I've got him convinced that would make him as popular around here as a Yankee carpetbagger would. The kid's a real hero. I made sure the word leaked he'd saved a damsel in distress."

"I appreciate the update, Don. Is there anything I can do for you?"

"It would be helpful if you could tell me how to get in touch with Miss Georgadoff. I need to take her statement about what happened and what a hero Danny is. I suspect that would go a long way in making the DA drop any thoughts about indicting the kid, once and for all. I suppose you'd prefer her writing something out to having her subpoenaed for her statement."

"I'll take care of it, Don. Thanks for everything."

"Don't mention it. My pleasure."

The cell phone rang again. Bob handed it back to Jack.

"Mr. Cole, Rutherford again. I've got the Virginia State Police Captain holding. Can I transfer him to you?"

"Put him through." Jack put his hand over the telephone speaker and whispered to Bob, "Virginia State Police. Maybe we're finally going to get some news about our boy."

"Mr. Cole?"

"This is Jack Cole."

"Mr. Cole, this is Captain Gary Woolsley. We got information on the stolen green Suburban."

Jack's pulse rate quickened.

"A green Suburban was involved in a minor accident on the 495 Loop Road. It sideswiped another car, then exited the freeway at State Road 7. A witness got the license number. It's the same vehicle we've been looking for. There were two people in the Suburban, according to several witnesses. The Fineberg woman may still be alive. At least that's what everyone here is praying for."

"I appreciate the information, Captain. Let me give you my cell number. I'd appreciate you calling me directly if you come up with anything else—no matter how inconsequential."

"Will do!"

Jack laid the cell phone on the table. "The way things are going, no point in putting this in my pocket. It would probably ring again as soon as I put it away."

"Jack," Bob said, "I've only got a minute; I need to get back to Liz. I want you to do me a favor."

"Just ask," Jack said.

Bob swallowed. He didn't like doing this, but he felt he had no choice. "It's about Michael. Miriana told us the guy who kidnapped her intends to go after my son. He threatened the same thing when he had me tied up in my bedroom. There's no doubt in my mind the man is from the Balkans. His features, his accent, even his clothes were a dead giveaway. We've got to get Michael out of there."

"Bob, I already contacted the Pentagon. They as much as said they thought I was being melodramatic when I asked them to ship Mike back to the States. However, I did get them to agree to keep him out of the field and as far south of the Macedonia/Yugoslav border as possible."

"Shit!"

CHAPTER FIFTY-ONE

As Vitas drove out of the old convenience store's parking lot, he noticed that the woman was regaining consciousness. Her head bobbed back and forth, as though moving to strains of music only she could hear. He grabbed her arm and shook her. She opened her eyes and looked at him.

"Please let me go," she pleaded.

"Maybe I will. What is your name?"

"Doris Fineberg."

"I think maybe it is a good idea to let you go, Doris."

"Really?" she said. Color began to return to her cheeks.

"That is what I said."

He turned into a wooded park-like area and stopped at a little clearing that contained a picnic table and a stone barbecue pit.

"Can I go now?" Doris pleaded, suddenly finding her voice.

"Here is the deal, Doris. I get out of the car and walk around to your side. You wait until I open the door, then you get out. You run until you no longer can see the car. I will then drive away. You walk until you find a telephone somewhere. Call your husband. Or call the police."

"No, no, I won't call the police," Doris said. "I promise." Her eyes widened in alarm.

He patted her shoulder. "Do not lie to me, Doris. Besides, it will not matter if you call the police. I will be far away by then." Vitas slid out of the car seat and walked stiffly around to the passenger side. It took him a long time. But she waited, like a stupid sheep. He opened her door and helped her out.

"Thank you," she said.

"For what? I stole your car, beat you, and scared you to death. And now I am going to kill you."

Vitas watched her mouth open in silent shock when he drove the knife blade into her stomach. He jerked it upward until it struck her sternum. She clutched his knifehand while he let her sink to the ground.

What an idiot! She could have run away, Vitas thought, grinning down at the woman. With this leg, there is no way I could have caught her. Vitas felt the slipperiness of her blood on his hand. A familiar thrill ran through him.

Two hours after nightfall, Vitas stepped from the blackness of the shuttered store's doorway and approached the car that had stopped a few meters away. He opened the car door. "Right on time," Vitas said, clumsily lowering himself into the passenger seat of Paulus' car.

"Jesus! What happened to you? There's blood all over your pants and shirt. Your hands."

"What do they say in America? All in a day's work, Paulus, all in a day's work."

The ride to the safehouse took fifteen minutes. As soon as they were inside, Vitas ordered Paulus to bring the first-aid kit into the kitchen.

Paulus knelt on the linoleum floor and raised Vitas' trouser leg. His hand shot to his mouth and he gagged.

"What's wrong, Paulus?" Vitas asked. "My wounds making you light-headed?"

"Holy shit!" Paulus said, looking down at the scabby wounds and seeping blood on Vitas' leg. "Who did this to you?" he asked, while he rose from the floor and fell into a kitchen chair.

"What difference does it make? Just clean it up."

"You need a doctor."

"I'll see a doctor when I get to Yugoslavia. Just do it!"

PART IV

1999

CHAPTER ONE

Michael entered the 82nd Airborne's Macedonian Headquarters tent, walked up to Colonel Sweeney's desk, and came to attention. "Permission to speak freely, sir," he said.

"Permission granted, Captain."

"With all due respect, Colonel, what's going on? Why doesn't my unit ever go out on patrol? Have I screwed up?"

Sweeney ran his hands over his face and then through his hair. "Sit down, Mike. No, you haven't screwed up; you're doing a great job. The reason you and your men haven't been doing patrols has nothing to do with your performance. It's because the Pentagon ordered me to keep you out of harm's way."

"I don't understand, sir."

"I don't either, Michael. Not completely, anyway. Apparently someone from the CIA called General Hightower over at the Joint Chiefs and demanded you be rotated back to the States. They worked out a compromise. You're to be kept away from the Yugoslav border. I've got no choice. Orders are orders."

Michael felt betrayed. He never would have believed his father would do such a thing. "This stinks, Colonel," he said. "What do I tell my men? Hell, what do I tell the other company commanders?"

"Nothing. You tell them absolutely nothing."

CHAPTER TWO

"Stefan, we must leave," Vanja said. She heard the fear in her own voice and regretted it. Stefan hated weakness, especially when displayed by his own family members. "The Serb Army is moving this way. It's all over the television."

Stefan turned his head and gave Vanja a blank stare. Then he looked back at the television.

Vanja stepped in front of him and knelt on the carpet. "You've been like this since you saw Miriana shot. You have to get over it. You don't know that she is dead. She could still be alive. Do you want her to learn her father just gave up, that he's a quitter? You will never know if she's alive if you let Serb goons kill you."

Vanja began to cry. She grabbed Stefan's arm and pressed her head against it. "What's wrong with you?" she wailed. "If you have no concern for your own life, don't you care anymore about us?"

Stefan looked at her again, eyes blazing now. "Shut up, woman!"

"No, I won't shut up," she screamed, her face crimson. "You've bullied me for thirty years. And still I loved you. Well, go ahead and let the Serbs kill you. Attila and I are leaving."

Vanja stood and rushed away, skirts swirling while she ran out the front door of the little, white-stuccoed house. Attila was in the yard, throwing pebbles at a tree.

"Attila, get the car," she ordered.

"Wh . . . where is *Babo*, Mama?" the teenager asked in his cracking, pubescent voice.

"He's not coming. There's nothing we can do. Now get the car."

The teenager bowed his head and stuck his hands in his pockets. "Yes, Mama," he said, before walking around the side of the house.

He looks so much like his father, Vanja thought, tears running down her cheeks. Just as tall. The same sharp features. But he's prettier. Softer. The door creaked open behind her. She whirled around, wiping her face with the sleeve of her dress. Stefan's tall, lean form filled the doorframe. Now in his seventies, he was still an imposing figure. He looked at least ten years younger than he was.

As he came toward her, Vanja turned her head to the side, expecting him to strike her. Instead, he put his arms around her and kissed her gently on the forehead. He had never done anything like that outside the privacy of their bedroom, she realized – and rarely even there.

"You've been the best woman any man could want," he said. "You've always stood by me. If you're determined to go, I'll go with you. Someone has to protect you and Attila."

Vanja smiled and pressed her body against him. Tears, now of relief, flooded her eyes. Just then, Attila drove up in the Mercedes, jerrycans of gasoline strapped to the car's roof rack. The boy stopped the car, got out, and gawked wide-eyed at his parents.

Vanja smiled. "What's wrong, boy? You've never seen a man and woman hold each other. Go help your father pack a suitcase."

The young man smiled. "Yes, Mama."

CHAPTER THREE

Eighteen-year-old Frank Murata walked around his car to the passenger side and opened the door. He tried not to be too obvious, checking out Ellen's legs when he took her hand and helped her out. Man, does she have great legs, he thought.

Sexual tension was driving him crazy. He tried to control his trembling. It was damned hot out, yet he was shaking as though it was freezing. He kept getting mixed signals from Ellen. One moment he thought she wanted to screw his brains out; the next moment he thought she might scream rape. Catholic girls, he thought. One minute they're hot for your bod, then they're thinking about what they'll have to say in confession.

Ellen Murphy was everything Frank wanted in a girlfriend: tall, blond, athletic, and funny. He was fairly sure she was still a virgin. Takes one to know one, Frank thought. Jeez! Eighteen and still as chaste as a nun.

He led the way through a stand of trees. "Watch out for the poison oak," he told Ellen, pointing at the waxy leaves of a bush on the side of the path. He knew where he wanted to go. There was a clearing just ahead. It was hidden on three sides from the road that looped through the park. It was too early in the year for many other people to be in the park. He hoped.

They'd just entered the clearing when Ellen said, "Ooh, what's that smell?"

Frank detected the odor, too. He let go of Ellen's hand. "Stay here. I'll check it out. Somebody probably dumped garbage." He followed the scent trail. It got stronger while he crossed the clearing, passed the picnic table and barbecue pit, and approached the far treeline this side of the park road. The stench was so strong now that Frank took out his handkerchief and covered his mouth and nose. "Why the hell did I have to play the big, brave man?" he murmured, when he suddenly heard scurrying sounds just ahead. His heart seemed to stop and his stomach erupted with the swirling of a million butterflies.

Something lay on the ground a few feet away. It looked white. He took another step forward and then moved to the side, out of the light from the full moon. Moonlight now shone down on the blue-white skin of a mutilated body. Pieces of clothing had been strewn around the corpse and chunks of flesh had been bitten away. Frank's stomach heaved. He turned to Ellen, but before he could say anything, he vomited down the front of his clothes.

CHAPTER FOUR

Jack entered his office waiting area and smiled at Miriana sitting in one of the chairs. Now wearing a cropped black sweater, jeans, and flat-heeled, black leather boots, she looked like any young American woman.

"You two getting along?" Jack asked, directing the question to his secretary.

She chuckled. "Just offering Miriana some hints on how to deal with you and the other macho types around here."

Jack laughed. He waved at Miriana. "Come on in; let's talk."

Once they were seated facing each other in the two easy chairs at the far side of the office, Jack looked quizzically at Miriana. "You look worried," he said.

"Have you seen news?" she said, hugging herself. "Serb Army is moving toward Kosovo. They will go through Mladenovac. Is parents' town."

"I'm aware of that. Meetings are going on at NATO right now about what kind of action we should take."

"Mr. Cole, whatever action NATO takes will be too late to help family. The Serbs know I was involved in Karadjic's abduction. They will make family pay for my treachery."

"We'll think of something, Miriana. I promise."

Miriana blew out a loud, exasperated stream of air. "Have you found man who kidnapped me? Who attacked Mr. and Mrs. Danforth?" she asked.

"Not yet. We found the neighbor woman's car. Then some kids found her body in the woods a few miles away from the car. But we haven't found him."

"You have to find him!" Miriana heard her own voice tremble.

"We're doing our best. We'll keep looking for him. I promise."

CHAPTER FIVE

Liz opened her eyes and looked around the unfamiliar room – white walls, stainless steel bed rails. A soft but steady beep-beep-beep sound distracted her. She was groggy and lost. "Bob," she whispered hoarsely.

She heard someone delicately snoring. "Bob?"

A sharp, slapping sound – a book hitting the floor? A scraping noise – a chair leg on linoleum? Then Bob brought his face into view.

"Liz, I'm here." He took her hand in both of his.

She tried to say something, but all that came out was a raspy "Wh . . .. "

Bob filled a plastic cup with water from a jug. He slipped a straw into the cup and guided it between Liz's lips. She raised her head slightly and sipped. Then she dropped her head back on the pillow.

"Where am I?"

"Bethesda Memorial Hospital."

"What happened?"

"Do you remember the man . . .?"

Liz tried to follow what Bob said. But her head pounded and the overhead lights hurt her eyes.

"You took a bad knock on the head," he said. "You've been in and out of consciousness for the past four days."

Nothing he'd said made any sense to her. She tried to force a question from her mouth, but nothing came. Her eyes closed despite her efforts to resist. She felt herself beginning to drift away.

CHAPTER SIX

Paulus Tomavic, whistling along with a melody on his car radio, was pleased he'd soon be rid of Artyan Vitas. Because of his injuries, the assassin had to stay in the U.S. longer than planned. This would be Paulus' last trip shuttling food and medicine to the madman. I'll deliver the forged documents to Vitas today, then wash my hands of him, he thought.

Traffic was light on this early Tuesday afternoon, and most of the traffic lights were working in his favor for a change. He gunned the engine when the next one switched to yellow, racing through the intersection. Checking his rearview mirror for police, he saw a tan sedan speed after him through the now red light. His stomach seemed to do a full gainer.

He diverted from his normal direct route to the Alexandria safehouse and weaved through a maze of streets. The tan sedan hung back – but it followed each of his turns. Two men sat in the front seat. "Dammit! A tail." He saw an open curbside parking space and hit the brakes hard to pull into it. He stepped from the car, walked around its front, crossed the sidewalk, and stood before a bakery's display window. He pretended to look at the breads and pastries, while he looked for the tan car's reflection. It slowly moved into a parking slot across the street.

After going into the bakery and buying a loaf of French bread he didn't really need, Paulus returned to his car and drove back toward the Embassy. He saw the same car in his mirror.

Two hours later, the vehicle gate at the Yugoslav Embassy opened to release a Lincoln Towncar. Agents Tommy Shapiro and Lee Ferguson, parked across the street in a tan Oldsmobile, craned their necks to get a view of the driver. It was a woman. They settled back in their seats. "False alarm," Shapiro said.

A minute later, an identical car exited the Embassy grounds. Again, a female driver. A third and fourth car left the compound shortly after. Male drivers. But not Paulus Tomavic. What the hell! Shapiro thought.

"Shit! We've been made," Ferguson said.

Shapiro pulled the toothpick from his mouth. "That's putting it mildly. Which one do you think Tomavic was hiding in?"

CHAPTER SEVEN

"Hi, beautiful," Bob said while pushing a wheelchair into the hospital room.

"Oh, I'm sure I look absolutely gorgeous," Liz said in a sandpapery voice. She smoothed her hair back and sat up a little straighter in bed.

Bob kissed her on the lips. "You look damn good to me."

He felt tears well in his eyes and tried to blink them back. When that didn't work, he quickly wiped them away with the palm of his hand.

"I'm fine now, Bob," Liz said, patting his arm. "Don't worry."

"Easier said than done," he said.

"I can't wait to get out of here."

"The doctor said you were ready to go home. I have your ride right here."

"Now?" Liz said gleefully. "I can leave now?"

Bob laughed. "You bet!"

A nurse came into the room. "So you're taking our favorite patient away from us," she said.

"You've all been great," Bob told her. "But you've had her for six days. Now I want her back."

"No argument from me," the nurse laughed. "But I want the privilege of wheeling Mrs. Danforth out. Besides, it's hospital policy that only a hospital employee can push a patient to freedom."

Bob walked beside the wheelchair to the CIA car parked at the hospital's front entrance. He nodded at the CIA agent/driver standing next to it. He kept his hand near the grip of the pistol in his shoulder holster until Liz was safely buckled into the backseat, he'd gone around to the other side and climbed in next to her, and the CIA man had pulled away from the curb.

CHAPTER EIGHT

Paulus looked at Vitas stretched out on the couch. The assassin's chest heaved and an animal-like rumble resonated from within it. His normal ruddy complexion now looked red – as though his face was on fire. The room stank with sour perspiration and . . . something else. Paulus couldn't place the odor. He knew he never would have been able to enter the safehouse and walk up to the man without being observed if Vitas were not sick. Thank God he would be leaving today – before he died on him.

Vitas jerked alert and sat up when Paulus touched his shoulder. "What the fuck!" he shouted.

"It's time for you to go. The plane is ready at the airport."

"About time," Vitas said. "Four days holed up in this fucking place."

Paulus almost corrected the man. He'd been there six days. But he decided to let it go. "You know we couldn't risk putting you on the streets with hundreds of policemen, the FBI, and the CIA looking for you."

"Yeah, yeah. What now?"

"I have a private plane, a Gulf Stream, waiting for you in West Virginia. About a five-hour drive. It will take you to Juarez, Mexico. From there the plane will fly you to Mexico City, then Madrid, and finally to Belgrade."

"All right, I'm ready," Vitas said, struggling to get off the couch. He favored his injured leg. He followed Paulus out into the night and got in the back of the Embassy man's sedan. He opened the back door and stretched out on the seat.

Paulus looked back over the front seat at Vitas. The man had already fallen asleep. He cranked up the air conditioner and opened the front windows. The stench of the man was overpowering. He was no doctor, but Paulus had guessed days ago that Vitas' leg had become infected. It was damn lucky he'd been able to hire a private jet, Paulus thought; no commercial airline would have let the man board one of their planes.

CHAPTER NINE

From Mladenovac, Stefan, Vanja, and Attila crossed the Morava River on one of the few bridges that NATO air assaults had left standing. It had taken them two days to travel the first three hundred kilometers. Refugees packed the roads and they'd had to stop on several occasions to allow the car's engine to cool off.

"These goddam peasants don't have the sense to get out of the way," Stefan yelled for the hundredth time, while hitting the brakes to avoid running over an old man limping along on crutches.

Vanja patted Stefan's arm. "Be patient, my husband," she said.

Stefan heaved a massive sigh and clenched his teeth in frustration, while he slowly drove the car ahead.

Passing through Serb town after Serb town, they saw little evidence of the war with NATO – other than the refugees from the north and from Kosovo Province straggling along the road. Buildings were undamaged; people seemed to be performing their normal activities. Life in the small towns and villages of Serbia appeared to be unchanged. Most of the bombing attacks, Stefan knew, had centered in and around the larger metropolitan areas and on the bridges.

When they approached Surdulica, just east of the southern part of Kosovo Province, the number of refugees increased to a swarm. Stefan identified ethnic Albanians, Gypsies, Bosnians, and even Bulgarians. There were also a myriad of other people whose clothing or features didn't make them easily identifiable. It took Stefan another two days to drive the last thirty kilometers from Surdulica to a point just north of the Macedonian border. Most of the refugees were on foot. Only a few traveled in trucks, cars, or even tractors. Stefan saw there were very few young men among the refugees. The Serbs must have found them, or they are fighting in the mountains, he thought. His car moved slowly, only as fast as the walking refugees moved. In Preshevo, almost at the Macedonian border, the mass of people came to a virtual stop.

Stefan got out of the car and approached a bedraggled old man.

"What's going on?" he asked. "Why isn't the traffic moving?"

The man just hunched his shoulders and turned away. Stefan grabbed an old woman by the arm.

"Do you know what lies ahead?" he asked her.

She shook her arm free. "Have you seen my Marika?" she asked plaintively. "The soldiers took her. Have you seen my Marika?"

Stefan shrugged and walked back to the car. No one seemed to know what was happening.

"Attila, move the car over to those trees where it will be cooler," he said. "And see if you can scrounge up some petrol. We're down to our last can. Vanja, get out the tent and set it up. We could be here awhile."

While Vanja and Attila worked to set up camp, Stefan circulated among the refugees. He listened to their tales of dispossession, murder, rape, and mayhem. An idea suddenly struck him. He walked back to their campsite and sat down with Vanja and Attila.

"Somehow I will scrounge up some writing paper," he told them. "We will interview as many of these people as possible. Since I speak Albanian, I will ask the questions and then translate their answers into Roma. Both of you will write it all down. We will record all we can on the atrocities perpetrated by the Serbs."

"What will we do with all of this information, O Babo?" Attila asked.

"NATO and the international relief agencies will kiss our feet if we can give them lots of eyewitness accounts of Serb atrocities."

"Do you hate the Serbs so much, O Babo?" Attila asked.

I don't hate anyone, and then again I hate everyone, Stefan thought. "That's not the point, Attila," he said.

CHAPTER TEN

Michael felt useless and alienated from the rest of the 82nd Airborne's units. His men resented the incessant kidding from the soldiers of other companies. They'd been relegated to performing administrative duties, doing KP, and pulling guard duty. The rumor was sweeping through camp that the battalion commander didn't have confidence in Captain Danforth.

"Captain Danforth," a voice called.

He turned and saw one of his men striding toward him. "What is it, Cox?"

"Colonel Sweeney's looking for you," Cox said breathlessly. "He wants you at headquarters right away."

Michael fast-walked to headquarters.

"Captain Danforth, this is Mr. Maxwell Hunter of the International Red Cross," Sweeney said after Michael reported. "He's got a problem, so we have a problem. Mr. Hunter, why don't you explain the situation?"

Hunter stood and put his finger on a map on an easel. "Here's our location," he said. He moved the finger to the right. "Over here we've got thirty thousand refugees along five miles of road. Some have been camped along here for days, with no sanitary facilities or medical supplies. The only food and water is whatever they brought with them. If we don't do something to relieve the pressure, we'll find ourselves in the middle of a typhoid or cholera epidemic, not to mention wholesale starvation. I'm sure the Serbs would love telling the world about the thousands of people who died because they fled their perfectly safe homes and found nothing but sickness and starvation in NATO's hands."

"So, what can we do?" Michael asked.

"That's where you come in, Mike," Colonel Sweeney said. "Your company will ride shotgun with the relief convoy we're sending in."

"Yes, sir," Michael said enthusiastically. Finally! he thought.

"I want you on the road at 0400 hours tomorrow."

"Yes, sir," Michael said again.

Hunter walked out and Michael started to follow.

"Hold a second, Mike." Sweeney leaned his chair back on two legs. He clasped his hands behind his head. "I'm sure you noticed the location Hunter pointed out – Preshevo – is right on the Serb border. There's been sniper activity all along there."

Michael nodded.

"You're the last company commander I've got who's not already on a mission. I don't feel I can wait for one of them to return. The condition of the refugees worsens with each passing hour. We've got to help those people. That's why we're here."

"I understand, sir."

"Be careful, Mike. If you get hurt, my career is over."

CHAPTER ELEVEN

His escape route out of the United States would have been trying even for someone in excellent health. West Virginia, then Mexico, Spain, and finally Belgrade. But Vitas realized he was in far from excellent shape. His fever would spike, then the chills would start, and then he'd feel the fever again. He stumbled on the tarmac at the small airstrip outside Belgrade. One of the pilots on his private aircraft caught his arm.

Vitas grunted at the man, pulled his arm free, and walked unsteadily toward the square block building that served as the flight center. Got to get some rest, he thought. But first I need to see a doctor. This leg is killing me. He limped into the building and slowly made his way across a cracked tile floor toward the exit door on the opposite side. He had been here before and knew the structure was no more than ten meters across, but the walk to the exit door felt like a journey through a tunnel with no end.

"Artyan! Over here."

Vitas looked around, trying to find who had called his name. There were only three people in the building, but their faces blurred as though seen through a distorted lens. It wasn't until Luka, the President's driver, slapped him on the back that Vitas recognized him.

"What are you doing here, Luka?" Vitas asked. "Some bigwig flying in?"

"No one bigger than you, Artyan. The President sent me to pick you up."

"How the hell . . .?"

"Our Washington Embassy told us you would be on that plane." He jerked a thumb toward the Gulf Stream resting on the tarmac. "I'm your welcoming committee."

"Luka, I never thought I'd be happy to see your ugly face. Where's your car? You must take me to a doctor."

"What's wrong?" Luka asked.

"I'll have to wait for the doctor to tell me."

Vitas couldn't keep up. Luka had to keep stopping to wait for him.

"You look like crap," Luka said. "Why are you limping?"

"It's a long story, my friend," Vitas said, not offering any further explanation.

Luka shrugged.

Vitas followed him through the terminal doors and slid into the front seat of the bulletproof sedan parked at the curb.

"You have a doctor you want to see or will the President's physician do?"

"Sounds fine."

Vitas closed his eyes and pressed the side of his face against the car window. The glass cooled his cheek. While they drove along Belgrade's rutted roads, the only sounds were the thump-thump-thump of the tires.

How do I tell the President I failed? Vitas thought. A spasm of pain suddenly shot into his thigh, and he rubbed the swollen area around the wound, noticing that his pant leg was damp. "That Danforth bitch," he murmured.

"What was that?" Luka asked, taking his eyes off the road for a moment.

"Nothing!" Vitas said, bringing his hands to his face and rubbing his weary eyes.

"That stink? What is it?" Luka asked, wrinkling his nose.

Vitas ignored the question. That's one of the reasons he needed to see a doctor. He'd noticed the odor coming from the wounds in his leg for the past three days.

CHAPTER TWELVE

The sun's upper edge peeked over the eastern hills. Michael got his first real look at one of the results of the Serb government's ethnic cleansing campaign. Thousands of people spread before him in a valley bisected by the road. Their crying and wailing sounded like thousands of bleating lambs. Gaunt, dirty, and dispirited, possessing only what they could carry, they formed a human river from one end of the valley to the other, waiting to be processed through to an uncertain future in Macedonia.

Michael ordered the supply vehicles to line up in a muddy field fifty yards off the road. He split his unit into four-man teams, with each team guarding one of the twenty two-and-a-half-ton trucks. He anticipated a riot when the starving refugees discovered food, water, medicine, and other supplies had arrived. But they surprised him by queuing up in an orderly manner.

After each truck was emptied, it returned with its guards to headquarters to be reloaded.

As the sun rose higher, the temperature grew so hot that he told his men to shed their fatigue blouses. He shed his blouse as well. He looked at the refugees' faces while they waited for food and water. Their expressions didn't change at all, even when they received supplies. Michael realized he was staring at despair.

"Let me through. I must see the American officer."

The strident yell reached Michael where he stood in the back of a truck. He saw two of his soldiers holding an elderly man by the arms. He looked at Hunter, the Red Cross representative, and said, "I'm going to find out what the commotion's all about. Be right back." He jumped down from the back of the truck and walked over to his two soldiers and the man they'd detained.

"What do you want?" Michael asked the elderly man.

"I have important information. But I will only give it to an American officer."

"Search him," Michael ordered.

"He's clean, sir."

"Okay, let him go."

"Are you an officer?" the man asked, looking at Michael's olive drab T-shirt.

"Yes," Michael answered. "A Captain, United States Army."

"Can we talk away from the others?"

Michael followed the man for a few yards. "This is far enough. What do you want?"

"What would you say if I told you I had two hundred pages of signed eyewitness accounts of atrocities committed by the Serbs?"

"I'd say I would take you to my superior officer and let him deal with it. But first, who are you?"

"Stefan Radko."

Michael felt a sudden excitement rush through him. "How do you spell your last name?"

"R-A-D-K-O. Radko."

"Do you have a daughter named Miriana?" Michael asked.

Stefan's eyes widened with astonishment. "How do you know my daughter's name?"

"We met in the United States. Are her mother and brother with you here?"

"She is alive? Miriana is alive?"

Michael smiled. "Yes, she's very much alive."

"Where is she? Is she well?"

"She's in the Washington, D.C. area. And, yes, she is quite well."

"How can we see her? We must find a way—"

"I'll take you to someone who knows about those things," Michael said. "You can discuss it with my commander when you hand over the information you said you have."

Radko nodded.

Michael watched the man's eyes narrow. A cunning, almost feral look came over his face. "There is a price for my information," Radko said.

Michael remembered Miriana had said her father was a sonofabitch. Now he decided to see how big an SOB he really was.

"I'm a soldier, not a deal maker," he said.

"It is not money I want," Stefan replied, a hint of impatience in his tone. "I want my family taken away from here. And I do not mean put into a refugee camp. I want us to be taken to America and reunited with Miriana. That is my price."

"Where's the rest of your family?"

"About a mile north of here."

Michael paused for a moment. Then he told Radko to wait, and walked back to the truck where Hunter distributed supplies to refugees. He pulled the Red Cross leader aside. "I need to go up the road. Why don't you come with me? We'll bring one of the loaded trucks along. Could take a little pressure off this site."

"Okay," Hunter said. "Give me a minute to tell one of my people."

While Michael waited for Hunter to return, he looked up at the soldier standing in the truck's cargo bay, rifle slung over his shoulder. "Kennedy, toss my fatigue shirt down here."

"Sure thing, Captain," the soldier said, reaching for Michael's shirt and tossing it down to him.

When Michael had it on and buttoned, he walked back toward Radko. He thought about Colonel Sweeney's warning, but he figured that as long as he didn't actually cross over into Serbia, he'd be okay.

"Are you ready, Mr. Radko?"

Instead of answering, Stefan gaped at Michael. He seemed to be staring at Michael's fatigue shirt. At the name strip sewn over the pocket.

CHAPTER THIRTEEN

"Well, well, you have come back to us, Artyan. What has happened to you? You look *siv*. Are you not feeling well? Please sit."

Vitas glanced around the President's large office, with its Oriental carpet and expensive-looking furniture. He sat in a leather chair across the desk from the President and thought about how nice it must be to give orders to others who have to do the dirty work.

"I feel as gray as I look, Mr. President," Vitas said, in a slow, weak voice.

"Can I offer you some tea?"

"*Da, molim.* I would appreciate it."

The President nodded to an aide who immediately left the office to fetch it.

"Luka tells me he took you to my doctor yesterday. What did that quack say?" the President said in a solicitous tone.

"Oh, you know doctors! He took some blood and said he would have tests done. He insists I have an infection of some sort. He gave me a shot and some salve to put on my leg."

"Good! You must do whatever the doctor tells you to do. He has always kept me healthy and strong."

"Yes, sir."

The President looked at him sternly and suddenly changed his tone. "What do you have to report from America?"

Vitas gulped. "I found the Gypsy girl in the United States and questioned her," he said. "She never implicated any others in the General's kidnapping."

"What was the Gypsy girl doing in America?"

"The CIA had her under protective custody."

"Bastards! What did you do with the Gypsy girl?" the President asked, a leer on his face.

Vitas opened his mouth to answer, but the aide returned carrying a brass tray. While the aide place two glasses of tea on the desk, the President paced the room, his hands clasped behind his back. By the time the aide left, Vitas had decided to tell the truth – with only a few embellishments.

"Well," the President said, "what about the Gypsy?"

"She escaped."

The President's eyes became slits, boring into Vitas. "She's alive?"

"Yes, Mr. President. But–"

"No buts, Vitas," the President boomed. "What about the man who planned the kidnapping?"

Vitas hung his head like a shamed schoolboy. "I had him – Robert Danforth. His wife, too. Tied up in their home. I was about to kill them. But a CIA assault team stormed the house. I had to leave them." He glanced at the President, hoping to see some sign of understanding.

The President's face reddened. Vitas thought the man's eyes might pop out of his skull.

"Twice you failed me," the President roared. "You didn't kill the girl. You didn't kill this man Danforth. I asked you to bring me vengeance, and all you've brought is excuses!"

Vitas swallowed. The next few moments would decide his fate. "I had to get out of there. Otherwise, I wouldn't have been able to tell you the best news. You can exact revenge in a way worse than death for the Gypsy girl and Danforth."

The President looked skeptical. "There's nothing worse than dying," he said.

Vitas knew that to be false. He had put many victims through pain so severe they begged for their own deaths. But he didn't think this was the time or place to debate the point. "Yes, Mr. President," he said. "Except for one thing: the vicious murder of a loved one. You see, the Danforths's son and the Gypsy girl's lover are one and the same man. He is an American soldier. The American press has reported that his unit, part of the 82nd Airborne, is with NATO forces in Macedonia right on our border."

A light seemed to go on behind the President's eyes. His complexion lost some of its lurid redness. "Who exactly is this man?"

Vitas surpressed a smile. "Michael Danforth, an Army Captain."

"You aren't making this up, Vitas?" the President asked suspiciously.

"No, Mr. President. It's the truth."

"So what do you propose doing?"

"Excuse me if I am being presumptuous, Mr. President. But I suggest you send a SPETSNAZ unit to snatch young Danforth. We will claim we found him on Yugoslav soil, then execute him as a spy."

The President put his hands to his head and rubbed his temples with his fingers. He was silent for a moment. Then he said, "I have a better idea. Why just kill him? We'll kidnap him and let his parents and the girl know that we have him and that he's being tortured. But officially we'll deny it. We can make them suffer forever."

CHAPTER FOURTEEN

Bob and Liz sat at their backyard patio table on one of those rare summer days in Bethesda when the humidity drops below seventy percent and a cool breeze takes the edge off the heat. There were glasses of chilled white wine, untouched, on the table. Cuts and bruises still showed on Liz's face. Bob knew that his own face also bore signs of the madman's attack. It broke his heart that Liz had not undressed in front of him in the two days since coming home from the hospital. He knew she wouldn't until the thin line the madman had drawn on her body with his switchblade had completely healed. She saw it as a mark of shame. That the man had seen her naked. That he had violated her in a way she never would have imagined. He wanted to tell her that the line was a badge of courage, a testament to her bravery. It just wasn't the time.

"How do you feel about accepting the Randells' dinner invitation?" Bob asked, forcing cheeriness he didn't really feel into his voice. "Sounded like they were really looking forward to seeing us."

Liz looked down at her hands, as though she was inspecting them for some stray speck of dirt. She slowly shook her head. "I don't think so. I've got so many things to do around the house. You know."

Bob reached across the table and covered her hands with his own. "Whatever you say, honey," he said.

Liz looked up, smiled, and then dropped her gaze again.

Bob felt rage bubble within him. It was becoming a more familiar feeling with each passing day. Find the sonofabitch, he silently prayed. Find this man named Vitas.

CHAPTER FIFTEEN

Stefan sat between Michael and the driver. The deuce-and-a-half slowly bounced down the rutted, refugee-clogged road. Hunter and four armed paratroopers stood in the supply-crowded cargo bay. The truck worked its way against a southward creeping human tide.

"How much further, Mr. Radko?" Michael asked.

Stefan didn't answer. He wasn't paying attention. How can it be? he thought. Impossible! Danforth! Gregorie's murderer. Now his son is here.

Michael repeated his question.

"What! Oh! It's just around the bend in the road. You will see an old, gray Mercedes on the right side."

"How'd you get a car this far south? The roads must have been crammed with people."

"We just drove at their pace most of the time. There is the car up ahead," Stefan pointed. "That is as far as we got before the traffic stopped completely."

Michael shielded his eyes from the sun's glare. The road and the fields on each side were wall-to-wall people. A woman and a teenaged boy stood next to the Mercedes, parked in the shade of a large tree. While the truck edged forward, hundreds of refugees rose from the ground and began to move toward it.

"Don't stop," Michael told the driver. "Pull over to the middle of that pasture." He turned to Radko. "As soon as we stop, go to your family and get them in your car. The road will clear a little when people crowd around the truck. When the truck is empty, I want you to follow it back out of here. I'll be riding with you."

"I do not want to just go back to that place where we met," Stefan said. "I want my family taken all the way to your headquarters, and then out of Macedonia as soon as possible."

"Those papers you say you have better be damn good if you expect tickets to the United States."

"They are damn good!" Stefan said.

"Why don't you let me take a look at them?" Michael suggested."

"And then maybe you will tell me how you know my daughter's name?"

"Fair enough," Michael agreed.

As soon as the truck came to a halt, Michael followed Radko out of the cab. While Radko walked toward his car, Michael ran to the back of the truck.

"Stay in the truck," he ordered his men. "Let them see your weapons. We don't need a riot."

He climbed into the truck to join his men, while Hunter began to address the milling, murmuring crowd in Albanian.

"Your attention, please." Hunter waited for his words to be passed back to those who were too far away to hear, and then he waited for the crowd to quiet. "We have food and water, and some medicine." Another wait for the message to be carried to the rear of the crowd. "If you will line up, we will pass out what we have. There is not enough for all of you, but—"

The sound of several thousand voices rose in complaint, and the sound grew when Hunter's words traveled through the crowd.

Hunter raised his arms for quiet. It took over a minute for the din to calm. "There are twenty trucks just like this one distributing supplies one and a half kilometers from here. Those of you who are strong enough to walk should go there. Please let children, the old, and the sick get through to us here."

The sounds of complaints rose again, but many of those in front moved aside to allow the weaker people to come forward.

"Amazing," Michael told Hunter. "Even after all they've been through, they still behave in a civilized fashion."

"I've seen the same thing everywhere I've gone since coming over here," Hunter said.

Michael just shook his head and jumped down from the truck.

CHAPTER SIXTEEN

General Dimitri Plodic handpicked the five-man Serb Army Special Forces team to infiltrate Macedonia. The Serb Special Forces had been modeled after the Russian SPETSNAZ. Like the American Green Berets and the SEALs, the SPETSNAZ troops were the best and the brightest of the Russian military forces. They were paramilitary forces that could operate in almost any situation, no matter how extreme. All the men he selected were at least bilingual in Serbo-Croatian and Albanian. A couple also knew English. And each had years of combat experience and other qualities Plodic valued: a pathological need for action, fearlessness, and no conscience. The fact that a couple of the men were borderline psychopaths only served Plodic's purposes.

The Serb Intelligence Agency provided each man with false ID and a fabricated personal history. Plodic told them not to shave, to look more like civilians, like refugees. They were to pass as Bosnian Muslims. The General personally explained the mission to the team's leader, Captain Mikhail Sokic, making his options clear: Succeed and be national heroes, fail and . . .. He left the alternative to Sokic's imagination.

"Captain Sokic, you have three weeks to prepare your men," Plodic said. "Intelligence Service personnel are available to you at any time. Use them! I want you to know everything about the Kumanovo area and about the 82nd Airborne Division – its location in Macedonia, its mission, its weaponry. Everything."

"Yes, General Plodic. We will do our best," Sokic barked.

"I hope so, Captain. The President wants this American officer brought to him. My career and yours are on the line."

CHAPTER SEVENTEEN

The day had been filled with budget meetings, which had strained Bob's patience more than usual. He thought more than once that, perhaps, he had come to the moment when he should put in his papers. At least that's what Liz wanted him to do. Retire. He'd thought a lot about changing careers — maybe go into teaching at the university level.

He breezed through the outer office, gave a half-hearted wave to his secretary, and walked into his office. He dropped into his chair and noticed an envelope lying on the middle of the blotter. He noticed the APO return address and Michael's familiar scrawl. Thank God! A letter, finally. He checked the date. It had been sent just five days earlier. Tearing the end of the envelope open and extracting the single sheet of paper, he walked to a window while standing in a ray of sunshine.

Dear Dad:

This is addressed to you alone because I have to get something off my chest. You can't imagine how angry and disappointed I am that you would interfere with my assignment and my career. The embarrassment and humiliation you have caused me is unbelievable. While every other company commander has led missions into the hills along the border to sweep them clean of Serb units, I've been kept behind the lines. While other companies do their jobs, mine stays in the headquarters area, safe and sound. And why? Because I have connections. Because my father has pull.

Never in my life would I have expected you to do something like this. I found out that someone at the CIA contacted the Pentagon about me. I must assume it was you.

Butt out, Dad! This is my life. Give me a chance to live it.

The letter was signed "Michael." No "Love" or "Your son."

CHAPTER EIGHTEEN

Michael got in the front seat of the Mercedes, next to Stefan's son. Stefan, seated behind the teenager, said, "Captain, this is my wife, Vanja, and my son, Attila."

Michael turned to look at Vanja and said, "Hello." The woman smiled and tipped her head in return.

As Attila pulled away from the side of the road and followed the U.S. Army truck, Stefan said, "Vanja, this is Captain Michael Danforth."

"It's nice to meet you," Michael said, noticing the woman's jaw drop and her eyes widen while she stared at him. She looked over at Stefan. Michael thought he detected nervousness in her expression. But he remembered Stefan reacted the same way when he saw his nametag. Maybe *Danforth* is a dirty word in their language, Michael thought.

Michael shifted his gaze to Stefan. "Now would be a good time to see your log, Mr. Radko," he said.

"Go ahead, Vanja. Show him what you wrote down," Stefan ordered.

Michael looked back at Vanja and watched her pull three thick sheaves of paper tied with ribbon from a large straw bag. Placing them on her lap, she took the top packet, reached out, and handed it to Michael. He untied the ribbons, removed a blank cover sheet, and noticed the handwritten words on the next sheet. "What language is this?" he asked.

"Roma," Vanja said. "The Gypsy language."

"How am I supposed to understand this?"

"You are not, unless you can read Roma," Stefan said sarcastically.

"So these could be love letters, for all I know?"

"Captain Danforth, you will just have to take our word for it," Stefan said. "Every one of those sheets of paper is a separate eyewitness account of a crime committed by one or more Serbs against a Kosovar Albanian, Bosnian, or Gypsy."

Michael again wondered, Can I trust someone whose own daughter describes him as a sonofabitch?

"Now that I have delivered what I promised, tell me how you know Miriana."

Michael swung around in his seat again and looked back at Stefan. Before he could respond, Vanja yelled something in a high-pitched voice and a language Michael didn't understand.

In a paternalistic tone, Stefan, using English, told her, "Now, now, dear. You must not be rude. English please."

"He knows Miriana?" Vanja cried, now staring at Michael. "How? Is she all right? Where is she?" She looked back at Stefan. "Why did you not say something earlier?"

Stefan patted her hand. "Give him a chance to answer." He had a smug look on his face.

Michael turned away from Stefan and looked once again at Vanja. Her face was etched with anticipation. Her hands were finger-laced together against her chest as though in prayer. Stefan moved across the seat, coming closer to Vanja and put his arm around her. But he was staring at Michael, slit-eyed, somehow triumphant. Miriana has her mother's eyes and nose, he thought, and her father's cheekbones and hair color. But her complexion fell somewhere in between her mother's fair skin and her father's dark coloring.

"Miriana's well," he said. "I don't know the whole story, but my father had something to do with getting her to the United States. She'd helped him with some assignment."

"She is okay . . .?" Vanja's voice broke.

"She's great," Michael said, seeing immediate relief spread across her face.

"Assignment?" Stefan demanded in a sharp voice. "What business is your father in now?"

Michael thought Radko's use of the word "now" was odd, but he brushed it off. "He's a . . . consultant," Michael said. "Anyway, I met Miriana at a party. She told me her last name is Georgadoff. If she hadn't told me your name, Mr. Radko, I wouldn't have made the connection."

Michael noticed a suspicious look in the man's eyes, a look that said he doubted Michael had told them everything.

Michael told Attila to park the car in front of a communications tent fifty yards off the road.

"Wait here," Michael said. "I'll be right back."

He stepped inside the tent and over to a Sergeant seated in front of a radio. "Sergeant, see if you can raise Colonel Sweeney for me."

"Yes, sir. This may take a minute, Captain. Where will you be?"

"Right here, Sergeant, waiting impatiently."

"Gotcha, sir."

"I am confused, Stefan," Vanja said, while the Radkos waited in the Mercedes outside the American tent. "Is the American officer who I think he is? Can that be possible?"

"The Americans have a saying: It is a small world." He smiled, but there was no joy in it. "Yes, he is exactly who you think he is." Yes, my wife, Stefan thought. And his father is the man who killed my son, Gregorie. The man who could have caused the death of our beloved daughter. And now his son *knows* Miriana. That look in his eyes when he says her name!

"*Babo*, Mama, what are you talking about?" Attila asked.

"Shut up!" Stefan growled.

Colonel Sweeney paced the wood floor of his command tent at the 82nd's base camp. He slapped the easel-mounted map and said to his operations chief, "Chuck, we got units covering a thousand square miles trying to assist the refugees. We can't spread our men out like that. I want our people in platoon-sized units. Nothing smaller. Get–." The phone on his desk rang. He leaped to answer it and barked, "Sweeney."

"Colonel, it's Captain Danforth. I've got an interesting situation here. I think you need to meet some people I ran into."

"What kind of situation?"

"One with political implications, sir. I'd rather not discuss it over the radio."

"Okay, Mike. Bring them in." Sweeney cut the connection. Now what? He thought. But his phone rang again with yet another problem, and he quickly put Danforth's comments in the recesses of his mind.

An hour later, Sweeney felt his pulse accelerate while Michael described what was allegedly written on the pile of papers lying on his desk. He tried to keep his excitement from showing on his face, but he couldn't keep his hands from trembling. He noticed the man named Radko standing on the other side of his desk staring at his hands and quickly moved them under his desk.

Sweeney stared at Radko and the woman and teenaged boy standing with him. "I can't read Roma," he said. "How can I know these papers are what you claim them to be?"

"There are several hundred Gypsies caught up in the mass of people on the road north of here," Stefan said. "Pull any one of them out at random and let him translate the papers. As for their authenticity, every one of the people we interviewed is also out on that road. Your men can find them – every refugee is being registered by name and village. The names of those we interviewed are in those pages. When you find them – in a week, or month, or so – they will verify the information in their statements. Every word we wrote down is true. It would take weeks for you to duplicate what we have already done. The International War Crimes Tribunal would love to get these documents. We can get more statements than these. Why not put us to work? We know and understand these people. We can get more out of them than your NATO clerks safe in their little offices would ever be able to get."

"Whoa, slow down," Sweeney said. The Colonel sat quietly in thought for a moment. "Mr. Radko, I'm going to do exactly as you suggest. If what you say is true, you and your family can be a big help to us."

He turned to Michael. "Captain Danforth, take the Radkos to the processing center. Move them to the head of the line. Once they're registered, see they receive housing. Assign one of your men to help them get settled."

CHAPTER NINETEEN

Jack looked around the BOQ room at Andrews Air Force Base and, for the first time, really noticed the stark furnishings of the place: vinyl-clad furniture, a throw rug over the linoleum-covered floor, and no pictures on the wall. This was no place for a beautiful young woman to spend her time. As soon as Miriana's safety was no longer an issue, he would have to help her find an apartment.

"We've finished debriefing you, Miriana," Jack Cole said. "Now we need to make arrangements for your future. Get you a job. Find a place for you to live. As soon as we are sure this Vitas character is gone."

"Mr. Cole, I cannot think about future until I know family is safe."

"We tried to find them in Mladenovac, but the neighbors said they left days ago. They could be anywhere."

"The Serbs will hunt them same as me. They will assume my parents were involved with Karadjic's kidnapping. You must get them out of Yugoslavia," she said. Jack noticed that her fingernails were bitten to the quick.

"Miriana, we'll do all we can, but I can't promise." She had dark circles under her eyes, and her clothes hung on her because she'd lost weight. He tried to change the subject. "What do you plan to do with the money?"

"Nothing! Money is to help family. When I am with them I will think about money."

"Miriana, there's one thing we have to do. You can't stay here forever. We need to relocate you, get you out in the real world."

"I think I would like talk to Mr. and Mrs. Danforth," Miriana said. "I want to ask advice."

"Okay, Miriana, I'll set it up." Jack walked out of the room and nodded at the guard sitting in the hall. He wondered what the odds were that the members of her family were still alive.

He slid behind the wheel and started the engine. The dashboard clock read six-forty-five p.m. Tromping on the accelerator, ignoring the posted fifteen mile per hour speed limit, he traversed the base and drove toward Washington, D.C. He picked up his cell phone and punched in Bob Danforth's office number. When no one answered, he tried the house.

"Hello!"

"Hi, Liz. It's Jack."

"He just got home, but he's in the shower, Jack. Can I give him a message?"

"How do you know I'm not calling to talk to you, gorgeous?"

"In the twenty years I've known you, how often have you called just to talk to little old me?"

Jack chuckled. "All right, Liz, you got me. Actually, I'm calling for you as much as for Bob. I just left Miriana Georgadoff at Andrews. We're about to relocate her somewhere outside the beltway. She wants to ask you two for advice."

"We'd love to see her! In fact, why don't you bring her here Saturday afternoon? We'll put some steaks on the grill."

"Liz, I'd like that, but I've got to catch a flight to the Balkans. I've got to sit in on the meetings between NATO and the Serbs. But I could have one of my people drive her over. He can watch the street while you visit with Miriana, and take her back to the base afterwards."

"Great! I'll let Bob know."

"Thanks, Liz."

CHAPTER TWENTY

Captain Sokic led his four men up the rocky Serbian hillside, setting a blistering pace. They'd all pushed the envelope during the past week, honing their physical condition, and today had been no exception. Their packs loaded with fifty pounds of sand, they'd already run ten miles. Scaling this cliff face would put them on the mesa above their base camp. From the top of the mesa they would run two miles to their barracks.

Sokic rehashed his plan while he dug his boots into spaces between the rocks. Like a chess player, he wanted to anticipate every contingency. Not only because he and his men would soon put themselves in jeopardy. But also because he knew General Plodic would question him, to be certain they were all prepared.

I still have two weeks before we execute the mission, he thought. By then my men will be ready. He would tirelessly train his unit. They would know what to expect from the Americans. They would be perfect imitations of Bosnian refugees.

Sokic already knew everything about Captain Michael Danforth's background and training. The Serb Intelligence Service had done its job well. He knew where Danforth had gone to school. What special training he'd had. Even what his grades were. Danforth was a highly trained combat soldier, but Sokic felt confident the man would be no match for his SPETSNAZ team. He and his men would succeed. And if they had the opportunity to kill a few Americans, maybe even some Albanian or Bosnian dogs along the way, so much the better.

CHAPTER TWENTY-ONE

Michael and another officer, Captain Khalid Ibrahim, from the Germantown section of Philadelphia, left the 82nd's base camp at 9 a.m., drove the mile to the refugee camp where they picked up the most current camp census, and then went twenty miles to Kumanovo. NATO military officers who had been working in the field with the refugees had been ordered to Kumanovo to brief NATO Headquarters representatives on their observations. The meeting lasted two hours and broke up at noon.

"What say we grab a bite here in town?" Khalid said when they walked out of the NATO offices.

"What's the matter, Khalid, tired of Army rations?"

"In a word, yes!"

"Me too," Michael said. He laughed and slapped Khalid on the back. "I hear there's a great place a couple blocks from here that serves Middle Eastern food. The owner of the place, like most of the people around the area, is probably Muslim. When he hears your name he'll treat you like a long-lost relative."

"I doubt he has any relatives of the African persuasion. And what, with my luck, if the guy is an orthodox Christian – not Muslim. He'll poison my food. So, do me a favor and keep your trap shut."

Now behind the wheel of the Jeep, Michael laughed while he drove through the narrow Kumanovo streets, until he found the Sultan Restaurant. Parking across the street, he followed Khalid onto the restaurant patio and sat opposite his friend at an outdoor table under a grape arbor.

"These places are all beginning to look the same to me," Khalid said. "Same small, square wooden tables and narrow cane chairs. Uneven brick floors on a sand base. Plastic flowers on red and white oil cloth-covered tables."

"Well, excuse me, Khalid. Maybe we should just go back to the base and eat in the mess hall."

"Asshole!" Khalid laughed. "I was about to say how much I love these quaint southern European restaurants."

As they sat talking, Michael noticed a phone booth across the street.

"I wonder how my folks would feel about a collect call from Macedonia?"

"Why, they'd consider you the most thoughtful, loving son in the world," Khalid said.

Michael smiled. "As usual, Khalid, you are a wise and thoughtful friend, and a fine student of human nature. You've made me realize I'd be a real bastard if I didn't pick up the phone and call home – collect."

He crossed the street and dialed the operator. In three minutes, he heard his father's deep voice, "Yes, yes, I'll accept the charges! Michael, Michael, can you hear me? Are you okay? It's four o'clock in the morning."

"Oh, Jesus, Dad. I didn't even think about the time difference."

"No, no. Don't worry about that. Are you all right?"

"I'm fine."

"I got your letter, Michael," Bob said.

Damn! Michael thought. I wish I hadn't sent it while I was still angry with Dad. "I'm sorry about the tone of the letter, Dad. But I was pretty steamed at the time."

Liz's voice suddenly came over the line. "Hi, I'm on the extension. What are you two talking about?"

"Honey, if you wouldn't mind, could you give Michael and me a moment?"

Michael heard silence. He knew his mother wouldn't like getting off the phone one bit.

"We'll only be a minute. Then you can get back on again," Bob said.

Michael heard his mother replace the receiver in its cradle a little more forcefully than necessary. "You're in for a tense evening, Dad."

"You don't know the half of it. Listen, I didn't tell your mother about your letter. No sense making her worry any more than she already is. She would've been sick if she'd thought you were upset so far from home." He paused for a moment. "I admit I asked Jack Cole to intercede with the Pentagon on your behalf. But he'd already called over there – before I talked with him. We both wanted you completely out of the Balkans. I'd be much happier if the Army sent you back to the States. But it had less to do with the war over there, than that the guy who kidnapped Miriana swore he'd go after you in Yugoslavia."

"Let him come. I'd love to get my hands on the sonofabitch."

"This isn't the time for testosterone overload, Mike," Bob said. "You could be at risk of assassination or abduction, especially if you were to cross into Yugoslavia. Your men could be at risk as well. Keep your head down, son."

"I haven't heard you say that in years, Dad. 'Keep your head down.' Not since I was a kid."

"You're still my kid. Now I'm going to call your mother back to the phone. Talk nice to her. I don't need her PO'ed more than she is already."

Michael laughed and said, "You can count on me, Dad."

"Oh, one other thing," Bob said. "Jack Cole's having someone drive Miriana out here this weekend, on Saturday. The three of us will have lunch together. She's doing great, by the way."

"Thanks, Dad," Michael said, his heart doing a trapeze act in his chest. "I was going to ask Mom if she'd heard from Miriana."

"I've kept an eye on her, Mike. I'll give her your address so she can write. I assume you'd like that."

"You assume right, Dad."

"I miss you, son."

Michael hesitated. He wasn't used to his father expressing his emotions so openly. "Thanks, Dad."

"I'll get your mother. Liz, you can get on now," Bob shouted.

Bob heard Liz pick up the receiver in the kitchen. "It's nice of you to let me finally talk to my son," she said sarcastically.

Michael hung up the phone after talking with his mother for a few minutes and crossed back over to the cafe.

"What's with the shit-eating grin?" Khalid asked.

Michael laughed. "Gonna have a little surprise for someone this coming Saturday." He felt a shiver of excitement course through him.

CHAPTER TWENTY-TWO

Colonel Sweeney finally found a Gypsy woman who could read and write both Roma and English. It took her a week to translate the statements that Stefan had gathered. But from the first pages onward, Dennis Sweeney knew he'd struck gold. He located many of the refugees Radko had interviewed, isolated them in a separate compound, then contacted the NATO field commander in Macedonia who, in turn, brought in people out of NATO Headquarters in Brussels. Investigators from NATO and the War Crimes Tribunal in The Hague, already in Macedonia, met with Stefan and Vanja.

"What motivated you to do this?" the Chief Investigator from The Hague asked.

Stefan looked surprised at the question. "Is it not our responsibility to bring the criminals committing these atrocities to justice?" he said with furrowed brow, trying not to laugh at the way he was playing this idiot.

"Of course, Mr. Radko. But few people would go to the effort you and your wife did. I compliment you. You saved us weeks of work, and the detail you have provided is amazing."

"We are happy to be of assistance."

"Is there anything we can do to show our appreciation?" the Chief Investigator asked.

"There is a favor I would ask: Help my wife, son, and me get out of Macedonia. We have learned our daughter has gone to the United States. We want to join her."

The Chief Investigator thought he saw tears in Stefan's eyes. "Yes, Colonel Sweeney already mentioned this to us," he said. "I'll do everything I can, Mr. Radko. But, of course, we'll need you to remain in Macedonia until we talk to all the victims and eyewitnesses you interviewed. I'm sure you'll get a great deal of personal satisfaction assisting us in the questioning, seeing this through to the end."

Stefan's mouth tightened, as though he'd sucked on a lemon.

CHAPTER TWENTY-THREE

"Mr. Radko," Michael said, having finally found Miriana's father crouched behind a tent near the inside of the refugee camp perimeter fence, playing dice with five Albanian men. There were neat stacks of currency and coins in front of Stefan. He had clearly been winning.

Stefan looked up at the interruption. "Can this wait?" he said coolly.

"I'm afraid not. You need to come with me."

Stefan blew out a stream of air. "My apologies, gentlemen," he said, scooping up and pocketing the dice and his stacks of money. "When our masters talk, we jump."

Michael suspected that most of the refugees there didn't understand Radko's English. He assumed the man had chosen to use English so Michael would understand. The man truly was a sonofabitch.

As Radko walked away with Michael, he began to laugh. "Another week in this camp and none of these peasants will have a coin left in his pocket," he said, slapping his thigh. "These are the easiest pickings I have had in years."

"Don't you feel bad about taking what little these poor people have left?"

"Sheep are meant to be shorn, Captain. Don't you agree?"

Michael just shook his head. How could this man be Miriana's father?

"So," Stefan said, "what is so important you interrupted the game?"

"I have a surprise for you and your family."

"You have arranged to get us out of here?" Stefan's eyes sparkled, and his smile seemed to extend from ear to ear.

"No, not yet."

"Well, what is it?" Stefan said, his smile fading.

"It's a surprise. I've already rounded up your wife and son. They're waiting for us by my Jeep."

"We are going for a ride? Where?"

"You'll see," Michael said.

Michael, talkative and in high spirits, couldn't hide his excitement during the ride into Kumanovo. It was a beautiful sunny day with just a trace of a breeze and the open country around them offered a spectacular view of the nearby hills and the distant mountains. Vanja and Attila, seemingly picking up on his mood, were more animated with Michael than either had been before. Stefan just glowered, sitting rigidly in the Jeep's front passenger seat.

Michael drove to the NATO field headquarters in Kumanovo. While he parked the Jeep down the street from the building entrance, the muffled sound of an explosion echoed through the town.

"What was that?" Vanja asked, looking around, then huddling against Attila.

Michael gave her a reassuring smile. "There are always guerrillas in the hills. Don't worry, we have patrols out." He turned back toward the building and led them to a small, first floor office.

"Ah, Captain Danforth, right on time," a short, stocky man in a German Colonel's uniform said in English. "And this must be the Radko family. Fritz Heinige," he introduced himself, shaking hands all around. "I have heard much about you Radkos. The information you provided has been invaluable. Now, if we can all sit down around the table?"

Once they were all settled in chairs, Heinige asked Michael, "Do you have the telephone number?"

Michael handed him a scrap of paper, then watched him lift the receiver and tap in a long series of numbers. Michael glanced at his watch: eight Saturday on night, Macedonia time, equaled noon on Saturday, Eastern Standard Time.

Heinige switched the call to speaker mode, replaced the receiver, and walked out of the room, leaving behind the sound of a phone ringing.

Then, a woman's voice. "Hello!"

"Mom, it's me, Michael."

"How wonderful! Is everything all right?"

"Everything's great! Is Miriana there with you?"

Vanja, seated between Stefan and Attila, gasped and slid forward in her chair. She grabbed Stefan's hand.

"Yes," Liz said. "Do you want to talk to her?"

"Sure. But there are some people here who should probably talk to her first. Could you put her on?"

There was an interval of mildly hissing static, then Miriana's voice filled the room. "Hello, Michael, is that you?"

Before Michael could respond, the Radko's erupted in rapid-fire shouting. Michael could understand only her name. "Miriana! Miriana!" But all the rest was Roma shouted back and forth.

Vanja and Attila kept raising their voices, competing to be heard. Miriana must have recognized their voices because she began screaming their names and shooting questions at them. Then Michael heard Miriana break down and cry, "Mama, *Babo*, Attila." When Vanja began crying and Attila jumped out of his chair, hurried to the telephone speaker and yelled, Stefan took control.

"Quiet!" he yelled. Like someone had turned a switch, the room fell silent. No more shouting or crying. "One question at a time," Stefan ordered. "Miriana, are you well?"

Michael jumped at the loudness of Stefan's voice. He wasn't used to the way the man dealt with his family.

"Yes, *O Babo*. Everyone here has been wonderful. Especially Michael's parents, Mr. and Mrs. Danforth. Are you all okay?"

Michael saw the worried look Vanja gave Stefan, but didn't know what to make of it.

"Yes, we are fine," Stefan said. "Everything will be perfect as soon as we get out of here and are all together again."

"When will that happen?" Miriana asked.

"Soon, I hope."

"What have you been doing?" Vanja interjected.

"That is a long story. I will tell you when we are together again."

After fifteen minutes, Miriana finally switched to English and asked to speak with Michael.

Michael picked up the receiver, taking the phone off speaker. "Hi."

"Hi, yourself. I should put your mother back on phone. She seems – how do you say it? – anxious to talk to you. But, before I say goodbye, I want to say finding family is most wonderful gift you could give me. This phone call has been so . . . .."

Michael heard Miriana's sniffling over the phone.

"I miss you, Michael," she said.

Michael felt a shiver run from his neck and down his spine. "If it wasn't so awkward at the moment . . . .."

"I understand," Miriana said, giggling.

Liz came back on the line. "From the look on Miriana's face, you must have made her day. What's going on?"

351

"I found her parents and younger brother. They're with me."

"Michael, that's wonderful! Are they okay?"

"They're all fine, Mom. They're nice people." When Michael said this, he turned abruptly in Stefan's direction. He caught a venomous, squint-eyed look that caused the hairs on his neck to stand up. Stefan's expression quickly changed to neutral, and he averted his eyes.

Michael turned again, putting his back to the Radkos.

In Bethesda, Bob picked up the extension. "Hi, son, what's happening?"

"I'll let Miriana explain it to you. Could you help her family get out of here? I know some refugees are being transported to the States. Can you get their names on the list?"

"I can't promise, but I'll give it a try. Let me grab a pencil and a piece of paper. Okay! Where are they located?"

"They're at the Kumanovo Refugee Camp. It's right near the 82nd's base in Macedonia."

"I guess that's all I really need to get from you. I can get their full names from Miriana. I assume the records there have the last name spelled, G-E-O-R-G-A-D-O-F-F."

"Miriana's mother and brother use that name," Michael said, "but her father's name is different. It's Radko, not Georgadoff. Stefan Radko." Michael looked at Stefan, just when Miriana's father laughed in short, grunting bursts that made Michael's skin crawl.

"What did you say?" Bob shouted, an odd tone to his voice.

"Radko," Michael said again. "R-A-D-K-O," he spelled.

"Michael, listen to me! Don't–" The phone went dead.

Bob desperately tried to reconnect the call, but without success.

CHAPTER TWENTY-FOUR

"Jack, I'm confident we can work out an agreement with the Serbs. It's *what* kind of agreement that's problematic," Major General Stan Ewing said, while he walked with Jack down the stone path leading from the Kumanovo Municipal Building to the American negotiating team's temporary offices.

"Remember, you're supposed to refer to the other side as Yugoslavs, not Serbs," Bob said, a facetious edge to his voice.

"More politicalspeak! The former Yugoslavia is run by Serbs at all levels. But now that 'Serb' has become a dirty word, they want to be called Yugoslavs."

"Stan, I understand. But the administration wants a deal. They don't want this thing to turn into another Vietnam War."

"If the administration expects me to kiss the Yugoslav generals' asses, they got the wrong boy. Besides, the White House is playing games. They hate the military and use us to deflect attention away from the President's extra-curricular activities."

"Spare me, Stan. You know your orders, so get the job done."

Ewing nodded, a disgusted look on his face. "What the hell are you doing over here, anyway?"

"The Director finagled me onto our team as an observer. That's my official assignment."

"And unofficially?"

"Now, Stan, you know better than that. Since when would I have an unofficial role?"

Ewing burst out laughing, slapped Jack on the back, and walked away.

Jack watched Ewing cross the compound to the building where generals and diplomats from both sides – NATO and Yugoslavia – would try to hammer out a peace pact. Then he backtracked and walked to the Jeep assigned to him and drove off in the direction of the 82nd Airborne Headquarters. While the Jeep bounced over the ruts in the road, Jack thought again about why he was so anxious to come to this godforsaken country. *I've watched that boy grow from a toddler to a man. His father is my best friend. If the Army has gone back on its promise to keep him in Macedonia, far from the Yugoslav line, I'll have some top brass ass put in a meat grinder.*

CHAPTER TWENTY-FIVE

General Plodic knocked on the door and, as instructed by the secretary in the anteroom, opened it and entered the Serb leader's office. He walked confidently across the carpeted floor, holding Captain Sokic's progress report in his hand.

"Plodic, what do you have to report?" the Serb leader growled, not even waiting for the General to get halfway across his office. The man stood behind his desk, his hands flat on the desktop, his eyes locked on Plodic like missiles locking on an enemy plane.

Plodic felt his confidence dissipate. Perspiration dripped from his underarms. He could tell from the President's tone and the scowl on his face that he was in a very bad mood. "Everything is progressing as per your orders, Mr. President. The Special Forces team will be ready to go in thirteen days. Right on time, according to the schedule you gave me. They're the best men in all of Yugoslavia. They'll be ready, I assure you."

"You have confidence in these men?" the leader asked, an implied message in his tone Plodic did not fail to comprehend. He knew the President had just warned him. If the mission failed, then Plodic's ass would be on the line. People who failed this psychopath had a habit of disappearing.

"Absolutely, Mr. President. They are the best trained men in all of Yugoslavia. True patriots." Plodic hazarded a smile, but quickly wiped it from his face. The leader's eyes were beginning to make his bowels feel loose.

"Good! Then they should be able to start in two days."

JOSEPH BADAL

CHAPTER TWENTY-SIX

Colonel Heinige rushed back into the room. "Captain Danforth, you should take the Radkos back to their camp. It appears we have Serb guerillas in the hills again, but this time they are close to the city. They must have knocked out the telephone lines. We are sending soldiers out to sweep the streets in case any of the guerillas infiltrated the city. You need to get these people out of here while you still can."

"Yes, sir!" Michael said. He turned to the Radko family. "Let's go. You'll be safer at the camp." He led the way out to the street and ran for the Jeep, leaving the Radkos in the building's doorway. After starting the vehicle, he backed it up to the building entrance. When Stefan and his family had climbed aboard, he sped toward the refugee camp.

Vanja and Attila seemed worried about the sounds of small arms fire coming from the hills above the road. Neither of them said a word until they were a couple of miles from the refugee camp, after they could no longer hear the pop-pop-pop of weapons.

From the back of the Jeep, Vanja placed a hand on Michael's shoulder and shouted over the noise of the engine and the wind rushing through the open vehicle, "I will never be able to thank you for what you did. You gave us back our daughter when we thought we had lost her forever."

"I was glad I could do it. As they say, it's a small world."

Michael ignored the grunting sound that came from Stefan sitting in the front passenger seat. He'd already come to the conclusion that Miriana was right. Her father was "sonofbitch."

356

CHAPTER TWENTY-SEVEN

By Monday evening, Stefan was sick of the refugee camp. And the men he had fleeced seemed to suspect his winning streak with the dice had continued too long to be mere luck. Where could he find a new group of suckers? Stefan left the camp and walked north on the road to Preshevo, in search of new sheep to shear.

Although just before dusk, there was still enough light for him to see the campsites along the road and in the fields to the west. Idiots! Stefan thought. Waiting like children for the great Americans to save them. He patted the wad of bills in his pockets and smiled. He was confident he'd double his money before he returned to the refugee camp later that night.

On the other side of the border, north of Preshevo, Captain Sokic and his men hid their vehicles in trees along a dirt track connecting with the main road. They walked back to the main road to mix with the scattering of refugees still moving south. It appeared that most had stopped and camped, now that night approached.

Carrying their gear in packs, suitcases, and canvas bags on their backs and shoulders, they continued southward.

Sokic watched his men dispersing among the refugees, melting in amongst the stragglers, dragging their feet and walking stooped as though exhausted and demoralized. They fit right in as they shuffled along at a snail's pace, their ragged clothing hanging on them like castoffs on scarecrows. Sokic trailed behind, placing himself next to a slow-moving, horse-drawn wagon.

While he walked, Sokic practiced his cover story – birth date, village, names of his family members. He had it all down perfectly, but Sokic was a careful man. At the outskirts of Preshevo, four hours later, he and his team encountered the first NATO refugee checkpoint.

After a long wait in barely-moving lines of refugees, they were cleared through to the next checkpoint. Most of the rest of the way, Sokic, his team, and a dozen other refugees hitched a ride on a tractor-towed flatbed trailer. Two kilometers north of Kumanovo, when it was fully dark, the Serb soldiers jumped off the trailer, climbed a hillside by the road, and rested among the trees.

"We wait here until all these Muslim pigs are asleep," Sokic told his men. "Then we'll go around Kumanovo and locate the 82nd's encampment. Dimitrov, you and Pyotr take the first watch. Vassily, Josef, get some sleep. The next shift will be in two hours. We leave at 0200."

By ten p.m., Stefan had unburdened several Kosovars of their money. He'd not gotten very far north of Kumanovo, but he wasn't sure where he was. He tried to remember how many shots of *raki* he'd drunk, but all he could come up with was "a lot." Although dead-tired, he felt ecstatic about the money filling his pockets. So many marks, so little time, he thought, laughing in the darkness, listening to his voice rebound off the hills on the east side of the road. At a curve in the road, he noticed a small group of men leave the crowd of refugees and climb a hillside into the trees.

Still more sheep, he thought. And no women with them. Good! No nagging wives telling their husbands not to gamble or drink. Rubbing his hands together gleefully, he thought, What the hell; I can't pass up suckers like these. An hour is all it should take. He shook the loaded die in his hand while he plodded up the grassy incline toward the flat crest of the hill, no longer feeling tired. He'd made it halfway up the hill, when a man stepped from behind a large bush and stuck the point of a knife under his chin.

"Going someplace, old man?"

Stefan had dealt with all manner of men; he could identify the victims from the predators, the sane from the crazies. The tone in this man's voice told him he needed to be careful with this one.

"Hello," he replied in Serbo-Croatian. "I was hoping you might share some water with me."

"Get fucked," the man growled. "We've got nothing for the likes of you."

Stefan began to turn around, when a second man appeared and placed a hand on his arm. "Who are you?" the man asked.

"Stefan Radko is my name. I'm staying at the refugee camp down the road. I got tired of the Americans' bullshit and decided to take a walk."

The second man just continued staring at Stefan. He didn't react to what Stefan had said.

"You look like you just arrived," Stefan said in what he hoped was his most congenial tone. "Perhaps I can be of help; I've been here for many days and I know the people at the refugee camp. The paperwork is awful, but I can help you with it."

"Thank you, sir; please join us," the man said, turning around and going back up. "We left our farms weeks ago and have been traveling on foot since then," he said over his shoulder. "We would appreciate your help in finding our families."

Stefan followed, thinking none of them would have much chance of finding family in the mob of refugees. He sat with the men and learned their names – always better to break down suspicions by using first names, appearing to be friendly. He told them lies about his own escape from Yugoslavia.

Stefan noticed that this group seemed somehow unlike the other refugees – dirty, with tattered clothes, but not so downtrodden. They seemed more . . . alert, better educated. The more he talked, however, and the more of their liquor he drank, the more comfortable Stefan felt. Soon he seduced a couple of them into playing dice. The mood of the group became amiable.

"Where's that other bottle of whiskey?" the one who seemed to be the leader said.

Another man took a bottle from a suitcase. Stefan smacked his lips. He would do more than his share in making the contents of this bottle disappear, too.

"Have you met any American soldiers?" one of them asked. "I hear they are well trained and equipped. We should be grateful they have come to protect us."

Stefan began to relish his role as adviser to this group of farmers. It was wonderful to have an advantage over them. He looked across the campfire and squinted, trying to bring the man's face opposite him into better focus. "Oh, yes, he slurred, "I met many Americans. Even the head of their 82nd Airborne, Colonel Sweeney."

Sokic glanced at Dimitrov sitting across from him and saw the soldier raise his eyebrows, as though to convey the thought that this old man was either the biggest blowhard in the world or they had discovered a valuable resource. Or both.

"What other Americans have you met?" Sokic asked.

"Many, many," Stefan said, throwing an arm in the air to indicate there were too many to name.

"I think you're joking with us."

Stefan shrugged. "Believe what you want," he said. "But one of the American officers has even fallen in love with my daughter."

"Big goddam deal," Pyotr said loudly.

Sokic narrowed his eyes with contempt while he stared across the fire at Pyotr. Stupid idiot! If the Gypsy clams up . . . The soldier shrank back and lowered his head.

"It's true; one of them has fallen in love with my Miriana," Stefan said. He spat into the fire.

The name tugged at Sokic's memory. General Plodic had spoken about Karadjic's kidnapping and how a Gypsy girl named Miriana was involved.

"Your daughter, is she beautiful?" he asked.

Stefan smirked. "You won't find a more beautiful girl in all of Yugoslavia."

Sokic laughed. "Spoken like a loving father," he said. "I hear the Americans are all rich. You must be pleased an American officer is interested in your daughter."

Stefan scowled. "He's the last American I would let my Miriana marry!"

"Why?"

"His father killed my son," Stefan slurred. "I curse the Danforth name."

Sokic was so surprised his jaw dropped.

CHAPTER TWENTY-EIGHT

Michael had arranged to have dinner with Jack Cole in the officers' mess tent on Monday night. His stomach growled when he walked into the tent at 2100 hours. He saw Jack sitting at one of the picnic tables lined up inside. The place was almost empty.

Michael sat and rubbed his face with both hands as though to wipe away the weariness he felt.

"You look beat, kid," Jack said.

"My company guarded convoys again today. We made seven trips between here and Preshevo. The road's still so packed with refugees, it takes an hour to go five miles. I'm physically exhausted and emotionally spent. Looking at their faces is . . . they've lost hope, Uncle Jack."

"That's why we're here, Mike, to give them hope."

"I guess. But from what I've seen and heard, I'd lay money that no more than half the Kosovars will willingly return to their former villages unless NATO stations troops all over the province. They'll never trust the Serbs to leave them in peace. What kind of hope do these people have if they can't return to their homes?"

"Let's get some chow, Mike, and talk about something less gloomy – like that lovely young lady who has a crush on you."

Michael's face warmed. He smiled, then laughed. "Miriana is a subject I can put my heart into. But, as for the food, prepare for more gloom," he joked.

Jack laughed when he got up from the bench. Michael led the way to the steam tables at the other end of the mess tent.

After picking from a selection of two meats, three vegetables – in addition to the ubiquitous potato – plus bread, dessert, and beverages, they returned to their table and sat across from each other, now the only persons in the dining area. Michael watched Jack remove his suit coat, exposing the .45 in his shoulder holster.

"What's the matter, afraid of muggers?" Michael said, pointing at the weapon with his fork.

"They should be afraid of me," Jack said. "But let's talk about you and your girlfriend."

"What do you want to know?"

After an hour's conversation, Michael began to nod off. "I think I'd better hit the sack," he said, "before I fall asleep right here."

Jack smiled. "I was hoping you'd talk through the night. It would help with this jet lag."

While they walked toward the exit, the canvas flap serving as the door flew open. Jack jumped, reaching for his pistol. Michael put a hand on his arm. "It's okay," he said. "Take it easy; I know him."

Attila stood in the tent entrance, next to an American Staff Sergeant with an MP's armband.

"Sorry to bother you, sir," the Sergeant said, "but this boy said it was an emer–"

"Captain Danforth," Attila interrupted, clearly agitated. "Mama told me to come find you. Papa has not returned to our tent. She thinks something happened to him."

"Calm down, Attila. I'm sure your father's fine. He's probably just visiting friends."

"No, no, something's wrong. He left camp–"

"He what!" Michael exclaimed.

"He said he wanted to find a dice game. He left more than four hours ago. He said he would walk north, toward Preshevo. Papa usually comes home earlier than this."

"I'd better go out and try to find Attila's father," Michael told Jack. "Sorry. We can talk some more tomorrow." Then he turned to the MP. "Sergeant, you can escort this boy back to the front gate now."

"You can't leave the camp at night," Jack said after the MP led the kid away. "Wait until morning. You're going to have to escort a supply convoy in that direction anyway, and you'll have your men with you then."

"I can't just leave the old man out there. What if he's gotten himself hurt?"

"Jesus, Mary, and Joseph," Jack said. "Think, Mike. It's dangerous out there. Besides, who the hell is he to you?"

"I'm sorry, Uncle Jack. I should have introduced you. That was Miriana's brother, Attila. It's his father, Stefan, who's missing."

"Stefan Georgadoff. Sounds Bulgarian, not Roma."

"Georgadoff is Bulgarian; but it's the mother's name. Miriana's father is Gypsy. His last name is Radko."

Jack's face went white. "Did you say Radko? R-a-d-k-o?"

"Right. Why? What's wrong?" Michael said.

"Nothing. I . . . I just thought I recognized the name. My Jeep's right outside the tent. Come on, I'll drive."

Jack's loyalty to the Danforths wrestled with his desire to tell Michael about Radko. He knew Bob and Liz had never told their son about the kidnapping in Greece. Would he be violating his friends' trust if he told Michael the truth now?

CHAPTER TWENTY-NINE

"Where is he, Bob?" Liz asked, her voice strained.

"It's a war zone, honey," Bob said, making a Herculean effort to remain calm. He understood the fear showing in Liz's eyes. The same fear had penetrated his gut. "You can't just look up a name in the phone book and call. I contacted the Pentagon. The duty officer said he'd try to contact Mike's commander."

"Well, then where's Jack? You've called him, too. Where the hell is he?" she shouted. "I can't believe the whole damn CIA can't find him." She walked back and forth across the den, wringing the dishtowel she'd carried from the kitchen.

"Liz, we know where Jack is supposed to be. But you know Jack. He's not happy unless he's got his nose stuck under some tent. Can you picture him sitting in those peace treaty meetings as an observer? He's probably out in the field somewhere doing real intelligence work. The damned cell phone relay towers are down, so his mobile phone is useless."

"Twenty-four hours have passed since we talked to Michael. We've got to get him away from that bastard, Radko." She began pacing around the kitchen table, her arms flailing the air. "That bastard!" she cursed, her voice suddenly quieter, the words coming out in a hiss.

"I understand, Liz. I left a message where Jack's staying. He'll get it sooner or later and will contact Michael. I'm just as worried as you are."

"Why don't you try calling the Pentagon again? They could get him to call us."

"They're working on it. We call again and we'll look like frantic parents."

"We are frantic parents!" Liz shouted.

"Jack'll know what to do," Bob said, putting his arms around his wife.

Liz again paced the length of the den and back. "That sonofabitch!" she said, clenching her fists and shaking them in the air. "How could he be back in our lives again? We should have told Michael about Radko years ago."

CHAPTER THIRTY

"What do you mean, he killed your son?" Sokic said, trying to keep a neutral expression on his face.

Stefan waved away the question. "Long story," he stammered. He tried to stand, but his head started spinning and he fell back to the ground. "Life plays strange . . .," he said, his words drifting off. He sat silent for several seconds, shaking his head as though to clear the fog that had settled over his brain, then said, "A man kills my son and now *his* son wants to take my daughter from me. I will kill Michael Danforth before he steals Miriana from me."

"We'll help you, Mr. Radko," Sokic said, taking his arm and helping him to his feet.

Leaning against Sokic, Radko mumbled, "How will you help me? What can a bunch of ragged-ass Kosovars do to help me?"

"Show us where to find him," Sokic said. "We'll take care of everything. You don't have to worry."

"What can you do to Danforth? He's a soldier and you're a bunch of farmers."

"Don't worry. We'll make sure he doesn't take your daughter away from you."

"Sounds goo--" Stefan's knees seemed to turn to jelly and he collapsed into a sitting position. In the glow of the fire, Sokic saw Stefan's eyes roll just before he sagged completely to the ground, curled into a fetal position, and began snoring.

CHAPTER THIRTY-ONE

Jack slowly drove up the road, his mind still in turmoil. He remembered Bob telling him the story years ago of Michael's kidnapping. The way Bob had spoken the name Stefan Radko then, the hatred in his voice, had imprinted the Radko name in Jack's memory. Should I tell Mike about Radko? Jesus, Jack thought, Bob and Liz must have had a reason to keep the facts from the boy. And now Michael had fallen in love with Radko's daughter.

"Why don't we check over there?" Michael said, bringing Jack back to the present. He saw Michael pointing in the direction of a campsite near the road. Jack steered the Jeep over to it. The shapeless mounds on the ground around the dying fire turned out to be blanket-covered refugees. One man still sat up, smoking a cigarette. In answer to Jack's questions, he told them in broken English that he had not seen any old Gypsy wandering around during the last few hours.

"Mike, this is the proverbial needle in a haystack," Jack said, pulling the vehicle back on the road.

"Yeah, I know. But let's go on for another mile or two."

They followed the meandering road north, stopping at fires along the way to ask about Stefan; but no one claimed to have seen him. They were about to give it up when Michael pointed to one more small fire on a hillside off to the right. "Someone's up in those trees," he said.

Jack stopped the Jeep and walked with Michael up the hillside toward the fire. A man started down the hill toward them, silhouetted against the light from the fire. Something about the way the man carried himself alarmed Jack. Erect, confident, the man moved almost cat-like toward them.

Jack dropped behind Michael, slipped his hand under his jacket, and released the safety on his pistol. Then he moved again to Michael's left side and walked next to him.

The man approaching them said something in what sounded like Serbo-Croatian.

"Do you speak English?" Michael asked.

"Yes," the man said.

"We're looking for an old man named Stefan Radko. He wandered off from the refugee camp near Kumanovo. Have you seen him?"

"We have seen many old men, but none have told us their names," the man said. "What does this Radko look like?"

Michael noticed the man spoke English in a stilted, very formal way – as though he'd had language training, but no real practice in an English-speaking country.

"About my height," Michael said. "Maybe a little lighter than me. White hair. Dark skin. Large mustache."

"If we meet him, we'll tell him you're searching for him," the man said.

Jack and Michael returned to the Jeep. When Jack turned the vehicle around, he noticed the man still stood where they'd left him.

"Who were they, Dimitrov?" Sokic demanded.

"Some American officer and a civilian – probably one of the relief workers. They were looking for this piece-of-shit Gypsy," he said, kicking dirt on the prostrate Stefan.

Sokic rubbed his chin, walked in a circle around the fire. "Did you see the officer's name on his field jacket?"

"No sir, it was too dark."

"All right, get some sleep. We leave in a couple of hours. I want to find Danforth before it gets light. This old Gypsy is going to make our job much easier."

"You seemed tense back there," Michael said. "Something wrong?"

"Oh, probably just paranoia. Did you notice anything about that guy?"

Michael tilted his head to one side. "Well, now that you mention it, he seemed cocky for a refugee, you know, confident, not scared like the others I've seen. Not at all nervous about our showing up this late at night."

"Uh-huh. Anything else?"

"I don't know, but I felt like the guy lied about not seeing Mr. Radko."

"That's what I thought, too. You should come back in the morning with one of your platoons and check him out again."

"It's a long drive back to the base, then to Kumanovo," Michael said. "Why don't you spend the night at the base? It's too late to drive me back, then go to your hotel in Kumanovo. My roommate's out in the field, so you can use his bunk."

"I'll take you up on that, Mike. I don't think I could stay awake driving back to Kumanovo by myself."

As they approached the gate to the 82nd's base camp, Michael said, "I wonder what happened to Mr. Radko."

Jack cringed.

CHAPTER THIRTY-TWO

Bob looked at his desk clock for the hundredth time. Four p.m. He pressed the intercom button. "Jeannie, have we heard from Jack Cole?"

"No, sir, nothing yet."

"Would you try his hotel again. It's midnight in Macedonia. He's got to be in his room by now."

She soon buzzed him back. "Kumanovo is on line two."

Bob snatched the receiver from its cradle. "Hello!"

"This is the Alexandria Hotel," a man said in heavily accented English. "How may I help you, sir?"

"This is Bob Danforth. I—"

"Ah, yes, Mr. Danforth," the man said, obvious pique in his voice. "You have called three times before. Mr. Cole has not yet picked up your earlier messages."

"None of them?"

"Correct. Mr. Cole has not returned to his room."

"You're sure?"

First a slight pause on the line, then, "Mr. Danforth, I make it my job to be sure of such things." Then the man's tone became louder as he said, "Please be assured I will have Mr. Cole call you as soon as he returns."

"I'm sure you will," Bob snapped, hearing the implied, *Don't call us, we'll call you.* He hung up the phone, opened a desk drawer, and took out a bottle of antacid pills. He popped a couple after swiveling his chair around to gaze through the window at dark gray storm clouds hovering above the woods just beyond the CIA compound.

CHAPTER THIRTY-THREE

After alerting Captain Danforth at the U.S. Army base and watching the Captain and the man named Cole drive off in a Jeep, Attila ran north along the road toward Serbia. His head hurt from the crushing strain of panic surging through him. What had happened to *Babo*? What would he and Mama do if something had happened to *Babo*? He also felt anger toward his father. Why had he gone out so late? This was a war zone. But then he felt guilty about his anger. Tears came to his eyes and his throat constricted. How could they survive without *Babo*?

Stopping at every camp, questioning one person after the other, he'd traveled miles before he realized he was on an impossible mission. *Babo* could be anywhere. He would never find him in the dark.

He stood in the middle of the road, sweat pouring from his brow. He wiped his face with his shirtsleeve, then turned back to the south. Maybe *Babo* is already back at the refugee camp. Attila had a sudden rush of elation. Yes, he's probably already in bed, fast asleep. And I'm running around in the dark like an idiot. He gave a little laugh.

But the elation disappeared as rapidly as it had come. Who was he kidding? Attila knew that was just wishful thinking. His father might have been robbed by refugees and dumped in some ditch. Or maybe Serb guerrillas had murdered him. Attila looked around him. There seemed to be figures lurking behind every tree, in every shadow. He again wiped his sleeve over his face, this time removing tears along with sweat.

CHAPTER THIRTY-FOUR

Captain Sokic and his men buried all their nonessential gear in a shallow hole and covered it with leaves and dead tree branches. Instead of the array of luggage his men had carried earlier, they now hefted only backpacks containing weapons, ammunition, water, and emergency supplies.

Sokic roused Stefan with a sharp kick in the thigh.

"Wha . . . what was that?" Stefan cried. Groaning, he sat upright. He rubbed his thigh. Then he dropped his head into his hands and shook it, as though trying to figure out where he was.

"Get up, old man. We have some distance to cover before it gets light."

"Where are we going?"

"You're going to take us to your friend Danforth."

"Are you going to kill him?"

Sokic frowned and raised his hands, palms out. "I'm insulted. Do we look like murderers to you?"

The six men set off from the campsite at a brisk walk. When Stefan couldn't keep up, he was carried piggyback-style by one of the soldiers.

Hungover and exhausted, Stefan fell into a half-sleep, despite the jarring ride. Suddenly, however, he was shocked awake by being dropped like a sack of grain. The lights of the refugee camp were just ahead.

"Where's the 82nd Airborne's encampment?" Sokic demanded.

Stefan pointed to the left of the refugee camp. "You see the lights shining there? The two camps adjoin one another. But there is no way you'll get past the guards and into the Army camp."

"Radko, we have no intention of entering the Americans' camp. You're going to bring Danforth to us."

"How?"

"Easy," Sokic said, faking a tolerant smile. "You'll give the sentries a message for Danforth. That you want to see him. That it's an emergency."

"And why do you believe he'll come out to see me?" Stefan asked.

Sokic snorted. "Remember," he said, "he wants to impress his girlfriend's father. I think he'll come running."

Stefan nodded. "Then what?"

Sokic patted Stefan on the shoulder. "You need not worry about a thing, my friend. We'll take care of the rest."

CHAPTER THIRTY-FIVE

"Halt!" a voice shouted.

"Don't shoot," Radko called out.

"Hands above your head!"

Radko complied while he walked forward. He stopped again within a few feet of the gate. The American soldier at the gate held a rifle leveled at Radko's chest. Another soldier frisked him.

"He's clean; no weapons," the soldier said after patting him down. "What are you doing here?"

"I have to talk with one of your officers," Radko said, lowering his arms.

"What's so important at this hour?" the soldier demanded.

"It is an emergency," Stefan said. "I must talk to Captain Danforth."

"That's the 'Charlie' Company Commander," the soldier who had frisked Stefan said to the other one, who lowered the barrel of his rifle.

The second guard said, "No way I'm bothering an officer at this time of night because some bullshit old fart claims he's got an emergency."

Radko shrugged. "I've got information about Serb guerrillas in the area. I'm sure Captain Danforth will be pleased to hear that you did not think my information was important."

The two guys eyed one another and then one said, "Send someone over to Captain Danforth's tent." Then he took Radko's arm and led him to a bench under a wooden canopy, just outside the gate. "Wait here," he told him.

Michael jerked awake as he snatched his .45 from under his pillow. The soldier who had shaken him by the shoulder jumped back three feet and hit his head on a dangling lantern.

"Jesus," the young man gasped, "don't shoot, sir. I called from outside your tent, but you didn't respond."

"Step outside," Michael said, keeping his voice low so he wouldn't wake Jack, still asleep on the other cot.

"Ruiz, sir, Delta Company, 2nd Battalion," the soldier said once they were outside, never taking his eyes off Michael's pistol. "I'm on guard duty. Got a message for you. Some old guy just came to the front gate and said he had to talk to you. Said it was an emergency. Something about Serb guerrillas."

Michael lowered the gun. "Don't worry, Ruiz. I'm not going to shoot you. But next time you might want to yell a little louder."

"Yes, sir! You scared the beejesus out of me, sir."

"What's this old man's name?" Michael asked.

"Radko. Said his name was Stefan Radko."

"Where is he?"

"He's still at the guard shack, waiting for you to come out," Ruiz said.

"You get back up there and make sure he doesn't leave. I'll be right there."

Michael quickly dressed in his fatigues and boots, strapped on his pistol belt, and slammed his .45 into the holster.

Jack stirred when Michael moved to the tent entrance. "Something up?" he asked, his voice thick with sleep.

"It's nothing," Michael said, as he closed the flap behind him. "Everything's okay. Mr. Radko's out by the gate. I'm going out to meet him."

Jack leaped from the cot and shouted, "Michael, wait!" The roar of a Jeep engine drowned his words.

"Damn!" Jack exclaimed. "Damn!" he said aloud again. He dressed quickly and began to run the two hundred yards to the front gate. But before he could get halfway there he saw, in the glare of the guardhouse security lights, an elderly man getting into Michael's Jeep. He yelled, but Michael was revving the noisy Jeep, and now moving away.

"Mr. Radko, where have you been?" Michael was unable to disguise his irritation. "We searched all over for you."

Stefan hung his head. "I found a dice game and wound up drinking too much. I passed out. Made it back to your gate. Could not walk another step. Guess I am getting too old to be out so late."

"What' about the Serb guerrillas you mentioned to the guard?" Michael asked.

"I need you to—"

"Hold it! What's that?" Michael said. Pointing ahead. Something lay in the road ahead – half on, half off the road surface. A body! He hit the brakes, stopped a few feet short of the body, and jumped out of the Jeep. He reached inside his field jacket for his pistol, ready to pull it if necessary. He bent over to see if the person was alive.

CHAPTER THIRTY-SIX

"Get the duty officer up here," Jack snapped at the gate sentries. "I got a feeling Captain Danforth's in trouble."

"Sir," one of them said, "I can't bother the duty officer just because you got a *feeling*." Not friendly at all.

Jack clenched his fists There was no time to waste.

His shoulders slumped in apparent defeat, Jack took several steps away from the gate. When he walked behind one of the sentries, he wrapped his arm around the man's neck and pulled his own pistol from inside his jacket. "Drop your rifles now, or I'll blow your pal's head off," he told the others.

They stared at him – wide-eyed, open-mouthed. "Boys, you got three seconds before I make mush out of this man's brains. DROP YOUR WEAPONS!"

Two of the soldiers looked at the third soldier – the one with the Sergeant's insignia. Jack noticed the steel-hard look on the Sergeant's face and knew this one could be trouble.

He cocked the hammer on his pistol and pressed it against the temple of the soldier he held. The man grunted from the pain. "Don't fuck around!" Jack shouted. "I'll shoot this man and then take out the three of you before you can react."

The guards looked at one another, looking embarrassed and uncertain about what to do. Finally, one of them lowered his weapon to the guard. The others followed suit. They all placed their hands on their helmets.

"Good boys," Jack said. "Who's got the keys to the HUMVEE?"

"They're in the ignition," one of them said. He sounded as though he couldn't wait for this crazy man to take the vehicle and leave.

"Okay, lie down on the ground," Jack ordered. This time they obeyed without hesitation. "You, too," he told the man he held. "When I'm gone, call the duty officer and tell him a nice man stole your wheels and went off after Captain Michael Danforth."

Before leaving, he tossed their weapons into the brush behind the guard shack.

CHAPTER THIRTY-SEVEN

Michael bent down, rolled the body over, and immediately froze. He knew he'd made the mistake of his life. The pistol aimed at his stomach and the smile on the man's face told him everything.

"Remove your hand from inside your jacket and step back!" the man said in a hushed, but firm tone.

Michael showed his hands, slowly straightened up and took a step back. Try to relax, he told himself. Remember your training. He waited until the man began to stand and grabbed his gunhand in both of his own, shifted his weight, and threw the man over his shoulder. The man slammed the pavement with a *whomp!* Then starbursts of light exploded in Michael's head and he felt himself falling. Then he felt nothing.

"That was careless, Dimitrov," Captain Sokic snarled, grimacing at the soldier wheezing for breath. But Sokic wasn't interested in a response. "Josef, you and Vassily put Danforth in the Jeep. Pyotr, you drive," he rasped. Sokic then turned to Radko who was standing off to the side of the road. "You've got two seconds to disappear before I shoot your ass." He watched Radko move off the road and go into the trees beyond.

Attila stepped out of the trees and slid down the embankment to the road. He was exhausted from his trek north and the return trip looking for his father. He saw the security lights of the refugee camp entrance far in the distance to his right and started to walk in that direction. But a slight sound distracted him. Off to his left, a vehicle was stopped on the road, just outside the ray of light cast by one of the security lamps mounted on the military camp's perimeter fence. Its headlights were on. Its engine idled.

379

Several figures stood around the vehicle. Suddenly, another figure ran away from the road, toward the woods. He recognized his father's walk and posture.

"*Babo*," Attila screamed. "*Babo*, it's me." He ran up the middle of the road toward where he saw Radko enter the treeline.

Pyotr was about to put the Jeep in gear, when Sokic grabbed his arm. "Wait!" he said. "What was that?"

Stefan had heard a shout, while running away from the Jeep into the woods. But he hadn't stopped. All he wanted to do was get away from the men who were obviously more than he'd originally thought they were. And they were damned sure not Bosnian farmers. It was okay with him if they murdered Danforth, but he didn't want to be anywhere near them in case American soldiers showed up. After he was hidden, he peeked around a tree and looked down at the road. Then he heard the same voice shouting again.

"*Babo!*"

Stefan looked to the right. Attila stepped into the beam of the Jeep's headlights.

"Go back!" Stefan screamed. He heard Sokic's voice shout, "Go! Go!" Then the sound of the Jeep engine revving. The vehicle shot forward. He watched the vehicle speed down the road toward his son.

Radko shouted again. "Attila, run!" His words sounded to him as loud as though they'd been screamed into a bullhorn. But he knew they were wasted. The engine shrieked as the vehicle launched forward and smashed into Attila. His son was flung over the Jeep's windshield like a pinwheeling sack of potatoes. He watched the boy land with a sickening thud in the middle of the road.

CHAPTER THIRTY-EIGHT

Jack saw the red glow of taillights vanishing in the distance. He goosed the HUMVEE and felt it surge forward.

Then his headlights revealed something on the pavement. He slammed on the brakes and skidded to a stop a few feet from a man bent over what looked like a heap of clothing. Jack pulled out his pistol and jumped from the HUMVEE. He saw flesh and blood in the heap of clothing. Walking closer, keeping his gun extended, Jack asked, "What happened?" The man kneeling beside the body did not respond. He just swayed back and forth.

Jack grabbed him by the collar, forcing him to stand, and shook him. "What's going on? Who are you?" The man stood hunched over, staring down at the twisted limbs of a teenaged boy.

"Dammit, who are you?" Jack screamed.

The roar of engines speeding toward him from the Army compound deflected his attention. He put his weapon away and put his hands on his head while three vehicles bore down on him. They jolted to a stop a few steps away and a gang of soldiers jumped out and surrounded Jack. One of them roughly frisked him and took away his pistol.

A lieutenant who seemed to be in charge pointed at Stefan. "Who's that?" he asked no one in particular.

A soldier – Jack recognized him as one of the sentries – said, "That's the guy Captain Danforth drove off with."

"So where's Captain Danforth?" the Lieutenant asked.

The sentry just shrugged.

"Search him, too," the officer ordered.

The sentry searched Radko and found his pockets stuffed with currency. He also found ID papers and handed them to the officer. The officer stepped in front of one of the Jeeps and held the papers down in the beam of a headlight to read them. "Your name is Stefan Radko?"

No response.

The officer repeated the question – louder this time. "Are you Stefan Radko?"

"Yes, I am Stefan Radko."

"You sonofabitch!" Jack cursed. He broke away from the two men guarding him, grabbed Stefan by the front of his coat, and jerked him forward. "Where's Michael, you bastard?"

Stefan glared at Jack. "He is on his way to hell," he whispered. Then Stefan began to laugh, but he suddenly stopped and sank to his knees.

"Get him back to the camp," the Lieutenant ordered, pointing at Radko. "We'll take this other one to headquarters for interrogation."

CHAPTER THIRTY-NINE

The Serb Special Forces team took the bypass road around Kumanovo and sped north to Preshevo. Sokic knew they had to put distance between them and the Americans. As soon as the Americans discovered Danforth missing, there would be a general alert. One Black Hawk helicopter would ruin everything; their mission would be a failure. Kidnapping Danforth was only half the mission. They had to get him into Serbia.

Danforth lay bound, gagged, and unconscious in the back of the Jeep. Sokic smiled with satisfaction at his target's still figure. Luck had been with them, so far.

The last of the moon could be seen low in the sky. A few refugees already on the road, hiking south, had to scurry out of the Jeep's path. Sokic tapped Pyotr on the arm. "Make sure you don't run into any of these scum. We don't want to damage the vehicle."

Pyotr nodded his understanding, but Sokic thought he saw disappointment on the man's face. It was still dark, so he couldn't be sure.

When Sokic saw the rutted dirt road leading to the spot where the team's cars were hidden, he yelled at Pyotr to make the turn. They stopped at the spot where they'd left the vehicles, camouflaged beside the road. But the cars were gone.

"Damn Muslim thieves!" Sokic growled. He turned to Pyotr and demanded, "How much gas do we have?"

Pyotr checked the fuel gauge. "It's on vapors," he said.

"We might as well dump it in a ravine," Sokic said. "We'll have to walk until we find another vehicle."

CHAPTER FORTY

Michael returned to head-throbbing consciousness. He had a moment of disorientation. Then the memory of what had happened hit him.

His hands, gone numb, were tied tightly behind his back. His tongue was dry and swollen. He tasted dirt. Michael remained still and opened his eyes only enough to glimpse his surroundings. It was still dark. Clouds obscured part of the waning moon. The slight breeze carried a chill with it. Two men stood a few feet away. All Michael could see were their boots and the lower part of their pants. Somewhere just behind him, a man said something in Serbo-Croatian.

Serbs! Michael thought. Stay calm, he told himself, as he assessed his situation: Bound and gagged, killer headache, stiff with cold. In enemy hands. I'm in deep shit.

One of the Serbs poured water from a canteen over Michael's face. He sputtered when some of it splashed into his nose.

"Well, our guest is finally awake," one of the men said. "Get him to his feet." Two men hoisted Michael by the arms. The apparent leader smiled at Michael. "I have a message for you from our esteemed President," he said in English. "He says, 'Welcome to Serbia, where you will spend the rest of your miserable life. Welcome to Hell.' "

Michael no longer felt disoriented. But he was confused. He felt as though he'd dropped into some Alice-In-Wonderland nightmare fantasy world. What the hell did the Serb leader want with *him*?

CHAPTER FORTY-ONE

Sergeant Sean O'Hara and Private Tyrell Robinson couldn't get Radko to say a word while they drove him to the refugee camp. The old man sat in the backseat, silent as a Sphinx.

"Ah," one of the NATO guards from France said, "it is Monsieur Radko. Where have you been? Your wife and son, they drive us crazy with questions. The boy has gone out to search for you."

Stefan just stared at nothing.

"What is the matter with him?" the other French guard asked.

O'Hara glanced at Stefan and lowered his voice to answer, "He saw his son get killed."

"*Merde!*"

"Where's his tent?" O'Hara asked.

The guard entered a wooden hut and came out looking at a sheet of paper on a clipboard. "Tent 346," he said. "Go straight ahead until you come to the Red Cross building. Then take a left and go for about a half-mile. The numbers are on little signs in front of each tent."

"*Merci*," O'Hara said. But it came across like "Mercy," in a West Texas accent.

"*I n'y a pas de rien,*" the French guard said, smiling.

As Robinson drove into the camp, he started laughing. "Nice accent there, Sergeant," he said. "No wonder the French think we're cretins."

O'Hara scowled. "What's wrong with my accent? And how would you know?"

"High-school French – four years."

"Huh! What did Peppie Le Pew say when I thanked him?"

"He said it was nothing. Must have been talking about your French."

They finally found tent 346 just when the sun peeked above the horizon. Robinson pulled in front. O'Hara helped Radko out of the vehicle, supporting him while he led him to the tent.

A woman stepped out into the morning light. "Stefan, where have you been?" she cried in English. "I have been so worried." She touched the patches of dried blood on his jacket. "Are you hurt?" she asked, looking accusingly at O'Hara.

"He's fine, ma'am. Help me get him into the tent."

Vanja stepped between Stefan and O'Hara. Robinson helped her move Stefan to a cot. Three cots took up most of the space within the tent. Suitcases and boxes were piled on the dirt floor in the remaining space. The only light came from two lanterns hanging from a rope strung along the top of the tent.

When they had Stefan sitting down on one of the cots inside, Robinson said, "Maybe you should sit down, too, ma'am."

She refused to sit. "What happened to my husband," she demanded.

"We think he saw your son get hit by a vehicle out on the road," O'Hara said.

Vanja covered her mouth with both hands. Then her hands flew to the top of her head. "Where is my son? How badly hurt is he?"

"I'm sorry, ma'am, he's dead."

Vanja's shriek filled the tent. She collapsed on the dirt floor, wailing.

O'Hara and Robinson had almost reached the camp's gate when they took a call on the Jeep's radio: "Eagle Four, this is Eagle One. Come in, Eagle Four. Eagle Four, can you read me? This is Eagle One. Over."

O'Hara picked up the mike. "Eagle One, this is Eagle Four. We read you loud and clear. Over."

"Bring Radko to Colonel Sweeney. Over."

"We already dropped the old guy at his tent," O'Hara protested. "Over."

"Well, go back and get him! Out!"

CHAPTER FORTY-TWO

Vanja sat up, patted her face with the skirt of her dress, and glared at Stefan. "What . . . were you . . . doing out there? Attila would have been safe in the tent if you hadn't left the camp."

Stefan was rocking mechanically back and forth on the cot.

"Answer me, husband!" she screeched in a voice that shocked even her. She'd never spoken to Stefan like this before.

"Nothing, woman. Leave me be."

"I want to know what happened!"

"I did nothing wrong! I was out getting us money. I was walking home when Attila found me. We were in the road. Some drunken American soldiers in a Jeep ran into him."

Vanja stood and folded her arms across her chest. She stared at him. He wouldn't meet her eyes. She knew in every cell of her body he was lying.

Suddenly, the same two American soldiers who'd brought Stefan to the tent minutes earlier returned. One said when he stepped into the tent, "Stefan Radko, you're to come with us."

"What is it?" Vanja asked. "What has he done?"

"Ma'am, I must ask you to stay out of this. Don't interfere."

"Please tell me. Why are you taking my husband away?" Vanja's chin trembled and her stomach contracted into a tight ball. She felt ill.

"Look, ma'am, you'll have to talk to our commander about that."

"Please," she said. "First you tell me my son is dead; now you want to take my husband. What is happening?"

The black soldier looked Vanja in the eye and said, "We don't know the whole story. But when we found your husband in the road where your son was killed, we heard something about Mr. Radko maybe being mixed up in the kidnapping of an American officer. A Captain Michael Danforth."

Vanja's chin stopped trembling. She clenched her jaw. Then she balled up her fists and whipped around and screamed at Stefan in Roma. "You lying, miserable bastard. You couldn't leave it alone. Twenty-eight years have passed and you had to pay Danforth back. It was *your* fault from the beginning. *You* were responsible for Gregorie's death. Kidnapping babies! This is God's punishment! And now our son, Attila. And if anything happens to Danforth's son, you'll have broken your daughter's heart, as well."

Vanja turned back to the soldiers and, with her finger pointing back at Stefan, yelled, "Get him out of my sight!"

She stepped aside and allowed the two soldiers to take Stefan. She watched them drag him outside. When they had gone, she sat back down on the cot and sobbed, even after she had no more tears.

CHAPTER FORTY-THREE

After contacting NATO Headquarters, Colonel Sweeney mobilized a battalion of the 82nd Airborne. He ordered it to move up to the Yugoslav border, to stop every person moving north into Serbia. At 0430 hours – one hour after the kidnapping – his senior staff waited for him in the headquarters building.

"Attention!" someone shouted when Colonel Sweeney entered the room.

All stood.

"As you were, gentlemen." Sweeney headed for a chair. "Jim, let's hear what you've got."

Major Jim Taylor, Sweeney's Executive Officer, cleared his throat. "The old Gypsy we picked up on the road outside the base entrance claimed five men kidnapped Captain Danforth. The men claimed to be Bosnian farmers, but he didn't buy their story. He thought they might be Serb paramilitary types. We've tried to get additional information out of him, but he's not cooperating. Our best guess is Danforth's abduction was a random act performed by a Serb special operations unit. Because of the heavy NATO night bombing missions, it's highly unlikely the kidnappers would take Danforth through Kosovo Province. Albania and Bulgaria aren't good alternatives either. And we know they wouldn't have gone south, deeper into Macedonia. So they're probably on the road running north toward Serbia."

Sweeney asked, "Jim, how do we know they didn't connect with a helicopter and fly out?"

"Because our radar units have detected no Serb aircraft activity within fifty miles of the kidnapping site."

"Good," Sweeney said. He looked at Captain Jess Dombrowsky, his Chopper Squadron Leader, and said, "I want gunships overflying the Yugoslav border from now on."

"Yes, sir," Dombrowsky said.

"So, what are our–" Sweeney stopped when Sergeant Major Luther Jewell walked into the room and nodded at him. Sweeney waved Jewell over.

The Sergeant Major approached the Colonel, bent down, and whispered, "I got a guy outside who wants to sit in with you. He's got CIA credentials. Name's Jack Cole. Says he's a friend of Captain Danforth's. What do you want me to tell him, sir?"

Sweeney scratched his ear. "Show him in, Sergeant Major. I'll take all the help I can get."

Jewell walked to the door, opened it and called out in his deep, rumbling voice, "This way, Mr. Cole."

"Please take a seat, Mr. Cole," Sweeney said. "Major Taylor here just briefed us on his analysis of the situation. It looks like the Serbs were looking to grab an American, probably for political and psychological reasons. Michael Danforth was in the wrong place at the wrong time."

"With all due respect to Major Taylor, I don't believe there's anything random about Michael Danforth's kidnapping," Jack said. "Stefan Radko's involvement–"

"Stefan Radko?" Sweeney interrupted.

Jack held up a finger and said, "Give me a minute, Colonel." He then continued and said, "Stefan Radko's involvement convinced me that this kidnapping is not random. We don't have time to go into all the details, but Michael Danforth has now been kidnapped twice in his life. The first time was when he was two years old. *Then* it *was* random. Stefan Radko was behind that kidnapping, too. Michael's father, now a colleague of mine, killed Radko's son while trying to rescue Michael. Radko has never forgiven him."

Jack paused to let his words sink in. He could see shocked looks directed at him.

"Recent events in the States," Jack continued, "lead me to believe the Yugoslav leadership, the Serbs running the country, also have a grudge against Michael's father because of a clandestine mission he headed up. Michael Danforth's kidnapping is a blatant act of revenge against a U.S. citizen. The Serbs in the Yugoslav leadership will never admit they have Michael. He's either going to be killed or will be kept in a slave-labor camp."

"Pretty fantastic story, Mr. Cole," Taylor said.

"Every word of it's true. And if we don't figure out a way in the next hour or two to find the men who took Michael, we'll never get him back," Jack said. "Once they get Michael into the heart of Serbia, it's all over."

"Any ideas, Mr. Cole?"

"Yeah, a couple. Let's assume our President isn't going to approve an invasion of Yugoslavia over the kidnapping of one soldier, and any operation of any size, approved or unapproved, would be detected by the Serbs — and the Russians, for that matter. And we don't need the political fallout that would bring. I think we should send in a Special Forces or Marine Force Recon unit."

"But, to where?" one of the staff officers asked.

"Good question," Jack said, running his fingers through his hair. "Before coming over here, I called Langley and instructed them to contact NIMA, the National Imagery & Mapping Association. They should be calling back soon."

"What do you have in mind?" Taylor asked.

"We're asking NIMA to run up some change detection," Jack said. "They'll compare current satellite images against past images over the last twenty-four hours from the Macedonian border with Serbia to a point fifty miles north of the border. The National Reconnaissance Office flies satellites all over the world. I'll bet they've got several in orbit over the Balkans. NIMA's got to have data off those satellites. They're going to look for anomalies — vehicles where they shouldn't be, troops moving on the road. Maybe something will turn up."

"We dealing with infrared, or something else?" Taylor asked.

"Probably Synthetic Aperture Radar. We should be able to get an SAR phase history analysis."

"And what if there's no imagery?" Taylor said.

Jack's heart seemed to become too heavy for his chest. The same question had come to mind during his call to Langley. "Then we're up the creek," he said. "We'd have to ask for tasking — get the NRO to change the inclination of one of its satellites. They probably couldn't do that without getting permission from the White House, or from CINCEUCOM, at a minimum."

"Oh shit!" Taylor exclaimed. "What about going to a commercial satellite operator?"

"Neither is a viable option," Jack explained. "Michael would be in the Serb capital by the time we got an answer from either one."

The room went quiet for a few seconds.

Finally, Sweeney turned to Major Jim Taylor. "Jim, call Colonel Mumphrey at the Marine detachment. Tell him I need to talk to him. I want his men on standby." He swiveled around and nodded to Major Harris

391

Krumka, his Intelligence Chief. "I want you to work with Mr. Cole. Get him a line to the National Security Agency and keep it open."

"What do you want me to tell our commanders up on the border?" Jim Taylor asked.

"Tell them to get their men ready in case we need to cross the border. This is top secret. I don't want anyone outside this room to know what we're preparing to do. Now get to it! Captain Dombrowsky, Mr. Cole, you'll stay here with me." Sweeney turned to Major Taylor who was leaving the room. "Jim, as soon as you make the call to the company commanders, come back here."

After the others filed out of the room, Sweeney walked to the door, closed it, returned to his chair, and said to Dombrowsky. "Jess, how quickly can you get two Apaches in the air over southern Yugoslavia?"

"You mean on the border?"

"No, I mean into Yugoslavia."

"How far into Yugoslavia?" Dombrowsky asked.

"No more than fifty miles."

"Jeez!" Dombrowsky exhaled. "No disrespect intended, Colonel, but why don't you just ask how long it would take me to fly to Belgrade?"

"Listen, Jess. I know I'm asking a lot. But one of our own is in trouble. As long as I'm in charge, there ain't going to be any POWs or MIAs from this unit."

"Don't get me wrong, sir. I'll do whatever it takes to get Mike back. But fifty miles into Yugoslavia! We're not going to be able to keep that quiet."

"Answer my question, Jess," Sweeney said, as Major Taylor walked back into the room and sat down.

"Forty, fifty minutes. I'll need to find three men who won't mind being courts-martialed, fuel the birds, complete preflight checks."

"You can get in undetected?"

"Possible. But, I'll have to clip the treetops."

"Do it, Jess!"

"Yes, sir!"

The pilot walked out of the room. After he was gone, Major Taylor squinted at Colonel Sweeney. "I think I was here long enough to get the gist of what you want Dombrowsky to do," he said. "With all due respect, Colonel, are you crazy?"

"Probably, Jim. I want you to type up orders saying I ordered Dombrowsky to cross into Yugoslavia. I'll sign them. And get Colonel Nye over at Air Force on the horn. Tell him we're putting two, two-man Apache crews into the Red Zone. We don't want the AWACS boys to report them."

Taylor stood and came to attention. "Yes, sir," he snapped.

After Taylor left the room, Jack turned to Sweeney and said, "If you lose your job over this, Colonel, come see me. I can use a man like you."

CHAPTER FORTY-FOUR

Vitas felt an Arctic-like wind seize him. His teeth chattered; his body shook. So cold. A fog seemed to cover his eye and nothing appeared real. Then the fever began again. He stewed in his own sweat. Then chills again, and then more fever and sweating. Something cool touched his forehead. Was that a hand on his arm?

He opened his eyes. The fog began to diminish – white room, ceiling fan, a blinking monitor. He remembered then where he was, and why. Damn raccoon! Damn Danforth bitch! he thought.

Then the Gypsy girl's face came to him. The chill returned, gripping his flesh and bone. But, as before, it gave way to heat, a flash of hotness so intense he felt scalded. And then a momentary reprieve.

A movement at his side – a human form loomed into view. Vitas squeezed his eyelids shut, then opened them, trying to focus. It still seemed a gauzy veil blurred his vision. Then he recognized the white cap and white uniform. A nurse. Vitas tried to speak, but words wouldn't come. His throat was parched, his tongue felt too big for his mouth. With a massive effort of will, he raised a quivering hand and weakly crooked a finger at her.

The nurse stepped close enough for him to make out her features. She had a professional but gentle smile. She bent closer, her face just inches from his. He inhaled the smell of her perfume, her shampoo, her flesh. He clutched the front of her uniform and pulled her to him. He squeezed her breast. He pressed his mouth against hers and bit her lower lip. But he couldn't continue and collapsed back onto the pillow.

The nurse made a sound that was almost a scream. Vitas felt and tasted her blood. He felt the woman struggle out of his grasp.

Then a thunderbolt of pain struck his chest. Every muscle in his body seemed to cramp. He opened his mouth and gasped for breath, and sensed the woman move away from him. Her screams sounded off the walls and ceiling.

Vitas tried to suck air into his lungs, but they didn't seem to work. He felt liquid leak from his mouth, down his chin, and onto his neck. And then the whiteness of the room faded away to blackness, to nothing.

CHAPTER FORTY-FIVE

Michael walked near the middle of a line of men spaced about ten feet apart – two Serb soldiers in front and three trailing. His wrists were tied together in front of his body with rope, and a second rope – a tether – was held by the man named Dimitrov. Whenever Michael lagged behind, the Serb jerked on the rope, sending a sharp pain from Michael's wrists to his shoulders, and dragged him along like a dog.

His arms and head hurt. He stumbled along the narrow forest trail, weaving first one way then the other. But Michael was nowhere near as dizzy and weak as he pretended. Staggering along the narrow trail through the forest, he intentionally fell every few minutes.

Through trees to the left, Michael could just see a ribbon of road meandering far below.

Ahead, the trail led out of the trees and edged along the brink of a steep hillside. He waited until the trail approached closest to the drop-off, then violently yanked the tether out of Dimitrov's hand and launched himself down the slope. He rolled and crashed through bushes and bounced off saplings, then slammed chest-first into a large tree. The pain made him gasp. It was as though a knife had been stuck into his ribs. He scrambled under a bush, breathing as shallowly as possible.

There were shouts from above, and then the sound of boots moving cautiously down the hillside. A small rock, dislodged by one of the Serbs, rolled past his face. Twice, someone came within a few feet of his hiding place.

Dimitrov finally found Michael. "You bastard!" the Serb hissed in English, while he dragged him out by the arm and began to punch him in the face and chest, sending shock waves of pain through him.

"Idiot!" Sokic snarled, grabbing Dimitrov's arm and shoving him aside.

Sokic spat an order and two of his other men lifted Michael off the ground and held him braced between them.

The Serb leader stood toe-to-toe with Michael. "I have had all the crap I am going to take from you," he said. "Any more delaying tactics and I will shoot you right here."

"Bullshit!" Michael blurted. "You already told me enough to know that's the last thing you'll do. You need me alive."

Sokic snapped an arm forward, grabbed Michael's throat, and squeezed. With his air cut off by the Serb's painful grip, Michael gagged and nearly passed out. Suddenly, the pressure let up. But Michael saw the bloodlust in the man's eyes and knew the Serb would have killed him right there if his orders allowed it.

CHAPTER FORTY-SIX

After hours of waiting in Sweeney's command post for news of Michael, Jack got a ride back to his hotel. He needed to shower and change. Then he'd return to the Army base. He dragged into the lobby and was walking toward the stairs when a man's urgent voice called across the lobby: "Mr. Cole!"

Jack turned tired eyes toward the voice and saw the desk clerk beckoning him. What the hell now? He walked over to the man.

"A Mr. Danforth called for you several times," the clerk said, handing Jack four message slips. "He wants you to call him as soon as possible."

Jack took the messages and mumbled, "Thanks." He felt heaviness on his heart like never before while he walked back over to the stairs. How could he tell Bob and Liz about Michael? His body slumped. He looked at his watch. Ten p.m. in Bethesda.

After he reached his room, Jack shucked his shirt and began unlacing a shoe, at the same time holding the telephone receiver to his ear and waiting for the overseas operator to make the connection. The phone rang on the other side of the Atlantic. Please don't be home, he prayed.

"Hello!" It was Bob, and not Liz, thank God.

"It's Jack."

"Jack, I've been trying to reach you all day. You've got to find Michael and warn him. Miriana's father is Stefan Radko. Must be the *same* Radko."

"Bob, I need to–"

"Let me finish. You know Radko hates my guts because of what happened to his own son. There's no telling what he'll do to Michael to get even with me. You've got to protect my son. You've–"

Jack interrupted. "It's already too late. The Serbs kidnapped Michael this morning. We're trying to find him before they get too deep into Yugoslavia. And Radko *was* involved. He set Michael up."

Jack waited for Bob to respond, but all he heard was a light buzz over the line. "Bob," Jack said softly, "did you hear me?"

"Yeah, I heard," Bob said, flatly. "Anything else?"

"No, that's it. I'm sor—"

"I've got to tell Liz," Bob said. There was a click, then a dial tone.

Jack forced away his fatigue. He stripped off the rest of his clothes, moving with renewed, anger-fed energy. He took a quick shower, shaved, brushed his teeth. After putting on clean clothes, he rushed downstairs and drove back to the American base.

CHAPTER FORTY-SEVEN

When Jack walked back into Sweeney's command post, the silence in the room told him there'd been no news of Michael.

Sweeney's face was a steel mask. "Nothing! Not a damn thing," he told Jack.

"Anyone question Radko?"

"Yeah. The sonofabitch admitted his complicity and seemed proud of it. He told us he at first thought they were just a bunch of farmers, but he figured, after a while, they were Serb soldiers. The bastards killed his son, and he still hasn't given the slightest indication he's sorry about what he did."

The phone rang. Jack noticed everyone in the room watching while Major Krumka, the Intelligence Officer, picked up the receiver, listened for a moment, then handed it to him. "It's for you," Krumka said. "NIMA's got something."

"Put it on speaker mode," Jack said. That done, he said loudly, "Cole here. Go ahead."

"Okay," said the voice on the line. "We couldn't see much with the SAR satellite until the sun came up. The last satellite pass went over the Preshevo area ten minutes ago. A couple miles north of the city, we saw a vehicle nose down in a ravine. Another of our satellites – an infrared unit – got a weak heat signature off its engine. With computer enhancement, we picked up U.S. Army insignia. It's the Jeep your man was driving when he got snatched."

"Any people around the site?"

"Nope! Not a soul."

Jack walked around the room, organizing his thoughts.

"You still there, Mr. Cole?" the NIMA man asked.

"Hold on," Jack shouted.

Sweeney looked quizzically at Jack. "What's . . . ?"

Jack cut Colonel Sweeney off with a wave of his hand. He stepped closer to the speaker. "Your IR satellites can't pick up anything in the dark unless it's hot or lit up, right?"

"Correct! A fire, a running engine, even a man or a large animal."

"So," Jack continued, "you said the satellite picked up a heat signature off the Jeep. Which means its engine must have been running pretty recently."

"Sounds right!"

"How 'bout going back over every satellite pass and see when you picked up the first heat signature coming from that location. Could give us an idea how long ago they dumped the Jeep. And while you're at it, check to see if any vehicles left the area shortly after the Jeep showed up."

"I see where you're going," the NIMA man said. "You think maybe they dumped the Jeep and took off in another vehicle they stashed there."

"And," Jack continued the thought, "if we don't find any evidence of other cars or trucks having left the site, it's damn sure they set out on foot. Depending on when the Jeep showed up, we should be able to figure out how far they could've traveled – by vehicle, or by foot. How soon can you get back to us?"

"Thirty minutes."

"We don't have thirty minutes. Make it ten."

CHAPTER FORTY-EIGHT

Bob had enough rank in the CIA to pretty much do whatever he wanted to do without a written directive from a superior, short of ordering wet work. So, demanding a company King Air on a moment's notice didn't raise any questions on the part of the Aircraft Control Officer. All the man asked was, "When do you need it and where are you going?"

"Yesterday," Bob answered. "I need the plane yesterday. I'm flying to Macedonia to join Jack Cole in the talks with the Serbs."

"Man, it's a mess over there," the Aircraft Control Officer said.

More than you know, Bob thought.

After getting off the phone to Langley, Bob returned to his bedroom and hesitated in the doorway. Liz was packing an overnight bag for him, mechanically going through the motions. Bob approached her, gently took her arm, and guided her to the other side of the bed. He made her sit, then cupped her chin and raised her eyes to his.

"You stay strong. I don't want to be worrying about you while I'm over there."

Liz cleared her throat. Then she placed her hands on Bob's chest, pushed him away, and stood. "There's not a damned thing wrong with me that getting our son back safe and sound won't cure." She wagged a finger at him and said, "I'm not that innocent young girl who fell apart in Greece years ago, when that bastard Radko took Michael. If I could get my hands on that sick . . .."

There was something showing in Liz's face that told Bob she knew he and the CIA had something to do with Michael's kidnapping. Her look and the tone in her voice came up short of accusing him of culpability. Nonetheless, Bob felt a rush of icy fear go through him as he thought of what might happen to the rest of his and Liz's lives if he didn't bring Michael back.

Liz suddenly, unexpectedly, stepped into Bob's arms and buried her face in his neck. "You bring our boy home. You hear me, Bob Danforth? You bring our boy home."

The flight to the U.S. Air Force field constructed outside Kumanovo for the war would take an agonizing seven hours. Despite being exhausted from worry and lack of sleep, Bob felt wired. He knew his and Liz's future and their mental well-being were tied up in how this mission turned out.

He'd taken a seat in one of two captain's chairs that bracketed a small round table near the bulkhead. He'd spread out a map of the Serbia/Macedonia border and studied it until his eyes burned. The men who took Michael were going north. He knew that with a certainty that came from years of thinking like the enemies of the United States. He'd participated and planned countless covert operations, and was the best the CIA had.

Bob assumed the kidnappers had stashed a vehicle somewhere near the border. Or a Serb helicopter would pick up the men once they crossed into Serbia. The latter alternative would be the worst. He said a silent prayer the Serbs would try to escape on foot or in a vehicle. A helicopter would be easy to detect. But if they got Michael on board a chopper and managed to take off again, there wasn't much the Americans would be able to do. An escape on foot or by motor vehicle would slow them down.

"Mr. Danforth," the co-pilot announced over the plane's intercom, "I've got a call for you."

Bob grabbed the telephone receiver from its place on the bulkhead. "Danforth," he said.

"Bob, it's Jack. I just called the house and Liz told me what you were up to. Are you nuts?"

"Any news?" Bob asked.

"Nothing yet. What do you think you're going to do?"

"Listen, Jack, let's not get into a pissing match over my flying over there. You don't like it, then fire my ass."

"Okay, okay, calm down," Jack said. "I'm at the 82nd's headquarters. I'll have a car pick you up at the airstrip."

"Have there been any Serb helicopters in the area of the border?" Bob asked.

"We've been watching. Not a one."

Bob sighed and, in a quiet voice, said, "Thank God." Then he said, "They've got to be going straight north. They wouldn't risk going in any other direction. They've got to get into Serbia as quickly as possible."

"We're assuming the same thing. When are you due to land?"

Bob checked his watch. "Three hours."

CHAPTER FORTY-NINE

The rising sun had brightened the sky above the valley, but the road was in cold shadow. Michael, his hands still bound in front and tethered to one of the Serb soldiers, noticed Sokic's men's disdainful looks at the scattering of refugees they were beginning to encounter. Their hatred toward the Kosovars was palpable.

One of the soldiers spat at a dirty, bedraggled man shuffling south, everything he now owned in the world on his back, in his hands. A couple of the others slung curses at the frightened people they passed, taunting them. The leader of the Serb unit told his men to shut up.

Michael looked at the refugees' expressions and saw the same fear and despair he'd seen thousands of times in the past few weeks. Their faces were open books, which Michael had learned to read. They'd lost everything and knew they had no reason to believe they would ever return to their homes. He wondered if they could see the same look on his face.

Michael had a sudden sinking feeling. He told himself he could never lose hope. His worst enemy was hopelessness. Never give up. But he knew the Serbs would commandeer the first vehicle they came across, and then his situation would turn from dire to hopeless. As long as they were on foot, they couldn't put much distance between themselves and the Macedonian border. But with a car or truck, even a horse-drawn wagon . . ..
And once they moved into a Serb village or town, U.S. planes would be unable to spot them – if there were planes out looking for him in the first place.

CHAPTER FIFTY

"82nd Air—"

"This is NIMA calling for Jack Cole."

"Hold on."

Jack had been pacing the command center like a caged animal. He rushed to the speakerphone. "This is Jack Cole."

"Matthews at NIMA. I think we got something. One of our satellites crosses over the area where the Jeep is located every twenty-two minutes. We zeroed in on the coordinates of that spot and checked every satellite pass from 1918 hours on. Absolutely nothing occurred until 0512 hours, your time. We saw the heat signatures of six people around one vehicle. At 0534 hours, the men are gone and the Jeep is lying in the ravine fifty yards away."

"How about the people?" Jack blurted. "Could you pick up their signatures moving away from the site?"

"Not on the same satellite pass. And, for whatever reason, we didn't detect them during the 0556 overflight. But at 0618, six separate heat signatures were picked up in the hills a couple miles north of the abandoned Jeep."

"Could be any group of people," Jack said, playing devil's advocate, although his instincts told him they'd located Michael and his captors.

"Yeah, maybe. But we'll have sunlight on the 0640 SAR pass. I may be able to tell you a whole lot more in . . . six and-a-half minutes."

"Okay, we'll continue keeping this line open until then. I'll see if I can hold my breath that long. And, Matthews, good work."

Matthews said, "I'll come back on the line the minute I have the next imagery."

Jack crisscrossed the room. He stopped suddenly after three circuits, spun around, and faced Colonel Sweeney. "Colonel," he said, "is there something we could be doing right now in anticipation of Matthews telling us they just took a picture of five Serb soldiers and one U.S. Army Captain. If they're still on foot, they can't be too far north of here." Jack smiled at Sweeney and said, "You wouldn't happen to have a helicopter that could check out the general area?"

Sweeney smiled back. "I'll see what I can do," he said, walking over to a second telephone where he dialed four numbers. "Jim, Dennis Sweeney here. No, nothing for sure. Listen, get Dombrowsky on the radio and tell him to get his two birds in the air. Tell him he's probably too far north."

Jack grinned at Sweeney and thought, thank God for military men with a balls-to-the-wall attitude.

"No, I don't know exactly where," Sweeney continued. "Just tell Jess to follow the main road south. Hopefully, I'll have more information in a few minutes."

Sweeney hung up and joined Jack in striding back and forth across the room.

Jack jumped at the sudden sound of Matthews' voice bursting like an explosion over the speakerphone. "You there, Mr. Cole?"

With Sweeney following him, he rushed over to the phone. "I'm here. Go ahead."

"We got six men taking a Sunday stroll up the middle of the main north-south road. One of the men is obviously tied up. Without a car, and considering the time sequence, I'd say it's your man."

"What're the coordinates?" Jack shouted.

"Check your fax machine. Our Photographic Intelligence Section sent you the last photographs. The coordinates are printed on the bottom of the pictures."

"Thanks, Matthews, I owe you one."

"Just let us know if you find our boy."

"You can count on it."

Bob's legs ached. He stood and tried to stretch them while walking back and forth in the airplane's cabin but the clearance was too low and bending over while he walked only made his back ache. He returned to his seat and collapsed into it. Less than an hour, he thought as he looked at his wristwatch.

407

CHAPTER FIFTY-ONE

Other than a couple hours sleep between dinner with Jack Cole and going out to meet Stefan Radko at the 82nd compound's gate, Michael hadn't slept for twenty-six hours. His head ached. Gingerly he touched his ribs. At least one was broken, he thought, from rolling down the hill and hitting the tree – or from the beating the Serb soldier gave him. He didn't have to pretend to slow down the Serbs anymore. Going slow now came easily.

Then he heard the sound of an engine approaching from the direction they were walking. His heart sank. He looked ahead at the curve in the road and waited for the vehicle to appear. He said a silent prayer: Please let it be a motorcycle, or a tractor. Something too small to carry all of them, or something slow. Don't let it be a car or truck.

The oncoming vehicle became louder, and then it came around the curve in the road and entered the straightaway. Michael felt lower than he already felt. It was a sedan.

The Serbs had lined up across the road. They pointed their rifles at the car. Sokic raised an arm. As soon as the car stopped, the soldiers surrounded it and began dragging the occupants – a man and a woman in their thirties, two small children, and an elderly woman – out onto the road. From the way the soldiers manhandled them, Michael assumed the people from the car must be Kosovar Albanian or Bosnian Muslims. Both hated groups. Less than human to the Serbs.

Sokic shouted orders to his men, three of whom herded the car's occupants into the trees beyond the road. They'd been gone only a minute, when shots rang out. The men returned a moment later, all smiles.

The soldier guarding Michael pulled on the tether tied to his wrists and jerked him toward the car, shoving him into the backseat. The other soldiers removed the people's possessions from inside the car and from its roof and tossed them into the ditch by the side of the road. They then piled into the car.

Sokic got behind the wheel. He had barely finished turning the car around, when he began cursing, got out of the vehicle, and walked to the rear fender. He opened the fuel door and unscrewed the gas cap. Then he went over to a sapling by the side of the road, ripped off a branch, and took it back to the car. He stuck the branch into the fuel tank and pulled it out. Only about a quarter of an inch at the bottom of the branch glistened with wetness. Sokic slammed his boot-tip into the car fender. He threw the stick away.

Squeezed between the Serbs in the backseat, Michael silently mouthed the words, "Run out of gas," over and over. This time his prayer was answered – a few miles up the road.

CHAPTER FIFTY-TWO

Major Jim Taylor picked up the radio transmitter. "Lobo One, this is Mother Goose." Then he read coordinates into the microphone.

"I copy, Mother Goose. Lobo One out," said Captain Jess Dombrowsky in his Apache helicopter, in the sky fifty miles inside Yugoslavia.

"You hear that, Ernie?" he asked through his headset.

"Yeah, Jess," his co-pilot, Ernie Patten, replied.

"How about you guys?" Jess asked, looking out his side window at the second Apache.

"Loud and clear," declared Scooter James, his wingman.

"Roger," Billy Herrera, Scooter's co-pilot said.

"Hold on while I input the coordinates," Ernie said.

Dombrowsky turned the aircraft due south and pushed the throttle to the Apache's maximum level cruising speed of one hundred eighty miles per hour.

The radio message had been sent in the clear. Dombrowsky knew that meant the Serb military might have intercepted it. But he had the upper hand – they wouldn't be able to react in time. Unless the bad guys had MIGs nearby.

Flying at this speed, his wingman and he would be at the designated coordinates before the Serbs could triangulate their location and get planes or troops there. He hoped.

The two Apache helicopters followed the road south, flying at an altitude of three hundred feet. Fifteen miles north of the coordinates they'd been given, the crews encountered a two-thousand-foot mountain intersected by a tunnel. Unable to continue following the road, they gained altitude to hurdle the formation. When Dombrowsky passed over the peak, he realized the rules of the game suddenly changed.

"Holy shit!" the Serb soldier screamed, abandoning his effort to take a leisurely piss against the outside wall of the radar site's command and control center. Running back inside the installation, he saw his teammate punching buttons on the target acquisition radar console. He'd already locked on the American helicopters. The soldier snatched a telephone from its cradle and called in the sighting to headquarters, while watching his partner at the radar console electronically transmit the enemy helicopters' locations from the target acquisition radar to the target tracking radar.

The soldier was sure headquarters would notify the Serb Air Force MIG 29 Fighter Wing stationed near Dimitrovgrad, just west of the Bulgarian border – about ninety kilometers northeast of the radar site. Within eight minutes of the radar team's warning, two MIGs could be racing down the runway at the Dimitrovgrad Air Force Base.

"Our luck just changed, Jess," Lieutenant Scooter James declared in a voice so calm he might as well have been telling Dombrowsky the time. "Do me a favor, will you, and don't remind me I volunteered for this mission."

Dombrowsky smiled and said, "It just gives us added motivation to get the job done quickly, Scooter. Tighten up on my six. We're going treetop."

The two Apaches banked off the crest of the mountain and roared down toward the road ahead. Dombrowsky noted the distance to the coordinates Patten had entered: Twelve miles to go – three-and-a-half minutes. Plenty of time, he thought. Unless the bad guys have MIGs close by.

CHAPTER FIFTY-THREE

Jack had somehow wrung enough self-discipline from his seemingly demented mind to force himself to sit in a chair. He didn't know how he would live with it if this turned out badly. He'd taken a seat when he realized his incessant pacing had started to grate on everyone's nerves. He'd always prided himself on his ability to control his emotions, to maintain self-control under the most arduous of circumstances. But this was personal. Michael Danforth was the son of his best friend. And he had been abducted in retaliation for the CIA's kidnapping of Antonin Karadjic. He'd authorized that mission.

"Colonel Sweeney, it's Colonel Nye on the horn," Sergeant Major Jewell shouted, holding up the telephone receiver, waving it at Sweeney. The tone in Jewell's voice and the tension evident in his body language caused Jack's skin to hurt. Every nerve in his body seemed on fire.

Jack watched Sweeney go over to Jewell's desk and take the phone from the Sergeant Major's hand. Sweeney sat on the edge of the desk, holding the receiver against his chest, as though he was preparing himself for bad news. He had obviously picked up on the strain in Jewell's voice. Jack moved closer.

"Hello, George," Sweeney said, after moving the receiver to his ear. "Wha—. Yes. Yes. Yes. I understand. Yeah. Let's keep our fingers crossed. Thanks, George. I hope your men are real close to their planes."

He slammed down the phone, looking meaningfully at Jack. Then he turned to Jewell. "Get Major Taylor on the horn. Have him radio Dombrowsky. The Serbs have jets in the air."

Jack groaned. The stab of pain he felt in his stomach meant his ulcer was acting up again. That always happened when something bad happened.

Things had suddenly turned awful. Then Bob Danforth walked into the room.

CHAPTER FIFTY-FOUR

Back on foot, Michael heard the whup-whup-whup of helicopter rotors. He knew the sound of the AH-64H, Apache Attack Helicopter, by heart. From the way his captors looked toward the sky, he could tell they recognized the sound, too. Michael felt a tingle run up his spine when the noise grew louder.

Sokic had stopped. He now cocked an ear upward. He looked at Michael. Michael smiled back, watching realization strike.

"Take cover," Sokic yelled. He dove into a shallow dry ditch beside the road. Dimitrov and Pyotr followed suit. Josef, tugging violently on the rope around Michael's wrists, dragged him into the ditch on the opposite side of the road and dove on top of him. Vassily dropped into the same ditch, farther down the road.

Helicopter noise grew louder and louder. Then Michael felt the beat of the rotors churning the air above him.

But the choppers moved away, farther down the road, taking Michael's desperate hope with them.

"Scooter, we're past the position where those men are supposed to be," Jess Dombrowsky shouted. "Let's turn around and make another pass to the north."

"Roger," Scooter replied, following Dombrowsky. "We can't hang around here much longer, though, Jess. Those Serb jets are going to join the party any minute."

"Damn, that was close," Josef said, starting to climb out of the ditch.

"Get back down," Vassily yelled. "The Americans could come back."

Josef fell back down. "Fucking Americans," he grumbled. But he raised his head and saw two specks on the horizon about a mile away. They seemed to be getting bigger.

Michael heard the Apaches coming back. It's now or never, he thought. He snapped his head backward through the half-foot of space Josef had created by lifting his own head. Michael felt the crunch of bone and cartilage when the back of his head smashed into Josef's face. A sharp pain shot through Michael's head, neck, and shoulders, making him forget for a moment about his busted ribs. He felt dizzy. Josef went limp and fell with his full weight onto Michael's back. Michael peeked over at Vassily through his now-cloudy vision. The Serb appeared to be facing away, his arms covering his head.

Rolling Josef off his back, Michael grabbed the Serb's AK-47 assault rifle and, with his eyes closed, checked the weapon's safety. It was off. He opened his eyes, then squeezed them shut, hoping to clear his vision. When he opened them again, he seemed to be able to see a lot better. He pulled the knife from the scabbard on Josef's belt and cut the Serb's throat.

He wiped the blade on his fatigue pants, propped the knife upside down between his boots and sawed the ropes on his wrists against its razor-sharp blade. The ropes parted while the Apaches roared overhead on their way back to the north. Their screaming rotors kicked up dust devils that screened Michael from the Serbs. Gripping the knife, he crept on his hands and knees toward Vassily, whose shape appeared dimly in the dust cloud. The Serb still had his head down, protecting his face from the blowing dirt. Then, as the choppers passed them, Vassily suddenly turned toward Michael. Shock showed on his face.

Vassily drew his knife – Michael was too close for him to have time to bring his rifle around. The Serb rolled away and came up on his knees.

They grappled, each with a grip on the other's knife hand. The Serb was bigger and stronger, but Michael was faster. He broke the Serb's hold on his wrist, twisted him onto his stomach, heaved himself atop, and drove his knife into the side of Vassily's neck. Pressing down with all his weight, he waited for his enemy to stop struggling, while warm blood splashed over his hand.

Then Michael ripped off his bloody fatigue shirt, picked up the AK-47 he'd taken from Josef, and crouched low, hoping the Apaches would return before the other Serbs discovered what had happened.

Dombrowsky focused on the valley below and the road bisecting it. The men they were looking for had to be down there. He checked the coordinates he'd punched into his controls. Correct. "Scooter, let's go back up the road one more time."

"Roger," Scooter replied. "But those MIGs are going to be on our asses any second now."

The choppers turned for another pass – to Michael it seemed like a miracle. The beat of the rotors drummed the still morning air. Michael looked across the road – no sign of the other Serbs. He stood and waved his bloody shirt in great, exaggerated arcs.

The Apaches raced by overhead.

"Did you see that?" Scooter and his co-pilot, Billy Herrera, shouted into their headsets at the same time.

"Yeah! I'm going back," Dombrowsky answered. "Scooter, you follow me around, but let's not fall into a trap. And Ernie, Billy keep your eyes open. Those MIGs could be here any second."

Dombrowsky steered straight for the man in the T-shirt still standing in the ditch. But now, instead of waving his shirt, he had an arm pointed across the road.

"Looks like our guy, Scooter," Dombrowsky shouted. "I think he's trying to tell us something. Hang back. I'll yell if I need help."

He hovered closer while the man in the ditch ducked back down, using the shirt to protect his face from the stinging dirt being whipped up by the aircraft.

Several men rose up from the ditch across the road and began firing their weapons at Dombrowsky. His hand already on the helicopter's M230 automatic cannon's firing grip, he let loose a barrage of 30mm shells that chewed up the edge of the road in a procession of explosions marching toward the men who were firing at him. One of the men flew backward, his torso erupting in a pinkish spray.

But then Dombrowsky noticed something wrong with the Apache. It wasn't responding properly. Black smoke began to fill his cabin. He could hear Ernie screaming. Despite its special armor, the Apache had been critically damaged.

Michael had watched the helicopter inch its way toward the road, like a giant, supernatural insect hovering and waiting for the sight of prey. Then the Serbs had fired on the aircraft and the Apache returned fire with devastating force. He felt elated by the turn of events. Then he saw smoke plume from the back of the Apache's cabin when it veered away from the road. Momentarily distracted, he almost missed seeing the dust-obscured figures of two men still standing on the other side of the road, continuing to fire at the fleeing, wounded helicopter. He raised Josef's AK-47 and fired through the dust screen. One of the men screamed and both dropped out of sight.

Crouching down and peering over his shoulder, Michael watched the burning aircraft stagger toward a hillside. He looked around for the second chopper. There was still hope, if the second aircraft engaged the Serbs hiding in the ditch.

There it was. The other chopper now hovered near its wounded partner. Still spewing black smoke, the chopper's engine whined sickeningly while the aircraft began to auto-rotate and lose altitude.

Michael looked across the road again. He rested his rifle on the top of the ditch and waited for someone to show themselves. But he was assaulted by a shock wave that shook his damaged ribs and froze the blood in his veins. Two jets with Serb markings shrieked overhead. He realized then he'd also have himself to blame for the destruction of the second helicopter and the deaths of its crew.

Scooter James was no coward, but he believed discretion really was the better part of valor. He couldn't help his crewman, wingman, or Danforth if he got blown to bits by a Russian-made rocket. He shouted into his headset while he turned tail. "Target alive! Lobo One is down. MIGs in the area. I'm outta here."

CHAPTER FIFTY-FIVE

Michael's heart sank as the second helicopter flew out of sight over a hilltop and the two jets came screaming around to pursue it. That helicopter had represented escape. Salvation. Life. Michael knew in his gut the helicopter was done for. No whirlybird could survive a two-jet attack. He concentrated on his own predicament. He snuck a look toward the opposite ditch and ducked back down in time to avoid getting a bullet in his forehead. Dirt and rock fragments exploded at the top of the ditch, inches from his head, sending what felt like thousands of needles into his face. It was time to move. He wasn't about to wait here so the assholes across the road could come after him.

Armed with a knife and the AK-47 – the extra magazine he took from Vassily's jacket pocket now stuck in his pants pocket, he began to crawl north along the ditch. Any place had to be better than hiding like a gopher in his hole. Maybe he'd be able to find a place to hide. Or a way out of here.

He paused twenty yards up the ditch and rolled onto his back. Peering at the hills to his left, he looked for a sign of the helicopter. Nothing. He couldn't even hear the sounds of the jets' engines. If he got out of this, he knew he'd have to live the rest of his life with the guilt of having been responsible for the deaths of two helicopter crews. But, he couldn't dwell on that now. He was a long way from making it back to the American lines. He was a long way from ever having the luxury of feeling guilty about anything ever again. Guilt was an emotion reserved for the living.

Michael rolled back to his hands and knees and moved farther up the ditch.

CHAPTER FIFTY-SIX

"Lobo One, Lobo One, this is Nighthawk flight leader. I've got you pinpointed on my screen. Hang in there, we're on our way." It was the voice of an F-16C's pilot.

Scooter felt he hadn't breathed for several minutes. His chest muscles ached from tension and fear.

"Nighthawk leader, this is Lobo Two. Lobo One's down. I got two MIGs after me and not enough juice to outrun them. I got to find a place to hide."

"Give us thirty seconds, Lobo Two."

Scooter's radar showed the MIGs were, at most, five miles away. He knew Russian-trained pilots tended to wait for actual sightings of targets before firing. Their target acquisition system was not nearly as advanced as the American system.

"Get us out of here, Scooter," Billy Herrera yelled.

Scooter focused on the terrain two hundred feet below. He spotted a large barn, nestled against wooded hills on the far side of a bowl-shaped valley. He dropped the Apache behind the barn and hovered just three feet off the ground. He eyed his radar screen while the two blips from the MIGs closed on him. Just when they were about to come over a hilltop across the valley, he turned the nose of the Apache away from the barn and lifted the chopper as high as the barn roof.

"Jesus, Scooter, what the hell are you doing?" Billy screamed.

In the zone now, Scooter heard Billy yell something, but he wasn't concentrating on anything but the jets. He knew the MIGs' radar had probably picked up the Apache, but hiding behind the barn would prevent the Serb pilots from sighting him. And they were flying way too fast to have had the chance to eyeball him when he lifted the chopper above the barn. If they'd spotted him, they would've loosed their heat-seeking missiles and turned the Apache – and him and Billy – into one great big piece of charred fused material.

When the jets roared overhead, Scooter hit the toggle switches on two Hellfire missiles. The Apache jolted when the heat-seeking projectiles exploded out of their pods. Scooter hadn't had enough time to lock on either of the MIGs; but he hoped the heat coming off at least one of the jets would attract the missiles. Both Hellfires zipped upward, following the heat trail of the MIG on the left.

The two jets took evasive action, peeling away from each other like two sides of a banana skin. Scooter guessed their missile warning alarms were whining in their cockpits and they would hit their antimissile counter measures, dropping metal chaff into the air in an attempt to confuse the missiles' guidance systems. The evasive action fooled one of the Hellfires, which drifted off target and disappeared. The second missile found its target and struck the MIG 29 in its afterburner. The plane exploded and fell to the ground in a shower of flaming metal.

The American F-16C pilots pushed the speed of their planes to near capacity while they raced across the Serb sky at twelve hundred miles per hour. The flight leader had both MIG 29s on his radarscope. Then the bloom of an explosion showed on the scope and one of the MIGs disappeared. The flight leader centered the crosshairs of his target acquisition system over the remaining MIG's image. In a fraction of a second, he considered the weapons choices available to him – 20mm multi-barreled cannon, two wingtip missiles, air-to-air missiles fixed to underwing hardpoints. He thought for a moment about getting into a dogfight with the MIG pilot – *mano-a-mano*. But this was enemy territory and his orders were to finish the job and return to base quickly. He selected one of the air-to-air missiles, waited for the electronic tone telling him he'd locked onto the MIG, and hit the FIRE switch.

The American pilot again checked his radar screen. The missile blip flashed on and off, moving in the direction of the Serb jet. Then he felt a rush of adrenaline, making his stomach feel as though it was filled with a thousand crawling creatures, when the MIG disappeared from his scope and the aura of a flash of light exploded over the hills in the distance.

CHAPTER FIFTY-SEVEN

Colonel Dennis Sweeney figured he'd already blown his career by sending two Apache helicopters into Serbian territory without authorization. But, candidly, he didn't give a shit. He'd been a brand new second lieutenant when he was assigned to Vietnam in 1972, near the end of the active American military presence there. He'd made a promise to himself he'd never leave one of his men behind, whether dead or alive. Just thinking about the MIAs in Vietnam made his stomach hurt and his heart ache. Now he had Captain Danforth *and* a helicopter crew down in Serbia.

Sweeney moved to the telephone linking him to Major Taylor. He got Taylor on the line and told him he wanted a helicopter ready to take off. He could tell from Taylor's reaction the man thought his commander had finally gone around the bend. But the man had the good sense not to object.

After looking around the room and seeing that everyone seemed busy, and that no one seemed to be paying special attention to him, Sweeney walked to the entrance door and slipped outside. He'd covered about ten yards, when he heard footsteps behind him. Turning, he saw Bob Danforth approaching.

"Going somewhere, Colonel?" Danforth said.

Before Sweeney could decide how to respond, Danforth said, "You can waste time bullshitting me, Colonel, or we can run to that helicopter and together try to find Michael. Don't try to stop me. I didn't fly all the way from the States to sit on my ass."

Sweeney shook his head. What the hell, he thought, in for a pence, in for a pound. He pointed at Danforth and said, "Wing tips and a Brooks Brothers suit. What the modern soldier wears into battle." He turned and ran for the landing pad, Danforth on his heels.

CHAPTER FIFTY-EIGHT

Michael scrambled up the ditch until it took a bend. Something just ahead flashed brightly in the morning sun. He peered around the bend and saw the shiny, open-mouthed end of a corrugated metal culvert running under the road.

He crawled to the opening and looked inside. It would be a tight fit. There was no light visible at the end of the brush-clogged tunnel. Slipping inside, he splashed through shallow pools of stinking, stagnant water. The culvert's corrugated skin, rippled every three inches with two-inch high ribs, made progress slow and painful – bruising his hands and knees.

He soon reached a mass of dead, water-sodden brush that completely plugged the culvert. He poked the muzzle of the AK-47 into it, braced the toes of his boots against the metal ridges of the culvert, and pushed. He managed to dislodge some of the debris, and then some more. Suddenly, rats as big as cats leaped, squeaking, out of it. He recoiled and banged his head against the top of the culvert while they ran past him and over him. He swatted one off his arm and it flew against the curved wall before following the others out.

Michael took several deep breaths, then slithered forward again to the debris plug. This time he broke all the way through it and crawled ahead toward now-visible daylight at the culvert's far end.

He slid halfway out at the other end of the culvert, blinking while his eyes adjusted to sunlight. This end of the culvert hung about eight feet above a pebble-bottomed creek bed. Michael looked to his left and saw he was well beyond and slightly below the road and the ditch that paralleled this side of the road. The Serbs were nowhere to be seen.

Michael carefully lowered the AK-47 to the steep slope from which the culvert projected. Then he pulled himself out of the tube and dropped to the creek bed with a grunt. He stretched upward to retrieve the automatic weapon from the embankment and walked crouching back along the creek until he reached the spot below the place he guessed the Serbs might still be hiding.

The dirt slope was dry and crumbly, difficult to climb. Halfway to the top, he lost his footing and fell on his damaged ribs, on top of the rifle. He let out an *oomph* and slipped backwards. He held his breath, heart pounding. If the Serbs were still there, they must have heard him.

Michael looked up toward the top of the incline and saw the Serb Captain stand up in the ditch, pointing his weapon down toward him. Michael continued to slip down the hillside on his stomach. But he managed to get his rifle pointed uphill and blindly fire.

One of the bullets smashed into the metal firing mechanism of Sokic's rifle and broke its magazine loose. The impact blew the weapon out of Sokic's hands and shards of lead from the shattered bullet tore into his arms, neck, and face.

Sokic roared in pain. He looked down at his rifle and knew it was useless. Grabbing the knife from his scabbard, Sokic climbed over the edge of the ditch and charged down the slope.

Michael had reached flat ground and regained his feet just when Sokic smashed into his already damaged rib cage. The collision drove the air out of his lungs, but he managed to deflect Sokic's knife by hitting the Serb's wrist with the rifle. The blow threw Sokic off balance and he fell back against the slope.

Sokic rolled and came immediately to his feet, still gripping the knife. He charged at Michael, who attempted to use the rifle to parry the thrust, but Sokic kicked it from his hands. Stepping back, Michael reached down to pull Josef's knife from inside his boot. Sokic kicked at the ground and sent a spray of dirt into Michael's face. Momentarily blinded, Michael tried to rub the dirt from his eyes with one hand, and groped for the knife with the other.

Sokic leaped before Michael could get the knife from his boot and drove him onto his back. Through his still-blurred vision, Michael saw the Serb raise the knife above his head, poised to drive it downward into his throat.

Michael believed he was about to die. He heard his own wheezing while he half-blindly raised both arms to try to block the knife. Then there was a loud *crack*! And time segued into slow motion. Sokic's arm remained extended above him as though in suspended animation, seemingly forever. Then he toppled over, plunging the knife into the ground three inches from Michael's left ear.

Normal time resumed. Michael pushed Sokic's body away and threw himself toward the AK-47 lying in the dirt a few feet away.

"I hope you're not going to shoot me," a man said.

Startled, Michael looked up at the road above. His eyes still blurred and stinging from the dirt, he had difficulty seeing more than the outline of a standing figure backlit by the sun.

"Not if you did this," Michael said, looking now at Sokic, a dark bloodstain rapidly spreading across the back of the Serb's shirt.

"Got here just in time, didn't I?" The man above chuckled.

"I'll say. Who the hell are you?"

"Captain Danforth, I'm Jess Dombrowsky, an illustrious member of the 82nd Airborne's Aviation Brigade. We've been looking all over for you. Nearly got ourselves killed trying to find you."

Michael picked up the rifle and carefully made his way up the slope, his breathing almost back to normal. There were two bodies lying in the ditch. He shook Dombrowsky's hand. "Thanks! Where'd you come from?"

Dombrowsky made a hitchhiking motion over his shoulder with his thumb, pointing at a column of smoke rising from a spot up against the nearest hill. "Parked my Apache over there," he said.

"That was you?" Michael exclaimed. "I thought you were a goner, for sure. Did your co-pilot make it?"

"Yes! He's back by the wreckage. Leg's broken." Dombrowsky sighed. Then his face went white and he collapsed in the ditch.

Michael dropped to his knees to check the man's pulse. It was slow but steady. He put his arms around Dombrowsky and tried to lift him, but his hands slipped. The pilot's back was wet and when Michael took his hands away he saw they were red with blood. He rolled Dombrowsky onto his side, took the knife from his boot, and sliced open the pilot's blood-soaked flight suit and undershirt. Blood seeped from an eight-inch-wide wound caused by a jagged piece of metal embedded in his upper back. Michael hefted the pilot over his shoulder, picked up the AK-47, struggled out of the ditch, and began walking toward the downed aircraft. He hoped a search-and-rescue team would arrive soon.

He'd just laid Dombrowsky on the ground next to his wounded co-pilot, when he heard the familiar sound of an approaching helicopter. Then the ear-splitting roar of jets filled the area between the low hills around them. Michael's heart sank at the thought of the Serb jets returning. But when he saw the American markings on the F-16Cs, he felt a chill at the base of his neck – the same feeling he got every time he heard the national anthem.

Michael looked at the co-pilot's leg and felt his stomach heave at the sight of white bone protruding through flesh. The man's face was pale to the point of being snow-white and his body shook. Damn, Michael thought, he's in shock.

An Apache helicopter whipped up clouds of dust while it set down seventy feet away. Two men climbed out of the helicopter and rushed over to where the injured pilots lay. One of them yelled at Michael over the noise of the helicopter's idling engine and the roar of the circling jets, while he looked at Dombrowsky's wound. "Scooter James. This is Billy Herrera. You guys all right?"

"You got a first-aid kit on board?" Michael yelled back.

"Yeah!" Billy ran back to the Apache, retrieved the kit, and returned to where Dombrowsky lay – still unconscious. Billy Herrera and Michael worked on cleaning Dombrowsky's wound, while Scooter covered Ernie Patten with a field jacket and wrapped the man's leg with a cotton bandage.

"I can't stop the bleeding as long as this piece of metal's stuck in him," Michael told Billy. "We're going to have to pull it out," Michael said. "Get ready with the pressure bandage."

Michael took a pair of forceps from the first-aid kit and clamped the ends of the tool on the edge of the palm-sized piece of shrapnel. He took a deep breath, then slowly exhaled. "Ready?" he asked. Billy nodded, his face gray. Pressing down on the forceps' grip with all the strength he had left, Michael pulled on the metal piece. He felt resistance, at first, then the shrapnel slid out of the wound. Blood suddenly erupted in a gush from the gaping slash in Dombrowsky's back. Billy slapped the pressure bandage over the wound. Once the bleeding had abated, Michael draped Dombrowsky's flight jacket over him.

They'd barely finished their first-aid work when Michael heard the rotor beat of more helicopters. He turned to see two more Apaches escorting a UH-60 Black Hawk helicopter. The Apaches hovered and formed an aerial perimeter while the Black Hawk landed fifty yards from the four Americans. Michael watched two men leap from the chopper, one with a large first-aid kit in hand, the other hefting a folded stretcher. When Colonel Sweeney exited the aircraft, Michael began to think he was hallucinating. He thought he'd totally lost his mind when his father followed Sweeney out of the Black Hawk.

"Man, am I glad to see you guys," Scooter said to the medics. "Take care of Jess; he's lost a lot of blood. Looks like Ernie's got a compound fracture and has gone into shock."

The medics were putting Dombrowsky on the litter when Colonel Sweeney and Michael's father ran up.

"Well, I guess we've had enough excitement for one day," Bob said to Michael, a strained smile on his face.

"Probably enough for a lifetime," Michael answered, a wave of fatigue hitting him while the adrenaline in his system subsided.

"You all right, son?" Bob asked. Before Michael could answer, Bob stepped to him and embraced him. When Bob finally released Michael, he stepped back and said, "What say we get out of here?"

"Sounds good to me," Michael said.

Scooter James interrupted them when he shouted, "See ya around." He laughed, while he and Billy Herrera ran back to their aircraft and climbed behind the controls.

"I hope so," Michael answered, knowing the pilot hadn't heard him.

Michael watched Scooter's Apache rise off the ground. Then he watched as Ernie Patten was carried to the Black Hawk to be placed next to the litter Dombrowsky was on. He and Bob followed Colonel Sweeney over to their ride out of Yugoslavia. Michael looked one last time at his surroundings, and over at the road in the distance. He couldn't make out the ditches, but he could imagine them. He knew he'd never forget this place.

Michael climbed aboard the helicopter. Bob followed, then Colonel Sweeney. The pilot looked over his shoulder from the cockpit and said, "Welcome home, Captain." Michael gave him a thumbs up sign and settled back against a corner of the aircraft's personnel bay, next to his father. He fell asleep before the Black Hawk lifted off, his head resting on Bob's shoulder.

CHAPTER FIFTY-NINE

"Liz, Michael's safe!" Bob shouted into the telephone. "He's safe."

"Oh, Bob," Liz cried. She dropped down into the chair next to the telephone. "I need to talk to him. I want to hear his voice."

"Honey, he's coming home "

"Thank God! Thank God! When will he be here? How soon can I see him?"

"Soon, honey."

Liz paused for a moment and asked, "Are you okay?"

"Couldn't be any better," Bob said. "I'm coming home, too. I'll be there tomorrow morning. I'll bring you up to date on everything when I get home."

"Okay, Bob. Just get here as soon as you can."

"Oh, and Liz, they got Radko. He's finished. He'll never be a problem again. Ever."

Liz replaced the receiver in its cradle. She brought her knees up to her chest and hugged them. The fear she'd carried with her for the last two days, since learning Miriana's father was Stefan Radko, sloughed off her like a second skin. She sensed the anger she'd borne for twenty-eight years, since Radko had taken her only child, would take longer to dissipate.

She rose from the chair and looked in the hall mirror. Strands of her graying blonde hair had escaped the barrettes and now lay over her face, across her ears. She reflexively moved her hands toward her head, her eyes meeting their twin reflections. And then her emotional dam burst. She broke down and cried with deep, quaking sobs.

CHAPTER SIXTY

The Serb leader's face appeared dark and menacing. His eyes looked red, satanic. He glared at the aide approaching the other side of his desk. The man stopped in mid-stride.

"I gave you an order," the leader said, his words unnaturally constrained, as though someone were choking him with a rope. "I told you to bring that sonofabitch Artyan Vitas to me. Where the hell is he?"

"I'm sorry, Mr. President," the aide said, his face flushed with fear. "He . . . Mr. Vitas is . . .." The man's Adams apple bobbed and his hands began to quiver.

"Speak up, you imbecile." The leader picked up the brass base to his pen set and hurled it across the room, narrowly missing the aide's head. The man dropped to the floor, cowering, his arms covering his head in anticipation of further missiles coming his way.

"Stand up, you sniveling dunce," the President screamed.

The aide scrambled to his feet. Sweat beaded on his forehead. He rubbed his hands together, all the while staring at the floor, an eye cocked in case he became a target again. "Mr. Vitas is dead. The doctor says he died of rabies."

The President hesitated. He couldn't believe what he'd been told. Artyan Vitas couldn't be dead. The man was indestructible. But he knew his aide was telling the truth. The sniveling idiot didn't have the guts to lie to him. Besides, if Vitas were alive he would have been here by now. "How appropriate," the President said coldly. "He always was a mad dog." A short, bitter laugh escaped his lips. "Well, don't just stand there. Bring that fat-assed General Plodic to me."

CHAPTER SIXTY-ONE

"Morning, Captain," Sergeant Major Luther Jewell said. "How ya feelin'?"

Michael sat on the side of his bed in the almost empty, giant hospital tent, holding his breath and slowly tying his bootlaces. He looked up at Jewell and grimaced. "Like I just played four quarters against the Washington Redskins – without pads."

"A little sore, huh?"

"Yeah, just a little," Michael said, groaning as he stood up.

"Jeez, Captain, you sound like my old granpappy."

"I feel like your old granpappy, Sergeant Major. But it could've been a lot worse. Now tell me what you're doing here. It can't be just a get-well visit."

"Colonel Sweeney wants to see you. He knows you're being released and wanted me to escort you to his tent."

"Well, lead the way. But take baby steps."

Jewell chuckled and set out toward the headquarters tent with Michael walking stiffly beside him.

When they reached Sweeney's headquarters, Michael waited just inside the entrance while Jewell walked across the enclosure and said a few words to Colonel Sweeney. The Colonel looked at Michael, smiled, stood up, and walked toward him. Michael met him halfway and came to attention. He started to salute, but he found he couldn't raise his right hand all the way up to his forehead.

Sweeney saw the grimace on Michael's face. "We will dispense with the military courtesy until you're fully recovered," he said with a smile.

"Thank you, sir. I don't even remember doing anything to my arm. I got aches where I didn't know I had muscles."

Sweeney laughed. "The surgeon tells me you're going to be fine. Just need a couple weeks of rest."

"The only way I'll get any rest is to get away from the field hospital. They checked for signs of concussion, cleaned up about a hundred cuts and abrasions, and hooked me to an IV for dehydration. That was bad enough. Now they poke me, prod me, and, every time I fall asleep, they wake me up to take my blood pressure or give me a pill, or something."

"How's the head?"

"No concussion, sir. But I've still got a bad headache, and a heck of a bump."

"Major Krumka briefed me on the report you gave him," Sweeney said. "You've done us proud, Mike. What you did out there took guts."

Michael blushed. "Thank you, sir. But if it hadn't been for those helicopter and jet jockeys, I'd be sitting in a cell somewhere in Belgrade right now. By the way, how are the wounded pilots?"

Sweeney smiled again. "Captain Dombrowsky's doing fine. No permanent damage. But I hear he's going to have a helluva scar on his back. Patten's probably going to have a limp. His flying days are over."

Sweeney touched Michael lightly on the shoulder. "Listen, Mike, the S-1's cutting orders for you. You're going back Stateside."

Michael's face dropped with disappointment. "But, sir, I'm fine. Just a little stiff, that's all."

"The Pentagon wants you out of here. You've been kidnapped once too often. I don't know the entire story; but the decision's been made. You're out of here."

Michael knew the meeting was over. This time he succeeded in getting his hand six inches from his forehead. "It's been an honor serving with you, Colonel."

"The honor's been all mine, Captain Danforth," Sweeney said, returning the salute.

Sweeney watched Michael turn and limp out of the tent. Then he walked over to Sergeant Major Jewell's desk. "You got the papers completed on those decorations for Danforth and the pilots?"

"Yes, Colonel," Jewell responded. "Distinguished Flying Crosses for the helicopter crews; Combat Infantry Badge and Bronze Star, with V device for valor, for Captain Danforth."

CHAPTER SIXTY-TWO

Michael hitched a ride back to his tent. His father and Jack Cole were there waiting for him, along with Miriana's mother, Vanja.

"We need to have a talk, Mike," Bob said. "I've got a story to tell you."

Michael sat down on his cot. He looked from his father, to Jack, to Vanja and said, "What's up?"

Jack turned to Vanja. "Why don't you go ahead?" he suggested.

The woman cleared her throat. She tried to speak, but only a squeaking sound came out. She cleared her throat again and began. "About twenty-eight years ago your father" – she looked at Bob – "was stationed in Greece with the U.S. Army. I was very young woman at the time . . . and Stefan's mistress. He was married to his first wife then and had one son, a teenager named Gregorie. The Bulgarian Communists employed Stefan to . . .." Vanja swallowed and looked down at the dirt floor.

Michael saw tears well in her eyes.

"Stefan and I worked for Communists," she resumed. "We kidnapped Greek babies, took them north, and sold them to Bulgarians. One day, our team make mistake and kidnap American baby." She paused again, raised her head, and looked directly into Michael's eyes. "That baby was you."

"What?" Michael gasped. His hands tightened, his knuckles white. "I was kidnapped?" He shook his head and, almost to himself, said, "My parents never told me about it."

Bob leaned forward and placed a hand on Michael's knee. "It's true, Mike. Let her explain."

Vanja squirmed on the cot. She said, "We carried you north to orphanage in Bulgaria. Your father and another man came to rescue you. They were in orphanage looking for you, when Stefan and Gregorie arrived to deliver another baby. There was shooting. Gregorie was killed. Stefan has always blamed your father for his first son's death."

Vanja stopped and looked at Bob. He took his cue and said, "A little over a month ago, I master-minded a CIA kidnap plot against a senior Serb General. We recruited Miriana to help us execute the kidnapping. She was acting as the Serb General's fortune-teller. Of course, we had no idea Miriana was related to Stefan Radko. Everything went off pretty much as planned. We got the General. And we also brought Miriana out. Based on what you told Major Krumka about comments the Serb Captain made to you, your kidnapping here must have been planned as an act of revenge. The order must have come from the very top. From the Serb President himself. Part of the plot was to kidnap Miriana in the U.S. They would've killed her if she hadn't escaped. You know about that. What you don't know is they also tried to kill your mother and me in Bethesda."

Michael mouthed the word "What!" but he made no sound.

"Mike, when they failed to kill us, they came after you."

"And Stefan was part of your kidnapping this time, too," Vanja said. "I don't know how Serbs made contact with him. And . . . .." Vanja lowered her head again and began crying. "And he got Attila killed. Stefan is so full of rage against your father that when he found out about you and Miriana he could not control himself. He could not stand idea that you – son of man who killed Gregorie – would take Miriana away from him."

Michael shook his head. Why hadn't his parents told him about his being kidnapped? But he understood almost instantly. Why give a kid nightmares about kidnapping, Communists, and Gypsies? And when he got older, they might have figured it just wasn't necessary to rehash old nightmares. He looked at Vanja again. "What about Miriana?" he asked.

Vanja put her hand on the cross hanging around her neck. "I swear to God, she knows nothing of this."

Michael suddenly felt disoriented, as though he'd been sucker-punched. He was suddenly exhausted.

Jack stood and patted him on the shoulder. "I'll come by later tonight to say goodbye. I know you're flying out early tomorrow morning." He took Vanja's arm and helped her to her feet.

As they left the tent, Vanja stopped and turned back to him. "I am sorry, Michael. I hope you will not hold any of this against Miriana. "

Michael could only stare at her.

Bob stood and looked down at his son. "If I'd been home, instead of at work, Radko could never have taken you away the first time. And none of this would have happened. I'm sorry, Mike." Bob turned and began to walk away.

"Dad," Michael said, causing Bob to stop and turn around. "Did you really sneak into Bulgaria to rescue me?"

Bob nodded and said, "Along with a very brave man named George Makris, who died in the effort."

"And you risked your life for me again yesterday when you flew into Serbia."

Bob just stared at Michael.

"You've sure given me some great stories to tell when I'm out with my friends. You think you could tell me the whole thing when we get back home?"

Bob laughed and said, "No more secrets, son."

As Jack Cole drove Vanja away from the 82nd Airborne's camp, she stared straight ahead through the Jeep's windshield.

"My son died somewhere on this road," she said.

Jack didn't respond. He didn't know what to say.

"What will happen to Stefan?" she asked.

"He's a criminal, Vanja. He helped kidnap an American officer. Maybe, because of his age, he won't go to prison. But there's no way he'll ever be allowed to go to the United States. He'll probably be deported back to Serbia. There's nothing I can do to help him."

"If he goes back to Serbia, the Serbs will kill him."

Jack shrugged.

CHAPTER SIXTY-THREE

General Plodic crossed the wide expanse of carpet and came to attention in front of the President's desk. He felt sweat break out on his back and roll down his spine. He silently cursed himself for his stupidity. He should have run when he had the chance. Now it was too late. He didn't have to hear the President say a single word. He knew what was about to occur. I'm sorry, Tatiana, my dear wife, he thought. I should have listened to you months ago. We should have fled to France.

"You useless pile of manure!" the President screamed, pulling Plodic away from his reflections. "Your men accomplished nothing. *They* were our best soldiers?"

Plodic flushed. Resentment swamped his fear for the briefest of moments. Five of his finest men dead, all because of this asshole politician's need to avenge the death of a psychotic General. But then the fear returned. He tried to control it. He didn't want to give the President the satisfaction.

"You shall be an example to all Serbs, my dear General Plodic. No one disappoints me. You hear me?"

Plodic pushed out his chest. He'd been a soldier his entire adult life. In spite of his fear, he wouldn't let this shithead speak to him like this. He would put the leader in his place. But when he opened his mouth to say the words that had formed in his mind, nothing came out.

The President rose from his chair and pressed a buzzer on his telephone console. Two burly uniformed guards stormed into the room and positioned themselves on either side of Plodic. The President turned his back. "Take him away," he said. "I never want to see him again."

CHAPTER SIXTY-FOUR

Jack Cole sat in the little eight-by-eight room and stared through the one-way window at Radko. The old man sat stiffly in a chair and listened to a second man in the room read from an official-looking document.

"Stefan Gregorovich Radko, you have been accused and convicted of complicity in the kidnapping of an American officer assigned to the North Atlantic Treaty Organization's peacekeeping mission in the Balkans. By the authority vested in NATO's War Crimes Tribunal, you have been sentenced to deportation. You will be transported to the Yugoslav border where you will be turned over to Serb officials."

Jack noticed Radko slump slightly upon hearing his sentence. But the man immediately recovered and resumed his ramrod straight posture. The second man left the room and Jack rose, exited the observation room, and joined Radko. The Gypsy looked up at him when he entered the room, but said nothing, and showed no emotion.

"Tough guy, huh?" Jack said, sitting down. "You're going to need to be when the Serbs get their hands on you." Jack let that thought sink in, then said, "But don't worry about your wife and daughter. I'll see they are well cared for. And I'm sure Miriana will have many beautiful children. She and Michael Danforth make a handsome couple, don't you agree?"

Radko's skin turned almost gray and his eyes seemed to go colorless.

Jack stood and left the room. He didn't think it would serve any purpose to tell Radko there was no NATO War Crimes Tribunal, nor had he been convicted in a duly constituted court. The Gypsy's trip back to Serbia had been arranged with an old Iron Curtain agent Jack had dealt with years before.

EPILOGUE

2000

A blinding flash of sunlight shot off the limousine window when the uniformed driver opened the back passenger door. Bob, standing on the bottom step in front of the church's massive carved stone entrance, raised his hand to shield his eyes. Then he turned slightly to the side and looked down at the well-wishers gathered near the curb beside the long white vehicle. He picked out the newlyweds on the far edge of the crowd and smiled – their journey together at its beginning.

He took in a shuddering breath. What a ride his own journey had been! What a ride! The words sparked in his brain. He couldn't have planned for, would never have conceived of the road he'd traveled. His heart seemed to hiccup for a moment. Would he have had it any other way? No! At least not the journey. But maybe some of the stops along the way.

Vanja stood off to the side, fifteen yards away from the wedding party and the other attendees. She mouthed the English word she'd come to love: *Serendipity*. She still couldn't pronounce it quite right, but she liked the way it sounded. And she loved its many nuances: Luck, happenstance. Hadn't her life been filled with all those things? She liked thinking about the good things in her life. If she thought about the sad things, she might go crazy.

She watched Michael sweep the long, white train of Miriana's gown off the sidewalk and help her into the waiting limousine. The crowd moved closer to the car, tossing rose petals and rice at the young couple. She wished Attila could have seen this. Her breath came in stutters and her throat tightened. This day, this wedding was a miracle, a miracle that could have been short-circuited at many stops along a lifetime of tragic events. And the legacy of her husband's perfidy had finally almost destroyed

Miriana. Her feelings of guilt about what her father had done to Michael and his family were almost impossible for her to overcome.

An image of Stefan came to her, but she shook her head as though to purge her memory of the man.

She saw Liz Danforth standing at the top of the steps near the church's massive carved wood doors. She wanted more than anything to tell the woman how sorry she was – for the part she'd played in almost ruining her life almost thirty years ago; about the role her husband played last year in bringing more nightmares to Liz's life. But she sensed Michael's mother wasn't ready to accept her apology. Her emotional wounds and the anger they caused were still too close to the surface.

Vanja stared again at Miriana and saw the complete, unreserved happiness on her face and gave a silent prayer for the gift God had given her daughter in the form of Michael's love. She waved at the limousine while it pulled away and continued waving until the car turned a corner and disappeared from view.

Bob sensed Liz beside him. He turned and hugged her, wiped away a tear at the corner of her eye with his free hand, and kissed her cheek. "I don't know why," he said, "but I was thinking about how I used to run around the yard in Greece with Michael in my arms, playing Superman."

Liz smiled. "Soup Man! Remember how he said Soup Man?"

Bob chuckled. Then he turned solemn and looked over Liz's shoulder at Vanja. "You know, for Michael's sake, you should try to mend things with Miriana's mother."

A sharp, angry look came to Liz's eyes and, for a moment, Bob thought she was going to blow up. But the look smoldered for a few seconds, and faded. "In time," she said. "In good time."

Bob met Liz's gaze. He knew, more than any other person, the emotions swirling inside his wife mind. He could tell when an errant memory came to her, one that took her back to the first kidnapping. A sudden look of panic would quickly cross her face, and would just as quickly segue into a clenched-jaw show of anger. But he also knew Liz was a loving, compassionate woman who would eventually make peace with Miriana's mother.

"Well, we've got a reception to attend," Bob said.

Liz nodded. She gave his hand a squeeze and started to turn. But she stopped and whispered, "Miriana's mother doesn't have a car. Maybe you should offer her a ride to the hotel."

JOSEPH BADAL

THE END

ABOUT THE AUTHOR

Joseph Badal has worked for thirty eight years in the banking and financial services industries. Prior to his finance career, he served as an officer in the U.S. Army in critical, highly classified positions in the U.S. and overseas, including tours of duty in Greece and Vietnam. He earned numerous military decorations.

Joe has been a member of the New Mexico House of Representatives and recently retired as a Board Member and Senior Executive of a New York Stock Exchange-listed company. He lives in New Mexico.

Joe's first suspense novel, "The Pythagorean Solution," was released in April, 2003. His second suspense novel, "Terror Cell," was released in July 2004. The paperback version of "The Pythagorean Solution" was released in 2005. His book "The Nostradamous Secret" was released in 2011. All of his books are available in digital format.

To learn more, visit his website at www.josephbadalbooks.com. You can see Joe's blog at http://josephbadal.wordpress.com.

CPSIA information can be obtained at www.ICGtesting.com
Printed in the USA
LVOW011636080213

319320LV00016B/572/P